CW00751354

The Sweepers

MICHAEL PATRICK COLLINS

UPFRONT PUBLISHING
PETERBOROUGH, ENGLAND

By the same author:
THE CREW
ISBN 9781844262915

Available now from

http://www.upfrontpublishing.com/view.php?book=105

All internet booksellers
And to order through good bookshops worldwide

THE SWEEPERS
Copyright © Michel Patrick Collins 2007

ISBN 978-184426-431-5

First Published 2007 by
UPFRONT PUBLISHING LTD
Peterborough, England.

Printed by Printondemand-Worldwide Ltd.

Michael Patrick Collins

For the long haulers. Wherever you are.

Michael Patrick Collins

Prologue
London, Friday 0400, 1ˢᵗ April 2000

'E thel' moved slowly up the river. Here the Thames was wide enough but you could never be too careful, especially after that horrendous collision of a few years back. Not that there would be too many pleasure boats out at this time of night, he thought. Actually she was really 'The Lady Ethel' but even 'Ethel' was inevitably corrupted further by the language of the river - here she was simply known as 'Eful'.

Certainly she had been 'Eful' for as long as Jesse had known her, and he had started on the, now very old, tug just after the war when his uncle Fred had been the 'Gaffer,' calling him 'Captain' was hardly appropriate for a vessel that spent its life hauling barges up and down what used to be the main artery of the city.

These days the only traffic that went this far up were the barges for the collection of the city's limitless supply of garbage and this morning Jesse, now the man in charge, had three scows trailing behind his old tug. These were twisting and turning in the turbulent flow as empty barges were inclined to do.

The tide was ebbing and the river was adding its formidable weight to the falling water level. The moon, slowly setting in the west, was just past full now, ensuring that the combined flow was close to its maximum and progress was slow.

Jesse didn't mind, he loved this river, apart from a two week holiday each year in Spain, he spent his life here. Nights like this made it all worthwhile; he looked up through the lights of the sleeping city, the sky was clear, lit only by the fading moon.

The yell, when it came, dragged him back from his daydream, although afterwards in the pub, describing the events of what was going to be an unusual day, he wondered whether it should have been called a night dream, given the time.

For the moment, his attention was entirely on the high pitched yell of his one crewman now running back along the port side towards the small wheel house in the stern. Naturally he was family, his brother's boy Alf, who he knew would eventually take over from him, as he had from his own uncle a few years back.

Right now though there was something far more pressing to worry about it seemed. The boy was running aft at the same time as he was trying to point back in the direction of the bow. Looking that way all Jesse could see was the looming mass of London Bridge. Puzzled, he checked his position; the lead's in lights on the left side were exactly correct? He glanced further his left, nothing coming through the centre arch, illegal but not unknown. In fact as far as he could see they were alone on the water. What the hell was the boy getting so excited about?

The lad arrived at the port-side door and, breathless, he just pointed at the centre arch; Jesse peered again into the comparative darkness of the bridge's shadow and now saw what had got the boy so wound up. Something was hanging there; it did not take too much imagination to see that it was a body or something very like one. He eased the power off and moved the tug to port aiming for the unused centre arch. Gradually the increased flow in the middle of the river and a slight reduction in power brought the vessel to a standstill under whatever it was dangling from a rope that seemed to be attached to one of the lamp posts that decorated this, London's youngest bridge.

Increasing power a little he slowly moved 'Eful' until the thing was hanging right in front of the wheel-house. As he got closer he could see there were shoes on it and, calling for the boy to hold the tug in this position he pulled out his mobile and pressed the numbers.

After the usual, 'What service do you want,' 'who are you' 'where are you?' bit, the police operator that he eventually ended up talking to told him to stay where he was and wait for the law to arrive. It took him some time to convince her that staying where he was, was not an option in this case and really he hadn't done it anyway. Finally she agreed he could wait at the garbage dock further upstream until they had spoken to him.

All done, he nodded at the boy and took the wheel back from his nephew. 'Well done Alf' he said 'Looks like we are in for a visit from the 'plod' later though, so if you have any of that 'wacky backy' anywhere I should lose it.' Alf grinned, 'You know I don't do that Uncle Jesse, Dad would kill me.' 'I know lad, and when he had finished with you I would too.' He smiled and opened the throttle. The old engine rumbled into life. Disconcertingly, as they got under way again, the legs of the body swung in the light breeze and the shoes hit the top of the wheel-house, dragging across the wood before swinging free over the stern. Looking back to see that the barges were still in line, Jesse could see the body now outlined against the lights of the embankment. It was gently swaying there.

As the last barge cleared the bridge the first flashing blue lights appeared on the north side of the river, slowing as they approached the centre of the bridge. More cars stopped at each end, the barriers already being hastily thrown up. Jesse, still looking back turned to his nephew. 'Good job it's Saturday Alf, it's going to cause a hell of a jam with that one out anyway. Hate to think what it would have been like on a weekday.'

★ ★ ★

The recently promoted Inspector had groaned when the call came in. It was almost at the end of his shift and he had been thinking about what he had planned for what was left of the weekend, now this. Uniform said it was apparently a jumper and like most cops he loathed them. Stupid bastards always caused more trouble dead than they had alive. Paper, paper, paper was the only result and he could see his Saturday sliding down the proverbial toilet as he took the call.

He walked over to his sergeant and shook him awake 'What's up Guv?' the man mumbled, still bleary with sleep. 'Got a bloody jumper, hung himself from London Bridge, called in by some barge driver a few minutes ago. Uniform are there, forensic on the way, as are we, if you can get your arse into gear, right.' He turned away making for the door. The sergeant sighed, another bad day on the way.

He had only been with this chap a few days and he was still settling in with the new man. The Inspector had been a recent promotion and transfer from Special Branch. At first everybody at the station thought he had stuffed up somewhere but far from it. This guy was apparently marked for greater things, the new position just a step on the way up the ladder, or so it was said on the grapevine.

Not that he was a bad bloke the sergeant thought as he moved to the now open door, just a bit testy in the early hours. Still who wouldn't be, he rationalised, and seeing as I'm going to be stuck with most of the bloody paper he is on about, suddenly I don't feel so happy either.

They reached the barriers set up on the north end of the bridge and were waved through. The sergeant stopped the car next to a small group of uniformed police on the eastern side.

A sergeant he recognised from the station walked over. 'Morning Guv just what you need to start the weekend with eh...?' He glared at the man, 'Bloody suicides! Why can't they just take a packet of aspirins and a bottle of Scotch and do it in the sack. Always got to make it as dramatic as bloody possible,' he grumbled. 'You got him up yet?' 'No not yet- thought we had better leave it until you got here.' He walked to the edge of the bridge pulled himself up on the parapet and looked over. Nothing much to see just the top of a head and the rope tied around the lamp post. 'Okay let's get him up and see who he is.' The uniformed sergeant called a couple of constables over and told them to pull the corpse over the wall. Each of them grimaced and then leaning over they grabbed the rope and began hauling. Eventually the body appeared but early rigor had already set in, as it always did with traumatic death, and it was with some difficulty that they manipulated the stiff body over the edge.

Eventually they managed to pull it over and laid flat on its back against the wall. One of them climbed back up to the lamp post and untied the rope, throwing it down beside the corpse.

The Inspector knelt down and looked at the face. It was distorted and unrecognisable from what looked like a savage beating, already the tissue was darkening. He felt through the pockets of what was clearly an expensive suit dropping the contents into the plastic bag his sergeant held open for him. Eventually he pulled a wallet from the inside pocket of the jacket and opened it up. The usual credit cards and cash were there, and then he saw something that stopped him dead.

He looked again at the card and gave a low whistle. 'I think this has just got a bit more interesting' he said to no one in particular, but his sergeant heard. 'Oh how's that Guv?' Saying nothing he stood up, holding the wallet open at the card that had attracted his attention for the man to see. This time it was his sergeant's turn to be surprised. 'Bloody Hell, see what you mean!' Closing the wallet he walked back to the car. 'I think I had better get back to the station and make a few calls. Stay here and get the forensic boys on to this as soon as possible. You can tell them it will have a high priority, any trouble tell them to ring me. Okay?' He nodded at the card, 'This guy is somebody special and you can be sure this is going to cause quite a stir,' he smiled thinly. 'Not just our weekend gone down the can after all. Suddenly I feel better. Get uniform to give you a lift back.'

Arriving back at the station he went to his office and closed the door. The only call he made was to his old employer, Chief Superintendent Simon Quartermaine, operational head of the Special Branch. It was 0600.

The phone rang for a few minutes before a bleary voice answered 'Quartermaine.' 'Charlie Phillips here sir, you may remember me. Inspector with the Yard now, thanks to you.' The senior man, still coming on line, replied, 'Of course I do Charlie, Christ I'm not that old yet, what's up?' 'Well sir, we have just pulled a stiff up on to London Bridge. Looks like he hung himself, bit like that Catholic priest bloke did a while back under Blackfriars, a Roberto Calvi wasn't it?' Quartermaine just grunted and the Inspector continued. 'At least I think it is supposed to look as though he'd hung himself, but the funny thing is his face was pretty much unrecognisable. He had been badly beaten just before, by the look of things. It was called in by the skipper of a barge who saw the body when he was going up river this morning at about 0400. I thought you ought to know because he has a top security clearance at MI6 according to the card in his wallet. I figured this is going to have some political fallout and that you ought to be in on it right up front. First question I have is why a senior MI6 man, having got himself badly beaten up, would then go off and hang himself from a bridge over the Thames?' Quartermaine, now sitting up and fully awake, asked the inevitable question and when he was told the name it was his turn to whistle. 'Okay' he said, 'Who knows who it is so far, I presume you have forensic down there?' 'Yes sir, they will have picked the stiff up by now; I told my sergeant that the results would be wanted today, given who he is, but I am the only one who knows the name - unless one of the others recognises him, but from the state of the face that is not likely sir. Of course, if he has done the school boy thing and put his name in the clothes there may be a problem.' 'Right, here is what you do Charlie.' There followed a long list of instructions which would all but fill the rest of the man's day, finally Quartermaine finished. 'And well done Inspector. If anything else turns up let me know, okay?' 'Will do sir' the connection was broken.

It was some time later as he was wading through the list of jobs he had inherited that his sergeant knocked and came in. He looked up, 'anything from the labs yet?' 'No not yet Guv, but one of the uniforms handed me this as I was about to come back. Says he found it jammed in the stonework near where the stiff was dangling.' He handed a card to the Inspector who looked at it for some time. It was a standard business card of good quality, completely black except for a stylised broom of the sort used in tree plantations to put out fires. This was a set in silver, as was the word at the bottom, 'Sweepers.' There was nothing on the back. 'Weird! Never seen anything like that before, probably nothing to do with this; still, put it in the bag with the rest of the stuff. I have to take it all over to Special Branch later and with a bit of luck they will take the whole thing off our hands and leave us in peace for what's left of the weekend. Keep me posted in the mean-time right.' Nodding, the sergeant walked back to the door, paused and said, 'Any idea who he was Guv? Thought I might know the name from somewhere, sounded vaguely familiar?' The Inspector looked up quickly 'Sod it, I had hoped that I wouldn't have to say this but the identity has been clamped by you-know-who. What about the others, any suggestions of recognition there?' 'No I don't think so. I mean he was a bit of a mess wasn't he?' 'Right' the inspector continued, 'You keep an ear out for any loose talk and make it quite clear what will happen to the individual who leaks this, clear?'

That afternoon he stood in Quartermaine's office. The contents of the plastic evidence bag were scattered over the large oak desk as the head of Special Branch sorted through it all. Eventually he picked up the card which had been hidden under the pile. Pausing to control his question he looked at the young inspector, 'And this?' 'Found by the uniform blokes, stuck in the stonework of the bridge close to where he was hanging sir. I only put it in the bag because it was so close, probably nothing to do with it, nice card though.' Quartermaine looked at it again. 'Quite right, probably just rubbish.' He placed it to one side. 'All right Inspector, well done. Special Branch will take over from here. I take it you have told all those who were involved in this what will happen if there is any loose talk?' 'Yes sir, all taken care of.' As he moved towards the door he turned. 'If that is all sir?' Quartermaine looked up, smiled and waved. As the door closed he picked up the card again muttering to himself. 'The last thing you would want to get is one of these things young man.' He pressed the intercom button. 'Angela get me Colonel Raff on the phone will you, it's urgent?'

Michael Patrick Collins

PART ONE
THE MEETING

★

Michael Patrick Collins

Chapter One
2300 Christmas Eve 1965
(Two hours before the mission)

The camp was only ten kilometers west of the border and about fifteen south of the small town of Helmstadt. This was the crossing place long associated with the route to Berlin from the British sector of the still divided Germany.

It was the forward base of the Lancers, an old and illustrious cavalry regiment of the British Army, currently equipped with light armoured cars. They were stationed here to provide an early warning to the British Army of the Rhine should 'Redland' get restive.

As the cold war had eased and the political temperature rose to something above freezing, their main role had changed to patrolling and inspecting the allied side of the fence of the aptly named Iron Curtain where so many had died attempting to escape the delights of the 'not so Democratic Republic' of communist East Germany.

The camp was really a small gathering of huts built around a central square and surrounded by the highest points in the Hartz Mountains, a range of hills, - 'mountains' was stretching things a bit, that straddled the border on a north-south axis.

The country was difficult to patrol and gradually the military had started to use helicopters from the Army Air Corps in support of the ground troops. It was this change in policy that was supposed to provide the cover for the current operation.

For the past two weeks the small square in the centre of the camp had been occupied by three Allouette II helicopters from 25 Flight. At least, that is what the commanding officer of the Lancers had been told.

In fact 25 Flight did not exist and the machines were, in reality, attached to an ultra secret department in MI6. Their role on this occasion was the extraction of an apparently valued agent from 'over there'. It was inferred, by those on the need to know list, that information on who exactly was behind the assassination of President Kennedy two years ago might be revealed, along with quite a bit else, it was hoped.

The pilots, hand picked, all having completed at least one operational tour, were under no illusions about this particular job. To say that it was risky was something of an understatement. The 'Volpo', the East German border police, were an unpleasant lot at the best of times. Something like this was bound to bring out the worst in them, if they managed to get their hands on the snatch team that is. The weather men, there to give a final update on the expected conditions, had been followed into the room by the spook from MI6, a short fat individual in a crumpled suit, wearing a tie of indeterminate origin. It was already stained with the residue of a hasty meal, but almost immediately the owner announced it to be that of the London School of Economics. The cavalry Colonel's laconic reply, that he had not realised anybody at the LSE had a tie, was not well received.

The MI6 man's weak chin and badly overshot top jaw was accompanied by the nasal whining of what was soon to become known as, 'Estuarine,' but which for the moment was the chosen idiom of a few upwardly mobile sycophants of the so called 'New Age'. It had caused the Irish pilot's hackles to rise; he sensed that the other two and the Colonel of the Lancers were equally unimpressed. 'The Operation is on for tonight,' the man from Whitehall had announced pompously.

Moving to the centre of the room he continued 'You', he had waived vaguely at the Irishman and his two colleagues 'Will be ready to take off at 0100. The package has been told to be in position by 0045, pick up is planned at 0120 and you should be back here by 0200 at the latest.'

★ ★ ★

Now, as the Colonel of the Lancers and the man from Whitehall waited for the return of the aircraft, the overheated room was quiet for they were the only two there, the weather men had returned to Detmold, the main forward base of Army Air Corps Rhine Army, as soon as they had completed the briefing.

'Have you considered failure?' the Colonel began, more to break an awkward silence than in expectation of a reply. 'All taken care of mate' was the answer. The Colonel frowned. He was not used to being referred to as 'mate' by anybody and this Whitehall creep, and all those like him, from a government he privately loathed, was typical of the so called new order. It was the main reason he had decided to resign as soon as this tour of duty was over. 'And how would that be?' he continued. 'Well, these damn Paddies are good for something after all you know. That's why I picked him as the one to go over. The other two are ours, but Fitzgerald is totally

15

expendable as far as I am concerned, so if it all goes tits up, which it probably will, we say it was a private venture by a bunch of mercenaries, show his Irish papers and a few other bits and pieces and deny all knowledge. They won't believe all that rubbish of course but knowing and proving are two different things in this game.' 'And the man himself?' the Colonel persisted. 'Oh, one less of those bloody 'Micks' will be no loss, and that one has the potential to cause us a lot of trouble if we ever lose control of him. One of the best they have apparently, but also one who is becoming increasingly difficult and outspoken. In some ways it would be a blessing if they did get him; bit awkward for the agent of course.' He finished with an irritating cackle that the Colonel supposed was the odious little man's attempt at laughter.

Each of the three helicopters had taken a different path to the border, ensuring that the first two would reach it a few minutes in front of the one tasked with the crossing. The two lead aircraft reached the open area on the western side of the first fence and rolled on maximum bank, one to the north, the other following the fence to the south. The point had been carefully chosen after weeks of checking. It was here that the nearest towers were at their furthest apart and here, on a night such as this with blowing snow from a bitter northeaster, that visibility would be reduced to a minimum.

They had spent the previous weeks doing fast runs at low level up to and along the fence for the entire length of that part of the border; it was intended to condition the Volpo. Along with the weather and the added distraction of Christmas Eve, it was hoped it would be enough to enable the third machine to cross the line of the fences undetected.

The pick up was ten kilometers inside 'Redland' and the pilot was under no illusions as to the chances of finding the rendezvous. He was all too aware that on operations like this everything had to go exactly right including the things that had not been considered. So far it was all going to plan though. He watched as the lead aircraft broke off left and right to follow the fence. At fifty feet below them, at tree top height and a little behind, at the maximum 115knots he passed over the first of the three fences that marked this isolated part of Winston Churchill's Iron Curtain.

Fifteen minutes into the flight he was already cold in spite of the Canadian Air Force kapok flying suit that he wore. They had taken the doors off the aircraft, so that the pick up would be as quick as possible, but no doors meant no heater and the outside air temperature was –5, at 115knots the wind- chill factor made it considerably colder.

Staying as low as possible he considered it unlikely that he had been seen either by the guards or radar. Certainly, there had been no string of tracer indicating discovery, so far so good.

He glanced down at the shoulder holster sitting uncomfortably across his chest; it had to be so because the shoulder harness of the aircraft seat made the usual position under his right arm useless. It contained his only means of defence, a large Browning automatic. He had wanted something more powerful but the request had been denied.

Two more minutes passed and he was staring ahead through the Perspex canopy into a horizontal tunnel of white when suddenly a torch flashed in the darkness, 'IV' the agreed signal. He eased the cyclic stick back, simultaneously lowering the collective lever, and as the Allouette's nose lifted slightly the speed began to fall. The pitch on the main rotor was reduced further with collective and the aircraft began its short descent into the small clearing barely visible in the light of a half moon frequently obscured by the wind blown snow. The speed and altitude continued to decrease as the nose attitude was held at a constant angle with the cyclic stick.

Simultaneously the lever, until then being slowly lowered to reduce the forward speed, was raised again to bring the machine to a slow hover taxi. The aircraft skids were just above the white surface and approaching the light, he intended to run it on to avoid the white out of a stationery hover over blowing snow. It was risky because he had no way of knowing the depth but he figured that the belly of the aircraft would keep it upright even if it did sink a little.

As the aircraft settled into the snow he watched as two figures broke out of the undergrowth at the edge of the clearing and stumbled through the snow towards him. His orders were one passenger - so who was the other guy?

As they approached, the man in front veered to the left side of the aircraft and away from him; clearly the intention was to enter it from that side. Momentarily distracted, he did not see the weapon the second man had raised, even the sound of the shot was unheard above the high pitched whine of the gas turbine engine. It was only as the figure in front fell forward into the snow that he glanced back to find the gun now aimed at him. Before he could react, the Perspex canopy was shattered by the impact of a heavy calibre bullet intended to kill him. He was saved by the old B20 compass bolted to the framework in the middle of the cockpit windscreen. It literally exploded in front of him, covering him with the debris and raw alcohol of its contents.

Realising that the Browning was out of the question he slumped forward apparently hit, watching the man approach his side of the aircraft. As he reached the edge of the disk, the plain of rotation of the helicopter's main rotor, the pilot pushed the cyclic stick firmly forward. He watched in fascination as the visible edge of the disc dropped down towards his intended killer.

Too late, the man glanced up, the brief look of horror replaced by a fountain of blood as the blades, rotating at 320 rpm, made contact. The man was thrown backwards by the impact, the body dropped into snow now stained briefly with a line of crimson, which, even as the pilot watched, was already disappearing under the snow.

He reacted quickly and with both the cyclic stick and collective lever screwed down the controls were now locked by the friction clamps. He released his harness and rolled sideways out of the open hatchway stumbling as he did so because the snow surface was now level with the floor. Awkward in the softness of the surface he pulled himself round the front of the machine to the rapidly disappearing body of the first man, face down in the snow. The black stain in the middle of the back was not encouraging. He rolled the body over, no exit wound apparent so perhaps there was some hope.

With considerable difficulty he pulled the body to the port side and rolled it in. Here at least, the fact that the floor was now level with the snow was some help.

He made no attempt to strap the body in, looking at the wound he did not think the stranger would stir and he had already noticed lights in the distance at the other end of the clearing.

The effort to get back around the helicopter and fit his harness took an age. The lights were much clearer now and his frozen hands made releasing the controls slow and difficult. Finally he was ready and pulling up on the collective lever the helicopter shook itself free of the soft clinging surface. As he eased the cyclic stick forward, moving the helicopter to avoid the white-out of re-ingested snow, the landing light broke clear and an increasing pool of light spread out in front. Looking up, the pilot was surprised to see that the other East German, far from being killed by the rotor blades, was on his hands and knees frantically searching for his weapon. How he could see through what remained of a face covered in blood which had all the appearance of a scalping, was anybody's guess. Nevertheless, the intention was all too clear. Increasing forward pressure on the cyclic stick but keeping the skids of the undercarriage close to the surface the pilot bore down on the man. Again too late; the man became aware of the sudden increase in noise and turned to face the helicopter now no more than a few feet from him. The right hand skid struck his already blood stained face and he was thrown backwards into the snow again. The pilot quickly lowered the lever but continued to move forward, using the machine's weight to drive the body into the surface of the snow.

Accelerating and raising the collective lever, he pulled the machine up over the trees just as two more star-like holes appeared in the Perspex canopy. The support team had arrived it seemed and he had only just made it out of the clearing.

Now faced with a night flight over hostile territory, with no compass, he looked up at the guttering moon and turned onto what he figured was a rough westerly heading. Without a compass to guide him the run out was going to be a hit and miss affair. Mostly miss would be his choice, he thought with a grim smile.

With the chaos of the pick up behind him he began to reflect on the betrayal. Clearly that bastard from Whitehall at the base would have some questions to answer. He figured he was just the man to ask them.

Following a shallow valley and maintaining a course roughly west, he estimated the first of the three border fences in about three minutes. With no clear idea as to where he was going to cross it he planned to fly directly over the nearest tower as soon as he could make it out. He figured that a low fast approach from behind would enable him to get over it before the resident Volpo realised. That way, the guards would be unable to fire at him for the critical period - Plan A he thought, and plan B, well at the moment Plan B was to see how Plan A worked out.

Ludwig Hieneman, private soldier in the border police of the East German state was not happy, certainly he had been asleep but then he had been on duty for 16 hours when the Lieutenant had found him, it was not his fault they were short of men. Now he was stuck in this blasted tower on a punishment detail, for the whole of the Christmas period looking at the West. Naturally all was quiet as usual. In fact it was dead quiet. In the people's utopia of communist East Germany, Christmas was not an official holiday, but, as the Lieutenant had known only too well, Ludwig was a local and his family had planned an evening's celebration. Now that was ruined for him by the extra punishment duty. So here he was freezing, bored and angry.

There had been some noise further south about 30 minutes ago, probably the damn Brits winding us up again with the helicopter patrols, he thought. They had caused some concern at first when they began a few weeks ago, but now they watched the antics of the British Army with increasing disinterest.

All he could hear now was the wind which, blowing from the northeast, forced him to the southwest corner to shelter from the snow. It was on the wind that he first noticed the sound, the whine of the wind enhanced by something else which gradually penetrated his senses. Reluctantly he shook himself and moved out of the protection of the wall and peered into the east and the wind and snow. He saw nothing at first, but the noise increased quickly as though a full blown gale was about to strike. Only at the last did he lower his head to see the helicopter, just above on the surface of the snow and moving straight at his tower at high speed.

Never the brightest card in the pack, he ran for the machine gun mounted on that side. Too late he realised the mistake and turning he leaped to the western mounted gun just as the helicopter pulled up over the tower. It was so low that the vibration and downdraft dislodged the accumulated snow of the entire winter. It fell from the roof, obscuring all vision for the critical period. Nevertheless, Ludwig managed one burst of fire at the machine as it crossed the last of the three fences and disappeared into the night. He thought he had seen a few hits but he could not be sure. Now fully awake he hit the alarm, and the sector of the fence either side of his tower was immediately a blaze of lights. Within minutes the mobile patrol arrived and the Lieutenant was first to the top of the tower. Hieneman was quickly replaced and hustled away for questioning. It was not to be his most memorable Christmas.

The pilot had seen the tower at the same moment the machine had left the shallow valley in which he had approached the border. Rolling on forty degrees of bank he lowered the collective to put the aircraft as close to the snow in the cleared area to the east of the tower as possible, at the same time easing the cyclic stick forward to increase speed to the maximum. He aimed straight at it and just as he raised the nose to pass over it his mind registered the movement of the guard as he reached the eastern side of the tower. Too late, he thought, dozy bastard. He took the helicopter right over the top and dropped rapidly to the ground on the other side as he crossed the final fence. Only at the last moment did he feel the impact of heavy calibre bullets from the guard's machine gun. Bugger!! Not quite so dozy after all. A quick inspection of the instruments revealed nothing seriously damaged, at least it still flew, but there had been at least three impacts.

After a few minutes the problem became clear, he was losing fuel.

The tank was supposed to be self-sealing, something the French manufacturers had built into the machine during the Algerian campaign in the 50's, but it was not working today it seemed. Must have been a very heavy calibre bullet, the hole too big to seal he reasoned. He started looking for a suitable landing place. Lucky it hadn't hit anything vital.

He saw the road just as the low fuel light came on, glaring at him malevolently with its single yellow eye; the best he had was five minutes to put her down. Lining up on the road he lowered the lever, easing back on the cyclic he ran the helicopter on at about twenty knots just as the engine died. The snow covered surface of the road cushioned the shock and the machine gradually slid to a stop. Only then did he notice the stickiness, the lever was slippery in his hand. Slowly the pain pushed through the adrenaline and he realised that the guard had been anything but asleep. Looking aft in the gloom he could see the hole in the rear seat back where the bullet had exited the large fuel tank behind it. Almost spent, it had still ripped through the heavy arctic flying suit into the flesh of his left arm. Oh Sod it! Now I am in the shit he thought.

Leaving his seat he moved to the rear bench seat under which the cause of it all very still and very pale. He pulled the body out of the cabin onto the ground on the lea side the helicopter, it offered a little protection from the wind and he needed to know if he was still alive. No point in humping a stiff, he thought. He rolled the body on its back, groaning as the pain of his wound hit him. Kneeling down, he brushed the snow away from the face. Pulling the scarf down to see if there was life, he stopped. 'Jesus! What the hell is this?' the face, pale and drawn as it was, clearly that of a young woman. She moaned and the eyes opened briefly, fear and pain flashed across her face. He leant down and whispered in his 'schoolboy' German 'Jetzt bist sicher, wir sind ueber der Grenze' [You are safe now, we have crossed the border]. Her hand clutched his fiercely, and he lent forward again, listening. 'Thank you, thank you,' and then in German 'Es tut so weh' the pain was all too clear in her face. He stood beside the girl, for that is all she was, talking to himself. 'OK Paddy, fine promises you've made; safe is she; so what are you going to do now you dopey Irish bastard?'

He thought afterwards that he must have stood there for about five minutes trying to figure out what to do. Slowly he became aware of the noise of the armoured car moving cautiously along the road. At first his instinct was to pick her up and run, only then did he remember that they had nothing to fear, these were his people.

It was a border patrol of the Lancers; the armoured personnel carrier drew to a stop a few feet away, the flood light illuminating the scene as the crew watched, summing up the situation. He called out, the Irish accent convincing them that this was indeed one of theirs. He found himself quickly bundled into the back of the vehicle with the girl beside him; it was cramped but wonderfully warm.

The crew medic started on his arm but he stopped him. 'Look after her, I'm okay. She has a bullet in the back I think. It is still in there, best do what you can to stop the bleeding. It happened about....' He stopped. God, how long ago was it, seems an age? 'I think it was about twenty minutes, something like that.' 'Don't you worry sir' the medic said, 'Sarge is going flat out to the base. We have a good medical set up there, should be able to get you both fixed up pretty quick'. This was said with more confidence than he felt. He reckoned the pilot would be okay but of the girl he was not so sure.

As soon as the APC stopped, the medical team had pulled open the rear door and gently eased the girl onto a stretcher. He had followed them into the building, the hand of the radio operator steadying him, loss of blood bringing a sudden dizziness.

His own injury was messy but superficial. The heavy flying suit, at least the top part, was cut away to reveal a tear in the muscle of his left shoulder. Clearly the round had been almost spent and badly distorted. Lucky really, as the medic who pulled the piece of metal from the fabric of the shoulder of the suit pointed out if it had hit him in the back it could still have killed him.

Now, bandaged up with remnants of the kapok jacket loose on his shoulders, he asked the doctor for a lift to the officers' mess. The doctor reluctantly agreed, with the advice that he should return as soon as he could. A man was detailed to take him over. As he left he picked up the Browning and slung the holstered weapon over his injured shoulder.

His entry to the ante-room of the officers' quarters caused an intake of breath from the four men sitting there. The other two pilots were the first to recover, leaping to their feet. 'What the hell happened to you Fitz?' the taller of the two exclaimed. The man from Whitehall, a thin smile on his rat like face, spoke. 'So what the hell did happen to you? Another Irish cock up I suppose and where, might I ask, is the package?' The pilot ignored him. Turning to his two partners he said, 'Total fuck up fella's, typical MI6 crap. I got the girl out but picked this up on the way.' He gestured to the shoulder whilst moving quickly to the chair in which the government man sat. He continued. 'Of course the real question is which of you slimy Whitehall bastards told the Volpo we were coming.' 'What! What are you suggesting? What happened?' The man from MI6 spluttered without too much conviction. 'What happened, you piece of Whitehall garbage, is that I was met. Oh, the girl was there alright, and by the way, did you know it was a young girl? Trouble is she had a friend with her and he tried to kill her and me. We only just got out. She is in the hospital, Doc says critical. She may make it but it will be touch and go.'

Recovering, the MI6 man spluttered 'And this girl, did she say anything to you? We need to know everything, you will have to be debriefed now, it is vital I am told everything.' the man from Whitehall persisted.

The Irishman looked down, utter contempt on his face 'And you can screw yourself. I'm telling you nothing of what she said until I know which of your lot stitched us up and when I find out I am going to kill him.' The MI6 man tried to get up but the pilot had the Browning automatic out of its shoulder holster and jammed into the struggling man's face, forcing him to sit again. 'You sit still; I am sorely tempted to put you down as it is. If I could be sure you were involved in this you'd get yourself a third eye right now.'

The Colonel of the Lancers, quiet until now, coughed lightly. 'Steady on Captain, people like him aren't worth a murder charge old chap. Why not let him crawl back to London with all the other vermin? As you say, something stinks to high heaven here, but knowing all the deviants that seem to infest the intelligence services these days, I doubt we will ever get to the bottom of it, s'cuse the pun gentlemen.'

The Whitehall man, in a fit of incandescent fury, again attempted to stand.

This time the pilot stood aside to let him. 'You're finished Paddy I will have you out of this man's army so fast your bloody great clod-hopping Irish feet won't touch the ground. And you, Colonel, can expect an interview with the commanding general as well. I think you can anticipate a new career in the near future. Not that superannuated Colonels from tired old cavalry regiments with more past than future could expect much, secretary of the local golf club about all you could manage I think,' he said with a sneer. The pilot moved, the gun raised to strike, but the Colonel, his voice an icy blast, hissed 'Actually, I own the local golf club, along with a sizable chunk of the county it is in. That is in spite of the best efforts of your political masters to destroy me and people like me, so I will not be spending too much time worrying about threats from an unpleasant, overshot little creep like you. Why, if you had been one of my dogs I would have had you destroyed. Not breeding material with a jaw like that you see, but then if my guess is right probably not your thing anyway-breeding, that is.' He finished with a wintry smile. This was followed by harsh laughter from the pilots and a spluttering series of incomprehensible threats from the man who, when he finally regained control of himself, turned to the other two pilots.

'You two are witnesses to everything that was said here, including the threats to my person from him.' He pointed at the Irishman. The taller of the two spoke 'Witness to what? I haven't seen or heard a thing other than the fact that you got drunk in the bar and fell over and broke your nose.'

'What? What the hell are you talking about?' he began, but the Irishman taking the hint swung around quickly, the barrel of the Browning hitting the man from Whitehall at the bridge of his prominent nose and dropping him like stone, silencing the whining bray at last.

'Serves the fat little shit right' the tall pilot said. 'Like you say Fitz, the bastard knows more about this than we do and the Colonel has probably hit home with the deviant thing. The creep looks like one, sounds like one, so in my book probably is one, and you would think that was something that was guaranteed to arouse suspicion in MI6 these days. Although word is that there are still some of them who would like to make it compulsory.'

He paused 'Of course it means we are all in for a difficult time for a while but then it is our word against his so I think the two of us can weather it out. You and the Colonel I am not so sure about; he will work at getting you two kicked out you can bet on it.'

It was at that point that the regimental doctor entered. 'Oh dear, somebody had a bit of a fall I see, what a shame.' This was said in a tone that made it quite clear that it was nothing of the sort, and giving a clear indication that the Doc had already met the man from Whitehall. 'Actually Doc, best you get our gallant spy master over to the medical section. Probably needs to be sedated for a day or so. Nasty bonk on the old 'snozzle.' Probably going to need quite a bit of surgery to get something like that straightened out, going to be quite painful too, don't you think?' the Colonel said, the tone decidedly optimistic. 'Quite so sir, I'll get a couple of my chaps on to it.' He turned to the injured pilot, 'Captain I have had the girl transferred to the divisional hospital in Hanover, she is on the way now and should get there pretty quickly, it being Christmas Eve and all, assuming the snow hasn't blocked the Autobahns of course. The wound was bad and the bullet is still in there as you said, but from what I could see it appears to have missed anything vital, they are fully equipped over there so it was for the best.'

* * *

The next few days passed quickly. Looking back, the Irishman remembered little of the detail. However it did stay in his mind as one of the more forgettable Christmases he had endured.

He had returned to Detmold later that day with the other two pilots in one of the remaining serviceable machines. The damaged one was quietly recovered the same day by the Lancers' recovery team. It was carefully hidden away in one of the large sheds used for servicing the armoured cars and APCs, for repair and collection later.

From the East Germans nothing was heard; it was as if nothing had happened at all.

The three of them slept in the old Luftwaffe officers' mess adjacent to the airfield for most of the day. He made a half-hearted effort to enjoy Boxing Day and on the 27th of December he had requested an interview with the wing commander and tendered his resignation.

Colonel Raff, his boss, once he had heard the full story realised that this man would inevitably be hounded out anyway and reluctantly accepted, expressing his regret but understanding.

'We never seem to be able to get it right with you folks do we Captain?

The Irish have done as much for this man's army as anyone, but we always seem to screw it up for you. I am so very, very sorry to see you go old chap. If there is anything I can do for you just ask.' 'Thank you sir, there is one thing, would a lift over to Frankfurt airport be possible? I think I have a plane to catch.' 'Certainly, my boy, are you going home for a spell?' 'No sir, nothing there for me, I am heading for the Far East for a while. I hear there is a little bit of action going on out there where my limited talents may be of use. I have to go to the UK for a brief visit to say goodbye to someone very special first though. No point in hanging around here until the dust of this mess settles.'

'There is one other thing Colonel' he continued. 'Could you check up on the girl for me, just to see if she is okay and all? I will let you know where I am, when I am, but keep that bit to yourself please sir.'

He spent his last few days in Europe tidying up his affairs, not that there was much to do. Since the time in British Guiana he had made a point of trying to keep things simple. After he had left South America, the attachment to the special operations department and 25 Flight and the frequent moves this involved had ensured that he had kept it so. He had only one remaining responsibility in the UK and once that had been attended to he would be on his way to a very uncertain future.

Chapter Two

Colonel Raff had a telephone call, about three weeks later from Bangkok. He had done as promised and kept a close eye on the girl's progress. He told the pilot that she was off the danger list and expected to make a full recovery. There was a little amnesia evident though, apparently she could remember nothing of why she was there, the reason for her escape lost forever it seemed. Inevitably this had caused considerable frustration for the MI6 intelligence team sent to debrief her.

Naturally they had come looking for the pilot as a result, but true to his word the Colonel just showed them the letter of resignation and said nothing.

Just before he finished talking he said 'We got her name by the way, she is an Ingrid Fritzen. They traced her origins in the East; I have a contact with the Green Slime' he used the rather unflattering nickname of the British Army's own intelligence service as opposed to the civilianised MI5 or MI6. 'He said she appeared to be the daughter of a Stasi head of station over there but she has said nothing except her name and to ask after you. As you know the Stasi are the secret police and just as bad as the old Gestapo by all accounts, hardly surprising as most of them probably are 'old Gestapo'. Heaven knows what the escape thing was all about, but it seems nothing has been heard of the father since that night. Nothing heard about the chap you gave a haircut to either,' he added.

On the telephone at the end of the bar in Lucy's Tiger Den on Surrawong Road, the chosen and very discreet bar for those involved in the business of war, the pilot smiled to himself. Good girl, you remembered.

He said goodbye and, putting the handset down, he turned to the American with whom he was drinking.

'So this job then, is flying what, where, and for whom?' Then, as an afterthought, remembering that he had now joined the ranks of the mercenaries, 'Oh and what's the pay?'

The two men spoke long into the night discussing the Irishman's options, as well as to give the American time to weigh up and assess this new face on the block. The conversation covered everything; childhood, politics, experience and most of all the reason he was here. As the story unfolded the American found himself warming to the man. How often had he heard the story, another REMF [Rear Echelon Mother Fucker] shafting the guys at the front? Yes, if he was who he said he was this one would do. God knows we need experienced pilots up there more than ever these days, experienced and deniable. The fact that Fitzgerald was not even an American made him even more valuable. It was not a one way street, however, and the Irishman had quite a few questions of his own.

They were mainly about the job, which seemed to revolve around the re-supply of certain people doing certain things in a certain place just northeast of here. The money was discussed but Fitzgerald showed little real interest, that it was enough was all that really mattered. He did not see an expensive lifestyle in the immediate future anyway.

The American got up to leave 'Just got to check up on a few details Shaun. "Here', he pulled an envelope from his pocket and passed it over. 'This is by way of a retainer.' I will be back in town in one week, see you here then, same time same place, okay? Keep out of trouble.' Shaun glanced up from the envelope containing 10 new $100 bills. 'Trouble? Me? Never heard the word. See you in about a week then, and thanks.' 'No thanks needed, plenty more where that came from, and good old Uncle Sam needs you,' he paused and smiled, 'I think.'

The week passed quite quickly for Fitzgerald, the days starting late as the nights tended to be quite long. He did get around the town a bit, seeing a few of the sights and taking the time to re-kit himself with more appropriate clothing than that with which he had arrived.

He also invested in a little personal artillery, of which there was plenty available if you knew where to look. His choice, the familiar 9mm Browning automatic together with a couple of boxes of ammunition, although he did not think there would be any shortage of that where he was going. Still it paid to prepare, to have the edge, when the 'Fit hit the Shan' again, he had no doubt that this would not be long in coming.

He was staying in the Montien hotel conveniently located across the road from what is still one of the main centres of Bangkok's night life.

He soon fell into the routine of spending the middle of the day at a bar called 'Napoleon' about half way along the street on the right hand side on Patpong 1. This, along with the Thai Room on the adjacent Patpong 2 and known to all as the 'Typhoid Room', were popular with the airline community. Not only was the Napoleon's beer cold and the food good but it had the right atmosphere, subdued lighting and the daily newspapers. The fact that the staff were not hassling you, as was the case with the other places on the strip, was another of the attractions. Not that he had a problem with the local girls, they were working in a tough business after all, but he wanted peace and quiet not the constant harassment usually associated with this end of town.

After a late lunch and a few beers he would either return to the hotel for an afternoon nap or drift down to the British club for a swim. The girls from Qantas and British Airways used the place and it was a pleasant way to spend the afternoons.

It was inevitable that one evening he was told of that other special bar at this end of town, 'Bobby's Arms'. Unlike 'Tigers' this one didn't move around at all, hardly surprising, given that it was almost impossible to find without detailed directions.

This place was the hang out of the professional aircrew passing through the town and it was hidden at the back of the first floor of a multi-storey car park off Patpong 2. You definitely had to be told it was there. The clientele were almost exclusively technical aircrew; there were a considerable number in town with all the R&R flights from Saigon that finished up in this country.

It was run by a couple of Brits, Pete from Yorkshire with an accent to match and his mate Greg who had a penchant for expensive gold bracelets. Of 'Bobby' there was never a sign. Some were adamant that he did actually exist, others were not so sure.

These two knew everything that was going on aviation-wise, invariably before the crews themselves. It was not unusual for one or the other to ring the bell situated on the end of the bar and call out for a crew or an individual to ring their operations.

He soon found himself in the company of fellow aviators and the fact that he was military didn't seem to make any difference, a large number had seen military service themselves although none were from his old outfit. The talk was invariably about flying. Contrary to popular opinion, women were only discussed when in the air.

Years later he was to reflect on the time spent there in that week. Little did he realise that this bar and the people he met there were set to figure in his life on quite a few occasions in the future.

The week passed quickly and he arrived back in 'Tigers' a few minutes before the appointed time. Hard to beat the habits of a lifetime, he thought.

He sat in a booth at the back watching Tiger Rayling, the owner, talking to a scruffy looking bunch of individuals at the bar. As he waited his mind drifted. He wondered what the American - what was his name? Chuck Anderson, yes that was it; what he had found out. It would have been quite interesting to listen to the answers the Yanks were getting. If they spoke to some of the people he had upset he would never get the job.

The door opened eventually and Anderson walked in looking around in the gloom, Shaun waved at him from the booth. The group at the bar had stopped talking as he entered then, recognising Anderson, they said their 'Hi's' and returned to their beers, pausing only to look again as he continued past them to the booth and sat down.

'Good to see you again Shaun, how's it been? Interesting town eh?' 'Yep, I reckon there isn't much you couldn't get fixed here. Place is wide open, not that I would want to stay here too long. Liver would give up in the end I reckon.' he replied They discussed the dubious merits of Bangkok while the American waited for his beer. Rayling bought it over himself and Anderson introduced him to Shaun. 'Tiger, want you to meet Shaun Fitzgerald here; hope he's going to do some work for us up country. Guess you may see him in here from time to time.' Rayling turned to the Irishman, smiled, said 'Hi,' then added 'you gotta be nuts to work for this guy, just make sure you don't get your butt shot off, but you're welcome here anytime buddy.' Shaun smiled and nodded acknowledgement of the greeting. 'Don't take any notice of him,' Chuck continued 'He's only pissed off because he is not in the business anymore. He won this place in a card game. Didn't realise until he sobered up the next day though and then they told him that Lucy and her kid came with the deal. He has been here ever since.' Tiger laughed. His reply, as he moved back to the bar, had much to do with travel and procreation.

Anderson took a sip of his beer and continued. 'Had an interesting week actually, seems you have made some good friends and bad enemies along the way. Your lot were actually quite open about some of it. Now tell me were you really knocking off the boss's missus and did you shoot him in the arse?' 'What!' exclaimed the Irishman 'Bloody hell, who told you that load of crap?' 'Well it was one of your 'friends' in MI6 actually, a bloke with a badly broken nose. When he spoke to our guys he could barely control himself; don't think he likes you much. He was certainly very interested in your whereabouts.' 'Ah I see,' Shaun said 'No, don't suppose he does. Hope he was still in pain. I reckon he was the one who set me up on the last op and we had words, at the end of it, he lost.' He paused, 'Then again I guess I lost really. He still has his job. You don't believe all that crap, do you?' 'No we're not that dumb. We went on and checked with your previous employers and found out the truth of it all.' With a hint of respect in his voice now he continued, 'As a result I am to make you an offer which we hope you will accept.'

London

His nose had still not healed properly and his colleagues wondered if it ever would. Many hoped not, for he was universally disliked. Secretly, they wished whoever had done it had finished the job but it was obvious to all this creep was a chosen man. He was destined for high office unless something went wrong. As a result none of them was prepared to take him on. The fact that he was well aware of this made his naturally objectionable manner even more intolerable.

There was a rumour loose now though that the business in Germany had gone bad on him, the result, not what was expected. They watched and hoped that at last something would wake the top floor up to the realities of this guy, and they would get rid of him.

Had they known the real truth they would have been horrified, for as well as moving in the highest political circles Gerald Frobisher, late of the LSE, was a little more left of centre politically than was acceptable even by the standards of the most recently elected bunch of political parasites.

It had begun some years before at university as it had with most of the sleepers that seemed to infest the intelligence services of late. He had already been a card-carrying socialist and the drift further left was barely noticeable, his new friends were at pains to point out that this was desirable if he was to achieve a useful position later, useful to them that is.

What had followed a change in government was a rapid appointment in the intelligence service, something which surprised the old guard but something about which they could do nothing as the sexual scandals of the Cambridge alternatives were still unfolding.

The new government of the new order had been very quick to make known its intention to eliminate the class-ridden and chromosomally confused elements with which the service appeared to be riddled.

This was a move which, understandably, had general appeal with a population thoroughly disgusted by the betrayals to which they had been subjected by a class of people who were generally seen to have had it all anyway.

If they had realised that all they were doing was replacing one load of vermin with another, albeit from a slightly lower level on the social spectrum, they would have been much less happy.

Frobisher, untainted by the usual associations and a friend of people who now found themselves at the front of the political trough was after all, from the LSE, here he had gained a modest degree in sociology. Although the wags were known to comment that how could a degree in sociology from anywhere be anything but modest? His origins and his apparently political correct orientation, were exactly what the new minister wanted. It resulted in a meteoric rise through the department after his initial appointment.

The fact that he had absolutely no knowledge of the business of intelligence was not seen as relevant either. To this government, at this stage in its ministry, the very idea of spying was abhorrent. Only later as the insecurities of power crept in, would they realise the value of knowledge, no matter how it was obtained.

His 'other' new friends had waited for a couple of years until their man was in a position of authority and trust. As soon as this had been achieved the flow of secure information had begun, nothing much at first but enough to establish that he was one of them.

The alarm call that had resulted from the recently botched mission had begun some weeks before in East Berlin at the headquarters of the Stasi where the escape attempt was first discovered. That it was a senior member of the organisation made it essential that it be stopped.

The East Germans had come up with the idea that the attempt could be used to cause the west some political embarrassment. Involvement in a hostile act against a sovereign power was always good for the victim's Press, even if it was mainly for domestic propaganda. The run was apparently planned to take place into the British sector, and this had made the involvement of their new man a certainty.

Discreet inquiry and surveillance then revealed that the target was not going to attempt to run himself. He was sending his daughter to make contact and presumably to show good faith with his new, would-be masters.

What was clear was that he would make sure she had something of value to trade, but the fact that she was there at all would give the west considerable leverage they realised.

It was decided that she would be allowed to get to the border and there she would be eliminated with as much embarrassing involvement of the West as possible. Of course they had no way of knowing the method the British would use to help the girl escape and this is where

Frobisher came in. While the attempt was being made the father would be picked up and dealt with as well.

The Stasi then had two pieces of good luck; first they found that the man the rogue agent had picked to escort his daughter to the border, a trusted friend it seemed, was in fact on the payroll of the ultra secret department tasked with spying on the spies. He was bought in and briefed on his new role, as much to see if the impending murder of his friend's daughter would cause him a problem as any thing else. It did not.

He was then sent to London for a clandestine meeting with their man in MI6 to be briefed on the method of extraction that the British were planning.

He had met Frobisher in the 'Borsch and Tears' Restaurant in Beauchamp Place in Kensington. It was popular with the immigrant Irish population and as a result the presence of two strangers dressed in suits led to a reasonably rapid evacuation of the surrounding area. Irish nationalism had a habit of attracting the unwanted attention of strangers and the arrival of any well dressed unknown face invariably resulted in a mass exodus.

The place itself was on two levels with a cellar that was dark, with discreet booths where conversations were private.

The exodus suited them and soon the booths either side were both empty. Not that there was much to discuss as Frobisher simply handed over the extraction plan, adding that he would personally oversee the operation and that if they could eliminate the man tasked with the rescue as well, it would be useful, as the individual he had chosen was proving to be something of a problem. This would naturally add to the embarrassment that HM Government would experience.

All that had been six weeks ago and well before the incident on the border.

This next meeting was on quite a different level. The German to whom he was speaking once again, was scarcely recognisable as his contact from before the operation. The whole of his forehead badly scarred, he wore a hat throughout.

Of course Frobisher had heard the story from the individual who was responsible for the injury, but to see the results at first hand was still a shock. As they went through the aftermath it was pretty clear that, while it had only been a partial success, there were some positive aspects to it.

Understandably his East German superiors had rapidly decided to forget the planned exposure of Western aggression, hardly surprising given that the escape had succeeded, but it left them with something of a dilemma; the daughter.

Only the amnesia of the girl had saved her life. She still maintained she could remember nothing of substance of her previous life, and the British authorities had eventually released her, although she was still monitored and prohibited from leaving the country.

The interrogation of her 'late' father had revealed only that he had given her basic information on the involvement of Stasi in the Kennedy assassination some years before and this, only after the most prolonged and vicious torture they could devise. Needless to say he had not survived.

His companion had suggested elimination of the daughter but Frobisher had vetoed the idea. It would only draw attention to the failed mission again and he had already had some difficulty covering his tracks.

There was a re-awakening of the general feeling in MI6 that there was yet another mole. How else could the East Germans have found out the details of the extraction?

Only the quick thinking of the pilot had saved Her Majesty's Government from a political disaster and now the bloody pilot had disappeared. If anybody knew anything it was him for he had been alone with the girl right at the beginning, and there was still the lingering feeling that something had been said.

The MI6 top floor and the Stasi were not the only ones who wanted to know the pilot's whereabouts, the man sitting opposite Frobisher had sworn to find and kill him for the disfigurement he had suffered.

He had been told that he had to accept that the reconstruction would take years and be very painful; even then he would always be badly scarred.

The inquiry from the American, Anderson, had come as something of a surprise; at first it had worried Frobisher. Another threat, he thought, but he soon realised that it was a simple request for information about someone he loathed. He did his best to destroy the Irishman's reputation with lies and innuendo. Unfortunately it rapidly became obvious that he had overdone it because he found out that the damned Americans had not only spoken to him, but also directly to the Army and some of his old colleagues.

He had stopped as soon as he found out but he realised that it was probably too late and the real truth about Fitzgerald was out.

He made quite strenuous efforts in turn to find out the man's whereabouts but the Americans would say nothing and left him none the wiser, except that the bastard was still alive out there somewhere and the lingering suspicion that he may know something.

Naturally he also passed all this on to his East German contact who resolved to see what he could find out from their sources in the American intelligence system. The Stasi were also unsuccessful and the whereabouts of the man he wished dead more than any other, remained a mystery.

Fitzgerald had, to all intents and purposes, disappeared off the face of the earth and, after a year of looking, the files on the case in East Berlin and the thin file in the private drawer in Frobishers's office on the south bank of the Thames were forgotten.

★ ★ ★

In the years that followed, major changes occurred and ensured that even the fact that there had ever been any interest in the man faded away.

Gerald Frobisher was put into deep-freeze mode and not approached by the East Germans again.

The collapse of the Berlin wall in 1989 had caused him some concern but a call late one night had quickly put him at his ease; only his employer had changed it seemed, it was now to the Kremlin that he was responsible. He was assured that all reference to his previous dealings with the defunct East German secret police had been eliminated. He would report to the Lubianka, on Dzerzhinsky Square, as and when it was required.

His now ex, Stasi control, disappeared and was never picked up by the West German department set up to trawl through the files in East Berlin.

The man did keep in contact with Frobisher though, and as the years went by there was the occasional private disposal required by the newly knighted Sir Gerald, this kept his erstwhile partner gainfully employed.

Frobisher found it most convenient to have the power to eliminate any threat to himself, not that it was a regular event one or two a year at most. The man was always very professional and in most cases 'natural causes' appeared on the death certificates, along with an occasional 'accidental death' none ever caused any suspicion and the elimination of any threat accelerated Frobisher's rise to the top.

Along the way he had polished the accent. No more the nasal whine of 'Estuarine,' now it was the plummy vowels of the cultured civil servant he saw himself to be. As the years passed few remembered him as he was and, when possible he ensured the early retirement or disposal of those who did.

He did make discreet enquires about the activities of his ex control and some-time employee with his new masters at KGB. He suspected the man was also on their payroll, if only as a casual, probably performing a similar function to that which he used him for. He was reassured by the Russians to learn that the man was under constant surveillance and would be eliminated if there was any suggestion of a threat to their most valuable asset.

Chapter Three
Thailand 1967

So Captain Shaun Fitzgerald late of Her Majesty's Army Air Corps, found himself standing on the airfield of Udon in northern Thailand wondering what the hell he had got himself into.

The organisation he had joined, Continental Air Services, flew alongside the more famous Air America. Air America was the not-so- secret air arm of the CIA, and had its own origins in this neck of the woods anyway; CAS was a totally deniable offshoot of it.

AA was involved in the business of sustaining the forces opposed to the enemies of the USA. Twenty years ago, it had been a different name and a different enemy; then Japanese, now the North Vietnamese and their Laotian stooges the Pathet Loa. The war had started here years before, right at the end of WW2 when the French had tried and failed to re-establish their colonial empire. Inevitably, American paranoia over the Communist plague had dragged them in to fill the vacuum left by the departing French.

Fitzgerald spent the first few days re-acquainting himself with the UH1 helicopter, the ubiquitous Huey; the chosen mount of much of US army aviation. It was destined to become synonymous with the war in South Vietnam.

He had flown them when attached to the Americans in Southern Germany a while back and was soon familiar with the machine again.

His fellow pilots had clearly been told of his background. Few questions were asked and those only about any specialist skills he might have that could be useful.

He had told Anderson that he was a trained Forward Air Controller [FAC] and an Air OP [AOP], therefore the airborne control and direction of fighter bombers and the directing of artillery were familiar to him, he had also given a detailed summary of other skills that might be of use.

Anderson had rolled his eyes and emphasised that the job was re-supply and 'casevac,' essentially civilian work. Military tasks were the province of a bunch of guys referred to locally as the 'Ravens'; these 'almost' ex airforce pilots were flying Cessna O1 Birddogs on FAC ops. He was expressly forbidden to get involved in that sort of stuff over there. Apparently the characters at the bar in Bangkok where they had met were a sample of this rather select and certainly wild bunch. Somehow Fitzgerald did not think they would really give a damn who did the fire control, as long as the bad guys were neutralised.

Time passed quickly. It became a blur of wild re-supply missions, frequently under fire and battle damage was a common event. The odd rescue job was thrown in for a change and these tended to be even more explosive, given the North Vietnamese habit of waiting while a downed pilot called for rescue and then giving the rescue chopper a hard time.

It was an unwritten law that if one of their own went down everything was dropped and everybody closed on the crash site.

Fortunately, on each occasion he had been involved in a hot pickup so far the local Raven had called in large amounts of airborne fire suppression and the waiting guns were rapidly reduced to smoking ruins with the associated human debris scattered about the site. Even so his two door gunners had expended vast quantities of .50 cal on most rescues.

It was in the last-but-one month of his contract that things finally caught up with him. The job was simple, a load of ammo from the secret city of Long Tieng in the southwest corner and just off the 'Plain of Jars' out to Lima 32.

The Limas were a series of landing sites which had been set up throughout the country a few years before by a Major 'Hienie' Aderholt, a USAF officer. Lima 32 was in the hills north east of the POJ, as the high plateau of central Laos was more usually known.

It should have been a milk run but, as he was well aware, the commies had been pushing south from the North Vietnam border for a few weeks, even though it was coming into the wet season. The usual pull back was going to be late this year, if it happened at all.

Tracking across the plain at 6000 feet he noticed the tell- tale signs on the ground and on the radio as the FAC Ravens vectored the fighter bombers on to the targets; targets that should have retreated north weeks ago.

As they reached the northern edge of the plateau the 'Karst' country began to rise up to meet them; these limestone mountains covered a large part of the region here.

The landing at Lima 32 passed without incident. The two door gunners pushed the boxes of ammo, food and medical stuff out for the waiting Meo guerrillas. These were the local hill tribesman, the Hmong people, real tough mountain folks who fought on the American side and generally showed up the lowland Laotian run army as the gutless bunch of bastards they really were.

He waived at the resident CIA liaison officer and started to pull up, when over the radio came the 'Mayday'. One of the FAC guys had taken a direct hit from ground fire and was going in, the position was about 10 miles to the west of Lima 6.

Already 'Cricket', the airborne fire control aircraft was calling for the nearest helo's and it took a few minutes to relay his own position and that he was on the way, as was every other AA and CAS chopper in the area. It soon became clear that he was closest and it was to him that 'Cricket' gave the latest coordinates.

Throughout, the damaged Raven was calling his situation. It appeared he had been at the beginning of a shoot and inadvertently flown into a flak trap, picking up a load of 37mm. It had taken out one cylinder of the engine. He knew this, he said because the whole engine cowling had gone too, together with the rudder and a chunk of the port wing. He was going in and was desperately trying to find somewhere a bit flat to do so. His back seat observer was dead or injured, he wasn't sure.

As Shaun approached the area he realised that it was infested with the enemy, fire suppression would be required if he was to have any chance of getting these guys out. The problem was that 'Cricket' had no replacement Raven within 20 minutes of the expected pick-up point, even though there were a dozen fighter bombers in the pattern overhead waiting to drop.

He called in 'Cricket, this is Tango 15.' 'I'll do it, they can use me as a bearing to the target and I'll get my door guys to hose the areas required with tracer. If they drop there I may be able to get in right after. Is the Raven down yet?' 'Roger 15, you able to do that? You know what's required?' 'Sure do, been doing it for years Cricket.' He heard the airborne controller calling a brace of F105 fighter bombers out of the stack. These aircraft, the last of the century series of USAF fighter aircraft, were affectionately referred to as 'Thuds.' It did not take too much imagination to know why.

They were to pick up the line of the Huey and drop when they were told to. The targets would be marked with tracer from the chopper. The Raven called in on his personal radio that he was down, he had got his Meo backseater out and was laid up behind a bank to the east of the wreck. The bad guys had appeared from the trees on the other side of the aircraft and were heading towards it, hurry would be good, was the rueful end of the message.

Shaun picked up the wrecked O1 dead ahead with the bank off to the right but as soon as he headed for it he started to take hits from the NVA on the ground. Pulling off, he called the fighters in, flying straight at the wreck about 2 miles up range from it with the gunners firing tracer directly forward. The leader called in that he had the O1 on the ground in sight and Shaun told them that this and the area towards the timber line was the target, the bank was to be avoided. He would follow the strike in and try and use the post-impact chaos to pick the guys up.

It worked like a dream. The closest NVA were caught in the open and destroyed. Hovering over the downed FAC guy, his door gunners pulled the unconscious and injured Meo observer in, followed by the Raven. He lifted off as soon as they were on board. Already the bad guys were regrouping and he could feel the first strikes of bullets on the aircraft.

Relaxing as the chopper pulled through 4000ft, the impact of the 37mm flack was an unpleasant surprise but not as unpleasant as what happened next.

It must have been one of the last rounds, as the shooting finished there was a loud bang from behind his head and the Huey lurched into what was close to a 90-degree bank to the left.

He only stopped the roll with full right rudder, which was really maximum pitch on the tail rotor. With the stick hard against the right hand stop and full power pedal, the machine took on a crazy attitude of about 30 degrees of bank with the nose stuck up in the air. The whole thing was gently turning back the way he had come and back into range of the ground fire.

Making a rather tense radio call he said that he appeared to have taken a hit in the lateral cyclic system, and that, as a result, they were in a slow left turn that was going to take them back over the ground fire.

'Cricket' called in a Raven, recently arrived, to put some markers on the flak guns that had done the damage, at the same time calling in the next two 'Thuds' to bomb on those markers.

By this time he had worked out, with a little careful experimentation, that the lateral cyclic system was not connected at all and the only means of directional control he had was with the pedals. Further investigation revealed that if he pulled up on the collective lever the lateral cyclic system had its range reduced by the swash plate moving up the main rotor mast and the aircraft stopped turning, as long as he kept full right pedal in.

The only problem with that was that the aircraft also climbed and he was not sure how he was going to get it down again, because the reverse was also true. When he lowered the lever the angle of bank and the rate of turn increased alarmingly.

As he got the situation stabilised he managed to coax the machine round to a westerly heading and call on the intercom. The right hand door gunner replied. His mate on the left was hit and out of it but alive. He had patched him up as best he could, the Raven was okay and swearing that he would never get in one of these things again; his back seater was still unconscious.

Shaun told the gunner to ensure they were all strapped in real tight and to sit away from the doors if possible as he had no idea how he was going to get down; it was unlikely to be smooth.

He listened as the Raven vectored another strike on to the guns that had done this to him and, when he could, he called in. 'Cricket, Tango 15, I've got this thing heading 270 at around 6000 but I can't descend without turning so I am going to continue on this heading towards and beyond Lima 22, if I can.' Lima 22 was another of their tactical strips, this one on the western edge of the POJ. 'If I get that far I will descend. This will be a spiral down over the strip, I hope. You got an 01 around who can shadow me? This thing is not flying so well and I may have to head for the dirt PDQ before then!' The operator in the control aircraft came back straight away 'Roger Tango 15, break, Raven 26 it's yours. Break, Tango 15 how you gonna land that thing with all that bank on? Reckon you can?' '15, Hell I don't know, don't think anybody has ever done this before. Just make sure there is a chopper there to pick us up, if we make it that is. We have casualties Okay?' 'Cricket, Roger.'

He heard Raven 26 call in that he had him in sight and was closing and the nearest AA chopper calling in as well.

All that remained was to try and figure out how to get down. Raven 26 was Charley Smitt that day and as he pulled up alongside he called. 'Tango 15, Raven 26, that you Shaun?' 'Sure is Charley, look can you see what's happened up round the main rotor mast, damage an all?' After a few minutes the reply came. 'Yep, looks a bit mangled up, there is a rod hanging off the lower swash plate. I guess that is the lateral cyclic run you've lost. The casing at the bottom of the mast has gone as well but everything else seems okay. You've got a lot of holes in you though, looks as though you are losing gas, any casualties in the back?' 'Just what I needed Charley. Affirm, port side gunner and the Meo back-seater at the moment, just hope I can keep it that way.'

He checked his fuel state and realised Lima 22 was no longer an option and as there was no way he could survive an auto rotation like this, the only hope was a landing with power while he still had an engine. The descent could not be delayed any longer. 'Gotta go down Charley only got about 10 minutes left and I need power if I am going to pull this off. See the clear area up ahead? I'll pass it and then start down. Have a look for the bad guys will you,' Charley Smitt, a man of few words, gave a 'Roger' and pealed off to check out the area he thought the crippled chopper might land in.

As Shaun slowly lowered the collective lever the bank increased alarmingly. He eased the nose down; fore and aft cyclic was still working. He set up a rate of descent of 400 feet per minute with about 40 degrees of bank, the nose of the machine was still pointing at the sky although a little lower than before. The chopper had started to turn as soon as he lowered the lever and continued through 4 or 5 rotations with altitude decreasing all the time. He had no idea where the actual touchdown point might be or even how he was to do it. One thing for sure, he doubted this old girl would ever fly again. Somewhere in his subconscious he heard Raven 26 calling in a couple of A6's, the old WW2 navy fighter bombers still in use here. There must be trouble down there he thought, as if I haven't got enough to worry about.

Passing through 200 feet he figured he had some idea of where they would hit and he called on the intercom for everyone to hold on. The ground rushed up at a crazy angle. He felt the main rotor blades strike the ground and pulled up on the collective lever. The chopper staggered into the air, trying to right itself and even climb away but as the left hand skid of the undercarriage hit the ground and dug in, all hell broke loose. The main rotor, which had briefly lifted clear as he had pulled on the collective lever, now struck the ground with considerable force. This caused the machine to turn and cartwheel on itself, sliding backwards and upside down for what seemed an age; eventually it came to a stop pointing in the direction it had approached from.

Shaun found himself lying on his side, the entire front of the aircraft had been destroyed, his feet still on what remained of the pedals. The intercom circuit was amazingly still alive on battery power and it erupted in an explosion of bad language as the rescued Raven let fly at all things rotary. 'Okay guys' he interrupted 'lets get out of here before she blows,' undoing his harness as he spoke. All he had to do was crawl out forwards, there was nothing left there to stop him. Once clear he moved around to the port side which, sticking up in the air was now really the top of the machine as it had rolled right over. Pulling himself up he looked down into the main cabin area. It was a mess of bodies in varying degrees of consciousness. The Raven was clearly okay, still swearing from somewhere in the middle of the heap. His starboard side gunner was hanging in the harness conscious, dazed but coming out of it quickly. The other two were going to need help.

Eventually they managed to get them out and lay them on the grass some distance away. Shaun turned to look at his chopper lying forlornly, almost upside down, pointing in the direction of landing now little more than scrap. He realised they had all been very lucky.

His emergency radio broke into his thoughts, Smitt was telling him some NVA were heading his way and that he should make for the low hill behind the wreck, pick up was on the way. Meantime the A6s' would entertain them with a firework display.

As they carried the Meo and helped the now conscious port side gunner to the pick-up point, the A6's bombed and strafed the NVA infantry that had been threatening them. Eventually - it seemed an age, but was probably only 5 minutes - an all black Air America Huey pulled into the hover above them. They quickly threw the inert Meo in, followed by the injured gunner, boarded themselves and were away.

As they levelled off he started to relax; Jesus Christ but that was close. He closed his eyes, opening them only when his gunner pulled his arm. He was pointing at Shaun's left hand side. Glancing down he saw the reason. Oh sod it, not again; the whole left hand side of his flight suit was a mass of blood. Between them, he and the gunner cut the cloth away. The wound was a mess and covered the one he had received on the German border crossing a year or so ago. Bloody hell, he thought, as the pain kicked in, bad enough getting shot twice in the same year but what sort of dumb bastard gets shot in the same place twice? Between them they strapped a dressing on and waited for it all to end.

They were offloaded at Long Tieng, put straight onto an Air America C47 and flown to Udon. Here the three of them Shaun, the starboard gunner and the Meo backseater, were taken off to the base hospital. But not before the rescued Raven had come over to offer his thanks, apologising, saying that he didn't really mean all the things he had said about choppers and their drivers. He promised to drift by later with a bottle to see how they were.

True to his word the rescued Raven came back a couple of days later, introducing himself as John Morgan operating out of Long Tieng having recently moved up from Pakse in the south. 'Explains why we haven't met before John, I thought I knew all the guys out there at spook city. Name's Shaun Fitzgerald by the way. I'm with CAS out of here.' 'You Irish then?' Morgan asked, he nodded. 'Long way from home eh?' 'Aren't we all John, aren't we all' he replied.

They sat sharing the bottle of 'White Horse' Morgan had bought with him. They hid it every time a nurse appeared but eventually got sprung as their stories got taller and the noise louder, having been joined by the port side gunner from down the ward. She quickly kicked Morgan out and gave Shaun and his gunner a dressing down.

He was in the place for another week. The doctor said that this time the stitches and the wound must be allowed time to heal under supervision, and that a spell of R&R was required after release. He thought about this for some time. The usual place the guys went to for a break was Bangkok but this time he thought he would try Saigon, for a change.

* * *

A week later found him strolling down one of the city's main roads. Having been designed largely by the French this part of town anyway, was blessed with wide boulevards. Naturally, being the Far East, this meant even more chaos as the never-ending swarms of humanity and metal tried to manoeuvre. The streets were full and it seemed everyone was in a hurry and each had a horn on car or bike and used it endlessly.

Eventually tiring of the noise he turned off into a side street. Here whilst the volume was lower, it was still wall to wall people.

What had changed was a lessening in the military presence. Gradually, he became aware of a distinct lack of western faces and he touched the heavy Browning automatic in the holster under his right arm. He had been undecided whether to carry it or not and had talked to the boys in Udon before he left. General advice was that while it was okay to go unarmed in Bangkok, in Saigon you have to be nuts to do so. For the first time since his arrival he was glad of the advice and the feel of metal under his arm.

Slowly, as he moved further from the main drag, the congestion and the noise eased. He could actually see to the corner of the block now thirty metres away in front of him. It was while he was stopped, undecided as to which street café to use, that the feeling began.

Something was wrong; his subconscious had picked it up. He moved to the edge of the walkway and looked up and down the street again. A cafe on the other side of the road had a couple of westerners sitting outside drinking: looks okay. His eyes moved on. People walking: nothing unusual there. Eyes moving again: a motor bike, static, rider sitting on it pointing towards the café and the two westerners, pillion rider looking into a large bag on his shoulder: wrong!

His hand was already moving to the Browning as he stepped out into the road, watching as the pillion rider removed the grenade. The rider started to pull away, slowly moving up to the café, the intention obvious, his mate pulling the pin and about to throw as they approached the place.

Fitzgerald moved rapidly to the middle of the road, the sight of the gun enough to make the traffic shy away giving him a clear field of fire. As he raised the weapon and fired he yelled, 'Grenade!' at the top of his voice. The two rounds hit the rider in the chest, throwing him backwards, pushing the guy on the pillion off the back of the bike. The grenade he had been holding ready to throw into the crowded cafe fell to the road beside the bike, now on its side, the motor revving madly. Fitzgerald dropped to the ground, aware as he did that the people in the café and just about everybody else in the street who had heard his yell had done the same. The explosion, when it came, was surprisingly muffled.

At first it was unclear what had caused this but as he struggled to get up he could see that the rider had apparently fallen on top of the thing and taken the full force of the explosion. It had just about cut him in half. The pillion rider, however, was anything but out of it. Staggering to his feet he was dazed but otherwise unhurt. Fitzgerald watched fascinated, as the man once again searched the satchel on his shoulder.

On his knees now and in the middle of the road Fitzgerald raised the Browning again and fired two more rounds: the first to the chest; the second, the head. He wasn't sure whether the man had armed the grenade this time but he wasn't about to take a chance. Yelling a second warning he hit the ground again counting a very long fifteen seconds before rapidly getting to his feet and running up to the two bodies. Both were very dead. He grabbed the satchel, looking quickly inside, confirming at least three more grenades.

He ran back to the café, looking for the whites he had seen at the kerb- side tables. The two men were swearing loudly as they struggled to extricate themselves from a pile of tables and chairs. Fitzgerald started pulling from the top, freeing them from the mess and helping them to their feet. 'Reckon we should get out of here fellas', he said 'before the locals make a meaningful decision and decide we are the bad guys after all. Come on!' They looked at him, nodded, and followed him quickly to the back of the bar and into an alley. As they reached it the sirens started. Saigon's finest had arrived; definitely time to be somewhere else.

The three of them moved quickly through the narrow streets and alleys, quick enough to put some distance between them and the increasing noise but not so fast that the locals took much notice.

They chose a direction that eventually brought them out onto another of the main boulevards that divided the city. Slowing now, as much to get their breath as their bearings, Fitzgerald turned to the other two, 'Probably wouldn't be a bad idea to get off the street for a while. Anybody feel like a beer?' 'Thought you would never ask,' grumbled the shorter of the two.

They sat at the rear of the chosen bar, facing the front door in the approved manner, having already figured where the rear exit was. As the large cold Carlsberg arrived they settled down to the business of introductions. 'Reckon we owe you more than a beer mate,' the shorter of the two began. 'Name's Digby, friends call me 'Digger;' you can call me that okay; we're from 'Stralia'.' Fitzgerald smiled, having already figured that out from the stream of bad language that he had heard from under the pile of chairs.

The other man held out his hand 'Jim Kennedy, pleased to meet you and what he says goes double for me. You saved our bacon back there for sure. We owe you.' Shaun embarrassed, introduced himself and they settled down to the intricate business of establishing what each did.

It was tricky because it had to be done without giving offence. This became very clear when Digger, while they were going through their lucky escape suddenly erupted with 'Christ, mate, where the hell did you learn to shoot like that?' and then quickly followed it with a very embarrassed, 'Bloody hell; sorry, none of my business.'

'No problem Digger' the Irishman said, but it killed the subject.

The three of them sat there for a couple of hours drinking, by which time they knew each other quite well. The two Australians were aircrew as well, but while they had been military and in Vietnam they were now civilians, still in Vietnam and still flying. As Jim pointed out, they were doing almost the same job but for a lot more money.

They had been transport crew. Jim was a pilot and Digger a flight engineer in the Australian Air Force flying C130 Hercules. They had eventually left the service to join another ex airforce guy called Reg Bartlett.

Bartlett had got his hands on a couple of old DC3s and started his own freight outfit operating out of Saigon. That was about three years ago. Since then the airline, 'Trans Pacific' was the chosen name, had grown at a spectacular rate, now it had five Boeing 707s as well as a couple of C130s and of course the two original Dakotas. Jim and the Digger were on the 707s, which at least meant that the airline could actually live up to its name and get across the Pacific, something that the original DC3 had stretched a bit.

They were currently flying the Rest and Recreation [R&R] contract flying troops on leave to the various places in the area. They flew them down to Sydney, Bangkok and Manila, Japan and of course back to the USA on a regular rotation.

Having told their story they waited for Fitzgerald to reciprocate.

He told them very briefly what he did and what he did it in, adding that a command rating on the DC3 was his heaviest qualification. He went on to say that while his contract was just about up he would probably have to sign on again as there was nothing else that he could do even though he was reluctant to commit to another year. Things got a little quiet when the question of just who he actually worked for came up.

'Prefer not to discuss that fellas,' he said. The other two, realising that they had touched the wire once again, offered their apologies. Both had been in theatre long enough to know that there were quite a few things about this shitty little war that were never going to come out and that it was probably for the best that they didn't.

Jim glanced at the Digger, receiving a confirmatory nod. 'Well mate, as we said, we owe you, and what's more we are very short of blokes at the moment. If you are interested I am pretty sure we can offer you something right away. Of course, I will have to clear it with Reg, but once I tell him the story I reckon there will be a job for you with us if you want it. I guess it would be on the C47 at first but I think you could bet on being over with us on the 707 pretty quickly. What do you think? It would mean you could probably avoid getting any more holes in yourself. We tend not to get shot at too often anymore and you never know, third time 'they' might get lucky. We wouldn't want that eh Dig?' Digger grunted an affirmative.

Shaun, a little taken a back paused, recovering from the surprise. He said 'That's an offer I would have difficulty refusing gents, and very generous of you. As I said my contract comes up in a month. I will have to go back to complete it once the leave is over but after that if the offer still goes, yes I am your man. Maybe you can let me know before I leave? I'm here until Monday. Is that long enough for you to clear it with the owner? Reg was it?'

Jim reckoned he could probably get an answer by the next day as Bartlett was due to arrive that night from a Manila shuttle. He went on to suggest that maybe they could all meet later in their hotel after he had had a chance to run through it all with the boss. If Shaun were to come over at, say, 2000 or so, they could well fix it all up then.

'You sure you don't want to give him the night to chew it over?' asked the Irishman. 'He might feel a little pressurised this way.' 'Nope, it will be okay' Jim continued, 'You don't know this guy, I can assure you he will decide to take you on straight away. You'll like him. One hell of a character, knows how to make decisions. None of this 'hold hands in the shower' touchy feely crap, with him, he makes a decision and sticks to it.

What's more he is smart enough to know that it is the blokes that make the business work and he looks after his people.'

They left the bar in a much more relaxed state than they had arrived, the drama of a few hours ago all but forgotten. Separating, they agreed to meet later at the hotel used by TPA for crew rest. Shaun climbed into a cab and headed off to his own more modest accommodation, reflecting en route on the strange turn of events that day.

An airline job would suit very nicely thank you. His current contract was almost up and he and had no real idea of what to do next. He had serious misgivings about Europe, and the UK was definitely out, so up until today he had reluctantly decided to renew. Whether he would survive another year of Laos he had grave doubts. Few did.

Now that had all changed. Yes, he would take the job if it was offered and from what Jim Kennedy said it was almost a done deal. We shall see, he mused.

The cab was crawling through the traffic, eventually coming to a halt at the very junction of the road in which the shoot-out had taken place. The driver, in broken English with an American accent, told him in lurid detail how some white guy had gone berserk and shot down two innocent Vietnamese and then run off with two other whites. Shaun leaned back in the seat, the police were still there and the usual chaos after such an event was still going on. It certainly confirmed that his decision to bug out was the right one.

The meeting with Reg Bartlett went well; the man was everything Jim Kennedy had said and more. He had sat and listened to the story of the afternoon's activities as described by Fitzgerald even though he had already heard the story from Kennedy. He had asked a couple of questions on the DC3 qualifications and hours on type. He had asked no questions of Shaun's current employment or location. It was pretty clear that the other two had already advised that this was an area best left alone.

'Okay Shaun' he began 'the job's yours. I gather you are contracted for one more month, and that fits in rather well. We will put you on the Dak out of Than Son Knut at first but, all being well, we'll right hand seat you on the 707 within 6 months or so. How's that?' He handed a single sheet of paper to the Irishman. 'Those are the pay scales you will be on. I would think they are a little more than what your current employer pays you and I can pretty much guarantee you will not be shot at'--- he paused, 'Quite so much,' he added, with a smile.

Shaun glanced at the figures and saw that he would indeed be substantially better off.

They spent the rest of the evening drinking on the balcony of Bartlett's room overlooking the heaving mass that was Saigon. They all agreed there was no hope for this place under the current regime. Corruption murder and mayhem were the rules here. The locals had no interest in defeating communism, happy to sit back and let their allies fight and die while they ran the rackets. But as Reg Bartlett said, it's an ill wind that blows nobody any good and at least they would get something out of the mess.

He confided that he was already planning the activities of TPA in the post-war era. He reckoned there was room in Australia for a second international carrier. At the moment Trans Australian Airlines and Ansett ran the domestic ops like Tweedle-dum and Tweedle-dee, following each other round the sky playing at competition. International operations were, however, the sole possession of Qantas, the government owned behemoth, and they were all well overdue for a dose of real competition.

TPA was running at least half of the R&R flights for the ANZAC contingent over in Vung Tao province and as such was establishing a useful and respected reputation with the governments of Australia and New Zealand.

Around 2300, Shaun excused himself. He was to fly out the next day. They agreed dates and locations, simply he was to be back here in 5 weeks and on the line soon after.

He thanked Bartlett, who would hear none of it. 'Way I see it Shaun is that if it wasn't for you I would be down two of my best men, so I figure this is by way of thanks from all of us, okay?' Digger, never slow, rumbled, 'Geez boss I didn't know you cared!' and was studiously ignored for his trouble.

They shook hands at the door and Shaun left, feeling better than he had for years.

Bartlett and the other two returned to the balcony. 'Interesting man there blokes,' he began. 'Bloody hell, you should see him shoot' exclaimed Digger. 'He didn't learn that flying choppers I can tell you.' 'So I gather Dig. Let's hope he doesn't have to any more. I'd say that young fella is long overdue for a piece of good luck. I just hope he gets through the next month in one piece and we can provide it.'

The return journey was tedious. He was obliged to fly first to Bangkok and wait there for three hours before hitching a ride on a DC3 from the military side of the airport up to Udon.

It was late afternoon before he finally threw his old bag on the bunk he hoped he would see the end of in four weeks.

He had just closed his eyes when the little Thai guy who looked after them shook him. 'Mr Fitzgerald' he said, although it didn't come out quite like that --'Midder Fitweral' was the best he could manage. However the meaning was clear, the boss wanted him.

Within the hour he was once again in an old Huey heading east over the border for the secret city. He hadn't taken much notice of what he was carrying or even the other crew members; they were not his regular guys is all he knew.

At Long Tieng he wandered over to the Raven hooch to get a beer. He realised he was going to be here for the night. Already there was something cooking up for tomorrow and he needed to catch up on the 'scuttle butt'. A lot seemed to have happened in the weeks he was away.

He met his new friend John Morgan at the bar and within the hour was just about up to speed.

It seemed the commies had given up with the advance that had been in progress when he had left but, whereas in previous years, the wet season had usually involved a significant pull back to the North Vietnam border, this year they were proving a little more obstinate. As such the POJ was still an effective combat zone and the Meo irregulars were having a hard time of it, as the monsoon made close air support increasingly difficult.

Morgan told him his old mate Charley Smitt had copped a packet last week while marking a target for a couple of A6s. Apparently Charlie had run right into a load of 37mm and gone down. He had been rescued by the skin of his teeth by a CAS chopper but his backseat guy had died. Charley was badly shot up and in the hospital back at Udon.

By the end of the next day, the R&R days in Saigon were just a memory. It was as though he had never left. What he knew was that the sooner he got out of this place the better. Flying back to Udon he realised how bloody tired of it all he was. It didn't seem to matter what the guys did, there was always some REMF back there in a safe little hole somewhere, ready to fuck it all up. In the entire time that he had been here nothing had changed.

The Commies were still here, the Meo were still dying, and the lowland Laotians were still doing anything they could to avoid getting off their backsides and defending their country.

The weeks that followed were a string of re-supply missions with the odd casevac thrown in. He had visited Charley Smitt as often as possible and usually managed to get thrown out by the duty sister when she realised he always bought a bottle in with him. Like him Charley had had enough and was calling it quits. He was going to return to the States and recover there; he was not sure whether he would fly again.

Shaun still managed to get his aircraft shot up now and again and he really began to wonder if the luck of the Irish would hold out.

He had already told Chuck Anderson of his intention to quit when the month was up. Anderson had made a half-hearted attempt to talk him into another year but, when Shaun told him of the offer he had, he realised that there was no way.

The actual day of his departure was something of an anti-climax as is usually the way of these things. He had had a few beers in the CAS hooch on the last night, some of his own people and a couple of the Air America guys had wandered over to say, 'So long', they had all got pretty pissed, reminiscing. The next morning, he was alone, the rest all away on some operation or other. It was only the little Thai who stood at the door to the hut smiling, as always, bowing and saying good bye. Shaun dug into his pack, pulled out a carton of smokes and a bottle of Red Label and gave them to the little guy, along with a wad of Baht from his pocket. Tears appeared in the old man's eyes and Shaun, embarrassed, patted him on the shoulder and turned away. Damn it, he thought, these are good people, and they really are worth more than this commie shit.

As he walked across to the makeshift terminal to pick up the scheduled DC3 to Bangkok, Anderson came over and shook his hand. 'So long Paddy. Been nice to know you, one hell of a year I reckon. You take care now.' He handed Shaun an envelope with his final pay. 'Bit extra in there too old buddy; reckon you've earned it.' 'Thanks Chuck, it sure has, might see you around. The first job is on the DC3 so it is quite possible I will be back, not quite so close to the heat this time though, I hope.' The American smiled 'Sure,' and turned away.

★ ★ ★

His arrival in Saigon and induction into TPA was complete within the week; he flew a couple of sectors with one of their training people and was passed out in command. The co-pilots were usually young Vietnamese guys with very low hours, while down the back it was usually a war-weary old load master on the freight runs, or a couple of young local girls on the passenger jobs. The flying itself was around the major towns in country, that and the large American bases. Naturally, given Reg's connections, they spent quite a bit of time going in and out of Nui Dat over on the coast in Vung Tau province, as it was here that the major part of the Australian and New Zealand contingent were based.

There was a scheduled daily run to Phnom Pen in Cambodia and then on to Bangkok with a layover there. Inevitably, as they stayed in the Montien Hotel, 'The Napoleon,' 'Bobbys,' and 'Tigers,' all close, became frequent places of refuge from the chaos of Viet Nam, although, as Shaun was quick to say when pressed and pissed even there, nothing came close to Laos.

In Saigon he frequently ran into Jim and the Digger on the trooping flights and they, true to their word, had reminded Reg Bartlett that he had promised an early transfer to the right-hand seat of the 707 for him.

It seemed like only yesterday when he got the call but he realised that he had already been flying the DC3 for 9 months in TPA when Reg called him in to the local office. He told him he was on a 707 conversion starting in Sydney Australia in a week, finishing up with a, 'If that's okay?'

PART TWO
OPERATIONS

★

Michael Patrick Collins

Chapter Four

S o began a career that was to span something in excess of twenty-five years during which the friendship of the three men was forged into a lifelong bond.

Shaun rapidly moved to the left-hand seat, although, given the vagaries of the industry he frequently found himself sharing the flight deck with his two friends. Reg Bartlett was also a regular on the flight deck.

However, it was with Jim and the Digger that he felt most at home and it was no accident that they quite often operated as a crew in spite of both he and Jim being command rated now.

It was on one of their many flights from Saigon to Sydney, towards the end of the war in Vietnam, that he had remarked to Jim that it puzzled him why they were always scheduled to transit Saigon in the heat of the day. The aircraft was inevitably at its maximum weight with a full load of returning troops and maximum fuel.

With temperatures in the high thirties and above, planning was a piece of fiction and just getting airborne more the result of curvature of the earth than anything else when they were expected to fly non- stop.

Jim had asked Reg about it and been told that as far as he knew it was a security matter. He agreed it made no sense at all and it had caused a diversion to Darwin on more than one occasion on the way south, but that is what the State Department wanted and he could not get them to change.

★ ★ ★

Time passed and the war was soon no more than a fading memory.

Shaun was in command of a brand new 747\300 on the long night flog to London out of Bangkok, when this particular puzzling question was finally answered.

He had received a request for a flight deck visit, from that rarest of beings, a respected political correspondent from the parliamentary press office in Canberra and in conversation the subject of Vietnam came up. Apparently this guy had been in the army at that time, something in intelligence and liaison he said.

Shaun had again asked why they were always tasked to leave in the heat of the day, saying that the security excuse did not seem to hold water. He explained that it had frequently caused extreme difficulty, with one aircraft actually receiving a couple of bullet holes from ground fire because at max weight and max temperature, the rate of climb was so poor that they had been very low and way outside the protected zone.

The guy had looked at him for a few seconds, 'Is that what they told you?' 'Sure is' he had replied. 'Bastards,' the man swore. 'It had sod all to do with security Captain, at least not the security you are thinking about.' 'What do you mean? Shaun persisted. 'Well, if you remember, it was not the most popular war we have had and all the politicians were really worried about was that the Sydney arrival should be in the early hours of the morning. Theory was the great unwashed masses of 'peaceniks' wouldn't be able to stay awake that long and there would not be a scene at the airport. Can you remember how things were when you arrived? Pretty quiet, would be my guess, just the families, I bet?' Shaun thought for a minute 'Yep that just about sums it up. It was always just that, a few women and kids, the usual hugs and tears, no media and certainly none of the great unwashed. Reckon there would have been a riot if that load of scum had tried it on with the young fellas we bought out. They were all pretty wired up from what they were reading in the papers anyway as I recall. You mean the bloody politicians were quite prepared to put us all in harm's way just so they could avoid a bit of embarrassment?' 'That's about the size of it,' the journo said.

He had sat there talking for some time while Shaun spent most of the time listening. He, like all airline pilots, had a natural antipathy towards the media having seen so much crap written by idiots who knew nothing about the business. However in this case he found himself warming to the guy. The man seemed to be more interested in talking than story hunting and his views on the way of the world were very much in tune with their own.

It was during a lull in this somewhat one-sided conversation that the journalist picked up the paper Shaun had been reading, looked at the lead story in the overseas news section and said, 'Well from the look of this at least somebody is doing something about it.' Shaun glanced down at the page.

OP 1

It was a story in the foreign section. Apparently the president of some tin pot central African republic, who had been robbing his people blind for years and who was even alleged to have resorted to cannibalism in the belief that it gave him the strength of his victims, had been assassinated.

The interesting thing was that while just about all the western governments had agreed the man was a pariah, nothing was ever done. It was dismissed as an 'African' issue for Africans to sort out. Naturally expecting any African Government to take on a housekeeping role like this was fanciful in the extreme. Most were so corrupt themselves that they could either see nothing wrong, or the thought that they might be the next candidate was enough to keep them out of it.

The fact that something had been done was therefore a complete surprise, especially as it seemed very unclear as to who had done it. However, it was what followed that got the media really excited. The initial story was that it was a thoroughly professional job and there was a strong suspicion that it had been organised from outside the country.

Apparently an empty cartridge case from a high powered sniper rifle had been found some distance from one of the many rallies the now very ex-president had used to give the world the impression that he had the support of his people. It was while he was engaged in the usual rant against the old colonial power, France in this case, that his head had literally exploded.

Naturally the local police were running around like idiots and nothing other than the cartridge case was ever found. The real twist though had come a week later when the man who had taken over, the chief of police no less, had embarked on a pogrom of unprecedented ferocity on the opposition and anybody else he took a dislike to. For no other reason than that the assassination of his predecessor provided a good excuse for one.

It was at this point that the world media worked itself up into a real frenzy because at his first rally, seeking to justify his actions, he too had been eliminated in exactly the same way. The story in this paper ended there, with the usual journalistic hypothesising, because once again no real evidence was found.

Nobody made the connection with the UN chartered French registered Boeing 707 freighter that had left immediately after each assassination.

The conversation between the two pilots and the engineer on the flight deck of the second aircraft as it climbed out over the South Atlantic that evening would have sent the editor of the London Guardian, among others, into a frenzy of sanctimonious scribbling on the democratic rights of the poor oppressed peoples of Africa, with the inevitable rant that all the continent's endless woes were the fault of the colonial powers; conveniently forgetting that there had not been a colonial government in Africa for at least fifty years and that the complete mess the place was in was entirely the fault of home grown corruption and incompetence.

The aircraft climbed westward into the gathering night and on reaching its cruising level of 35000 feet it turned north to re-cross the coast en-route for Paris.

By this time, the three men on the flight deck had settled down to an involved conversation on the attributes of the rather attractive girl thoughtfully provided by the organisation to look after them. The operation was now forgotten.

The thing that would have really got the world's media interested was that all three were black Africans and they spoke French as their native tongue.

The effect of losing two 'Presidents' quickly had the desired result and the opposition leader, having barely survived the previous week soon formed the next attempt at government.

It was as this man sat at the large desk in the presidential palace that his secretary walked in. He was still in a state of wonder at the turn of events; only recently he had been hiding in the jungle with the remnants of his party.

The man handed him a letter. He stared at it, it was addressed to, 'Mr President' and the postmark was local. Opening it, he looked inside, seeing nothing he turned to the man standing there, puzzled. His secretary pointed at the desk. On it a single business card, black with a strange symbol and one word in silver on the front, had fallen from the envelope. He turned it over and there written in French were the words, 'We will be watching you.' He reversed the card again, looking intently at it. The single word on the front, in English this time, was 'Sweepers'.

None of that was ever reported of course, and the media frenzy quickly died down as the world shattering news of some brainless football star's latest indiscretion pushed it from the front page.

The journalist had sat there for a while longer discussing the ways of the world and Shaun found, to his surprise, that this one anyway, was indeed, a fellow traveller.

When Shaun returned to Sydney at the end of the trip he had discussed the Vietnam business with his friends and then with Reg Bartlett, even though Reg was now retired and critically ill. All had expressed their disgust. It was pieces of life's puzzle like this that led them and most of their colleagues to the conclusion, that as far as aviation was concerned, the last people on the planet you would ever trust would be a politician or a public servant.

The airline was undergoing massive change throughout this time. Within weeks Reg Bartlett had passed away after a long battle with cancer; a lifetime's work left to a son who was anything but a chip off the old block.

It took time for the rot to set in because his father had created an airline of quite exceptional strength and structure. However, Reg Bartlett had always flown and as a result always understood that it is the line pilots, cabin crews and engineering that really are the power that keeps an airline going. The son knew nothing of the front end of the business, preferring to wallow around with the new age garbage. He surrounded himself with that quite useless fraternity of individuals with degrees in sociology, human resources or that ultimate irrelevance, Occupational Health and Safety. All of these added nothing to the profitability of the company, and it was obvious to all at the front end that these people were engaged in nothing more than an elaborate job justification scheme.

Even the corporate language changed to that constipated syntax that was to become so common and which only demonstrated that the user had absolutely nothing of value to say, but was determined to spend as long as possible saying it.

The ultimate result of all this remained some time in the future and in the meantime the company appeared to perform well in spite of the growing lunacy. Certainly the line operations were producing comfortable profits, and Shaun and his friends where enjoying a stability unknown in their earlier lives.

As is always the way that was about to change.

Board Room TPA, Sydney, Australia

Neil Bartlett would never be considered the equal of his respected father. In fact, seeing them together, few would realise that they were father and son. Young Neil had gained nothing from him, the strength of character; will power and raw courage of Bartlett senior were all missing. Neil was an overweight, ugly man with a weak chin and even at the age of thirty there was still a tendency to break out in acne when under stress, something that was quite frequent these days.

Those who had known Reg's ex wife were well aware from whom the son got his character traits, like his mother before him; there was little that could be considered good.

Reg had tried, God knows he had tried, but the best schools and university had only produced an educated arrogant idiot who, because he was used to the best, never realised how utterly useless he really was.

Naturally, any suggestion of criticism was dealt with by removing the critic. Having surrounded himself with the usual self-serving slime bags that always surface in this type of corporate cesspool, as things started to go wrong he did what so many of his type do, and blamed everybody else.

He had been running TPA for about two years now, having taken the company over six months before his father's death. The first few months had passed quickly and, with Reg, ill but still looking over the boy's shoulder, there were some who thought he might just make it. However, as soon as the old man passed away 'the wheels had started to come off the wagon'.

He had never come to terms with the special relationship the line crews had with his father, resolving to instill a far more rigid and remote structure, quickly distancing management from the front line. His first move was to introduce a bonus scheme for his managers, with extra incentives for those who reduced cost by figures he plucked arbitrarily from thin air.

His main targets were the wages of the front line staff. He began with the cabin crew whose contracts were rewritten in such a way that wages were halved.

Engineering followed, and the current meeting of his board of directors was to determine a policy of attack on the salaries of the line pilots.

To achieve this he had slowly marginalised his father's original flight crew, they had all been close friends and used to direct contact with the old man as such they were seen as a threat to the new order.

The fact that, as a result of this special relationship, any operational problems that arose were quickly fixed with the minimum loss of revenue was totally ignored by the young Bartlett and his fellow travellers.

He demanded respect, never understanding that his father had got it because he had been there and done it. Something young Neil would never be able to claim.

He had quickly replaced all his fathers' old friends in management with people who would do what he wanted.

At a price of course, but if it resulted in what he considered that overpaid group of bloody pilots getting what they deserved, it would be worth it as far as he was concerned.

So now, as he sat at the head of the boardroom table, the cushion he used to increase his height had been placed on the seat by his secretary before the others had entered the room, he looked at the people on each side before beginning the meeting.

To his left were the departmental heads, with the Flight Operations Manager immediately on his left, this man was new. His predecessor had been removed for daring to suggest that the massive productivity bonuses, in the order of 60%, recently proposed for the top end, would be seen as unacceptable by the staff, who Neil was determined to keep to the maximum of 3%, and then only if he could get significant offsets.

This item was dealt with in relatively short order, hardly surprising as he was surrounded by the very people who would benefit from the 60% end of the equation. He then moved on to the next item of business which was far more critical in that it directly affected him.

The large reserves his father had accumulated and which had made TPA a strong and healthy company had been slowly frittered away and now he needed help. That help, such as it was, occupied the right hand side of the table in the form of the major shareholders, led by an odious individual called Francis Meldrum.

Neil never quite figured out how and why Meldrum was here. He knew that he represented a group of the major stockholders but his elevation to the board had come as something of a surprise and not a pleasant one at that. What made him uncomfortable was the feeling that Meldrum could see right through him. The knowledge that these were the only people in the room, who he could not threaten and intimidate, only increased his feeling of unease.

For once, the meeting went well. Meldrum was unusually quiet as Neil outlined his plans to attack the wages of the line pilot force. He voted in favour of all the devices proposed by Bartlett junior and his totally controlled, Chief of Operations.

The meeting had closed quickly; all agreed to the plan to present the weak, Pilots Association with a 'take it or leave it' ultimatum.

The proposal to set up a freighter wing, separate from the main line, and to staff this with those pilots approaching the end of their careers was seen as a master stroke, in that if it worked, the pilot body would lose the experience and wisdom of the very people who knew anything about the business and who were, of course, also the last link with his father. This would make further inroads into the conditions of the remaining mainline pilots all the easier.

He had left as soon as the meeting concluded. He needed to get home. Even success was not enough these days and today he felt that, in spite of getting his way, he was being manipulated by Meldrum and his cronies.

He slumped in the back seat of the limousine, snarled at his driver to get a move on and chewed through another set of finger nails.

He barged his way through the security check of the harbour-side apartment block. If you own the penthouse and a couple of the lesser apartments you were above all that he reasoned. Entering the place he pushed the duty bimbo aside. She had, on hearing the door, rushed to meet him, although as soon as she saw the mood he was in, she quickly retreated to the kitchen.

Moving through to the master bedroom he yanked open the drawer at the bedside and grabbed the plastic bag. Moving to the bathroom he spread the white powder on the cistern of the toilet. He cut it into lines with the razor he kept in the package and then, taking the straw, also there, he inhaled deeply. The drug kicked in immediately. That was the beauty of coke the relief was immediate and as his system slowly absorbed the stuff he called for the woman; time to relieve the rest of the tensions.

She appeared in the bedroom door reluctant to get too close, she knew the mood. He snarled at her and reluctantly she approached the bed. He was lying there naked, it was not a pretty sight but she knew what he wanted. She also knew that in his present mood and with a large dose of coke in his system she was likely to get far more than the usual sex. It had happened before. In the morning he always paid her more to ease the guilt but the sessions were getting more violent and she was scared.

OP2, Sydney

The murder had been horrific. An innocent young woman abducted on her way home from work had been forced into a stolen car, taken to an abandoned warehouse in the west of Sydney, and brutally raped by her two attackers. Having subjected her to the most degrading assaults, they had then indulged themselves in a fit of violent torture until eventually she had died.

The body had been found the next day by a homeless man seeking shelter and, true to form, the media immediately assumed that it was he who had committed the crimes.

The police reaction was somewhat different because they already had a report of a young woman, matching the victim's description, being forced into a car in a badly lit street in the Redfern area of the inner city by two men described as being below average height and of swarthy complexion. In fact the anonymous caller had suggested they were of eastern Mediterranean appearance, but the community liaison officer, a civilian appointed by the State Premier, whose job it was to filter out what he considered racist elements in police press releases, had made no mention of ethnicity.

However, added to this information the police already had a file open because there had been a series of similar, although less violent, attacks in the last couple of months. In each of the previous cases the victims had survived and given descriptions of two men who were thought to be Lebanese. Inquires had been started in the close knit Lebanese community in the suburb of Bankstown.

Predictably, the leaders had trodden the well-worn path of denial and then, as the police had persisted, the inevitable accusations of racial discrimination, finally suggesting that the girl had probably deserved it, declaring that western women should learn from their Islamic sisters and dress more modestly.

At the same time the local members of parliament were lobbied and the police were told by the vacillating State Premier to 'lay off'. After all, he had said, Bankstown was a swing seat and there was an election due.

On this occasion though the feeling inside the force was one of anger and contempt and the instruction was ignored, enquires continued, albeit with a little less publicity.

The breakthrough came as a result of two things. The DNA samples taken from the shattered body of the girl had clearly identified her two assailants, although just who they were remained a mystery for a few more weeks.

It was a car chase and the subsequent accident that gave the police the lead they had been waiting for. Two youths had stolen a Holden V8 Commodore from outside a railway station and in the subsequent high speed chase through the streets of the city they had eventually lost control of the powerful car and crashed. The driver had conveniently managed to kill himself but his passenger had survived with serious injuries. He had been taken to hospital under escort where he was given a blood transfusion. The preliminary procedure to this had required a blood test and the results of that were routinely run through the police computers. Much to their surprise, they had a match.

This individual was one of the two men they were looking for. Nothing was said but the guard was doubled. In spite of this the Lebanese community found out about the arrest and an angry crowd had quickly gathered outside the hospital. The fact that this individual was at least a car thief did not enter into the equation. The attitude seemed to be that they could do what they liked and any suggestion that they should abide by the same laws as the rest of the country was to be countered, as always, with the racist card.

For once the chief of police had anticipated this and deployed the riot squad around the building. He had then ordered the leaders to a private meeting and here he had informed them that there had been a significant development. He had emphasised that this made a mockery of their anti establishment rants and accusations of the previous weeks. They had sat there stunned, some even now denying that this horrendous crime could have been committed by two of their own. Eventually wiser heads had prevailed and a degree of co-operation was established.

The crowd had been addressed by them and had dispersed, but not before a gang of youths had tried to get into the place and release the prisoner. The police inspector responsible for the action had said afterwards, that it was odds on that the other wanted man was in amongst that group.

The State Premier was quick to claim the credit for the arrest, at the same time endeavouring to distance himself from the local politics. Behind the scenes though, he quickly contacted the State Attorney General and instructed him that, when and if the second man was found, the inevitable trial was to be dealt with as soon as possible with minimum sentences applied.

This, he reasoned, would enable him to go to the election with a demonstrated even hand and should, he felt, repair some of the inevitable damage with the party's following in the Lebanese community. For the innocent victim and her family he did not have even a passing thought.

The Attorney General put the phone down at the end of the conversation, deep in thought. He was from a long line of lawyers and his promotion to his current position had been a foregone conclusion as soon as he had joined the party. He was at something of a crossroads he realised, for he had just been told to meddle in the process of the very laws for which he was ultimately responsible.

It did not take him long to come to a decision, having convinced himself sometime before that his true role was that of party leader. If massaging the law was required to achieve this then so be it.

He now pondered the list of judges available to try the case. What was needed was a colleague who was either ambitious or vulnerable; he had quite a few to choose from.

The second man was soon picked up by the police, the community now very much interested in getting the business over with; the only exception being the men's immediate families, who still claimed it was the girl's fault. The second man was inevitably a cousin of the one already in custody. As soon as the cell doors were slammed shut they were both claiming that the girl had been a willing party, even in the face of the evidence of the witness to the original violent abduction.

It was leaked by the police to the papers that while being questioned they had made the statement that all western women were to blame because they provoked this type of behaviour. Later, as the gravity of their situation sank in they turned on each other, each blaming the other, in spite of the DNA evidence proving that both had been equally responsible.

The trial, which, in accordance with the Premier's wishes, was brought forward to place it well in front of the coming election, was over very quickly and the entire country waited for the verdict to be handed down. A guilty verdict was inevitable on all counts and life imprisonment anticipated. Many in the community were calling for a return of the death penalty as the real details of the crime were released into the public domain.

The presiding judge, who throughout had appeared uncomfortable with his lot, had received the last of a number of telephone calls the previous evening. It had been made quite clear to him exactly what was required. It had not been necessary to mention his drug addiction, this time it was the carrot that was extended with the suggestion of a number of lucrative appointments after the trial..... assuming a satisfactory sentence of course.

A week later in front of a packed court with a very heavy media presence he had handed down this sentence. Each of the defendants was given life as expected. This had resulted in relief for the parents of the girl but the Lebanese activists in the court had made their displeasure very obvious. It was only after order had been restored that the judge had been able to complete the sentence, setting a non parole period of an unbelievably lenient five years.

Once again the court had erupted, only this time it was the Lebanese who were cheering. The father and mother of the girl looked on in speechless horror, with the woman finally breaking down and weeping. The media stampeded for the telephones.

London

The old colonel, long retired, sat in his London club reading the newspaper, skipping through the usual domestic drivel. Was he really expected to give a damn what some fourth rate musician thought about world poverty? He was becoming increasingly bored with it all when suddenly the story of the verdict in a vicious murder trial in Sydney, Australia, caught his eye. He read it through and then read it again. Finally, placing the paper on the table, he leaned back deep in thought.

The steward had eventually touched him lightly on the shoulder, having had no success in attracting his attention. 'Colonel Sir, there is a call for you. It's from overseas, will you take it here?' 'Oh--- what? Sorry old chap, miles away. Yes, plug it in would you.' The steward leaned down, connected the line to the socket and passed the old man the hand piece.

'Raff,' he said. 'Sorry to bother you sir' the voice said. 'It's Omar.' 'Hello my boy what a pleasant surprise, where are you?' 'In Beirut Colonel,' there was a pause. 'Sir, have you heard about that business in Sydney?' It was Raff's turn to pause, 'I take it you are referring to that trial they just had down there Omar. As a matter of fact I have only just finished reading about it. Can't say I am very impressed. The whole thing stinks to high heaven from what I have read up to now. Your thoughts would be along similar lines I presume?' 'Yes sir, in fact we are concerned that these two will be seen as heroes by the youths of the local community and as a result bring us all down to their disgusting level. We wondered whether you, or should I say we, could do something to eliminate that possibility?' 'Interesting thought, leave it with me will you. Have to say it does look as though it is something we could be interested in. Do I presume that if we decide to go ahead you chaps will want to be involved?' 'Very much so Colonel, in fact I think, forgive me sir, but we would like to insist upon it.' The Colonel smiled to himself, honour had no ethnic boundaries he realised. He would look at this and if they decided to make it a mission he would make sure that Omar and their other Lebanese associates were given the chance to clean up the mess.

He sat there for awhile deep in thought. Their next meeting was scheduled for Tuesday and he decided to make the Sydney situation an early item on the agenda.

He spent most of the intervening days researching just what had happened. All his Australian sources had been in agreement. There had been a gross miscarriage of justice, and there were definite suggestions of political interference in the legal process. The presiding judge was a known heroin addict, something the establishment conveniently kept quiet, largely because so many of them were also involved in dubious practices and it was always a good idea to have a tame judge with a weakness on the team.

The following Tuesday the Colonel finished the briefing with the suggestion that it would be a good idea to task the Beirut team with any clean up operation that might be agreed upon.

They discussed at length the possible methods and the requirements to achieve the objective. Once the decision had been agreed the appropriate calls were made.

The first was to Manaus Brazil and this resulted in a helicopter taking off and heading westwards across the virgin green of the greatest forest on the planet. After an hour it set down in an isolated Amerindian village. The pilot was ushered into the presence of the head man and the warmth of the greeting was a clear indication of the trust and affection that existed between the two men. His request, however, was met with a puzzled expression and some concern. After being assured that he would treat the thing he wanted with great care, the chief eventually barked a stream of orders and a couple of his men quickly disappeared into the forest. Returning two hours later, the small vial of yellow liquid was passed to the pilot and after a brief farewell he was airborne, heading east into the gathering gloom of a tropical evening. Landing back at Manaus he called at the aircrew hotel in town and within twenty minutes had handed the small package to the captain of tomorrow's flight to the south.

In Buenos Aires Argentina, arrangements had been set in place for the package to be delivered to the captain of the following evening flight to Sydney.

At the Australian end, detailed enquires had taken place into the exact circumstances of the two criminals and the judge. Plans were made and within a few days all that was required was the arrival of the aircraft one from Beirut and the other Buenos Aries.

★ ★ ★

The 747 classic freighter aircraft had finally arrived at Sydney's Kingsford Smith airport. The inevitably protracted vectors associated with an arrival at this place had taken the best part of forty minutes to negotiate.

There were very few line pilots who had regular contact with the Sydney system who were not aware of the old story alleged to have been the words of a captain with Continental Airlines on his last flight from this place who signed off with, 'Thanks Sydney you are the second best air traffic control system in the world.' To this, the unsuspecting reply had been, 'So who is the best?' there was the inevitable pause here and then the American said 'Why, everybody else!' The stony silence that followed ensured that this immediately joined the lexicon of aviator stories.

They were directed to the freight terminal, to park at a gate adjacent to the most northern of the passenger terminal fingers where an A340, recently arrived from Argentina, was also parked. Leaving the aircraft in the freight area the three men of the crew soon negotiated the arrival procedures. It was always easier when you were on a freighter they knew and it was only about thirty minutes after they had parked the aircraft that they were in a taxi taking them to their hotel.

After a few hours' sleep and at an agreed time the captain's telephone rang. Still groggy from the long night, he managed a grunt 'Omar?' The Latin American voice rapidly bought him to the surface and a meeting was arranged.

The men, two Lebanese and an Argentinean met briefly in the bar that night and the packet was handed over together with a whispered warning on the handling of its contents, this done, the South American left.

The Lebanese crew had a three day layover in Sydney and the next day was spent setting the plan in place. Calls were made to the relevant authorities and a prisoner client meeting was arranged for both men.

Unfortunately while one was incarcerated in Long Bay, the jail situated in the city the other had been sent to a prison in the Hunter Valley at the town of Singleton, some three hours to the north. As it was essential each meeting occurred at roughly the same time, one of them would have to leave early the next morning.

This man was accompanied by an Australian who drove the hire car and at the agreed time of 1200 each of them sat in the secure holding room of the respective prisons, waiting for the prisoners to be brought in. In both cases their documents had been closely studied before they had been allowed in but their cover as attorneys representing the men, preparing for the appeals, was foolproof.

After the initial introductions the conversation was continued in Arabic, something that the guards were irritated by but were not confident enough to stop. Word was out about these two and if you valued your job it was best to turn a blind eye to certain things. Not that much of interest was said, some papers were shown and returned signed and after a brief conversation, the 'lawyers' made to leave. As they did so each fumbled in their respective briefcases and removed a pack of Lebanese cigarettes and receiving a confirmatory nod from the guards they handed them over to the prisoners. 'Something a little special for you,' each of them said, 'probably not a good idea to share them around.' Both prisoners grabbed the respective packet and in each case it rapidly disappeared in their prison overalls.

Within five hours the freighter was sitting at the holding point of Sydney's main runway 16 Right and, as the tower cleared them for take off, Omar eased the thrust levers forward and the heavy 747 lumbered onto the runway, lined up, and was gone. As it turned westwards into the setting sun en-route for Singapore and then home the two men let out a collective sigh of relief. Reaching the cruising level Omar turned to his companion 'Honour restored,' he paused, deep in thought 'a little.'

New South Wales. The Jails

They were both in solitary confinement. The authorities were only too aware that criminals guilty of this type of crime frequently did not last long in the open areas of the tougher jails where a rather rigid code existed.

As a result it was not until the guards went to let them out for the evening meal that the bodies were discovered. In each case the cell was a mess of blood and mucous, each had clearly been in agony before death eventually occurred. Subsequent medical opinion was that the whole process had taken three hours, although they could not be sure because the exact cause of death was proving very difficult to establish.

Initially each case was seen in isolation and it was a couple of hours before the news that both men had died in similar circumstances was out. As the days passed, the possible significance of the two lawyers meeting them at the same time was realised. This was confirmed when enquires with the legal firm tasked with the appeals denied all knowledge of the meetings and of the men themselves.

It was as the authorities were once again going over the few things found in the cell, that the cigarette packets first attracted attention. It was the distinctive brand, and then the butts of the one cigarette each had smoked before death and finally the single card found at the back of the packs, the size of a normal business card, jet black with the symbol of a broom in silver. In each case on the back were written two words 'Insh Allah.'--- 'Gods Will.'

It took many weeks to identify the toxin and when it was eventually isolated it caused uproar in the media, for it was an extremely rare poison secreted from glands on the back of a particular tree frog that inhabited the outermost reaches of the Amazon basin. Quite how it came to be injected into the cigarette each man had smoked remained a mystery. Nobody was much interested in trying the other ones in the pack but when these were analysed, all were found to be similarly doctored. The opinion from the investigating toxicologist was that it would have been just about the worst way to die, initial paralysis preventing any call for help. Not that it would have been any good anyway as there was no known antidote.

As the poison got to work, the internal organs were literally liquidised, causing massive internal bleeding not unlike that caused by the Ebola virus. Except with this toxin it was quicker and silent as a result of the paralysis.

No sooner had this got the media all wound up when they had another cause for a feeding frenzy. The body of the presiding judge in the case was found slumped in his car in the garage of his house with the engine still running. A hose pipe had been forced onto the exhaust and from there into the vehicle. The verdict was suicide but the police were not so sure because a rather distinctive business card had been found on the floor of the vehicle, and his housekeeper had told them of the visitor on the evening of his death. She thought he had been an Englishman. After he had left she had noticed that the judge had been in a highly agitated state. No, she had not heard their conversation.

The commissioner was called to the Premier's office soon after and asked to explain what the hell was going on. He had to admit that his men had not come up with anything apart from these. With that he placed the three identical cards on the Premier's desk. The man on the other side went white, fear evident in the bloated face. The policeman, concerned, asked if he was all right. The politician said nothing, picked up an envelope that had been on the desk and tipped it up. Out fell a business card, identical to the three already there, except that on the back of this one was written one word 'Resign.' He did so the next day.

His replacement was no surprise to the party hierarchy; it was the very powerful and much feared Attorney General who now sat in the premier's office.

The state police commissioner had thought long and hard on the evidence and eventually, as the days passed with the investigation completely stalled, he made the decision.

Leaving the airport terminal in Canberra the national capital and home of the Federal Police, he got into the official car waiting at the kerb. Nothing too conspicuous just the usual white Holden Commodore, the driver in civilian clothes. The short drive to the Federal Police HQ was over in a few minutes and he was soon ushered into the office of his Federal equivalent. This man stood from behind the desk, coming round to shake the extended hand. Relations between the two had not always been too warm but the 'Fed' was intrigued, the request for a meeting had given nothing away. Coffee appeared and then the door was closed.

'Now what can I do for you?' he asked 'Difficult to know where to start actually' the State Commissioner began. 'I suppose the beginning, as far as I know it, would be the best.' the Fed said nothing. 'Well it's these murders, the two Lebanese scumbags and the judge. The investigation is going nowhere, we are not even sure his lordship was murdered, although it does seem likely, given the way the other two were got rid of and the stink of the whole case.'

'Normally' he continued, 'we wouldn't be too concerned about the garbage, or that particular judge for that matter, he was already on the watch list. It was just a matter of time before he slipped up so badly that his friends dumped him, and with the recent early retirement of 'you know who', he lost his main protection. Digressing for a moment I have to say on that score, we may have got rid of one dud, and inherited something far worse. This one is not only bent but smart. We are going to have to tread very carefully there. I don't think any of us are under any illusions on that score.' 'No,' he continued 'It's really this or rather these that are bothering me and make me wonder at the so called suicide.' With that he placed the four cards on the desk.

Without pausing he went on to describe where they had been found explaining in some detail that it was the arrival of the fourth that was the catalyst that had caused the early retirement of his late boss.

The Fed controlled his expression with ease, although the sight of the cards had been something of a shock. Only last week he had received a brief query from Interpol on whether there had been any activities where just such evidence had been found at the scene and here he was being presented with four.

It was against unofficial policy to share too much with the State authorities and thought for a minute before continuing.

'What I am about to tell is between you and I, okay? It goes no further, if you feel you may have a problem with it, say so now.' The State Police Chief looked at him thinking what the hell was all this about? He agreed, 'Right,' The Fed continued 'But I think I should tell you that if you let it out we will hear about it.' He paused again, this time all he got was a nod.

'These things started to appear all over the world some three years ago apparently, always after some high profile scumbag had been disposed of. It has always been either a large scale criminal who has managed to avoid justice in some way, a totally corrupt poly, or a member of the judiciary who has been, shall we say, elastic with his responsibilities. In each case subsequent evidence has surfaced more than justifying the elimination.

They have occurred all over the so called civilised world, all continents except, until now it seems, here. Each case has been investigated and nothing, absolutely nothing, has ever been found. The methods are as varied as the hits. There is never any evidence or suspects. All we ever get are these cards, some with a warning some without.

'Ironically the Prime Minister mentioned this at the last State Premier's conference. I seem to recall he made some remark along the lines that it would not be a good idea to get one of these in the mail, which would, perhaps, explain the recent hasty resignation.'

'And what about the rule of law, natural justice, innocent until having been proved guilty, that sort of thing?' the State policeman asked. 'Yes, it does seem to cross a few boundaries doesn't it,' the Fed agreed. 'The trouble is, when you read each of the case histories we know about you very soon realise that all that lovely fluffy stuff has completely failed in each one.'

'For one reason or another, every customer so far, has more than deserved it. Official thinking is, we may not like it, certainly the lawyers hate it, their bread and butter of course, but the world is always just a little better for the removal of each one of these creeps. Anyway the main reasons the lawyers hate any direct action like this is because, not only does it get their greasy little paws out of the pot of gold the law has become, but in quite a few cases it is they who are the, eh shall we say, candidates.'

'What I suggest is that you read this file and then see if you still have a problem. If so, we can discuss it further. Have to get you to read it here if you don't mind. I can't let it out of the office; feel sure you will understand.'

It took the state policeman about an hour and a half to go through the file and at the end he looked up, face clouded in thought. Eventually he spoke. 'Christ, I knew there was some shit in this world but some of that makes even those two Lebanese creeps look like angels.' He paused.

'What do you want me to do about it all?' 'Why-Nothing, nothing at all;' the other man said. 'For appearance's sake I would perhaps continue with a low-level investigation for a while, if only to keep the press off it, and then just let the matter die.' 'Right, consider it done, and these?' He pointed at the four cards on the table. 'Ah, yes,' the Fed said, 'probably best if I keep those, put them in the file, if that is okay with you?' A nod sufficed, they shook hands and he got up to leave the room.

'One question' the man from the State Police said. The Fed waited. 'Why? If they wanted to knock those two off, why did they go to all that trouble? I mean it could have been done by a couple of thugs in the nick much more easily couldn't it?' The Fed paused a few seconds before replying. 'That's the whole point isn't it? From wherever you look at this, it was international. They use an exotic poison from South America, two apparently Arab assassins, who actually get them while they are in our most secure jails, and then they just disappear. Then a mysterious Englishman is seen in the company of a crooked judge and he also just disappears after a rather doubtful suicide. They are sending us, and through us, all the real scumbags on the planet a message, and I know it is not one I would like to receive in the post, would you?'

The Federal policeman waited a few minutes after the door closed, let out a big breath and picked up the phone and began dialling a long series of numbers beginning with 0044. As soon as a voice answered he said, 'Canberra all okay.' The handset was replaced at the other end without another word.

Chapter 5
Bangkok

It was during this period that Jim Kennedy's life took a twist. He had arrived in Bangkok on the way to London on what was until then just another trip. However, whereas it was usual for the tech crew to socialise, on this occasion the others were all occupied and Jim found himself alone. Usually a visit to Bobby's or the Napoleon would turn up an old friend, but again, there was nobody around. Then Pete, the barman, mentioned that a new bar called Club 99 had opened up a little way up Surawong Road and Jim, with nothing better to do, drifted up there to take a look. You could never have too many watering holes was his basic philosophy.

It took him a while to find it but eventually he located the place on a street corner and went in. First impressions were a cross between the standard Bangkok girlie bar and a night club, but the music was not overpowering and he decided a beer or two would give him a chance to check the place out.

Sipping the icy cold Kloster beer and thinking about nothing in particular, the tap on his shoulder came as something of an intrusion. Turning, he was surprised to see a woman standing there, even more when she spoke to him.

'Would you mind if I had a drink with you?' she said, and then seeing the puzzled look on his face she continued, 'It's just that I am having a little trouble with that French guy over there and I told him I was meeting my boyfriend and then you walked in and, well,' she faltered 'I told him you were he.' She waited and then snapped, 'Look, if it's a problem forget it.' 'Hell no, it's not a problem, just a surprise.' He paused. 'Jim Kennedy,' he said, remembering not to stick out his hand. An expected boyfriend would hardly shake hands after all!

She smiled, watching as he came on line with her situation. 'Don't want me to have a chat with him do you?' he asked, without much enthusiasm. 'God no! It's just that my girlfriend has the 'hots' for his mate and he has the idea that I am part of the deal. You don't mind talking to me for a while do you?'

He eased back on the bar looking at her as he did so. Bloody hell, she was something else that was for sure; beautiful no argument, but the eyes were the thing that held him, deep pools of dark liquid gold. 'Okay' he said 'I don't know who the hell you are but with eyes like that you can stay here as long as you like.' She smiled again, the eye thing obviously an expected reaction.

'Maria Fernandez,' she said 'and would you mind if I kissed you Jim Kennedy, after all we are supposed to be an item.' She leaned forward and without thinking he kissed her, vaguely aware that the French guy, who had been watching them, was showing all the signs of being a bit pissed off as he came up for breath. She stood back and looked at him, her eyes glowing in the half light of the bar.

So far he had known this woman for less than five minutes and he had yet to get control of things, his mind was racing. This just doesn't happen, what's the catch?

He started to look around the bar trying to find a reason. Noting the exits, at the same time realising that, in spite of Shaun Fitzgerald's advice from long ago to always go for a place with an easy exit, he had unwittingly placed himself just about as far from one as was possible. Stupid wanker, he thought.

However, apart from the rather dejected looking French guy there was nothing. The woman just stood there looking at him, seemingly well aware of what he was thinking. The barman placed a drink in front of her and she picked it up sipping it slowly, as he relaxed.

'So, Jim Kennedy,' she began, 'what do you do and why are you in this den of iniquity?' It was the eyes that did it, mesmerised, he told her.

They had been speaking for about fifteen minutes when Maria's girlfriend, a girl called Tina, came over saying she had had enough and wanted to leave. There was a rather hurried exchange of telephone numbers and Jim found himself alone once again.

His immediate reaction was to check out the Frenchman but he had recovered quickly from the loss and was busy moving in on a rather attractive Thai girl.

Jim, his mind slowly settling after what he reckoned was quite an experience, looked hard at the piece of paper in his hand. Probably the local cop shop he thought, I doubt I will see her again, pity really. He shoved the piece of paper into his shirt pocket.

Finishing his drink he wandered back to Bobby's, where by now a couple of crews had arrived and he soon forgot the brief encounter.

It was not until the next morning that he found the note in the pocket of last night's shirt. Why not, he thought I'll give it a go.

She answered immediately, clearly pleased. A meeting was arranged for one week ahead as he was leaving that night.

Slowly replacing the receiver she smiled to herself. I wonder if he will call again she mused.

It rapidly developed into an intense relationship. Jim's old friends, initially sceptical, had met Maria and been captivated as quickly as he was. Each agreed he was a lucky bugger and did not deserve her. They were pleased that their old friend was happy, no matter how long it lasted. In this game there was always a time limit, you just had to get the most out of it while it did.

Jim and Maria became regulars at Bobby's and were all but inseparable while he was in Bangkok.

Inevitably confidences were shared and it was here that, for Jim anyway, the first concerns appeared, for Maria had slowly opened up on what it was she and her girlfriend did and who they did it for.

The company for whom they worked was apparently owned by a Syrian, or at least he was the one that ran it. In Thailand there was always a Thai partner with the majority shareholding. Invariably the Thai did nothing, just took a percentage and satisfied the local ownership laws. That was certainly the case here.

The actual business was import and export; initially she had not thought too much about it but when Tina started making journeys to North Korea she became a little concerned, that and the fact that there was a subtle change in the merchandise she dealt with at about the same time.

At first it had all been locally produced textiles and other innocuous things. One night, for example, she had turned up with a garish and bizarre collection of what she described as 'novelty' condom samples of different shapes and sizes. These, she said, were destined for the Yugoslavian market and Jim, no lover of the communist world, had followed in Churchill's footsteps and suggested that even the largest be marked 'small'.

As the months passed however she had became more worried and eventually confided in him.

The business was now dominated with recycling manufactured goods from North Korea. The procedure was that a consignment of, say, garments would be re-labelled as having been manufactured in Thailand, thereby making them acceptable purchases in the west with the USA as the main market. However as well as this illegal operation, there was an even more sinister element involving cargoes of unspecified machinery which both she and her girlfriend suspected were munitions. These particular shipments, while they were processed as having passed through Thailand and, having done so, were therefore sanitized, in actual fact never even came near the place.

If that were not enough, she stumbled across an invoice one day giving the destination of one particular shipment as Iraq. Puzzled because she had no recollection of dealings with this pariah state, she investigated further only to find the same shipment was in her own records as something completely different, and this time the declared destination was Kuwait. She was horrified when, on checking the authorisations, it was her signature in both cases. In fact on checking further she found that every shipment that could be considered suspicious had been signed off by either her or Tina. The only time the Syrian's name appeared anywhere was on the obviously legal invoices.

The two women had discussed this at length and in private and further investigation by both revealed the true horror of their situation. Everything, that could be considered the least bit illegal, had been tied to one or the other of the women. Tina's position was even more exposed than Maria's, as it was she who had actually dealt with the North Koreans. Neither doubted that all this would become known eventually; exposure was just a matter of time.

They began to plan their departure. With Tina most at risk, it was she who wanted to go first.

It was here that they ran into yet another problem. The Syrian would quite obviously not want either of them to go if he had the slightest inkling that they had found out the true nature of his business. They were already aware that he was well connected with enough of the Thai establishment to make an exit impossible if he had a mind to. What could happen next terrified them. People did disappear in this place after all.

In one important way Tina's position was better than Maria's, for a large part of her job involved travel. She had made up her mind that she would jump ship when on her next overseas trip. That way she could avoid any hassles with the local authorities. For Maria there was no easy way out and she resolved to discuss it with Jim on his next visit.

He was due in the day after tomorrow she would talk about it all then.

Approaching Top of Descent 160 miles from Bangkok, Eastbound.

Shaun stirred in the left-hand seat and finished the last cup of tea he would have before touchdown. He had just read an article about the recent disposal of two thoroughly unpleasant little pieces of shit that the establishment had seemed incapable of dealing with. 'Interesting piece in that,' he said. 'Glad there seem to be some people prepared to fix up some of these creeps.' He tossed the folded paper to his First Officer. 'Here, have a look at that when we get on the ground, makes good reading.'

He leant down and pulled out the relevant Jeppesen charts for the runway 21 left ILS approach that the airfield information had indicated was their expected arrival. He discussed the salient points with his young co-pilot and the flight engineer and then asked the F/O to get them a descent clearance.

This was rapidly given by the Thai sector controller followed by the instruction that they were radar identified and were to take up a heading of 050 for vectors to the final approach course.

As the 120 mile point was passed he reached across to the thrust levers, disengaged the auto throttle and eased them back to idle all that would be required for the next twenty minutes or so. The dull roar of the four Rolls Royce engines, which had been with them since departure from London's Heathrow some twelve hours ago, slowly decreased to a rumble.

As they were to be radar controlled, the Instrument Landing System frequency of 110.3 was dialled up and identified by them both, the locator beacons tuned and identified as well, and with little to do for a few minutes, they sat looking into the early sunrise over Cambodia.

The mist, lay like a blanket over the miles of rice paddy that surrounded the city of Bangkok, it was already stirring in response to the heat of the coming day. It was not unknown for dense fog to form for a short period at this time of year. Shaun quickly checked the fuel situation. The run down to Utaphao was only ten minutes and as it was on the coast it was usually clear of the fog. He glanced at the F/O. 'You got the Utaphao weather Al?' 'Sure did skipper. It's fine. You thinking this may cause us a problem?' 'No, I think we will make it okay but the guys behind might have one.'

Al Hitchcock sat back in his seat having done everything required and he again watched the coming dawn. 'Bet you've seen a few of these boss, you were over there a while back weren't you?' Shaun paused. Like most people who had been 'there' he was reluctant to talk much about it to the youngsters, finding all too frequently, that their ignorance did not stop them being both experts and highly critical on the subject. Al, perhaps sensing this went on 'My Dad was there too. He was Army and he told us all about it. Said he wanted us to know what it was really like not the 'crap' the lefty media were shoving down our throats at that time. We were just kids and I think the idea was to put us off the whole rotten business. Not sure it worked though. We realised he was quite a guy, and something to live up to.' 'Your dad was right, it was a rotten business and if you can avoid anything similar I would. Course, I also know that a young fella like you would totally ignore that advice as well!' He paused, 'Maybe I'll tell you about it someday, okay?'

The sector controller handed them on to Approach on 119.1. Alan dialled in the new frequency and made the call. 'Approach, Transpac 102 out of 150 for 10000 heading is 050 we have information Victor.' The new controller gave them a descent clearance and a new vector of 100 degrees from which they were to intercept the final approach course of 208 for the ILS and the runway. They reset the altimeters to the local pressure at the transition level and began the first of a series of checklists. Shaun continued to slow the big aircraft down and eventually called for increasing amounts of flap. Then, as the glide slope bar on the flight director commanded the initial descent, the landing gear was lowered and the noise level increased considerably as eighteen wheels were lowered into the airflow.

Shaun eased the thrust levers up to counteract the extra drag, adding to the noise. Another frequency change to 118.1 put them with the tower controller who cleared them to land, emphasising 21 left.

The final check list was completed as soon as the flaps ran to 30, and a few minutes later the aircraft settled onto the runway.

As the speed brakes extended, Shaun pulled in idle reverse thrust. They had to roll the full length on this runway and there was little point in all the roaring and vibration of a full application if they then had to apply thrust to taxi to the end. Similarly, as the aircraft slowed, he squeezed on the brakes to disconnect the automatic system. Timing it just right, he cancelled reverse thrust by lowering the levers and, with a gentle brake application, he slowed the big airplane sufficiently to negotiate the ninety degree turn that took them off the runway and onto taxiway Sierra, which ran between the two strips. He stopped just short of runway 21 right, watching as a departing aircraft was getting airborne.

They glanced sideways at the golf course the Thai military had placed between the runways. Already there were people playing. 'Must be bloody keen,' Fred the engineer said, 'Bloody early, bloody noisy, and bloody hot I reckon. Rather have a cold beer any day.'

As the tower cleared them to cross the runway and call ground on 121.9 they moved slowly to their allocated bay, stopped, and shut the great engines down. Shaun stretched, the long flight over once more. Swinging round in the seat he said, 'So, you blokes can take two days off. I will be over at Bobbys tonight if you're desperate. Jim Kennedy and The Digger are due in from Sydney today so I think they will be a session.' Young Alan winced. Bloody Hell, he thought. I'll go, but I will have to leave early I can't keep up with these old guys and these three were something of a legend in the company, particularly when they got together. 'Okay boss' was all he could manage. Fred on the other hand said, 'Right. That little bugger Digger owes me a beer.'

Shaun showered and changed and was ready for a drink. The message Jim Kennedy had left for him had said that he and Digger would meet him in Bobbys as soon as he could get there. He figured Maria would also be there as well and it amused him to think on what Alan Hitchcock's reaction would be. Usually the young guys just sat there with their tongues out in her presence. She had that effect on men. Even he, cynic that he was, had to admit she was pretty special. All he hoped was that it would not end in tears.

He met Fred and Alan in the lobby and they left by the main entrance of the Montien, crossing the road they dived into the labyrinth of Patpong. The market was in full swing and it took them a while to negotiate all the stalls. Eventually, about halfway along the street they came to the crossover to Patpong 2. This led directly into the car park at the back of which was the bar. Climbing the few wooden stairs which he figured must have felt the tread of more aircrew than the average ops room; he opened the door, waiting for his eyes to adjust to the light.

He waved a hello to Pete behind the bar and then spied his old friends in the corner. As expected, Maria sat between them and had already attracted the attention of the other crews in the place. Jim, sitting on her left, and Digger on the other side kept the wolves at bay. She loved it all of course, although he thought he detected something in her manner that he had not seen before.

The two men stood up and shook hands with him and his crew. He then leant forward to kiss Maria on the cheek. 'Good to see you again' he said, and then on a whim added quietly 'you okay?' She stiffened visibly, her usual radiant smile tightened and she gave an almost imperceptible negative movement of her head.

He pulled up a chair, having introduced his crew to her; already Alan was gazing longingly. It gave Shaun time to glance at his old friend and the raised eyebrow clearly indicated that something was up. For the moment a few beers would suffice; they would talk later and in private.

It was obvious that Jim, The Digger and Maria had been discussing something that was worrying her before they arrived. Each made an effort to put it aside but

Shaun knew his friends too well not to wonder what the hell it was.

The crowd thinned as people began leaving to eat elsewhere. Fred and Alan excused themselves as well, sensing that there was something going on to which they were not a party. Alan was reluctant, only going when Fred threatened to tell everybody he was a SNAG, a Sensitive New Age Guy, who couldn't handle Patpong.

It was as the room cleared that Shaun became aware of the man. He was sitting at a table in the dining area, shielded from view by the other drinkers (until now), but as the room cleared Shaun caught him looking their way.

He was unsure at first but as the smoke thinned he recognized him. 'Well Bugger me!' he said to no one in particular, then turning to his companions, 'Scuse me for a minute folks, just seen a face from the past.' With that he pushed the chair back and walked over to the table. The man half smiled as he approached. 'Hi Shaun, long time no see.' 'Must be at least ten years, Chuck. Like to say you haven't changed a bit, bullshit of course' he replied. Chuck Anderson's smile broadened as he stood and they shook hands.

'Sit a while old friend tell me what's been going on.' 'Okay, I will if you will' Shaun replied. 'Hope you're not still living in Spook city?' Anderson didn't reply at first, and the pause was enough.' Oh I see, still at it eh. Okay that aside, it's good to see you,' Shaun continued. 'You want to come over and meet my friends?' Anderson looked a little awkward, 'Perhaps not yet Shaun. Thing is, could we have a quiet word? I have a bit of a problem here it seems?' 'Okay I'll just tell them to go on without me and then maybe we can get a bite to eat here, if that suits you?' 'That would be fine.' Anderson paused, 'Oh,

Shaun, no need to mention the spook business to them okay' 'No sure.' He turned, puzzled. He quickly made his excuses with the other three and they got up to leave. Jim, sensing something said, 'we'll be at the '99' later mate, okay? Do need to talk to you tonight if poss, old buddy.' Shaun nodded, but it was Maria who had his attention. She had not taken her eyes off Anderson from the time Shaun had walked back to the table, and what he saw in her eyes was fear.

He returned to Anderson's table as the others left, noticing the backward glance from Maria as she reached the door.

The two men spent a few minutes studying the menu and Pete came over to their table with two more large Kloster beers. 'Eating here tonight Shaun?' he asked. 'Yep Pete I think I will have a steak, usual bits and pieces. What about you, Chuck?' 'Steak will do me to thanks, medium with fries.' Pete collected the menus and left. 'Okay Chuck, what's it all about? You've got the girl scared out of her wits so spill it:' 'Oh you noticed,' the American began. 'Well I guess that makes it easier in a way. I'll start at the beginning but before I do, what is the connection between her and your two mates?' Shaun explained that these were the two men to whom he owed his current position, making it clear that he would not take kindly to any threat, adding that the same went for the girl who was very special to all of them, particularly Jim. 'Well that didn't stay easy for long.' The American smiled ruefully. 'In fact it makes my position very difficult. As you guessed, I am still with the company, or at least a part of it. Right now we are investigating an illicit flow of arms and ammo, along with quite a bit of other even nastier stuff which we would rather did not move around.' He took a sip of the cold beer and continued.

By the time he had finished Shaun was pretty sure he knew more about the Syrian and his 'Business' than even Maria did.

'So what are you lot going to do about all this then?' he asked, Chuck waited for some time, before replying. 'Not sure I should tell you this,' he started. Shaun waited saying nothing. 'How much do you know about 'wet' ops?' 'Enough,' the Irishman whispered in surprise. Then continued, 'Jesus you're not telling me you lot are thinking of taking them out? The women I mean?' Again the American was quiet and Shaun ploughed on 'Is that why she was scared shitless when she saw you. Have you spoken to her already? This is not going to happen Chuck, not now you know we are involved, got it?' Anderson looked very uncomfortable 'Problem is it is already authorised, we had no idea you guys were involved. How could we? You know what this place is like. This Syrian bastard is connected right to the top here. If we ask the locals to do something he will be gone overnight then it will all start up again somewhere else. You can see that, surely?' 'Yes I can, but why the women, Chuck? Christ they're only the front people as far as I can see.' 'Housekeeping buddy, that's all.' Shaun thought for a minute 'Okay, she obviously knows you are on to them, even if she doesn't know who you are so here is what I want you to do. I am seeing them all later and I reckon, from the way Maria was behaving tonight, this business is what we will be talking about. I am going to suggest to her that we get her out with us in a few days along with the other girl, Tina I think it is. You tell me here and now that you will not move on either of them, okay! What you do with the Syrian after we have them out is up to you.' The American chewed on his steak thinking. 'Okay Shaun, seeing as how it is you, I will put the whole thing on hold for one week. That is all I can promise. If you can get them out before then we will forget it, although I will tell you this, the Thais already have a handle on them and they will be looking for a fall guy, or rather girl, in this case. You realise from what I said, the Syrian will get away if it is left to the locals. All they will be interested in is having someone to blame, someone without money that is.'

They sat in silence finishing the meal, although Shaun had lost his appetite. His mind was already forming a plan.

It was as they were finishing yet another Kloster beer that the 'Sky News' came on the big-screen TV. Shaun glanced up and nodded to Pete who happened to be looking their way. He turned up the volume a little for them.

The lead story involved a particularly unpleasant criminal in London, a man involved in all the usual hobbies: drugs, prostitution, and of course murder. This one had just got off on a conspiracy and murder charge with an apparently hung jury. Even the reporter was disgusted, making a not too veiled suggestion that the jury had been got at.

As the man finished the story the Irishman said 'Time we set something up to deal with that type of scum. It's pretty clear the law can't or won't deal with it. Reckon we should just get in there and waste them ourselves.' Getting no response from his companion he looked up, Chuck, a thoughtful look in his eyes, whispered, 'We have' he paused 'and we do.'

He said no more but reaching up to his shirt pocket he withdrew a card and slid it across the table towards the Irishman. Shaun picked it up. All that was on it was a picture of a large broom. This was depicted in silver against an all black background. Along the bottom, again in silver, was just one word- 'SWEEPERS'.

Chuck got up to leave, 'Like to talk some more Shaun. Can we meet somewhere tomorrow? How about lunch at the Napoleon, say 1200 okay?' It was agreed and he moved on.

Chapter 6
London

S ir Gerald Frobisher was also watching the BBC news in his large apartment in Kensington Gardens. It was a grace and favour perk of his position at MI6. The obvious luxury with which he was surrounded caused him no moral discomfort. His burning urge for equality from the early years had long since been rationalised. Not that he had given it up entirely; he still trotted out the ideology of his younger days when required and it was still preached with the usual reforming zeal by his few remaining associates from that time. He was, however, well aware that they would have been very surprised if they could see him now.

No, it was more a case of equality being desirable for everybody else, something he supported at every opportunity. The punitive taxation of the bourgeoisie was necessary to achieve this. Naturally the idea that it should also apply to him never entered his head, and in reality, as his current home was to all intents and purposes free, his modest 'public' salary caused no eyebrows to be lifted in the shrinking circle of left leaning friends from his younger days. Of course it did not expose him to the very taxation he wished on others either.

Sir Gerald Frobisher had no trouble at all with the idea that the upper echelons of the public service were above the rules that were required to keep the 'hoi poloi' in their place, particularly the 'old money'. He, like his friend, Prime Minister Warren Simpson, loathed them and together they did everything they could to destroy the wealth of these people. He knew he would never even be considered for membership of that particular club and this only increased his determination to do everything in his power to eliminate it.

He leaned back as his servant bought him another gin and tonic; the news was moving on to the latest football match riot. Who was it who had said sport was the opiate of the masses? Some obscure and long-departed Australian poet he seemed to remember? Well the colonial chappy, whoever he was, had been dead right. The inane cackle that passed for his attempt at laughter at the pun caused his manservant to glance around from the well-stocked bar. At least it stopped the troglodytes thinking about the things that really mattered. Frobisher smiled.

'Good job they don't know about my latest little caper,' he said to himself. But then it is a good job they don't know about anything I am up to, he mused.

The lead BBC story had been all about the release of a certain Cyril Smith, well-known London gangster, thought to be involved in all sorts of unpleasant behaviour. He reflected that the comments of the reporter were entirely inappropriate. How dare he suggest that the jury had been got at. He made a note to ring his tame member of the BBC board tomorrow. The man would be sacked.

Of course, he anticipated, the board member would object, freedom of the media and all that rubbish. That would be until he mentioned the little flat in Chelsea of course. Always paid to have the goods on people, he had learned that a long time ago and his position in MI6 made it easy.

The last thing he wanted at the moment was anybody looking into charges of jury rigging in this case. Because of course it had been, and he had been well paid for the information that had made it happen.

He had watched the case unfold over the previous weeks and realised the opportunity when it became clear that Smith would go down for a long time.

Discreet calls had resulted in the agreement that, for the addresses of three of the jurors, the sum of £100,000 would be appearing in a particular Swiss account.

All that was required then was to check out the chambers handling the prosecution and find the weakest link.

Easy, as it turned out, because the head of this particular legal cesspool was already a known curb crawler having an unsavoury interest in young boys. The fact that it had never been made public was as much the result of the incestuous legal fraternity as the individual's equally unhealthy relationship with certain senior members of the establishment who were themselves members of the same very private associations.

Sir Gerald's call in his official capacity, suggesting a meeting, had been met with resignation by the recipient.

It had not been necessary for him to lay it on the line, the man knew who he was and guessed what he knew. The required information was on his desk the next day and as quickly passed on.

By evening a little shop in the town of Reading had been burned to the ground; the pictures of a second juror's daughter leaving her school were delivered, and the life support system of the last juror's mother had inexplicably failed at the nursing home in which she was a resident.

Sir Gerald smirked as the verdict was repeated, at the end of the news it was declared that three jurors had voted not guilty. 'Well' he thought, to himself, there's a surprise, a £100,000 one to be exact.

It left him with one piece of housekeeping that would require reasonably rapid attention. The curb crawling lawyer would have to be disposed of. After all, he was the only link between the case and Frobisher himself.

As the man servant was stood down for the night he waited until he heard the front door close and then moved into his study to make the call.

He no longer needed to look up the number; he punched in the long series of the Swiss code, the area code and the rest, from memory. There was a pause and the familiar voice answered. 'Ya?' The conversation that followed gave a detailed description of the customer, the work and home addresses, the required time scale and a couple of suggestions as to how it might be done.

Frobisher knew the man too well to insist on any given method, but it never hurt to provide a little guidance, and in this case he wanted the man, not only disposed of but totally discredited. The suggestion of some sort of seedy liaison, followed by his demise, was made. This, he felt, would attract the media's attention, and the fact that he had recently lost, in the prosecution of the high profile Smith case would be forgotten.

If the removal of a rent boy was required to add some 'window dressing' to this, he suggested a small supplementary payment. An initial figure of £10,000 was agreed which left him £90,000 in front. Not bad for a couple of telephone calls and a drive over the river to the city. And, he reflected, I am doing the community a service by removing this disgusting individual and probably one of his odious little playmates as well.

Of course he completely ignored the fact that his actions had also set loose a far more dangerous animal.

Bangkok

Shaun had placed the card in his pocket and left soon after the American. He found his three friends at Club 99, the mood still subdued. His suggestion that they return to the hotel for a counsel of war, was met with resignation.

They went to Jim's room, where they agreed to hear Maria's story first. As she finished she looked at Shaun. 'The American in the bar, is he a friend of yours?' Shaun nodded, and she went on, 'He came to the offices when the Thai staff were alone there the other day. He was asking questions. He said he was with the US government and that they would all be in trouble if they did not help him get some information about us. He specifically mentioned Hadad, the Syrian, but he also said he wanted information about Tina and me. I only know this because I passed him on the way out and when I went back to the office that day. The Thais were in such a state that I got it out of them.'

The Irishman looked at her and said, 'You have every reason to be worried Maria. Your boss has dropped both of you well and truly in it. In fact, up until tonight the plan seems to have been to remove all of you. They really only want him, you two were seen as no more than 'fellow travellers' but the result was going to be the same. Tell me one thing, did you tell your boss about Chuck's visit?' 'No' she said quietly, the full significance of what she had just heard, sinking in. 'And Tina?' 'Yes she knows, that is why she has gone already.' 'And what about the Thai staff will they tell the boss? I don't know.' She said. 'I think one of them will in the end; things are very tense there at the moment and he will notice, but he is away at the moment and is not due back for two days.' 'Well, that is something,' Shaun continued. He looked up at his old friend, 'The problem we have Jim, is that the Yanks have put a stop notice on the three of them from tonight. It is a good job Tina has gone or our own problems would double. Maria, as soon as we finish you must get on to her and tell her that under no circumstances is she to return to Thailand. In fact tell her to get back to the UK ASAP. Okay;' The woman nodded. 'Jim, what I am going to suggest is highly illegal but it is the only way I can think of getting Maria out of here. If she stays she is going to be the fall guy for all of this, even if they get the Syrian. It seems he is so well connected here that if there is any blame being dished out she will get it and he will slip away. That's assuming the Yanks don't get him first of course. As it is, I get the feeling they would rather just remove him, save a lot of embarrassment, but to do that they have to make sure his Thai mates are not smeared with collateral crap. Having Maria here to take the fall would be very handy.'

'So what's the plan mate?' Digger, silent until now, spoke up.

'Oh Christ, sorry Dig' Shaun said 'I just assumed you would be in on this, sorry old son.' 'Don't be daft Shaun of course I'm in on this, sounds like a great caper, so what's the bloody plan?'

The Irishman smiled. 'Okay here it is. Jim you and Dig are doing the freighter to the UK tomorrow night, right? So what I reckon is you get on to ops in Sydney tell them I need a route check or something. I displace your current F/O and the three of us fly it up to London. I'm due to passenger home tomorrow night anyway as young Alan Hitchcock, my F/O, is doing a command assessment flight with George Cooper, so I won't be missed. All they will have to do is passenger your F/O home. That way we keep it in-house and none of the youngsters will get into trouble if it all goes tits up, Oops! Sorry Maria, secret men's talk.' She smiled for the first time that night, and not for the first time did he envy his old friend. Christ, a bloke would do anything for a smile like that.

'And how does this help Maria, Shaun?' 'Well Jim, I reckon you and her have got to nip across the river tomorrow to that street that specializes in copies of everything. You take your company ID card with you and you get a copy of it made up for her. They can do the pictures of her over there and as long as you work out a seniority number and a plausible date of joining it should do the job. You must use the real data though, same passport number, name and all for the rest of it. She won't need any bar codes on the card though, because one of us will be with her all the time and we can open anything that requires opening.' He leaned down to the briefcase he had bought from his room and pulled out a sheaf of papers. 'These are the general declarations and customs forms for here on departure and the arrival in the UK. Get them to place our names and details on copies of them. I have written my stuff at the top. Dig you do the same. Then all you have to do is put yourself on and then Maria on as a flight attendant, with the details to match her ID and passport, and then run off a dozen copies. Maria' he continued 'You can bring one suitcase with you. Jim will give you some crew labels for it. Do you have, or can you get by tomorrow night, something resembling our girl's uniform? It's pretty simple, particularly in the tropics slim navy skirt and a white blouse should do it, and black shoes. Does that sound about right fellas?'

They each looked at him bemused; asking pilots to describe women's clothes was not something that had a great future it seemed. Eventually, having looked at each other he got a 'Yep, sounds about right,' out of the Digger, followed after a pause with, 'I think'

He smiled, 'Well if you two dopes can't remember I don't suppose the security people at the airport will either. Then tomorrow night we all go out there as a crew. You three go straight down to the freight terminal once we have done all the security and emigration crap. I'll do the plan and see you there later. I reckon once we are on, that will be it.

At the other end we take the general declarations and clear customs. Only here we have two sets: one with her on, the false set, and one without her. If we get a rumble from customs in Heathrow we use the ones with her on if not, the others. That way, assuming we don't get inspected, she just disappears and we are away.

If we do get pulled over we use the papers with her on them, and even then we will have to be very unlucky because it would require a cross check all the way back to Sydney and I don't think that will happen.'

'Bloody brilliant mate,' Jim burst out 'What do you think Maria, any problems with any of that?' 'Is it going to get you into trouble?' she asked. 'Only if we get caught,' Shaun said, smiling.

The look of relief on her face was a tonic for them all. Then, practical as ever, 'Where am I going to get a plain blue skirt and a white blouse? I don't usually do plain.' The men laughed 'Bloody women' Jim said, earning himself an affectionate clip round the ear as she stood up, thinking.

It was the Digger who summed it up, 'All I can say is it is a damn good job it's the freighter. We would never get away with it otherwise.'

Jim got onto operations in Sydney straight away. It helped that it was well past midnight and that the duty crewing officer was an old friend who knew better than to ask too many questions. The changes were quickly made and he agreed that the spare F/O from Jim's crew could passenger back in Shaun's place, as expected.

However, once the new arrangements were in place he couldn't resist a look at Shaun Fitzgerald's training record. As he thought, the Irishman had only done his annual route check last month. I wonder what those old buggers are up to he thought, no good I'll bet. Still, they were all good blokes, he would make damn sure it all got buried in the paper work before the end of his shift; he owed them that for past favours.

Jim unwound his long legs and went to the bar. Up until now none of them had felt like a drink. Having given everybody what they wanted he looked at his old friend, 'And you Shaun, what are you doing tomorrow?'

There was a significant pause then he began to tell them a little more about Chuck Anderson, and in the end he told them just about everything right back to the incident on the East German border and his time with Anderson and Continental Air Services in Laos.

The three of them sat and listened without interruption, enthralled, only at the end did Maria, ever the romantic, ask 'And this girl, Ingrid, wasn't it? You never saw her again?' A wistful smile on his face Shaun replied quietly. 'No Maria, in fact I never heard anything about her or the incident again. I don't even know if she lived.'

'What I do know is that if I ever get the chance that Whitehall bastard is going down. I'm damn sure he set us up, just couldn't prove it. Of course, if it had been a few months later in Laos he would have been disposed of then and there. Still, I hope 'they' would have woken up to that prick years ago and got rid of him; certainly I've heard nothing of him. Guess I should ask Chuck, seeing as how you mentioned it, he might know. Wouldn't say no to a few minutes with that back-shooting bastard on the border either, while I'm at it,' he concluded.

'Holy Cow Shaun, how come you never told us about all that before,' Digger exclaimed

'Dunno mate, it's all history now and I guess I didn't think you would be interested.' 'Bullshit, of course we are interested, at least it explains why you can shoot like that,' the engineer said. 'Like what?' Maria piped up. Shaun had discretely left out the incident in the back street in Saigon and now he glared at the Digger, who quickly and without much conviction, mumbled some lame explanation that even Maria realised was utter crap. She was smart enough to leave it though. Of course that did not mean that Jim was not going to get the third degree when she got him alone which explained why he too was glaring at the hapless engineer.

'And tomorrow mate?' Jim persisted, conveniently changing the subject. 'Ah yes, tomorrow. Well tomorrow I am going to see the man from 'Spook city' at the Napoleon, where I am going to tell him what we are all going to do. I will ask him to make sure, as far as he can, that there is no trouble, always good to have someone on the inside. I will tell him that Tina is away already. Maria you will not forget to call her okay? Then I will ask him about this.' He slowly pulled the card out of his pocket and handed it to the Digger, sitting beside him. Dig looked at puzzled, said nothing and passed it on. Jim looked at it with a frown and did likewise to Maria who said quietly, 'Where did you get this?' 'I got it from Chuck Anderson.' He went on to explain the news item they had both been watching and the comments he had made that had resulted in Anderson passing him the card 'Why?' he looked at her. 'Have you seen one before?' 'Yes' she said 'One was left at the office by your friend the day I saw him there. What does it mean?' 'Don't know, Maria maybe all will be revealed, tomorrow. But I'd bet getting one would not be good news.'

The next day passed in a blur for Jim and Maria. Getting moving early they had got breakfast in the coffee shop and then set off for the river.

Crossing it on the ferry, they had then caught a cab to Khao San Road where you could get any forged document you wanted made up. All you had to do was come up with an original and the locals would copy it with whatever name you required. Even an original was not required in some cases. They already had the masters for a lot of the more common things like the driving licences of the major western countries or student discount cards.

In this case though, Jim had to explain what he
wanted. He also took the precaution of standing over
them while the work was done, ensuring that his was the
only copy. Looking at the card afterwards he was amazed
at the quality. Apart from the lack of an active bar code
on the back it looked real. Maria's details had replaced his
own, with the data they had agreed placed on it below the
picture.

The general declaration and customs forms were a
much easier job and as he leafed through them to ensure
he had it all, he reflected on the ease with which it had
been accomplished. Makes a complete mockery of all that
bullshit the security people go on with he thought.

Crossing back over the river he took her to the shop
where he got his shirts made, explaining to the Indian
proprietor what type of blouse and skirt was wanted for
her. Here they were in luck, as the man did a lot of
alterations for the cabin attendants who were unhappy
with the way the company issued uniform looked. It
would be easy for him to make up one of each. Tactfully
he did not ask why they wanted them. He also agreed to
bring the finished items to their hotel as soon they were
completed. So, as soon as the measuring was finished
they returned to Patpong to get something to eat,
avoiding the Napoleon, as he did not want to interfere in
his old friends business although he did admit that he
was very curious as to what was going on over there.

Finally they went back to Maria's house so she could
get her possessions together for the journey home. She
sorted through her wardrobes and rejected all the tropical
items; somehow she did not think she would need
anything like that, for a while at least. She packed her
case, keeping the jewellery separate in a small bag she

would take on board with her. She then went to a cupboard and took out her passport, a few other papers she thought she might need and what cash was there. 'Doesn't look much for two years in this place does it love?' she said, looking at the lone suitcase. 'God what a mess.' She started to cry, and Jim moved to her, holding her tight he whispered 'Easy now it's going to be fine. By tomorrow you will be home with your folks and all this will begin to fade you'll see.' She looked up at him; the mascara had run a bit. 'What about us Jim?' He smiled. 'We'll be okay, just a different place is all. And I love the streaky look,' he said. Puzzled, she saw herself in the mirror and started to laugh 'Bastard,' she hissed 'Why do I put up with you?'

It was as they were about to leave that the phone rang. It was her office.

The Syrian had returned early and was demanding to know where she was, the secretary said. She sounded upset and, when Maria pressed her as to why, she whispered that he had been trying to talk to Tina in Hong Kong and that it seemed she had not been seen for two days. Now he was after Maria to find out what was going on. The fact that she had not been there when he arrived at the office had sent him into an uncontrollable rage. Thinking, she told the girl to say she was seeing a doctor and would be there as soon as possible. Then she put the handset down. Jim glanced her way. 'Trouble?' 'Yes that was the office' she went on to tell him what had happened 'I think he is already nervous about Tina's disappearance. He wants to make sure I am here. Do you think I should go in?' 'Hell no!' Jim exclaimed, 'We go to the Montien and stay there until call time, then we do the thing as per the plan.'

Shaun had slept late that day; he had arranged to meet the Digger in the Napoleon at 1500 for a beer, he figured that he and Chuck Anderson would have finished by then and if there was anything that needed doing as a result of their conversation it would be useful to have the two of them to do it.

Opening the door to the bar at 1155 he was pleased to see that the American was already there. He ordered a couple of Klosters and carried them over to the table reflecting that a beer for breakfast was a novel way to start the day. The initial small talk covered the ordering of their food and then he got down to business.

He told Anderson the plan, up to the point of their arrival in the UK. He left out the manner in which they were going to get the girl through customs. No sense telling anybody, who did not need to know, just how easy it was to make someone disappear. Although, he thought, if anybody could make someone disappear this man could. Not in quite the same way though.

Anderson had listened without interruption. 'It's as easy as that is it?' he said finally. 'We really haven't got a bloody hope have we?' Shaun smiled, 'Well, I'll let you know just how easy or not it is when we get there. Although if it all goes 'pear shaped' I suspect you will hear about it sooner than that.' There was an awkward pause 'And now what about this other business Chuck I'll admit you have aroused our curiosity.' 'Our? You mentioned it to your mates did you?' 'Well----' Shaun continued, 'There are a couple of things I haven't told you. First the other girl had already left for Hong Kong and by now she should have left there as well. She is under strict instructions not to come back to Bangkok, as you advised.' 'And the other thing? you said a couple.'

the American persisted, 'Yes well that is more interesting. At the end of our planning session last night I showed the boys your little card, naturally they were as ignorant as me. But the girl wasn't, she had seen it before, you left one at her office the day you put the fear of 'bejeesus' up her staff didn't you? Now why would that have been, Chuck?'

The American thought for a moment. 'Difficult to know where to begin.'

He looked down at the half empty beer, the condensation from the cold glass, was already pooling on the table around it.

'I suppose it all started years ago when we were in Laos. I reckon, like the rest of us, you would have come out of that with a pretty cynical view of the way things were being done in the world, eh?' 'Sure did,' the Irishman said. 'Well, I guess it was talking about it amongst ourselves that gave me the first indication that I was not alone in the belief that, no matter how hard the good guys tried to fix things up so that the bad guys got what should be coming to them, the real baddies always seemed to get away with it. Pretty soon we went on from recognising the problem to what we thought we could do to fix it.

I guess the real start of it all was way before that though, when I went to the UK and Germany to check you out as a matter of fact. I never told you this but I met your Colonel, a guy called Raff. I also met the other guy, the one who ran the cavalry outfit that was stationed on the border when you had your little shindig there. That was a Colonel Fitzroy-Gibbons if you recall. Actually I saw them both at the same time, F-G came over to the BOQ, Officers Mess you guys call it, at Detmold to see me. I seem to recall Raff had asked him to be there when he heard what it was I was coming to see him about. Quite a place that, isn't it, certainly put the CAS hooch in LT to shame.

Anyway we talked a little about you, quite a lot about the guy I had seen in London, Frobisher you recall. Boy he sure did not like you. These two soon straightened me out though, and you had the job after about five minutes of listening to them.

The evening didn't end there though; as the other fellas hit the sack we sat and talked, once the barman had been stood down, interesting tradition you have there where the barkeep gives the keys to his customers; anyway I guess I got a bit pissed, never seen old blokes put it away like those two. To get to the point, I started telling them about how 'shat off' we all were with the way we never seemed to catch up with the real bad bastards. I recall things went a bit quiet around then and I do remember the look they gave each other. After a while they obviously agreed something between themselves and asked me if I had any thoughts on what could be done about it. I think it was F-G, I call him that, the full thing is such a bloody mouthful. Any way, it was he who finally made the suggestion.

It seemed his career was about to come to an end, mostly as a result of that border business but I think he was pretty fed up with the way city hall was running the show now anyway. For all that, he wasn't too happy with the prospect of sitting around watching the vermin get away with it for the rest of his life.

What they suggested was the establishment of a very small, select and very secret group of like-minded travellers who would take on the role of cleaning up a little of the mess.

Of course, they were well aware that with the best will in the world the removal of a few bad guys would have little impact on the rot, but at least they would be doing something that the police and the law seemed incapable of.

They reckoned the elimination of the occasional high profile criminal, together with the odd corrupt politician or member of the establishment, might just scare a few of the other creeps a little, and if it didn't, then they could always be brought up the target list if required.

They emphasised that removals would only be sanctioned after detailed and thorough research, and on some occasions the individual would even be given a chance to reform.

Thinking back I must have been really pissed because I was very enthusiastic, even suggesting that we recruit from as much of the world as possible. After all, it was never intended to be just a UK-based thing; corruption was as universal as anything else.

We went on to discuss the men we would need and where we could get them. Right from the start ex military was the preferred option, if only because of the training.

We also reckoned the ability to travel without attracting too much attention would be useful. They went on to suggest as broad a net as possible with, say, a couple of guys on the payroll in as many of the major countries as possible. The thinking was that no individual would be tasked with a removal in his home country. It would always be done by a foreigner even though the research would be local of course. So, for example, an

Australian 'customer' could be dealt with by a guy from the US or the UK.

It was later that we came to realise that aircrew had just about all the desired criteria, especially as many of them were ex military anyway. They were certainly able to move in and out of most countries much more easily than a regular passenger, and the fact that they were crew meant there was never going to be a need to explain their presence or their sudden departure. Interestingly, what you have just told me more or less confirms that doesn't it?'

Shaun just nodded, not wishing to interrupt the American. 'Well it took us a few years to set it up and the activities have been limited to about three a year so far. Each one has been successful and we like to think the world is a little better for the work we have done.

There was the usual reaction from the civil rights loony's after a couple of the ops- you know the stuff, innocent until proven guilty, and all that crap, along with the usual hysterical ravings suggesting that vigilantes were on the loose. I must say we quite liked that one, it added to the effect of getting one of these in the post.' He picked up the card that Shaun had placed on the table.

'Naturally these creeps conveniently overlook the fact that in all cases so far the customer has been in a position to manipulate and circumvent the law. In some cases it has been the very lawyers themselves who were bent,' he smiled at that.

'Seems there are quite a few people out there who have trouble coming to terms with the idea that the very political and legal establishment whose job it is to enforce the law, can itself be corrupt. Nobody has yet explained to us how you bring a corrupt lawyer to justice.

Although,' he paused, 'we have, on a couple of occasions.'

Shaun looked up, 'Why do I think you are going to make me an offer I can't refuse? The Irishman said. Chuck smiled, 'Yeah I guess it is pretty obvious, eh. I'll not say anymore but, if you are interested and you think your mates would be, we would very much like to have you on the team.

Thing is, one of our Antipodean men has retired recently and we are a little short in that part of the world. If you don't like the idea I know I can rely on your discretion.' Shaun thought for a minute, 'I can't speak for the other two of course but, as it is, you can count me in. I'll put it to them today.' 'Okay,' the American said, 'I would ask you not to mention any names. Either way, I will want you and them, if they want in that is, to meet with Raff and F-G when you get up to London. They will fill you in on the detail far more than I can, if that's okay with you?' 'Sure, what, when, where, and who?' Shaun said.

The American pulled out a blank card and wrote a telephone number on it followed by two words and passed it over. Shaun glanced at it, underneath the number he had written a name, Martin O'Grady. 'That's the guy you ask for. It's a pub in the county of Hampshire about 70 miles south of London and it's called 'The Jolly Farmer' and he runs it. He will know to expect the call and he will give you all the instructions you will need to get there. You have a free day up there?' 'Yes the day after our arrival, that will be Thursday. We leave on the evening of the third day.' 'Right, well ring that number when you arrive and fix up the transport for the next day. As I said if the rest of your boys are interested they would be very welcome.'

'One more thing' Shaun continued, 'this op here with the Syrian, is that part of this or what?' The American looked a little embarrassed. 'I rather hoped you weren't going to ask that. No it's not, its official, in the sense that it is 'The Company' not 'Sweepers.' I just thought to get us, 'Sweepers' that is, a little free publicity is all.'

'Messy game you're playing there Chuck.' 'Yeah I know and in retrospect probably not one of my better ideas. Still no harm done, I have the card back and whatever happens to Haddad now will not be connected to any of this.'

They talked a little more, then having finished the meal the American excused himself agreeing to meet in a few days on the homeward slip.

Shaun stayed on as it was almost 1500 and Digger was due anytime. He sat alone deep in thought. This was a turn up for the books that was for sure, still it had appeal, there was no doubt about that. The idea that they might be able to clean up some of the garbage there was on the planet was something he was pretty sure would appeal to the others as well. He hoped so. Going into something like this without them would not be the same.

He looked up as the door opened and the squat figure of Digger filled the entrance. He waved and the engineer threaded his way through the mostly empty tables, to the booth. 'Better get us a couple of beers Dig, I have something to discuss with you. It may take a while.

Chapter 7

The Swissair flight from Geneva touched down on London Heathrow's runway 27 Left, and, as the MD82 cleared, the co-pilot switched to the ground frequency and called. They were told by the new controller to move across to the inner taxiway and return eastwards to their allocated stand at the old Terminal Two.

The man sat in economy at the rear of the cabin, he glanced at his watch. You had to give it to the Swiss; they were right on time, as usual. Pity they were such a boring race. He thought it was probably something to do with living in a place surrounded by mountains, either that or cuckoo clocks, he smiled to himself.

Still Switzerland had been his home since the collapse of the wall and the regime with it and he was well aware that he had been very lucky. Some of his colleagues in the Stasi had not faired so well, especially those that his West German counterparts had got hold of. He was under no illusions though, well aware that if it suited them his new masters in Dzerezhinsky Square would sell him out. As a result he had spent the last few years ensuring that the sell out, if it came, would be short of the main piece of merchandise, namely himself.

He had set off for the UK first thing in the morning, managing to get the last seat on the first flight of the day out of Zurich. Frobisher wanted this cleared up quickly it seemed.

That Frobisher still had a use for him was encouraging. He wondered who was to be removed this time, not that he really gave a damn, it was just a job like any other to him. He did sometimes wonder though, whether all Sir Gerald Frobisher's requests for elimination were sanctioned by Moscow Centre. Still, why should he care, the man paid well and on time and that was what mattered.

He quickly cleared the customs area. As usual he had nothing on him of any interest to anyone. In fact he did not even need to carry an overnight bag, having already reserved a business class seat for the return on the last flight that night. He did not anticipate that this would take long.

Catching the fast train to Paddington he was soon on the concourse of that great Brunellian masterpiece. He took care to keep his hat pulled well down for he was very aware that the City of London was one of the most intense users of security cameras. He was pretty confident that he was unknown but it never hurt to avoid setting up a pattern. With the computers the security people used these days the fact that he had used the station and the airport train before, and intended to on his return, might just attract the interest of a watcher, and the last thing he needed was to attract anyone's attention by establishing a pattern.

He reminded himself that the next airport city journey would have to be the Piccadilly line, much longer and tiresome, but the only real alternative as the airport cabs were far too easily traced. Even so he knew he was taking a risk as this time he planned to return through Paddington later that day.

He had considered this and realised that it was the only way he was going to make the last flight of the day. The decision was made; the risk of retracing his steps was less than staying in the place overnight, best to get out, you never could be sure.

He moved to the small booth that sold prepaid mobiles, purchased one for cash and dialled the number. Frobisher answered immediately, giving details of the expected location of the target that evening. He already had a picture of the man, faxed over last night. Now all that was required was to arm himself and wait out the rest of the day.

The business of finding a suitable weapon was simple; he took the subway to Notting Hill station and located a shop that specialised in selling knives for all occasions. He smiled to himself, he rather thought the intended use of the one he bought, again for cash, might not quite fit into the expected or acceptable use.

As knives go it was nothing special just a rather ordinary kitchen blade about four inches long with a serrated edge, certainly not your Rambo Randal or big Bowie but, as he well knew, just as dangerous in the right hands.

He had been told that the lawyer had a frequent haunt on Hampstead Heath, the men's toilet a known point of contact with the rent boys he used, his regular Thursday evening appearance had been easy to confirm. It was this information that Frobisher had passed on with the expected time of arrival. The man used the Circle line of the London subway system to get to Kings Cross where he changed to the Northern line finally getting off at Belsize Park. From there he made his way through the city streets to the 'Heath' itself. He had made sure he was in position about an hour before to reconnoiter the area, establish an exit route, and ensure that he could see the target arrive.

Positioning himself about twenty metres from the building, with a view of the approach road and the car park, he waited watching the activity. He soon realised that it was a quiet evening. Good; the last thing he wanted was witnesses. Almost fully dark now and the target was about ten minutes behind schedule. Looking at his watch for the third time he heard the low noise of a vehicle engine and then a car slowly pulled into the parking area. It was the target he was sure. The car, a Volvo, matched the detail he had been given.

Even before the target had moved from the front seat of the vehicle a figure had appeared from the other side of the building and moved to the male entrance, waiting there until the lawyer got out. As soon as the rent boy, he assumed that is what he was, recognised the lawyer he went inside. The lawyer hurried across looking nervously around as he entered the building.

The man waited a few minutes. No sense rushing in, best to ensure the area was clear and the targets were otherwise engaged. He used the few minutes to pull the surgical gloves on.

Moving slowly across the grass he reached the doorway, pausing again to make a final check. He had allowed five minutes for the disposal and as far as he could see there was nobody within that time scale of his position, in fact there was nobody in sight at all.

Stepping quietly into the light of the building he waited again, this time it was to allow his eyes to adjust, at the same time locating the only cubicle with the door closed.

Removing the knife from his pocket he moved quickly and now, standing in front of the door, he aimed the kick at the lock side. The door burst open with a splintering crack. It struck the lawyer in the back, throwing him forward on to the boy who was sitting in front of him. The German pulled the man's head back and slashed across his throat with the knife. As the main artery was severed a great stream of blood covered the rent boy. Still holding the dying lawyer's hair, he pulled him to one side and before the adolescent could make a sound he hit him in the throat with a blow so hard that the wind pipe was crushed. Throughout the German had made sure that he was not splashed, no mean feat as the cubicle was now awash with blood. He stood back and watched as the rent boy died slowly of asphyxiation, the eyes bulging as the lungs tried desperately to get air through the crushed plumbing of his throat. Looking at the two still - twitching bodies he thought how he could make it look like a sexual encounter gone wrong. Difficult really, any decent 'scene of crimes' pathologist would see that what had happened here required a third person, still no sense making it too easy. He pushed the lawyers rapidly cooling body down between the toilet and the side wall, face forward, and then placed the knife in the rent boy's hand.

Looking at his handy work he smiled, job done, with the suggested bonus as well. You never know he thought, the whole thing could be hushed up, given the obvious circumstances and this being a well known member of the legal profession. Either way, in this area, once the police worked out that it would have required a third person, the likely conclusion was going to be that these two had been interrupted by a like-minded individual and a fight had ensued. He was quite sure that the initial enquiry would be in the homosexual community and, anyway, he would be long gone.

He moved to the doorway of the building and stopped again to get used to the darkness, using the wait to check the area and remove the gloves which he carefully placed in a small plastic bag bought for the purpose. He left the 'Heath' moving at a reasonable pace to the tube station at Hampstead itself, one away from his arrival point and well away from the scene.

Before entering the lighted area of the station he pulled an old cap from his pocket, putting it on in such a way that his face was obscured. The damn cameras were everywhere. The only way to beat the system was to hide your face and change clothing regularly, ensuring that what was seen did not lead back to him. He made his way back to Paddington station and the high- speed link to Heathrow.

Within an hour he was standing in the queue for the last Swissair flight to Zurich, having flushed the plastic bag in the station toilet and ensured there were no stains anywhere on the shirt he wore. The hat and distinctive coat of the day were long gone, replaced by a slightly crumpled suit that had spent the day in a baggage locker at the station. To the casual observer he looked like nothing more than a rather tired business man returning home after a long day.

The last thing he did before boarding was to dial the number again and say three words 'Done with bonus.' Frobisher on the other end said nothing. The man switched off the mobile and placed it in his pocket; he would destroy it in Zurich.

Montien Hotel, Bangkok

The shrill noise of the telephone woke him from a deep sleep. The room was dark; hardly surprising as it was 0100 local. The freighter was obviously on time tonight. Pity, he thought, I could have done with a couple more hours. Yawning he threw the bedding off and stumbled into the shower. Within thirty minutes he was in the lobby fixing up his bill.

Jim and Maria were already sitting in the lounge much to his surprise; each had a cup of coffee in front of them. He wandered over. 'Didn't expect to see you two down so early,' he said. Jim grimaced 'Bloody woman made me put an early call in for her. I've been awake for ages' he paused, 'Well that's what it feels like.' 'Oh stop moaning darling. It was only half an hour and I have to try and look like one of your regular girls don't I.' Shaun looked at her. Stunning came to mind and the girls in TPA were pretty special anyway but he had no doubt Maria would sit near the top of the stack.

She had managed to turn a plain white blouse and a tailored blue skirt into something of a fashion statement. He didn't have the heart to say that a slightly less impressive appearance would have been his choice; the last thing they really wanted was anybody at the airport actually remembering her.

Just then Digger turned up 'Bloody hell Maria, look at you' he said. Maria confused, looked at herself alarmed. 'What's up, Dig, have I done something wrong?' 'No love, just never seen the 'hostie' bits look so good before.' 'Okay children,' Jim growled 'Perhaps we should get this show on the road.'

The journey to the airport only took 45 minutes these days, the new toll way system had quickly eliminated the two-and even three-hour saga's of a few years back. Arriving at the terminal, Shaun went to planning alone as agreed. The other three proceeded direct to the aircraft, having completed emigration, that way Maria's presence would go unnoticed by the company staff. Jim pulled a trolley over and placed the four suitcases on it. Digger, having already moved up to the X ray machine, unloaded them onto the conveyor and Jim pushed the trolley to the other end where Digger reloaded them. He then wheeled the bags over to the dedicated check-in desk and placed them on the scales while Jim and Maria walked across the concourse to the crew desk. As usual the forms for all the departing aircraft that night were placed on the unmanned counter and it took a couple of minutes of searching before Jim located the correct list. Naturally there were only three names on it. He scrawled a signature and ID number next to his name and for the sake of any cameras made Maria go through the motions as well although she only pretended to write on the form. Digger joined them and the three of them moved through the security check. The uniform and the ID were enough to let them pass without question. Moving through the terminal they made their way to gate 51 from which the transport to all the off terminal bays was run. After a few minutes a shuttle bus pulled up and they were on their way to the south of the long line of buildings that made up Bangkok's international airport, for the freight terminals were all at the southern end of the complex.

The aircraft, an old 200 series 747 converted to a freighter, was parked under the sodium arc lights, the humid air made it glow. It was in the process of being loaded, the large cargo door aft of the port wing wide open as a long line of containers was rapidly disappearing into the fuselage.

They made their way to the flight deck on the upper deck. Jim told Maria to stay there with him for the moment while the Digger completed the first of the long series of preflight checks and then left them to complete his walk-round inspection of the outside. They were soon joined by Shaun with the night's flight plan. He sat in the right hand seat; as Jim was the original Captain it seemed prudent to leave things the way they should be. He started loading the initial nine waypoints into the Carousel IV Inertial Navigation System but as Maria left the flight deck to look around the upper deck area behind it, he turned to his old friend. 'Jim there was a bit of a disturbance in the terminal as I came through, a lot of pretty serious-looking cops turned up and from what I could get out of the agent it seems they have been tipped off that a wanted alien might be trying to leave the country. He seemed to think it was an English female wanted on fraud charges. I reckon it might be an idea to show Maria around the galley, that way things will look a bit more realistic if some company ground pounder comes along.'

Maria, her brief look around complete, returned as Jim said, 'Not a bad idea. Come on love, time to make you into a hostie.' He got out of the seat and followed the girl back through the door into the small galley area, where he spent 15 minutes or so showing her where everything was and how to turn it all on. She listened intently and when he had finished looked up at him with a smile. 'Just can't wait to tie me to the kitchen sink can you Captain Kennedy? Next thing it will be kids you'll be wanting,' she said in her best Irish accent. Jim far too street-wise to even reply to that, just smiled and pointed at the flight deck doorway.

Digger, returned from the walk round inspection, said that the loading was complete and the big cargo door was now closed, the lower deck doors would soon follow and they could be on the way in ten minutes. He then added that it was probably a good idea to get out of here ASAP as he had heard that the police were inspecting all departures at the passenger terminal at the moment. Logic said that if they did not find what they wanted there they might start poking around at the freight end of this place. Maria, sitting behind Jim leaned forward and gripped his arm 'Do you think it is me they want?' she whispered. Jim looked at her, 'It would be one hell of a coincidence if there was another person on the run don't you think? I reckon we must assume it's you love and we get out of here now, like Dig says, okay Shaun?' 'Yep let's go. I'll get the clearance and we accept whatever level is available okay.'

His hand moved to the frequency selector panel and he dialed in 121.80 the frequency for clearance delivery. Keying the mike through the control column switch he called, 'Delivery Trans Pac 922 for London Heathrow filed Flight Level 310 standing by for clearance.' There was a pause and then in the usual quite appalling English they were informed that for Flight Level 310 there was a wait of 40 minutes and that the only level immediately available was 240, or 24000 feet. Shaun glanced at his friend who nodded, 'Trans Pac 922 roger we will take 240, go ahead with the clearance.' There was another pause and then the tower replied, 'Trans Pac 922 cleared to London Heathrow via the Limla 4 departure, flight level 240 and squawk 3107. When ready call ground on 121.90.'

The pre flight checks complete, they quickly ran through the before-start check list and within a few minutes having called the ground controller for a start clearance, the four engines were running, and the airplane came alive.

'Trans Pac 922 taxi' followed the after-start checks, with the ground controller directing them onto the outer taxiway and then to the holding point at runway 21 Right and to call the tower on 118.1 when they were ready. As Jim maneuvered the big aircraft out of the freight area they all saw the line of blue flashing lights leave the passenger terminal and speed towards the freight apron. Only just in time they realised now if they could just get off the ground before someone started asking awkward questions about recent departures.

Taxing at the maximum 30 knots allowed they soon reached the holding point. With take off flaps now extended and the pre flight checks complete, Shaun selected the tower frequency and called that they were ready.

'Trans Pac 922 cleared for take off, turn right on to 160, maintain 5000 and call departures airborne on 125.5.'

Jim eased the four thrust levers forward and the aircraft moved slowly onto the runway and turned through ninety degrees. It was now lined up with the full length of 21 Right. Keeping the machine moving he pushed the thrust levers forward at the same time calling, 'Set thrust.' The Digger, leaning forward, completed the final application of take-off power. The great engines, until now a dull rumble, roared at full rating take-off thrust. Rapidly gaining speed, Shaun called '80 knots' indicating to Jim that he now had rudder authority, 'V1' that he was now in a go situation if an engine failed and finally 'V2' as the aircraft left the ground and achieved the minimum speed for flight. The landing gear was retracted and climbing out at a speed of V2 plus ten knots the 800 feet point was soon reached and the flap retraction sequence soon completed.

Once they were established on the required heading of 160 degrees Shaun again changed frequency to departure control and called in, they were instructed to maintain a heading of 160 degrees to 25 DME [25 miles from the airport] then resume the Limla 4 departure.

With the after take off checks complete, the rest of the climb to the relatively low initial cruise altitude of 24000 feet passed quickly. It was just before they passed out of range with the Bangkok controller that they were asked how many people were on board. Shaun, feigning communication difficulties, told them Trans Pac 922 was changing to Rangoon and any further query was lost as, at this low level, radio ranges were significantly reduced. The early frequency change to 118.7 Rangoon control was made and nothing further was heard.

Settling into the cruise it did not take long to negotiate more altitude with sector controllers and by the time they had reached Calcutta they were at flight level 310 [31000 feet] which, at the current weight of the airplane, was as high as they could go anyway. They had rapidly settled into the familiar cruise routine of long haul, both pilots were of the same mind here. Each agreed that the volumes of extraneous work so loved by some of their more insecure colleagues served no useful purpose.

Their shared philosophy was that when it was all going well run the human systems at something like 30% power, leaving 70% available should the 'Shan' decide to have another fit. Not that much got by them, they just didn't believe in making all the fuss some of their colleagues loved.

One of the great advantages of flying the freighter was that the scheduling insecurity, so common in the marketing departments, that resulted in all airlines trying to depart at the same time did not exist in the freight world.

The freight did not seem to mind when it arrived and as a result they were usually at the end of that night's passenger traffic to Europe.

Not for them the delights of getting stuck behind the SAS 767 which always left Bangkok in front of a line of 747s, all Europe bound and cruising at Mach .86 while 'Scandy 972' sat there blocking the max achievable altitudes at a lumbering Mach .78.

There would be few in the long haul fleets of the companies flying this route on a regular basis that had not fumed and cursed over that particular piece of scheduling. Nor was it idle frustration, because a 4000' altitude block all the way to Copenhagen or Stockholm could make the difference between getting to London and having to slip into Amsterdam or Frankfurt for fuel.

Timed, as they were, to follow the night's passenger carrying aircraft they listened to the 'Tail end Charlies' of that night's stream far ahead, trying to find a way round the slower aircraft. If it was not the SAS 767 causing trouble it would be a Virgin or Cathay small engine A340, neither capable of much above Mach .79. Not for the first time did the three of them wonder why the aircraft manufacturers did not get their act together and build machines that were capable of similar speeds.

However tonight it was not their problem and they sat back in silence and watched the dim lights of India pass beneath them.

Soon after passing Delhi they crossed the vast electrified fence that formed the border with Pakistan. Clearly visible from 7 miles up, it stretched into the night haze to the left and right of the aircraft. They each wondered at the stupidity of mankind that tolerated such a colossal waste of energy, particularly in this part of the world where most of the populations, on either side of the thing, relied on oil lamps and animal dung for light and fuel.

Shaun had been known to ask how the first worlds, 'do good' brigade, always seeking money for the latest famine somewhere, would rationalise that. They agreed that no matter how it was done it would always be the west that was blamed. As far as these people were concerned a sociology degree from a third rate university qualified them to place blame without any real knowledge of the facts.

As the hours drifted by they were handed on to the next controllers in the long line from South East Asia to Europe, until they reached the edge of the continent on the western shores of the Black Sea. Here things were ramped up a little as the traffic volume increased significantly and would continue to do so as the more densely populated West appeared over the horizon. Running with the dawn, the sun took longer than usual to appear but as it finally burst through the haze over the vast Russian Steppes far behind them, the flat lands of eastern Romania were briefly bathed in a golden glow.

Maria sat behind Jim looking out, mesmerised as the mighty Danube appeared weaving its timeless course across the plain. Do you ever get used to this? She asked. Jim waited, thinking. 'You know it's this, and a thousand mornings like it that make this job the best in the world. I reckon you will always find that there are some people in all the other professions that wish they had done something else, but I can honestly say I have never heard a long hauler say he wished for anything else, ever. What about you Shaun?' His old friend sat there in an apparent trance watching the con trail of the Qantas Airways 747 4000 feet above them reflecting the early morning light. Eventually he dragged his eyes away 'Nope' was all he managed before refocusing on the stream of white condensation they were following.

Bartlett Penthouse, Sydney

Neil Bartlett stood stark naked looking out over the multi million dollar view of the harbour, the well known opera house to the right and the even more famous bridge to the left. Not that he really appreciated it, and certainly not at the moment.

He had just got up, it was 1300 and he knew he should have been in the office at 0800 for yet another meeting with Meldrum and his cronies. Trouble was he had gone to his usual club last night just for a quickie and ended up with anything but.

Sitting at the bar he had already decided to ditch the current bimbo, so when the two women sitting beside him had made it quite clear they were interested, the suggested return to his place was a foregone conclusion.

Once here they had taken over, at least at first; a quick snort of coke had, in his mind anyway, restored his dominance. He found sex with two women at the same time more than doubly stimulating, there was a word for that, what the hell was it, he thought? Got it, Synergy, well he reckoned he had more than proved that with his performance last night.

Both women were still here. The younger had cried a little last night; he liked to hurt them, nothing too obvious of course. He had been enjoying himself with her when the older girl had distracted him with another snort of coke.

It was good stuff, the best that money could buy she told him. They had come equipped and looked at his supply with ill-disguised contempt. They got theirs through a Chinese supplier from Cabramatta in the suburbs. Mary, the older of the two told him. It was so good compared to the stuff he was able to get that Bartlett had been adamant, he wanted access to their supplier and she had promised to do what she could.

Scratching himself, he walked back to the bed where the women were still asleep. Looking at their nakedness stirred him and he climbed onto the bed, forcing himself into the younger one. She hardly woke from the drug induced stupor before he was finished with her, and he moved on to her now, half awake partner. This time it took a little longer but eventually he rolled off exhausted, no longer interested in them.

Both of them were fully awake now and they made their way to the bathroom leaving him lying on the bed, the sweat and stink of the night drying on him. The noise of the telephone broke through into his subconscious. Picking it up, he managed a 'Bartlett. This better be good' It was his secretary with a call from Meldrum, did he want to take it? He groaned, Christ he hated that bloke, always catching him when his guard was down. 'Oh all right put him through,' he said.

There was a pause as the girl transferred the call and then. 'Neil, Francis here, are you well? We missed you at the meeting this morning, been a few little changes that you might find interesting.' 'Like what?' he managed. 'Prefer not to talk over the phone Neil it's a bit sensitive you see. Thought we might drop by to go through it with you at your place, half an hour okay?' Rapidly coming to his senses and looking at the apartment clearly the sight of an evening's orgy, he spluttered 'Not really convenient at the moment Meldrum make it two hours alright? I am a bit tied up at the moment.'

Back at the TPA building on the north side of Kingsford Smith airport, Sydney's gateway to the world, Meldrum replaced the handset and smiled. Looking at his colleague he said, 'Wants us there in two hours reckons he is a bit 'tied up.' I wonder if that means we can add masochism to the list of our little boy's deviations. We know he likes to rough them up, might be useful if there is more there we could use, don't you think.' His colleague just smiled thinking, Christ, you can talk Meldrum. Was there anybody who didn't know you liked the little boys? 'Stones and Glass Houses' came to mind, but he said nothing.

'Have to get young Mary in for a chat,' Meldrum continued, 'Find out what went on and whether they have fixed him up with the supplier they use. I suppose we will owe them some extra, no doubt the spotty little bastard has gone over the top again.' He looked at his gold Rolex. 'Fix the car for 1600, we will arrive just a little early and give our boy the good news.'

At the apartment Neil Bartlett had quickly got rid of the women, their suggestion of some form of gratuity met with indignant laughter. Neil Bartlett did not pay he said. He was a stud and they should consider themselves lucky to have had the experience. As the door slammed he punched in the numbers for housekeeping and snarled down the line that he wanted the place cleaned right now or else. He then went to the shower, wasting thirty minutes there; he tried to clear his head. What the hell had Meldrum got to say that could not wait until tomorrow?

As the cleaners left, and now dressed, he was about to fix himself a drink when the ground level security called. He looked at his watch; 15 minutes early damn them, done it on purpose of course. He told the security people to send them up and poured himself a large whisky.

The chimes of his apartment door sounded and he moved to let them in.

Meldrum pushed past him hand extended. 'Good of you to see us at such short notice Neil; I know you must be very busy running the airline and all.' The sarcasm lost on him, Bartlett replied 'Well yes, I am, as a matter of fact.' He spluttered, finding himself repulsed, like many before him, by the soggy wetness of Meldrum's handshake. The man who accompanied Meldrum just nodded and followed them into the room.

They walked through into the lounge and, without waiting to be asked, sat down. Refusing the offered drink and opening the small and very expensive attaché case, Meldrum began. 'Probably a good idea if you sat down, Neil,' were the ominous opening words.

Chapter 8
Cavalry Club Knightsbridge, London

They had agreed to meet for lunch at the club, it was discreet anyway but the quiet booths in the smoking lounge offered another level of privacy. It had the added bonus that almost the entire membership had been written off as 'has beens', relics from a past that definitely did not fit in with the current government's idea for the New Britain. As such those departments, in a government bureaucracy becoming increasingly paranoid as the next election approached, wasted none of its assets sniffing around the place.

Nevertheless, Raff paid off the cab a block away and walked in the opposite direction from the cloistered entrance of the club. No sense making it too easy he thought, stopping to take an innocent look around. He was sure he had nothing to worry about because the street was empty; there was not a soul in sight, a tails nightmare he smiled. He continued to the end of the block, turned left and walked around it to approach the entrance from the other side.

Removing his hat he approached the desk 'Colonel Raff for Colonel Fitzroy-Gibbons,' he said. The porter checked the list 'Smoking room sir on the first floor, he is expecting you.' Raff nodded his thanks and walked across to the staircase.

He stopped at the door, looking for his old friend; seeing him in a booth on the far side of the room he walked over. F-G stood up as he approached, hand outstretched, 'Good to see you again Peter, been a while. I gather there have been developments?' 'You too Alistair, yes you could say that, some quite surprising ones really.'

Alistair ordered his friend a drink and continued, 'I suspect you are referring to that sordid business on Hampstead Heath. Must say I was a bit surprised at first, then I realised it could not be us, timing and method all wrong.' 'Right on the mark Alistair, as you know we had that piece of legal garbage down as a long overdue customer. I was in the process of selecting a location and an operative when, well, it was taken out of our hands, so to speak.'

He continued, 'Damn nuisance really, I would have liked to ask a few questions because while I was sniffing around I got a little involved in the man's last case. If you recall, he prosecuted that thoroughly unpleasant Smith character who got off, what the Crown Prosecution Service had told everybody, was a rock solid case. At the last minute three of the jurors decided, in spite of all the evidence to the contrary, that Smith was innocent. I wondered about that and had a little poke around in their, the jurors that is, affairs. Guess what I found?' Alistair glanced around the room 'Nobbling would be my guess; Smith was quite capable of that. Question is of course, how he found out who they were. I thought that case was subject to strict security rules to guard against just that sort of thing.' 'And you would be right Alistair in fact the juror list was known only to the presiding judge, the head of the CPS, and the prosecuting attorney and you can guess who that was. Apparently, right at the end of the case, just as the jury retired to consider their verdict, three things occurred. First, a small shop in

Reading was torched and totally destroyed, and then there was a child abduction scare, photos of the child leaving school sent to the parents with the usual suggestions. Finally the life support system of an old lady in hospital was mysteriously switched off and she died. I am sure I do not need to tell you what the connection with those three incidents is.'

'The real question is, how the hell did Smith's thugs find out whom and where these people were? And there is an interesting development here.' F-G looked grim, 'Let me guess: leaks in high places.' 'Not just high Alistair, the highest. If I am right, and identification is difficult, we are talking the inner circle of the establishment here.' Raff paused. 'Why on earth would someone at that level want to see a piece of garbage like that free on the street again? Surely it can't be money can it?' 'On the contrary Peter, I think it is quite possible that is exactly what the motivation is. Not that it would necessarily be needed, just its acquisition is enough of an incentive with some people.' 'Well, if that is the case Alistair we have a very dangerous individual on the loose and the sooner we identify and neutralise him the better.'

'The initial leads for this I got from our ex learned friend's secretary. She remembered passing a call from an unlisted number a few days before the verdict but she was sure it was from somebody known to her boss. She intimated that he was not only known but that the man was afraid of whoever it was. She was quick to point out that that she had not listened in; it was her boss's manner that led her to think this. A rather hasty meeting had been arranged and she was instructed to bring in the file for this case and leave. She eventually admitted that, along with everything else, the addresses of the jurors were in that file.

They stopped talking as the steward bought them another round of drinks. As he left F-G began, 'You implied there was another matter Peter.' 'Ah yes and much more pleasant it is. How do feel about a run down to darkest Hampshire tomorrow to see our mad Irishman again?' 'Well I think I can manage that. The two of us is it?' 'Yes it would require both of us.' 'I had a call from Chuck in Bangkok. Seems he has run into a very old acquaintance of ours who he thinks may well be interested in our little crusade and who may well be bringing in two like-minded colleagues as well.' 'Know him do we, so who is it?' 'Indeed we do Alistair; no doubt you recall Captain Fitzgerald and that fiasco in Germany, back in the '70s? You should, it is one of the reasons we are sitting here after all. Well it seems our Chucky boy was sitting in a bar called,' he glanced at a note in his hand, 'Bobby's Arms'. He was watching a female suspected of working for some Syrian the CIA have had under surveillance. Plan seems to have been to neutralise her as well as the Syrian, you know how the cousins are. Anyway, he is sitting there in full spy mode when he notices a fellow looking at him; of course, it was Fitzgerald. Apparently, after they got over the initial surprise and a fair bit of catch up, it appears they went through quite a lot in Laos together after Fitzgerald's Germany thing, then the inevitable questions came.

To Chuck's embarrassment, it turns out the girl he was watching is heavily involved with one of Fitzgerald's buddies and Fitzgerald made it quite clear what will happen to him if any move is made against her. Next thing that goes wrong for him is that the girl actually recognises him as well and is scared silly. Then, Chuck, watching the whole thing unravelling before his eyes, has a bit of luck. Apparently they were half watching the Sky news, the usual death and destruction of course. Something Fitzgerald said after a particular story made him think he might be interested in our little organisation, so he sounded him out.

From what he said the three of them appear to be ideal, all ex-military, all technical aircrew on long haul ops and all arriving in London,' he looked at his watch, 'about now.'

'All being well, Martin should get a call from them tonight and we will make haste to Hampshire tomorrow for an evening meeting.' 'Well, if nothing else, it will nice to see young Fitzgerald again, always wondered what happened to him,' F-G mused. 'Have you spoken to Simon about it?' he asked. 'No, haven't had the chance yet, poor bugger's up to his eyes with the asylum seeker terrorist threat and trying to get the politicians to see there are some bastards on this planet you cannot cut a deal with. Trouble is, it's never them, or the stupid judges who keep letting them out that get blown up, more's the pity. Soon change their tune if it happened to one of their own.' he stopped embarrassed 'Touched a nerve there Peter sorry, however I do agree with you old chap. After all, why we are here really, don't you think?' 'Exactly so, sorry' Raff said.

Special Branch HQ London

Chief Superintendent Simon Quartermaine, head of Special Branch, sat at his desk in a state of utter frustration. He had just returned from a political meeting, something always guaranteed to destroy any 'bonhomie' the day may have had up to that point. This time had been just about as bad as it could get though. He had presented the Prime Minister, Warren Simpson, with a list of undesirables who he recommended should be extradited immediately, or failing that, be taken into custody using the new laws on incitement the government had been so quick to introduce but whose subsequent use had been nil.

They had listened as he read the list and gave the reasons. Certainly the names were well known because, before he had finished, he noticed the weak and vacillating Home Secretary squirming in his seat. However, the real trouble was always going to be that creep Frobisher, from MI6. He knew full well that the south bank lot had the ear of the PM not least because Warren Simpson seemed to think the sun shone out of Frobisher's butt. Something to do with their shared past at the LSE, he seemed to recall.

Sure enough, as soon as he had finished, Frobisher had started. First, Special Branch was over reacting again, and then many on the list were already under surveillance and providing useful connections to overseas terrorist elements. Their removal would stop that flow of information. Then the Home Secretary chimed in with the usual crap about not wanting to antagonise the racial minority groups, suggesting the problem was being exaggerated as usual. After all, there had been no real trouble had there? His own comment of, 'So now we wait for the bastards to start killing people before we do anything do we?' was not well received.

The upshot of it all was Simpson ordering the formation of yet another committee, headed by some superannuated senile old idiot from the judiciary, to investigate the list and recommend a course of action. Which, he well knew, translates into, let's do sod all— again.

Rubbing his eyes, trying to ease the fatigue he felt, he took a deep breath and leaned forward to buzz the secretary. 'Any calls I need to know about?' he growled. 'Only one I think you might be interested in. It was from Colonel Raff, said to tell you there had been a couple of developments you might like to talk about when you have the time, and that he and F-G were probably going down to Hampshire tomorrow.' 'Right, thanks Angela, I will call him right away, err.. Do you know where he is at the moment?' 'He said he and Colonel Fitzroy-Gibbons would be at the Cavalry Club until 1600, if that helps.' 'Yes thanks.' He broke the connection and leaned back in the chair. I wonder what those two old buggers were cooking up now he thought. He was a member of the same club and it was here he had met them both and from that meeting become involved in the organisation. Never at the operational end, of course, it was information that was needed, he had still insisted on being part of the decision-making process for all the UK originated missions.

In fact he was highly respected and his opinions were sought on every mission suggested no matter where in the world they were planned. For Peter Raff to call indicated that there was something they thought he should be made aware of and in which his input might be required.

Cavalry Club

F-G glanced at his watch. 'Lunch, Peter?' Just at that moment one of the stewards approached with a telephone. 'Call for you sir, Chief Superintendent Quartermaine.' 'Thank you.' F-G picked up the handset, 'Simon. Good to hear from you, how is everything?' 'Hello Alistair SNAFU as usual. Thought I might join you two for lunch if that is okay, be there in 15 minutes or so?' 'Delighted, Simon, we were just about to go in but we'll wait for you.' As he broke the connection Raff called for another round and advised the slight delay and the extra person to the steward.

'I think Simon is having a bad day,' he said, 'He usually likes to get away if the polie's have been getting up his nose, should make for an even more interesting lunch Peter.'

It turned into quite a prolonged affair with the two ex-army men going over the latest developments. Of the potential new recruits Quartermaine said little, knowing full well that he could trust the judgment of these two old soldiers, and in fact he needed to keep some distance between himself and this most secret of organisations anyway.

It was when the conversation turned to the Smith affair that Quartermaine got really interested. He was aware, of course, that the suggestion that the jury had been rigged was gathering pace, particularly as mobile phone traces had shown that each of the changeling jurors had received calls from the same handset from an area close to Smith's home.

As Smith had been in custody at the time, he was effectively off the hook; however the connection was beyond coincidence.

It was the death of the lawyer that had them all puzzled, mostly because he was actually being looked at by them anyway. The question that faced them now was the motive of the unknown killer; somehow they all doubted it was the simple street cleaning operation they had planned.

Raff's information on possible corruption in high places, gleaned from God knows where, only added to Quartermaine's interest.

They sat long into the afternoon discussing the next moves. All agreed that the early removal of one Mister Cyril Smith topped the list. Not only would this remove an odious individual that the law had had a chance to clear off the streets and once again ballsed up, but more importantly, Smith's demise may well help to flush out the high profile individual behind the mans release and who clearly had a vested interest in some 'deck clearing' by removing the one individual who might have connect him to the business.

Two hundred miles east of London

Shaun had programmed the old Carousel IV INS systems with the expected Lambourne 5A standard arrival procedure for a landing on London Heathrow's 27 Left and, as was usual on west bound tracks over

Europe once they had been handed over to Maastricht centre from which most of central west European airspace was controlled; they were cleared direct to a position called REDFA which was the boundary with the

UK airspace. Calling London on 127.82 they were then cleared to descend to Flight Level 200 and, after another frequency change, down further to FL 70 and direct to Lambourne. As they reached the 10,000 point Jim began a speed reduction to arrive at the Lambourne VOR at the requested 250 knots. Throughout the descent phase a series of check lists associated with the approach and landing were carried out. To Maria it all looked so easy but she realised that these men were thorough professionals and that it was this that made it seem so. The amount of information that came in was confusing to her. She heard what she thought was their call sign a number of times but of the information that followed it she understood nothing only realising that it involved them as she watched the two pilot's action whatever it was they had been asked to do.

They passed the Lambourne VOR, the beacon over which traffic in- bound from the east was either held or vectored to final approach, and now talking to the Heathrow Director, the radar controller who would steer them on to finals. The lazy S track allowed them to slow further and Jim bought the great machine back to 190 knots with the first stage of flap extended. He waited until radar turned them onto a southerly heading, and then called for a further extension to five. After a few minutes 'Director' cleared them to intercept the 27 left ILS, the instrument landing system that would guide them to the runway. Shaun glanced at Jim who gave a brief nod. Shaun selected the flaps to ten then, as the aircraft rolled level with the two needles settling to a perfect cross on the attitude direction indicator, he called the tower and told them that Trans Pac 922 was established 27 Left. The reply, as usual, was to maintain

170 knots to the marker. Maria, becoming a little more familiar with the complicated panel of instruments, looked across at what she now knew was the airspeed indicator. It did not surprise her to see that Jim had anticipated this and the needle was exactly on the 170 line.

The landing was smooth enough to be barely noticeable and as they were destined for the freight apron, well up 27 Left and off to the left at block 79, Jim only used idle reverse. He had left the auto brakes off as well, no point in subjecting the undercarriage to the jolt required to disengage them on the roll out. The end result of all that was that they arrived with hardly any noise at all. He slowed as they approached the taxiway. Digger fired up the APU and Shaun was occupied with bringing in the huge flaps and generally shutting down systems that were no longer required. Jim quickly manoeuvered to the allocated gate and stopped. The ground crew pushed the chocks in place and called the flight deck, and Jim selected the four fuel control switches to cutoff. With the fuel removed, the fire in the engines died and they slowly whispered to a stop.

On the flight deck the three of them stretched, 'Another one down eh fellas,' Jim said. Shaun looked across at him. 'Not quite, better not relax until we're sitting in the bus on the M4 motorway today I reckon.' With that he got out of the seat and began to rummage through the bag containing the ship's papers, placing each set of the General Declarations and the already filled-in customs forms in separate piles. On one set Maria was listed, on the other no mention of her was made. 'I'll keep the false ones in the left pocket and the real ones in the right okay? Just make sure I don't get them muddled up.' With that he opened the flight deck and descended to the main deck to monitor the opening of the left one door, something done by the ground crew but only after they were cleared to do so. He was relieved to see that there was no customs officer in the group of people standing there. He greeted them and then returned to the flight deck where the others had gathered their stuff together. Handing him his bag, they left the aircraft, walking over to the small combi van provided as crew transport.

The 'in hold' bags had been loaded already and within a few minutes they were on their way to the customs control point for arriving aircrew.

If there was going to be a problem this is where it would be, but as Shaun got out of the vehicle and entered the inspection room he relaxed. The customs officer showed little interest, accepting the real paperwork from his right hand pocket. He cast a disinterested glance at the 'nothing to declare' against their three names. Slightly more animation when the subject of the flight up was mentioned, then a polite 'good day' and Shaun was quickly out of there.

Finally they cleared the security gate, where some, overweight spotty youth in the inevitable yellow jacket that, according to the OH&S idiots, was a more powerful defence against accidents than a Superman suit, had slid open the side door and forced his way into the cabin. This individual, convinced that he was protecting the entire UK from some unknown threat by glaring at the men and leering at Maria, eventually got off. They all breathed a sigh of relief, partly because he had a chronic body odour problem, but really because that gate represented the last hurdle.

The journey down the M4 into London took about 40 minutes, quicker at this time of day. Having checked into the hotel, they stayed at the Gloucester in Kensington, and now in the room, Shaun lifted the suitcase onto the stand provided, snapped it open and distributed the things he would need.

Opening his briefcase he located the card that Chuck Anderson had given him. No time like the present, he thought. He dialled the exit code from the hotel and the number for the 'Jolly Farmer'. The girl who answered went off to get the man they were supposed to meet tomorrow. After a few minutes the handset was picked up. 'Martin O'Grady, what can I do for you?' the Irish accent quite pronounced.

Introductions over, it was clear that O'Grady was expecting the call. Accommodation for the three of them was arranged for the following night. He advised that they were to use the train from Waterloo, getting off at the Southampton Airport station, telling Shaun to call when he had an arrival time. He would then arrange to have them collected. That settled, Shaun called the other two and arranged to meet them that evening in the lobby for dinner. Finally after a shower he went to bed for a few hours' sleep.

The Jolly Farmer

Standing in the narrow entrance to the lounge bar of his public house, an area referred to as 'The Tardis' by the locals because it resembled the telephone box made famous by the BBC series Dr Who, Martin O'Grady was deep in thought. Interesting development, he mused, certainly need a few more people, and another Irishman would be a double bonus. He smiled to himself. Better let the Colonel know. He punched in the number for the Cavalry Club and after a slight delay Raff answered. 'Martin O'Grady here Colonel, your boys have called in and they are coming down tomorrow. I have them here for the night so you can get here anytime.' 'Thanks Martin' Raff answered. 'Alistair and I will arrive at about 1800 so, if you can organise dinner for us all in the back room there, we will see if these chaps are interested and up to it. You will be able to attend won't you? Need you to check them out as it were. I presume you will have enough room for the two of us as well old chap?' 'Of course Colonel, made a point of keeping everything available, seemed like a good idea not to have any strangers around, and I will let my people know that I will be indisposed for the evening.' 'Thanks Martin, see you tomorrow then.'

Raff looked up at his companions. 'Good man that, thinks of everything. We see these chaps tomorrow night over dinner. Leave about 1530. Okay with you Alistair; I will collect you if you like?' F-G grimaced, his friend was a notoriously fast driver and the old Bentley he insisted on using was well able to scare the crap out of any poor devil in the passenger seat. Resigned he managed a rather reluctant 'Yes, fine.'

Raff continued, 'Simon we'll call you the next morning to let you know how it turned out. In the meantime perhaps you could give some thought to the when, and the who, in the matter of our Mister Smith. I think the sooner the better given the ulterior motive don't you? This could be one for our South African friends I think.' Quartermaine agreed and with everything done they went their separate ways.

Bartlett Penthouse, Sydney

Twelve thousand miles away and twelve hours later Neil Bartlett was struggling to come to terms with what Meldrum and his partner had told him. Cutting through all the corporate bull about stock ownership and debt control, it was clear that he no longer had an airline. In fact, as it had just been laid out for him, his sole remaining interest in his father's company was a miniscule 5% of the stock, the other holdings over which he thought he had control had all been taken over by Meldrum and his group.

Meldrum did a good job of disguising the pleasure he had in destroying the man, even offering to let Bartlett keep his position as Chief Executive Officer, although he was careful to add the poison 'For the time being and until you find something more suitable' to the olive branch.

Of course there was some benefit in retaining Bartlett in the top position for a while. For one thing he was determined to push through the assault on staff salaries, in particular those of the technical aircrew for whom he shared with Bartlett a particular loathing, about the only thing they did share.

There were other changes intended too, some of a more delicate nature involving the relocation of the wealth he had found in the company. This wealth, in spite of Neil Bartlett's best efforts, was still considerable and Meldrum was determined to see as much of this as possible placed in a more personally advantageous position. Naturally he would look after his fellow travellers but as far as he was concerned, the rest of the staff were there to be fleeced, and that is what he intended to do.

It would be very convenient to retain Bartlett as the fall guy for this, for a while at least. Meldrum was working on at least a year to strip out the wealth and screw the staff. He figured it would probably be that long before the various departments realised what was happening; all the usual corporate waffle, times are hard, cost rising, unfair competition, oil prices etc, should keep the peasants quiet for at least that long.

However, as soon as the industrial unrest began he would remove Bartlett, blaming him for the situation, stating that the new order, with himself at the helm of course, would restore the conditions as soon as possible but that things were in such a mess, as a result of his predecessor's incompetence, people must not expect too much too soon.

This, he reckoned, would probably gain his regime a further year before the remaining goodwill of the staff was completely used up and things really began to get difficult. Of course, by then he intended that all the wealth of the company would have been stripped out of it and he and his cronies would move on to something else, leaving a valueless shell ripe only for the vultures. If, he smirked, they could find anything after he had finished with the place.

He watched as Bartlett grappled with his new found poverty, although 'poverty' was a relative term in this case for by any standards five percent of TPA stock would keep him comfortable under normal circumstances. Of course Bartlett's 'habit' could change all that very quickly and nobody would have ever described his lifestyle as 'normal' anyway.

It was the loss of the airline that Bartlett was finding it difficult to comprehend. He had never given a thought to a situation where 'it' and the staff in it would not be there to provide him with the lifestyle he knew he deserved. Now this loathsome individual had stolen his company and had the gall to 'allow' him to stay on as CEO.

However for once in his life Bartlett managed to keep his mouth shut. Meldrum rattled him and he decided to wait until they left and then make a few calls of his own. He did not believe that there was not a way out of this.

As soon as Meldrum and his partner had gone he was on the telephone and after a series of calls to his brokers and banks and the few he considered friends, he realised that everything Meldrum had said was true, if anything it was worse. It was obvious that they had systematically collected every debt he had as well as all the stock that had remained outside their control, it was his reliance on this that had enabled him to control the influence of their original holding.

It was also soon very clear that even the few friends he did have were distancing themselves. He was rapidly reduced to swearing and abusing them over the phone, something which invariably terminated the call, only adding to his frustration and fury.

Realising that he was powerless to save himself, he lapsed into a bout of self pity, blaming everyone but himself for the position he was in. It was not long before the need for a fix surfaced and then the memory of the previous night gave him something to focus the blame on. After all if those two whores had not distracted him, he convinced himself, he would have been at the meeting and could have saved the situation. Clearly it was their fault and they must pay, quite how he was not sure but the first step was to get to the club and ask around.

Meldrum was way ahead of him as usual. Anticipating the tortured process of blame Bartlett would go through, he had rung the older of the two women used last night, discussed briefly the little bit extra she reckoned they had earned, and then suggested another visit to the club he used, in anticipation that he would turn up again. This time Meldrum had specific instructions for her and the payment agreed was considerably more.

Chapter 9
London

That afternoon they had all made their way to Waterloo station and after a rather emotional goodbye with Maria, Shaun and the Digger had moved along the huge concourse to platform eleven. Here, the train to Bournemouth was already waiting. Jim stayed with her for a few minutes more, promising to call tomorrow before they left for the long journey home.

Over dinner the previous evening the three men, rested from the long flight had discussed the plan for today. They agreed a time of departure and the position they would take when they met the mysterious friends Chuck Anderson had arranged for them to see. Maria had been with them and Jim had been adamant, she was not to get involved in this; she had reluctantly agreed that she would go home.

As it was, the call she had made from the hotel that afternoon had come as a complete surprise to her folks, naturally they had wanted her home that day, and it had been with some difficulty that she had convinced her father that she had to stay in London for one more night.

The three men moved along the platform to the carriage in front of the buffet car. The Digger stood by the open the door, anticipating that a beer on the way would be a good idea as the journey time was about one and a half hours. 'This one will do us eh fellas?' They followed him through the large door at the end and moved into the seating area and sat in the middle of the car, the only other occupant was a rather distinguished elderly lady seated just at the entrance. Other than her the carriage was empty.

Right on the published time the train moved out. There was only one stop planned apparently, at a place called Woking about thirty minutes into the journey. After that it was non stop to their station at Southampton Airport where they were to be collected. Shaun had telephoned O'Grady with an ETA as soon as they had purchased their tickets.

At up to 100 miles an hour and as smooth as silk the train ate up the track. Even the stop at Woking was brief and, with acceleration better than a lot of the early aircraft they had flown, it was quickly up to cruise speed again. They were quietly impressed.

The trouble began soon after leaving Woking. In that brief stop four scruffy youths had got on and noisily parked themselves across the aisle from the elderly woman. They had the usual trappings of the modern feral Yob: the inevitable, quantity of scrap metal hanging off their ears eyebrows and noses, haircuts that your average chicken would have been proud of and of course, lots of noise. The three men had been quietly dozing and it took them a few minutes to lock on to the cause of the disturbance. By then the yobs, bored with their own barely literate conversation, punctuated with swearing of the most offensive kind, had started to turn on the elderly passenger across the aisle.

The Digger, sitting in the aisle seat and facing backwards, watched, eyes narrowing, as the two mental cripples closest to her demanded she hand her purse over. The engineer looked at his two colleagues 'Time for a beer I think gents,' 'Trouble Dig?' Shaun moved to go with him. 'It's okay I can handle it,' he said and moved down the aisle. He stopped just before the occupied seats and saw the pleading look on the woman's face. 'Bit noisy there boys, kind of like you all to keep it down, right. Might get you to leave the lady out of it too.' The youth opposite looked him up and down and leered, 'An' what yer fink yer gunna fuckin do about it Grandad? Old bag's got money and we wannit. Same goes for youse if youse don't fuck off, right!' As he said this he pulled a knife from the filthy anorak he wore and the yob opposite yelled excitedly. 'Go on, Wayne, stick the bastard.'

Digger said nothing but his left hand moved like lightning. Grabbing a handful of the knife-carrying youth's greasy hair he pulled down hard, slamming the face into the table that separated the two bench seats of the booth the youths occupied. At the same time he swung around and with his right hand chopped the mouthy one sitting opposite under the nose immediately drawing blood. With the occupants of the aisle seats out of it for a while, the two at the windows found it just about impossible to move, not that it stopped them trying of course and Digger, with the first youth's hair still in his hand hissed, 'Tell your mates to sit still sonny or you'll get some more.' Stupidly the yob swore and told them to get him, or at least he started to because Digger pulled the head up and as quickly slammed it down again, this time with considerably more force. The sound of the nose breaking was followed by a howl of pain soon silenced as the Digger repeated the movement, only this time he pulled the head slightly to the side and the impact was in the mouth. The yelling was replaced by the sound of breaking teeth and then rapidly reduced to a whimper. This youth was pulled upright at last, the face an unholy mess of mucous, blood and broken teeth. 'So boys,' Digger said quietly, 'Now we understand each other we'll do it my way okay?' The two in the window seats looked at the mess of their friends faces and mutely nodded. The one beside Digger was barely conscious, his nose bleeding profusely. To ensure no further interest from this one the engineer pulled the hood of the coat he wore over his head and down to the surface of the table, then taking the knife that lay there, he stabbed it hard through the cloth, effectively pinning its wearer face down. 'Right you' he pointed at one of the two still-intact youths 'You will now apologise to this lady for your foul language and threatening behaviour and you will turn out your pockets and give me your cash, sort of a fine for you. See lads, we can't have you two getting away with no punishment can we now?' They began to object until the Diggers grip on the hair of the yob on his left tightened again and another slamming session was imminent. The youth with the now very flat face, screamed 'Give it to him for fucks sake,' only to be pulled hard down on to the table once again. 'Watch yer language sonny, not much of your face left as it is, so less of the swearing okay!' As he said it his hand again tightened on the hair and the once mouthy yob sobbed, 'No more mister, please.'

Gathering all the cash they had he went on. 'Okay lads, just one last thing, I want you all to take your pants off now.' The immediate protests of the intact pair were quickly silenced by the barely understandable whimper of 'Do it,' from their mate.

It took some time to get the incapacitated pair undressed but when it was done he gathered the four pairs of equally filthy jeans. Standing there he looked at them. 'So boys, a sad lesson for you, next time have a little respect okay.' With that he continued to the end of the car opened the window and threw the clothing out.

Returning, he found the two who could still speak making a grovelling apology to the woman opposite. He threw a little of the small change he had taken from them onto the table. 'Should be enough there for a call or two.' Then turning to the woman he asked where she was going, well aware that with scum like this any contrition would be short-lived once she was alone again. Fortunately she was getting off at the same place as the three of them, so he moved her forward to sit with them and left the four youths to lick their wounds.

The rest of the journey passed without incident, the conversation from the end very subdued and frequently interrupted by groaning. The Digger smiled at the elderly woman. 'All okay now? I don't think those four will bother anybody for a while and we will put you in a cab when we get to the airport. Seems they have very kindly offered to pay for it. They had tickets to the stop after yours I think, Southampton Central? She nodded, 'However, seeing as how I have ditched the tickets with the rest of their stuff, I think the arrival will be interesting, especially with no pants an all.'

His two friends shook their heads and smiled. 'Doesn't pay to piss the Digger off, eh Shaun?' Jim laughed and quickly apologised to the lady who smiled and then surprisingly asked 'who the hell are you?' So they gave her a potted history, which bore no resemblance to the truth, stating that they were South

Africans in the UK working for an oil company, although much later Jim admitted that he did not think she was fooled for a minute. It was pretty obvious the old girl had been around and knew an Australian accent when she heard one, not that she had let on of course.

As they left the train at the airport station they walked passed the four youths still on the train and were highly amused to see the conductor standing over them demanding an explanation for their condition and the lack of tickets. 'Wait till he notices they haven't got any strides,' the Digger smiled, 'Something tells me those four dickheads will remember today for a while.'

Seeing them on the platform, the two at the window were frantically pointing at them, clearly trying to get the guard to understand that the cause of all their troubles was just walking away.

At the station entrance they said their goodbyes, again the woman thanked them and Digger paid the cabby with the cash donated by his recent acquaintances.

As soon as she left, a man, who had been standing back watching, walked over and in the accent of County Tipperary introduced himself. 'It's Martin O'Grady so it is and would you gentlemen be the three I've come to collect?' Shaun smiled with pleasure and, slipping into an accent of old, confirmed that they were indeed. 'Sure it will be nice to have another Paddy along. The car's over there shall we go?

On the short drive to his pub O'Grady explained the schedule for the night, suggesting they get settled in then come down for a beer or two. He explained that the two Colonels to whom they were going to be introduced would be arriving a little later and that they would all have a private dinner together to talk the business through.

M I 6

Sir Gerald Frobisher was just about to leave the office when the intercom buzzer sounded; looking at his watch he answered irritably 'What is it?'

'I have head of internal security here sir. He wonders if you could spare a minute?' his secretary announced. 'Damn it, doesn't he know what the bloody time is I'm due at the club in an hour?' Outside, the girl raised her eyes and mouthed a silent apology to the man standing by her desk. Working for Frobisher was not the most popular job and even though she had only been there for three months she was already making efforts to move on to another Department. 'He says it is a matter of some concern to you sir. Shall I send him in?' A grunted affirmative was all they got.

As the man entered the room Frobisher announced to his visitor, even before he had reached the large desk, 'I can give you five minutes Carrington that is all, clear?' Frobisher was determined to avoid the familiarity of first names, something that he had lovingly cultivated in his early years as an underling but now that he was at the other end of the seniority system he was convinced that undue familiarity, even with a fellow head of department as was the case here, was something to be avoided.

Pat Carrington, the head of internal security, smiled, only too aware of the man's ego and even more of his humble origins. It would take a lot more than bad manners from this idiot to ruffle his feathers, and it was going to be interesting to see if there was any reaction to his questions.

'What is it?' Frobisher demanded. 'Well Gerald,' he paused letting the use of first name sink in, 'seems we have a leak of sorts. Had Special Branch on the line, a low level inquiry into whether we had an interest in that criminal case recently. The one where the gangster chappy, Smith was the name I think, anyway he got off from what was supposed to be a watertight case.'

The head of internal security had not expected much of a reaction really, it was only a low level query from SB after all, and as a result, Frobisher's behaviour came as quite a surprise. Initially nothing, just a blank stare, then a visible paling of the face followed by nervous fiddling with the desk furniture and finally an explosion, 'What the hell do you mean by coming in here and accusing me of something like that? How dare those idiots across the river ask questions of us?' Taken a little by surprise, Carrington quickly recovered. You did not have to be a genius to realise that something unpleasant had just surfaced. 'Actually Gerald,' he continued 'It was just an enquiry as to whether we had an interest. Seems the Metropolitan Police have been checking telephone records and they have come up with a couple of our numbers, no names of course but it appears somebody was in contact with the bad guys from two of your department's external numbers while the man Smith was still in jail.' Frobisher said nothing so Carrington continued. 'Apparently, as his acquittal was as smelly as Billingsgate fish market on a Sunday morning in August they have been checking all the contacts made by his associates around that time. Probably got the numbers wrong I would think nothing to worry about. I mean it's not something we would have an interest in after all,' he paused ---'Is it?'

Treated to another dose of bluster, the head of internal security was more intrigued than ever. However, Frobisher, his mind working at the speed of light, recovered quickly 'Absolute nonsense, of course Pat, we agree. Naturally you will let me have the reports on this. Should have a look at them anyway I suppose, look and destroy I think, don't you?' The sudden switch to his first name and the nervous cackle that followed this, confirmed that while Frobisher would certainly have the reports, they would only be copies and that a little further investigation into this was now a certainty.

Before he left Carrington made one further comment. 'Thing is Gerald, we have no idea who could have made the call, even if it did come from here; almost impossible to find out actually.' The look of hastily covered relief this comment caused was further confirmation, if any was needed, that this was going to need a little look at.

Just as he reached the door a now totally composed Frobisher called out 'Just as a matter of interest Pat, who was it in SB who made the enquiry?' 'Funny you should ask that really Gerald, it seems one of their chaps, a Detective Sergeant by all accounts, was over at Scotland Yard. Word is he was just having a chat on some unrelated issue with an old buddy of his from the Met squad handling the case and while this guy was going through the telephone records he just happened to recognise the numbers, amazing piece of luck really.' 'Yes amazing, and his name?' Frobisher persisted. 'Can't say as I can recall it at the moment,' Carrington said 'probably in the file.' 'Yes, well ASAP with that to me if you would, don't like this sort of thing wandering around loose in my department. Sure you understand!'

The head of security was pretty sure that he did not understand – yet; but he would dig around a bit and find out just what the hell was going on here. One thing was for sure, the name of the Special Branch DS was not going to appear in any report this creep got his hands on.

Frobisher waited a few minutes after the man left his office and then pressed the intercom button. His PA took a few minutes to answer as she was about to finish for the night herself. 'What kept you Rogers?' was the abrupt query, followed by an instruction to call his club and cancel his appointment. 'Certainly sir, will that be all? I was just leaving.' 'Yes you may go as soon as you have made the call.' She poked her tongue at the office door and began looking for the number of the club. As soon as she had done it she left.

Pat Carrington was standing in the hall at the main door to the building deep in thought; he saw her leave the lift and beckoned her over. 'Got time for a drink Sally? Like to have a chat with you, if you have time?' Carrington was reckoned to be one of the more eligible and likable bachelors in the building, and a little flustered she said okay, but she would have to make a call first. Cancelling everything she had planned for that evening she went back to him. 'I don't know what you said to my boss Mr Carrington, but as soon as you left he got me to cancel his club appointment and he was even more testy than usual.' She blushed at this and hastily added 'Oh I shouldn't have said that.' 'That's okay Sally, we all know Frobisher is a prize wanker and it's Pat, right? Now let's get ourselves a drink or two.'

They had grabbed a cab and went to a quiet pub he knew down on the river, and having settled into a discreet booth towards the back of the room he left her and went to the bar. She had wondered what to ask for on the way over in the cab while he filled in the time with small talk. She decided on a safe small gin and tonic. He had been telling her of his early life in the Army on the way over, nothing too specific but enough to interest her. She had a feeling this evening was going to be something of a crossroads for her.

Returning, he placed the drinks on the table and said, 'Would you excuse me for a minute Sally, just got a call to make?' Taking the hint, she stood 'Do it here, I want to powder my nose anyway.' As she left for the ladies' rest rooms he pulled out his telephone and dialled a long series of numbers. A woman answered. 'Chief Superintendent Quartermaine if he is there please, it's Pat Carrington.' There was a pause and then, 'Hi Pat how's things?' 'Fine Simon, although there has been a rather interesting development actually, well, perhaps development is a bit strong, more a door opening when it shouldn't have and then slamming shut in a rather meaningful way if you get my drift. Probably best not to discuss it here and I am bit tied up next week. Perhaps we could meet on Friday next. How does that suit you?' 'Fine, it's not urgent then?' 'No, not really, I will have to have a poke around at the office first of course, and if I find anything urgent I'll call and we can bring it forward but at this stage Friday will be soon enough I think.' Quartermaine interrupted 'Oh! By the way Pat, we may have turned up something on the CCTV cameras, nothing specific but there is an anomaly. I will know more on Friday, okay. What have you got planned for the weekend then?' 'Funny you should ask, Simon, a little research which may well prove interesting in a number of ways,' he said and Quartermaine, who new him very well, laughed. 'Randy old bugger got some poor girl in tow have you?' 'Something like that,' the man from MI6 agreed and seeing the girl returning said ,'Got to go, see you next Friday if not before, bye.'

Looking up, he smiled as she arrived at the booth. She really was quite a looker, he thought, and then blamed the policeman for planting the idea of something a little more than a drink into his head.

He stood and was amused at the look of surprise on her face. Not used to old fashioned manners he thought. The evening passed quickly. She told him about herself: how long she had been with the firm, Oxford before that, a first in political science, and how she had been approached; all of which he knew of course because as head of internal security it was his business to know. Throughout this and the occasional foray into his own past he placed the odd question about her current employer, nothing too obvious but enough for him to get an idea of recent contacts through the office. The subject of the recent murder came up and here he struck gold, for she told him that she seemed to remember Frobisher calling the lawyer and that a meeting had been arranged soon after. She also mentioned that she thought she recalled that a file had passed over her desk which appeared to have some information on the trial. Although why her boss would be interested in a sordid piece of domestic crime like that she had no idea then or now.

Drinks led to dinner and inevitably his flat. She well aware that the 'firm' frowned on intra office relations and resigned herself to the fact that if it got out her career might suffer some damage, but he was almost impossible to resist and, who knows, it may lead to something more. Although she realised that his interest in the goings on at the office were the original reason she was here, she felt it had moved on a little from that now.

As the morning light penetrated the drapes of his very male bedroom she woke, the warm feelings of a night of quite extraordinary sex replaced slowly with reality, and then as the circuits came on line, with a rush, God! What time is it? Where the hell am I? It was only as her movements disturbed him that he soothed her mounting panic. 'It's Saturday Sally. You don't work today Dopey.' They collapsed on the bed with laughter and when they finally got up it was to take a leisurely lunch at yet another place on the river that he knew. This time there was no office talk and when she left him there really was the hope of something more meaningful in the future.

For his part, having put her in a taxi, he walked slowly down the river bank back towards his apartment, deep in thought. Half of him cursed, another relationship to complicate things, he would never learn. The other half was admitting that this one might be different and the third half, he laughed to himself, was even more curious about the activities of Sir Gerald bloody Frobisher than he had been last night. As he was now up to one and a half he reckoned it had all been worth it.

Recalling his call to Quartermaine he increased the pace. Think I will have another chat with him before Friday, he thought. If there was something going on we had better get it stopped quickly, a look around the office first and then a meeting, he decided.

The object of his attention had also had quite an interesting evening. It was with mounting panic that he had spoken to the man in Geneva, once he had got home.

If the conversation in his office had not been enough, as he left the lift on his way to the car park he had seen Carrington walk out of the front door of the building with his PA and he was under no illusions as to what that was all about.

He had got to his apartment and immediately picked up the phone. He found himself almost pleading with the man to fly to the UK as soon as possible.

This was a rush job. No he couldn't send any details. Yes, he would have them on Monday and he would see him when he arrived and hand the details over to him then. It was a matter of life and death, he finished rather dramatically. He was not amused when the voice on the line laughed and pointed out that it always was at least half of that. A meeting place and time was agreed, together with a provisional price, and then the connection was broken.

Seven hundred miles away the man sat looking out across the lake. Interesting, he thought, Frobisher, very close to panic. Clearly something he is involved in is in danger of exposure and the most likely thing was the recent removal of the lawyer. As a result he could also be in danger. He wondered if the authorities had picked up anything that could lead them to him. That prospect was enough to cause him some concern.

He was not in the least interested in the demise of Frobisher. If it happened it would mean the end of a quite lucrative source of business of course, but the thought that through Frobisher they may find a connection to Geneva may well require some drastic surgery and this was of considerably greater concern.

He picked up the phone and dialled Swiss Air reservations 'One Business Class return to London Heathrow for the first flight on Monday,' and then, 'No, I will require a ticket valid for a week,' he said, realising that this might take a few days and none too pleased at the prospect. He liked to get in, do the job and get out, and this, coming so close to his most recent visit, concerned him but he could see no way around it. If there was a leak he needed to know about it, stop it, or terminate the connection. Either way he could not contract it out, if it involved his own security, he knew he had to take care of it himself.

The Jolly Farmer

Martin O'Grady stood up as the three men entered the bar. 'What would you like to drink gentlemen?' Shaun settled for a pint of best bitter while the two Australians stuck with their more familiar lager. Having settled in the right hand bar, which was separate from the larger dining room, they were watching the early evening news on the TV, waiting for the two colonels to arrive.

In the segment on local news there was a piece about a serious assault that had occurred on a Bournemouth-bound train that very day. It appeared, as far as the TV station was concerned, that four totally innocent young men had been badly beaten up by a larger group of men for no apparent reason. The police were reported as being very concerned at what was seen as an unprovoked assault.

There followed an interview with one of the youths, who, incidentally, displayed no damage whatsoever and who, in the familiar dialect of the feral yob, described in lurid detail how they had tried to defend themselves against overwhelming odds from a group of what he described as 'old bastards'.

When an increasingly sceptical reporter suggested that they may have done something to warrant this, he denied it vehemently, going into great lengths about how two of his mates 'was' in hospital with severe injuries.

'Amazing how you have become "Overwhelming odds" there Digger. I mean, I know you're a bit odd but overwhelming, that's a bit unkind don't you think Shaun?' 'Sure is Jim,' he smiled, 'why don't you ring the TV station and tell them to call the old lady. She could square things away.' He paused, 'Then again perhaps not, these creeps are just as likely to take it out on her if they were to find out where she lives and then, the way the law is in this country, some 'dumb arse' magistrate would have her charged with being an accessory. Seems to me the low life's are always the innocent victims and the victims are the guilty parties here these days.

Remember that poor bloody farmer a while back ended up being found guilty of murder. The judge never explained just what an old guy who had been robbed twice already and finding himself confronted by three creeps in the middle of the night was supposed to do. Only problem I had with that was why he didn't get the three of them. World would be a better place that's for sure. Pity nobody asked that stupid bitch of a Prosecutor what she would have done in a similar circumstance as well. The answer to that would have been interesting, don't you think?' Jim agreed and continued, 'Of course until it starts happening to these legal dipsticks, lawyers, judges and lets not forget the bloody politicians, nothing is ever going to be done. Reckon the reaction to that lawyer who got topped over here a few days ago should be worth watching, a few more incidents like that and things would change very quickly. First thing the politicians would do is clear the do good brigade idiots out of the legal cesspool if it were them and their mates who were the victims. It's getting like this all over the first world; this place would be the worst, but Australia is not far behind I reckon.

'Too bloody right,' growled Digger while Shaun just nodded.

Martin O'Grady smiled to himself. These guys were going to fit in very well he thought. He would tell Raff what he had just heard when he got here; in the meantime he would find out just what had happened on that train. He had his own connections with the local police and all it would take was a call.

The dull rumble of the V8 engine in Raff's Bentley pulling up outside broke into the conversation and O'Grady got up excusing himself. 'I'll just get them settled in then we can adjourn to the back room for something to eat and a little chat. You guys have another round of drinks and then get young Maureen here to show you the way.' He turned to the very attractive barmaid, 'The boy's drinks are on the house Maureen okay,' Jim glanced up 'Thanks Martin, our round later then.' O'Grady nodded and left them.

They had moved through to the back room as soon as they had finished their drinks and here O'Grady introduced them to the two military men. Of course Shaun knew them both. He shook hands with Raff his old CO. 'Good to see you again sir.' It had been a long time, but he found himself slipping back into the old ways of the military. 'Gentlemen, can I introduce my two closest friends.'

Having recently heard the story from all those years ago it did not take long for the other two airmen to relax in the company of the two military men. The six of them sat at the long table there and the first course of what turned out to be an excellent dinner was served. The quality of the food was no surprise as the two chefs of the 'Jolly Farmer' enjoyed an enviable reputation.

Over the meal and after a run through old times with Shaun, the two old colonels moved on to outline the organisation they had created. They made it clear that the original idea had come about from as long ago as the immediate aftermath of the border incident in which Shaun had been involved all those years ago. Each admitted they had been thinking along the same lines for some time, but it was the meeting with the American, Chuck Anderson, that had provided the catalyst required to form the beginnings of an organisation.

From those early years and the establishment of quite rigid terms of reference, the first operations had taken place. Initially these had been carried out by one of them, but as the years slipped by age had made it desirable to recruit younger men. The two of them had, at what was soon to become only the UK end of things, reluctantly been retired to the planning and recruiting staff.

Not that this was a bad thing as it turned out, because the organisation had grown to include operatives in South Africa, Australia and the Far East to add to the initial UK and the USA members.

One of the main criteria was always the ability to move in an out of countries with the minimum of fuss and it had soon become clear that aircrew involved on international operations were ideal candidates. Raff had paused here and looked at the three of them. 'I am sure I do not have to tell you how easy it is to get into the UK as aircrew.' Each of them immediately felt a little uncomfortable. It was pretty obvious that Anderson had already informed them of yesterday's little caper with Maria. Just to confirm it, after a further pause, he continued. 'Don't worry gentlemen, your secret is safe with us, but I think you will have to agree it does demonstrate rather well the truth of what I am saying here, don't you think? Of course we are well aware that not all countries are as porous as this, one of the dubious advantages of the current government I think.

The fact remains that you move across national boundaries with considerable ease and, from a long period of watching, we have established that in any search for individuals that have attracted the attention of the local authorities, the list of transiting aircrew is almost never consulted. This is partly the result of the use of separate procedures from those used by passengers of course, but it is also a fact that the establishments assume that most aircrew are law abiding types. Either way it does mean that you gentlemen make ideal candidates for the type of work we have in mind.' Jim coughed lightly 'And what would that be exactly Colonel?' 'A little more detail and then I will come to that Jim,' he replied.

They sat there with the residue of the meal in front of them, the vintage bottle of port making a second slow circuit of the table. The three airmen were soon fully aware of what they were being asked to join.

Raff, who had done most of the talking, looked at each of them in turn. 'Of course we do not expect you to decide right now and should you have reservations we will quite understand. We will be very disappointed because from where we sit you three are ideal. I think I am right in saying our activities do seem to fit rather well into your declared misgivings with the current state of things in the world today. I should emphasise that no operation is ever undertaken without the most detailed analysis of the customer.' He smiled at this and then continued. 'Before any operation is approved we make a point of running the history of the individual through one of our other branches. This we do to avoid any possibility of undesirable influence from governments. You can be assured that once candidates have been put through our selection process the decision to remove them is more than justified. Similarly, for reasons I have explained, the actual operations are almost always carried out by foreigners who are removed from the scene immediately, which is why we favour aircrew of course. Anyway gentlemen, sleep on it and as you are all heading south again tomorrow perhaps you will let us know your decision when you get to Sydney.'

'Reassure us Colonel,' Jim interrupted, 'This organisation is not some secret government agency is it? I am pretty sure none of us would be interested if it is. We tend to share firm views on most politicians and the people who work for them. The way we see it, quite a few of them would make good subjects for some of your special attention, if you get my drift.' The other two nodded in agreement and Raff smiled. 'You don't have to worry on that score Captain. I gather Shaun here has not filled you in on all of our shared history so I will bring you up to date. When your friend left us he also left something of a mess behind him. Alistair here had all but made up his mind to leave anyway, but the run in with that rather odious individual from MI6 made it impossible for him to stay on. Fortunately, as you know Shaun, the girl you fished out never said a word and this left Frobisher looking pretty stupid. After all, a very risky operation had gone bad and his name was all over it. All they had to show for it was a young female with amnesia, an expensive helicopter with a bloody great hole in it, and, initially anyway, the likelihood of all hell breaking out in Redland once the story got out.

In the first few weeks of that New Year the noise of the metaphorical umbrella's opening was almost deafening. Frobisher found himself more and more isolated and inevitably he was looking for scapegoats. He had already decided to do a number on you and Alistair here, but he thought he would throw me in for good measure. It was not long before I was made an offer I could not refuse as well. Of course the one person he really wanted to destroy was you Shaun, but you had disappeared.

Interestingly there were quite a few other people who were sorry about that but for very different reasons. It soon became clear to certain more enlightened individuals that you could have probably shed a little more light on exactly what happened. Frobisher called in a lot of favours from his political mates, among which was our current Prime Minister, the oh so photogenic Warren Simpson no less. Needless to say, he managed not only to escape the fallout, but actually to get a leg up in the agency. It will not please you I am sure,' he looked at Fitzgerald, 'to hear that our mutual 'friend' is currently running the Russian desk at MI6 and worse, if rumour is to be believed, he is in line to take the top job once the current occupant retires. There are quite a lot of us who have serious misgivings about that for a number of reasons, but given the political cesspool that is currently running this country the odds are that he will get the job.'

'Well you're dead right there Colonel' the Irishman began. 'I really thought the fall out from all that would finish the fat little creep. Destroys your faith in the system it does, not that I have had any faith in anything much for quite a few years now and that's for sure. Now you tell us he is up for the top job. You know I was pretty certain he had set us up, that is, the girl and me. I never did tell you what it was she said did I? Well it wasn't much, just something her father had told her before she left him that night. He was adamant that she was not to trust a man called Frobisher, was all she said, anybody but him, she did not know why. It was that which convinced me he had set us up. It seemed pretty clear to me afterwards that the last thing he wanted was her father appearing in the West. Remember the brief was one male escaping; anyway Frobisher did not want it to happen, that much was clear from his reaction when I told him about the girl. I recall he was as surprised as we all were. Just as a matter of interest,' he paused 'Whatever happened to her anyway?'

Raff thought for a moment, remembering, 'As far as I can recall she was kept under surveillance for a while. I only know that because I had a contact in the intelligence corps and, as there was quite a bit of feeling about the way Alistair and I were being railroaded, he used to let me in on some of the things Frobisher and his cronies were getting up to. Anyway, they watched her for quite a while then she just disappeared. Last contact I had with her was quite some time before that though. She came to see me just before they slung us out; it was right out of the blue. She wanted me to tell her what I knew about that night and about you.' He paused again, deep in thought, 'Yes that's it, she was very interested in you. Wanted to know where you had gone and all, seemed to be carrying something of a torch for you actually, knight in shining armour, that sort of thing. I said nothing of course, couldn't be sure that the MI6 creep hadn't turned her. What I did say was that she might like to consider telling her story to the newspapers, just to protect herself. I reckoned they would be less likely to make her disappear if the whole thing was known about. Anyway, apart from that she left me empty handed and then – it would have been nearly a year later, the story was published. It only ran to one page and interest had died in a week, you know how things are. City Hall was a bit pissed off with her but there was nothing they could do, the only person that could have kept the thing alive was you and clearly you did not see anything about it. Soon after that I heard that they had terminated their surveillance and let her go on her own, after that nothing' again he paused thinking 'Although there was a rumor that she may have been given a job overseas somewhere, nothing too sensitive of course. If it was true it would have only been done so that they could keep an eye on her I think. Told you the name didn't I? Inger Fritzen I think it was. Sorry, can't tell you anymore old boy.'

Before Shaun could reply Digger guffawed, 'Knight in shining armour? The lass doesn't know you at all mate! I wouldn't trust you alone with a sheep if there was a full moon and that's for sure.' It broke the rather sombre mood that had descended and the rest of the evening was spent 'shooting the breeze'.

Eventually the airmen looked at each other, and the other two nodded at Jim. 'I reckon we could give you an answer now Colonel,' he said 'I think we are all far enough down the road to see that what you are doing is something that should have been done years ago. If it weren't for the 'Politically Correct' world we live in these days, things wouldn't have got in the mess they are. It is our opinion that the establishments of the western world are infested with people who would rather the innocent suffered than tackle the real troublemakers. Digger here reckons they, the establishment that is, are really shit scared the ordinary folk will eventually realise how useless they all are and start taking the law into their own hands and that it is this that creates the culture of blaming the victim and protecting the guilty. Anything that evens things up a little will get our vote.' He looked at the other two, 'Right fella's?' Another nod from Shaun and Digger confirmed it. 'However, we are all cautious men,' Jim continued, 'So if it is okay with you we will talk it through on the run home as you suggest and let you know then just how far we want to go with this then.'

Raff made no effort to hide his pleasure standing up and shaking each mans hand in turn, 'And it is Peter and Alistair by the way.' He continued, 'Before we leave this and get on to less serious subjects gentlemen, can I just say that what you have just said Jim is very true. We are only here because modern societies are very obviously incapable of keeping their respective houses in order. You do realise, I hope, that we are not alone. We have some very powerful people in high places who we consider to be fellow travellers. Not all of them are as near the centre of things as you will be. In fact, some of our sources would have serious misgivings if the use to which we put certain information they give us became associated with them. It suits us, and them, to be at arm's length. However, without them our operations would be very difficult and in many cases impossible.'

He looked across at Fitzroy-Gibbons who leaned down to the briefcase he had beside him and removed a small pile of cuttings from newspapers which he handed to Raff. 'I would like you to have a look at these. Understand that we certainly do not react to the ravings of the press but these stories will, I think, give you a clear idea of the sort of customer we would consider.'

Shaun spread the cuttings out in front of them. The story described was one of a bungled criminal prosecution where the evidence was said to be bullet proof but at the eleventh hour the criminal had got off. 'Nobbled jurors' was how one paper put it. Incidentally that paper had promptly been advised it was to be sued by Mr Smith's lawyers.

The Attorney General, a product of the current government's appeasement policy, had very quickly started waffling on about the rule of law and that justice had been seen to be done, adding all the legal excuses for doing absolutely nothing and finishing with the usual explanation that the legal profession must be totally removed from personal responsibility.

The story was, of course, the recent trial of one Mister Smith, with the addition that one paper had even made the connection to the more recent murder of one of the lawyers associated with the case, in the toilets on Hampstead Heath.

Watching them finish reading, Raff then placed a file on top of the pile.

'And that, gentlemen, is the real truth on our Mr Smith and his lawyers, take it with you and read it, and let me know what you think.'

Chapter 10
Monday Morning

Swiss Air 950, Zurich to London Heathrow, had passed over the Dover VOR, the vhf omni range beacon on the hills behind the ferry port, already in a descent from the cruising level of Flight Level 290.

The clearance had been a Biggin 1 Foxtrot standard arrival and the A320's flight management computer had been programmed for this. As Dover slipped behind, the aircraft was already rolling out on to the new heading of 243 degrees which it would hold for 13 miles to the next position 'Sandy'. Here it again rolled into a gentle turn, right hand this time, until the nose was now pointing at the beacon at Biggin Hill. This was of course, the airfield immortalised as one of the bases of 'The Few', in the Battle of Britain in World War 2.

Twelve miles before this the A320 had slowed to the required 250 Knots and the crew were listening to the continuous chatter on the radio endeavoring to anticipate whether they would be required to hold here. Today they were lucky because, as they approached the point at which holding would normally be required, the controller told them to call Heathrow Director on 119.72. The First Officer flicked the pre selected radio frequency into the active window of com 1 and called. Two Radar vectors put them onto final approach for Heathrow's runway 27 Left.

Quickly leaving the southern runway the aircraft was soon parked at Terminal 2. Like all the terminals at Heathrow it seemed to be in a perpetual state of rebuilding. The wags often commented that you could never be sure whether the legions of workmen who infested the place were actually putting it up or pulling it down. The general opinion was that the latter would be a better idea. The only real progress, if it could be described as such, was that now they all wore the little yellow vest so loved by the occupational health and safety freeloaders.

None of this really bothered the man; he glanced at his watch again reassured that they were, once again, on time. As the front door was opened he stood up and joined the queue to leave the aircraft.

He had done what he could to change his appearance, the brown hair now grey, the eyes blue. He did not like contact lenses and as soon as he had passed through the customs area he would get them out. Apart from that, his dress was that of a rather tired old hippy-type, lurid but well worn shirt, old jeans, the inevitable earring and some rather scruffy sandals. He did not think the computers would strike a match but as an added effect he did what he could to change his walk and manner.

Today he was a German. His perfectly genuine German passport, should it even be inspected, would trigger no alarm bells, one of the great advantages of having friends in Moscow Centre he reflected. However today, as expected, having collected his bag, he passed through the customs area without even seeing a customs officer. Not that he was naive enough to think they were not there; the cameras were everywhere. You just had to know where to look and, of course, remember not to.

A quick walk to the desk for a prepaid mobile and he was soon boarding the train on the Piccadilly Line to the city. This was going to take over an hour so he made a point of finding a carriage to himself at the front of the train. He realised it would not stay empty for long so as soon as the train moved off he called the number.

The relief in Frobisher's voice was evident even on the mobile. A meeting for that night was arranged, the venue known to both of them from times past, the 'Borsch and Tears' off the Brompton road. Inevitably, Frobisher asked where he was staying. The frosty silence following the query enough for him to say, 'Oh yes, quite so, probably best I don't know. Sorry, see you at eight then.' The man said nothing, pressing the kill button on the phone.

Nothing about this left him feeling confident. He had known Frobisher for years. He had lost count of the number of 'difficulties' he had resolved for him but this time it was different. He did not know why, a feeling, something; he resolved to get the job done and get out as quickly as possible. It would be quite a while before he returned, he decided.

Frobisher put the handset down frowning, looked at the clock on the wall, 0900. That bloody man Carrington should be in by now he said to himself. He punched the intercom button, 'Rogers get me Carrington, Internal Security, now! I assume you know the number,' he snapped. Sally Rogers winced, it was going to be a bad day, the price she had to pay for a fantastic weekend, she figured. She had completely missed the slight emphasis her boss had placed on 'Her' actually knowing the number.

This was going to be a little awkward. Just how did one address the head of internal security when one had spent most of the weekend in his bed? Taking a deep breath she touched the numbers. A rather weary voice answered, 'Carrington.' 'Eh, it's Sally Rogers from Mr Frobisher's department here sir,' she said, going for the safe option. A sexy chuckle made her blush. Quickly looking around the office, stupid woman she thought, of course I'm alone. 'Bit formal Sal what's up?' Carrington asked. She relaxed a little, 'He wants to see you Pat and he is in a pretty foul mood.' 'Okay be right over, I bet I know what it is about. See you in a mo.' He replaced the receiver, thinking.......

He looked at the clock on the wall, 0905, early. He must be rattled about something and the only thing he could think of was the Special Branch business of Friday. Well, he was not going to like this then, Carrington thought, because there was no way he was going to divulge any names or specific detail until this had been sorted out.

Entering the outer office he looked at the girl; beautiful hardly described her even on a Monday morning after a very active weekend. He had to mentally shake himself, get his mind back on the business at hand; it would not pay to underestimate Frobisher. Unpleasant creep he undoubtedly was, but he was also as cunning 'as a shit house rat'- with the added protection of some very powerful political friends. He walked over to the desk, allowing himself the indulgence of a quick peck on the girl's cheek. He stood back as Sally, smiling, pressed the intercom button and announced his arrival.

'Enter,' was all that was said. Carrington frowned and walked to the door. Inside Frobisher sat straight-backed in his chair, the large desk forming an effective psychological barrier between them. 'Morning Carrington,' and after the briefest of pauses, 'Good weekend I trust, get up to anything interesting?' Something about this last set the alarm bells ringing; he looked hard at the man behind the desk but the expression gave nothing away. 'Yes fine thanks, just the usual, since you ask.' Frobisher stared at him and the pause made it even clearer that he knew something. Eventually, as he rearranged the pencils for the umpteenth time, he started 'Got something for me on that little piece of business on Friday I hope, most anxious to have a little chat with the Special Branch chappy. I was probably a bit hasty on Friday; fellow was only doing his job after all. Like to give him a call and thank him, so if you can just let me know then we can consider the incident closed don't you think?' It was Pat Carrington's turn to pause. 'Afraid there is a bit of a problem there Gerald.' he said. A frown quickly formed on Frobisher's face as the head of Internal Security went on, 'I shall have to hold on to the file for a week or two, I really need to take a closer look at this telephone business, sure you understand old boy. I will call the SB and pass on your thanks. I'm sure they will be most appreciative after all, not often one of us says thanks to them, is it?' As he was pretty certain Frobisher had never thanked anybody for anything ever he said the last with a wry smile. Frobisher was clearly unhappy with this and asked for the name again, but Pat said that he could not remember, repeating that he would deal with it.

He left the office and, after arranging to meet Sally that night as he left, he was soon sitting at his own desk with two files. One was the rather thin report from the

Special Branch referring to the mysterious phone calls, the other the police file on the case against Cyril Smith, which included the details gathered on the pre trial activities of his people or as much as they had been able to find out.

As he sat there trying to make some sense of it all, at the other end of the building Frobisher was hastily clearing his desk.

It took about an hour to deal with the urgent stuff and sideline the rest and as soon as he had finished he pressed the intercom. 'In here, Rogers' he snarled. When she had entered the room he let her stand for a while and just at the point where she was starting to feel very uncomfortable under his stare he began. 'I am leaving the office, for the rest of the day. You are to re-schedule anything needing me until tomorrow is that clear?' and before she could do any more than nod he continued, 'I want you to take care of this stuff, the rest can wait.' He pushed a pile of files towards her. She picked up the papers and walked to the door. Reaching it she turned to him 'Can I say where you will be sir?' 'No you cannot!' he snapped 'All you need to know is that I will be away all day. Should you need to contact me for anything, leave a message on my mobile, is that clear?' As the door closed he stood up and walked to the small safe in the corner of the office. Only he knew the combination and quickly dialling the numbers he pulled open the door and removed the new file he had started on Friday. Glancing at the contents he quickly placed it in his briefcase.

As soon as he was clear of the building he made the call. There was the usual click and the familiar voice said 'Ya?' 'We need to meet as soon as possible. There has been a slight change of plan. I think lunch instead of dinner, in the usual place,' he paused, 'unless you have a prior engagement that is?' The man at the other end smiled to himself; sarcastic bastard he thought what prior engagement? Even so, he did not like changing plans. However, if this one brought forward the business he would be able to get out more quickly and that was a positive. '1200 suit you?' 'Fine.' The contact was broken.

As he moved into the restaurant, taking the stairs to the basement, it was 1130; he always arrived early just in case there were any unpleasant surprises planned. For the same reason once he reached the bottom of the stairs he purposely moved to the very back of the room taking a dark booth by the fire escape. He manoeuvered himself into a position from which he could see the whole room, whilst he remained in the shadows. Taking his time he inspected each of the other customers. After about five minutes of this he began to relax; just the usual load of student types intent on their own conversations. In fact, this time even his own appearance had attracted little notice, he was after all, dressed in a very similar garb to that favoured by the other occupants. He wondered what effect Frobisher's arrival would have, he somehow doubted the man would have the sense to dress down and he anticipated the usual exodus. Not that it mattered, once he had the target details he did not intend to stay. The waitress came over and he ordered two glasses of the house red.

Exactly on 1200 Frobisher appeared at the bottom of the stairs and the man was amused to see he had at least made some effort to be a little less conspicuous. Nevertheless heads turned to look and the hostile glances made it clear he had failed. Slowly most of the others got up to leave as the object of their irritation moved through the tables to the booth he was sitting in. By the time he had got there, those remaining were just the ordinary lunch time regulars. The rather obvious city gent in casual clothes talking to the old hippy attracted no attention. The dull whispering of conversation quickly resumed and the two men sat looking at each other for a few seconds. The man was trying to remember when he had last seen the Englishman; it must be at least three years ago he thought. All recent contact had been very much at arms length and he suddenly realised that this difference was in no small way why he was feeling so uncomfortable with this mission. The other thing that struck him was how much his client had aged- the last few years had not been kind to Frobisher it seemed.

Frobisher also took a few moments to assess the man with whom he had been associated for so long. Only here, the picture was quite different. The German had changed little. The hair was slightly longer, the large scar less obvious, but still the same ice-cold dead eyes that immediately made him feel uncomfortable. He quickly cleared his throat, wanting to get the business over with and get out of there. 'As I said,' he began 'Slight change of plan. Here are the target details, suggested points of contact and a couple of ideas on method.' He paused. 'Also, enclosed, your fee plus the bit extra you will no doubt require when you see the details. US dollars are acceptable I imagine?' The man looked at the file and then slowly opened. Frobisher glanced around nervously. 'Have to look at it here do you?' The man looked up, 'Just a quick flick through to see if I have any immediate queries,' he replied. It took him about ten minutes to absorb the information in the package. He did not bother to count the money, that it was right went without saying. Putting it all back into the envelope he said, 'You seem to have got yourself into a bit of a mess this time Frobisher. Not the usual run of the mill job this at all, is it? Usually something like this would attract a much higher fee but as I am also going to benefit I will accept what you have provided.' He paused, 'And the time scale?' Frobisher barely disguised his relief. 'As soon as possible, today even, -- certainly before the weekend; that is why I made a few suggestions. I can probably supply anything you might need. However it is quite important that the suggested cover story be adhered to. We really do need to point Special Branch in the wrong direction when this is done; don't want them thinking too much about this. Ironic really, if they had kept their bloody noses out of things that didn't concern them none of this would have been necessary. You will note the address and the combination; the information I wish you to obtain will be there I am sure and it is imperative you get it. This has got to be stopped now.' The German finished repacking the bulky file.

'Today is quite out of the question, tomorrow as well, I will need to check the target out and decide just how it is to be done. I am inclined to the car option you suggest at the moment; nice and easy to apply and no requirement to be there. I presume collateral damage is not a problem?'

'Not at all, more the merrier given the cover story.' Frobisher paused, 'So you will let me know what you want then?' 'I can do that now,' the man said and pulling a slightly stained beer mat towards him he scribbled a few words on it and passed it over. 'Is that all?' 'For the moment yes.' If I think of anything else I will call you.'

With that he stood and left Frobisher sitting there, the untouched glasses of wine in front of him. The beer mat instructions were safely tucked away in his inside pocket.

Herat, North West Afghanistan 37,000ft eastbound

Jim yawned and stretched in the right hand seat of the 747. Shaun sat equally relaxed in the left, in that comatose state in which long haul crew spent a large part of their working lives. The sun was just pushing its way through a low overcast. The mountains of Baluchistan were still in shadow to starboard, while the western end of the mighty Himalaya was already reflecting the increasing light of the coming dawn. Jim had just changed the radio frequency to Kabul, made the call, and now there was nothing much to do for the time it took to transit western Afghanistan. In twenty-five minutes or so he would call again, only this time it would be the controller in Multan Pakistan. Here, the on board computers would turn the aircraft onto an easterly heading which, give or take a few degrees, they would hold all the way to top of descent into Bangkok, still almost six hours away.

They had left London Heathrow the previous evening at 1900 local, grateful that, as this flight was destined for Melbourne, the lack of curfew at that airport allowed them to leave at a reasonable hour. This had put them ahead of the nightly 'bomber stream' destined for Sydney where, because of the archaic curfew system that was in force there, they would have been obliged to leave any European port as late as possible and all at the same time.

The fact they were able to avoid all this made the flight unusually quiet and gave the three of them ample opportunity to talk through what had happened during their time in London.

They each recognised that they were at something of a crossroads. It was one thing to sympathise with those proposing a more robust reaction to the state of play in the world, but to get actively involved in fixing it did require more thought.

The clincher was the dossier on the London thug, Cyril Smith. They had read it and it was a story of continual and increasingly violent crime spanning a period of some thirty years. Whilst some of what was written was inspired guess-work, the number of murders or disappearances with which he had been connected amounted to thirty. As was said in the summary, even if the figure was only half this it was enough to place the man in the category of a mass murderer. In reality the document went on to suggest that the actual figure could be higher.

As well as the death rate Smith was heavily involved in all the established cesspools. First, as usual, was prostitution; he had apparently recognised very early on the vulnerability of the young women in the slowly opening countries of eastern Europe and it was reckoned that his people-smuggling operation was involved with the shipment of young women from there.

They were quickly and forcibly addicted and were then put to work in the most appalling conditions. At the inevitable end of their very short working lives they all joined the ranks of the 'missing'. As there was never any record that they had existed in the first place they did not even figure in these statistics.

On the question of drugs, the one preferred for the women was heroin. It was immediately addictive and the women became easily controllable. The other drug he supplied was cocaine, favoured by the increasingly affluent middle classes of Britain and Europe.

He had apparently had some difficulty with the Colombian cartels at first. They had rather naively thought to run the European operation themselves. Quickly arranging the termination of the men sent from there to establish the market and in one case sending the head of a particularly uncooperative Colombian back to Medellin in a freezer box, he had then approached them on what he considered equal terms. An agreement had been reached. The result was that he now controlled virtually all the cocaine flow into the UK and Western Europe and much of the distribution.

In the last twenty years he had been prosecuted six times for crimes increasingly more violent and on each occasion cast iron cases had failed as witnesses disappeared or refused to testify. So desperate had the Crown Prosecution Service become that this last case was to have been held in the most secure environment possible, with the witnesses only known to the judge and the two top lawyers involved. That the usual collapse had occurred pointed the finger squarely at the legal people involved. It was this and the subsequent murder of the prosecution attorney, a known curb crawler, that was occupying the police at this time.

In the meantime the operation to control the activities of Cyril Smith had understandably lost some of its momentum. There seemed little point in pursuing another case against the man until the leak had been identified and eliminated. The fact that the lawyer had himself been removed indicated quite clearly that there was another leak.

That was, at least, the position of officialdom. However, the report they had then gone on to suggest that there was clearly another way. It proposed direct action to remove the source of the problem. Nobody was under any illusions that another 'Cyril Smith' would eventually crawl out of the sewer but eliminating as much of the top end of the current organisation would slow things down for a while and that, it was suggested, was a positive.

It went on to give a detailed analysis of the movements of the target, focusing on points of possible exposure, the most likely of which seemed to be a particular pub in south London. It appeared Smith had grown up in the area at the time the Kray family were making a name for themselves and one of their 'locals' had been where Smith had eventually become established in a life of violent crime.

It was now a monthly ritual to meet there with the senior members of his organisation apparently. So far, all attempts to infiltrate the staff there and through them the lower orders of his organisation had ended up with another body in the river. Knowing full well that the authorities were unable to take direct action, Smith's only remaining concern had been with his rivals; now it appears even they had all been eliminated. The report suggested that the complacency of total control might provide an opportunity for infiltration.

The three men had talked the whole thing through, this case and the general concept. It was pretty clear that there was a well established and well connected organisation here, with contacts in high places in quite a few countries of the world. Eventually they had all agreed that a decision could wait, at least until they had got home.

By this time the Indian capital, Delhi, was past and the long green line of the mighty river Ganges was out to the left. It would be with them all the way to Calcutta.

After a couple of days off in Bangkok they left on a direct flight to Sydney. Nothing had been said there on the activities at the beginning of the northbound flight. The only item of interest was in the paper on the morning of their departure, where the death of a wealthy Syrian businessman was reported. His body had been found in one of the city's many canals, his throat cut. At present the local police were at a loss to find a reason although there were rumours that some of his activities did not exactly suit the establishment.

Recognising the name, Jim had called Maria with the news. There was a distinct tone of relief in her voice when the significance of it all sank in. He did caution her that this meant that if there was any residual investigation both she and her friend Tina were still 'in the frame', at least in Thailand. It would not be a good idea to plan a holiday there for a while!

A few days later found the three of them sitting on the balcony of Shaun's harbourside apartment in North Sydney in the late afternoon, sipping a cold beer and trying to make some sense of what had happened to 'their' airline.

When they had left ten days ago, it all seemed to be very much business as usual, but on arrival they had been greeted with the news that Reg Bartlett's son Neil, was being eased out, although that wasn't quite how the ground engineer who had met them put it.

As a result of this there had been an initial feeling of relief in the company. However this was soon tinged with increasing cynicism about the real motives of his successors. Few of them knew much about this Meldrum character. While the optimists were saying that he could not be any worse, the realists thought maybe otherwise because Meldrum had all the markings of the corporate raider.

His early words were the usual staff motivating 'Ra Ra' bullshit of 'pulling together', 'sharing the rewards', and any number of other clichés these people used to con a workforce into thinking they actually gave a damn. While it undoubtedly worked on the fragile egos of the IT or Banking world, this industry was considerably more down to earth. Here actions actually did speak louder than words and even the more impressionable youngsters soon started looking to the old guys for guidance and seeing the increasing cynicism, quickly lost their initial enthusiasm. The realists were in wait and see mode.

One of the first changes he had instituted was the establishment of a separate 'freight only' wing, to be flown, it was proposed, by the senior pilots in the company, thereby allowing them to go past their normal retirement date and opening up mainline to younger men.

The other immediate change had been the chief pilot. Ken Hayward had been due to retire anyway; he had been with them all from the very beginning. A much respected man, he had spent the last few years doing his best to protect the company and its staff from the lunacy of Bartlett junior. Lately he had made no secret of the fact that he had had enough, suggesting a couple of pilots who he knew would handle the job well as replacements. Inevitably both were passed over and an individual called Nigel Mainwaring got the job. Almost universally disliked and distrusted by those who flew the line, his appointment was met with dismay by the few remaining optimists and wise nodding from the rest.

In fact Mainwaring's only claim to fame was that he was universally distrusted by all the line pilots. The copilots and junior captains were always worried by him, his reputation in the junior ranks was one of a self serving bully who could not be relied upon. This, coupled with a low skill rate made the job of flying with him hell on earth for a copilot, knowing full well that no matter what the idiot did, he, the First Officer, would get the blame.

Among the senior pilots it was no better; here he was treated with contempt and generally ignored.

The three of them had spent the first couple of days playing catch up with the rapidly changing scene and were soon up to speed.

This morning, however, they had each had a telephone call from the new Chief Pilot's secretary calling them in for a meeting. They had arrived a couple of minutes early in the time honoured way and Mainwaring had, as expected, kept them waiting in a pathetic attempt to establish some sort of childish superiority. An exercise in futility with these three because almost immediately, at Shaun's suggestion, they had all wandered off to the crew room for a coffee and a chat with their colleagues, telling the hapless secretary to call them there when her boss was ready. When they did eventually get into his office Mainwaring was obviously livid but, just managing to control himself, he said nothing.

He was now determined to get rid of these three at the first opportunity. However he was well aware that they were amongst the most respected members of the company's line pilot fraternity and that it was not going to be easy.

Actually, the reason for the meeting could well provide the early stages in the planned isolation and eventual disposal of the three of them and the other remnants of the original pilots and engineers. What he proposed to them was that they be amongst the first to transfer to the new freight operation.

He knew that to get people to transfer willingly he was going to have to make it an attractive package, and in discussion with his new boss, Meldrum, it had been agreed that anybody who did make the move would receive their current line pay plus ten percent, while all other conditions were to remain the same. Meldrum had reasoned that such a promise was nothing that he could not very rapidly renege on once the individuals had made the transfer. At the same time he would make sure that it was a one way ticket as well. Of course the agreement of a return to main line, should there be a need, would be made but there would never be any intention to allow this to happen. Once they had got the old guard out of the main line system the plan was to systematically reduce the various long-standing agreements with the younger line pilots, bringing in individual contracts enabling the rapid removal of any dissenter or critic. This would be coupled with a rapid increase in the rostered hours to the maximum permissible.

In the meantime, the fact that the pilots in the freight operation were on a marginally better pay rate for apparently less work would be emphasised in an attempt to drive a wedge between the two groups. When this had been achieved he would then rapidly reduce the conditions in the freight wing as well in the certain knowledge that most of the old pilots there would then leave, at which point it would be shut down.

At this stage though, the freight operation was being sold as a jewel in the crown, for pilots approaching retirement. An honourable finish to long and distinguished careers, the chance to be involved in the establishment of a great new enterprise that would stand as a legacy to them once they had gone.

Finishing this little speech Mainwaring had been quite proud of himself, that is, until he re-focused on the totally dead-pan expressions of the three men on the opposite side of his desk. Each had slipped into a posture of bored indifference. Jim Kennedy was looking out of the window, eyes glazed over. Shaun Fitzgerald was getting visibly irritated by his inability to undo a knot in the lace of his shoe and Digger was puffing away on a large and smelly cigar, creating his own Vesuvius-like pile of ash on the immaculate carpet and in spite of the prominent no smoking sign on the desk in front of him. Infuriating as this was it was only later, when he was informed by the chief engineer that Digger didn't actually smoke, that the full magnitude of the insult sank in.

Only just keeping control Mainwaring managed, 'Well, what do you think? Are you interested?' He looked at each in turn but it was Jim who spoke for them all.

'Actually Nigel I reckon the whole thing stinks and the reason I reckon it stinks is no more than the fact that you are so keen on it. As it stands I can't see what the problem is, but you forget I have known you for years and I wouldn't trust you further than I could throw an elephants turd.' This was followed by a vaguely interested nod from the Irishman and a guffaw from Digger resulting in yet another cloud of ash falling on the carpet. 'Having said that,' he continued, 'you put the package together and we will have a look at it.' He stopped and looked at his two friends. 'Don't know about you guys but I've heard enough of this stuff for one day. Anyone feel like a beer?' The other two got to their feet without a word and moved towards the door. As he joined them Jim turned, 'Oh, you were finished weren't you Nigel?' Purple with anger, the new chief pilot managed a guttural croak which Jim took as an affirmative. 'Good, okay, we will let you know once we have seen the complete proposal. We may require a few amendments of our own. Oh and Nigel open a window will you. This office stinks of cigars.' With that he followed the other two out of the door.

Mainwaring had been summoned to Meldrum's office that afternoon to report on the mornings meeting. Predictably he put a positive spin on the whole thing, seeking to ingratiate himself with the new order. He told Meldrum that he thought they would agree and that inevitably once these three were seen to have accepted the idea, others would follow. Meldrum said nothing recognising the type. It was the main reason he had been chosen for the job after all.

As Mainwaring closed the door he called in his closest confidant, now the Head of Operations, and the two men discussed the details of the long- term plan. They knew that it was quite impossible to initiate the asset strip and liquidation of the organisation on their own. They would have to ensure that the Board of Directors was on side, and the only way that could be achieved was to ensure they were not only paid off, but equally liable. The carrot and the stick as Meldrum put it. He had no doubt that if the stockholders ever became aware of the real intention, he and all of them would be in jail for quite a long time.

It was towards the end of this discussion that the telephone rang and after an initial acknowledgement he had said nothing; however his colleague noticed a tightening of the knuckles as he listened.

He slowly replaced the receiver and the Ops Director looked at him, 'Trouble?' Meldrum's eyes slowly came back into focus. 'You know what that little prick Bartlett is trying to do? He has been ringing around town trying to convince the institutions that they should realign their stock with him again and reinstate him as the actual CEO as opposed to the paper position we have created for him. That was the top man in Zebra Insurance who, as you know, holds enough stock to make life difficult for us. He wants to know what the hell is going on. At the moment he is quite happy. The announcement of the new freight arm has pushed everything up but, as I have just been told in no uncertain terms, if the news that Bartlett is trying to regain some real control gets out, all that gain in the stock price and more will soon disappear. I have just been told to sort it out or else and I do not like being spoken to like that. I think young Neil has just gone past his use by date. Pity really, it would have been nice to have had him around to carry the can for the trouble that is coming, still no matter.'

He flicked through his personal list of numbers, found what he was looking for and dialled. Leaving it on the speaker, the woman's voice was heard by both men. 'When have you arranged to meet our mutual friend?' he asked. 'I think I will need to see you before you do. Shall we say the usual place at,' he looked at his watch, '1500 this afternoon?' Another pause, followed by a testy, 'Of course that's three o' bloody clock! Make sure you are there, and just you, is that clear!' The phone crashed down and he looked up at the Ops Chief 'And that stupid bitch is rapidly approaching it too.' The Ops Chief raised his eyebrows. It looked as though they were in for another of those 'interesting times.'

He had been with Meldrum for years and had seen it all before. It did not bother him a bit just so long as the money kept rolling in. He had to admit to himself the evil bastard had an uncanny knack of making that happen, always at a cost of course, the list of bodies both real and corporate was already too long to remember. He had no doubt young Bartlett's demise would be spectacular and soon.

Meldrum finished the meeting, saying no more about the business of the afternoon. He left the building soon after but instead of using his normal limousine he walked a little way along the street, hailed a passing cab and directed the driver to an apartment block in the Point Piper area of the city.

This area had become some what confused with its identity of late. Long the chosen suburb of the obscenely rich, its proximity to the red light district of Kings Cross had led to an increasing number of people engaged in far closer encounters with the rough end of life moving in. They were equally wealthy of course; it was just that the source of their wealth would not stand up to much of an inspection by the local dowagers.

Not that this bothered Meldrum one bit of course. He just wanted to see the woman, give her the good news and get out of the place. He slipped into the little wine bar on the ground floor of the building and waited. She was there within about ten minutes of the appointed time; he looked at his watch and glared at her. She muttered, 'Woman's prerogative,' with more confidence than she felt.

The conversation lasted no more than fifteen minutes, one cup of the usual over-fussy Cappuccino, which he loathed. It always took so long to make and the noise was more suited to the steam engines of old. The frothy mess that was the end result hardly seemed worth the bother. That the inhabitants of Point Piper drank the stuff by the gallon only added to his irritation. He left her with clear orders as to what was expected that night and a mobile number she was to ring after the job had been completed.

Chapter Eleven
Sydney the Bartlett apartment

B artlett stood looking at the harbour, deep in thought he saw nothing. The day had not been entirely without hope he thought. A couple of the calls for support had been met with, if not outright agreement, at least the suggestion that if he could get some of the other major stockholders on line they would hear him out.

He had realised quite early on in the call marathon that while Meldrum was undoubtedly a force to be reckoned with within the financial circles there were quite a few who had their doubts on whether he could be trusted. Ironic, he laughed, after all he was not exactly lily white himself; lesser of two evils, he reasoned.

Glancing at the gold Omega he shook himself out of the mood. He had decided that tonight the two women he still blamed for his predicament would be made to pay; one hour to go he thought.

He had been quite specific when she had answered his call that morning. Wonderful evening and a desperate need for an encore, more generous this time. He was convinced his chat had won her over.

He was going to meet them both at the club in one hour, a few drinks there and back here to the apartment for a real session. He would very quickly establish who was in charge this time. The young one, Sharon, first- he liked the way she was quick to cry. Then as her older friend moved to distract him he would sort her out.

Once she had been brought to heel he would get back to the young one. Yes, he thought, tonight would make up in part for what had been a disastrous week.

He had planned to arrive early, having read somewhere that this was what you did on these occasions, to case the joint, whatever that meant, but to his irritation he saw that the older woman was already there and talking to the barman. He walked over and after the briefest of greetings enquired as to where her friend was. 'Not sure she will be able to make it. You caught us on the hop and she had something lined up, but she is very keen to see you again. She said she will try and get over to your place a little later if that is okay? Seems you made quite an impression there,' she lied. His ego kicked in immediately. 'I bet I did,' he laughed. 'And that was nothing compared to the 'impression' I have planned for tonight.' and then in a more conspiratorial tone, 'Did you bring the stuff?' She smiled. Too easy, she thought, a slight nod and he was happy.

Deciding to see just how far she could take this she said 'Of course you know we can't let you have this one for free don't you? We girls have got to live after all. We will need to have something up front, at least to cover the, eh.... well you know.' 'How much?' he growled, the mood quickly changing. 'I think a grand would just about cover it.' 'A thousand bucks,' he scoffed. 'Well, the stuff is top quality as you ordered so if you cover that we can discuss the rest in the morning.' she said. He pulled out his wallet and handed over ten of the green one hundred dollar bills. As he did this she could not help but notice that what remained in there was considerably more.

If this goes to plan, she thought, it could be my lucky night and no need to share this one, for as soon as she had left Meldrum she had called her younger partner and told her it was off. No witnesses and now no split either; she was almost looking forward to this.

Her supplier, Lee Chin, had assured her the stuff was top quality of course. Even better than usual; he had told her. She knew she was lucky to have direct access to the Chinaman, the result of a long relationship between the two. Lee liked sex with western women and she was more than happy to oblige, for not only did he pay her well but it gave her access to a regular and prime quality supply quite literally from the top. She was under no illusions that if she had to go through the normal process the stuff she received would have already been cut. That Vietnamese bastard Tran Van Sah, Lee's second in command, would have seen to that.

They had a couple of drinks and she realised he was getting impatient. 'Come on, let's go. I don't want your mate to turn up at my place and find we are not there.' Not much chance of that she laughed to herself, at the same time picking up her wrap and sliding out of the booth. The barman watched her follow him to the door. Raising a conspiratorial eyebrow as she caught the glance, she just winked at him, holding a finger to her lips. He nodded; he had not seen her tonight if anybody asked.

The cab stopped at Bartlett's luxurious harbourside apartment building and they made their way across the empty lobby to the rank of elevators on the rear wall of the entrance hall. She had purposely placed herself to the right of him so the security guard could not see her clearly from his desk over in the left- hand corner of the entrance hall. Leaving might be a little trickier but she had a little plan for that. The security man's polite greeting and curious glance was met with the usual surly instruction to get on with his job and mind his own bloody business.

The man watched as the elevator doors slid shut. 'Arsehole,' he said to himself. Another hooker just like the other night, hope his one has the biggest dose of pox possible, which would serve him right. Trouble is these rich sods never got a dose; their girls were far too expensive for that, unlike me, he thought. Returning to the sports page of the Daily Mirror he absent mindedly put another penicillin capsule in his mouth. One week to go and with luck he would be able to piss without the pain.

As Bartlett closed the door she moved into the large lounge area. She was drawn compulsively to the balcony, the view must come close to one of the most sought after in the world. Her brief moment was soon destroyed though. 'Okay I didn't bring you up here to gawp out of the fucking window. Get the gear off. I want it now!' With that he quickly stripped and moved towards her. She realised that she was going to have to endure this once more though she did make one attempt to avoid the inevitable. 'Don't you want to take a line first, boost the performance you know?' 'No, later.' With that he began to pull at her clothes. She moved back quickly. 'All right, I'll do it,' she said and undressed quickly. He pulled open the door to the balcony and pushed her out. For a moment she panicked, God he's going to throw me over, but then he turned her round at the rail, roughly kicking her legs apart. 'You want to look at the view? Well, there you are. I have other things on my mind.'

When he had finished he walked back into the room. 'Some fucking view that eh?' he laughed at his pathetic little joke. 'Now let's get a drink and then we can really get started.' He glanced at his watch, frowning. 'Doesn't look as though your mate is coming, means you'll have to work harder for your money, right?' She grimaced.

While he busied himself at the bar she opened her purse and removed the two sachets, one pink one blue. Moving to the large glass table in the corner of the room she opened the blue packet and gently tapped the white powder out onto the top. Expertly cutting and re-cutting the small pile she used the credit card to form it into the required line. 'Straw?' she asked, 'Or are we going to slum it with a one hundred dollar bill?' Laughing, he pulled a straw from a jar and brought it over. 'That's yours,' she said, 'I'll just get mine.' She walked slowly back to the bag for the pink packet. She wanted to avoid taking it if possible. Best to keep her wits about her and while hers was already cut she knew that there would still be an effect. She relaxed as she heard him sniffing the white powder; no need to bother now, just get him onto the bed.

Turning round and walking slowly back to him she put her arms around his neck. 'You know, I think I'll wait, you're always so good after a hit and I want to be able to enjoy it. Come to bed.' He laughed, pulling her after him into the room, the effects of the drug already evident.

God that is good stuff, he thought, I haven't felt like this for years. Almost throwing her onto the bed he forced himself into her, encouraged by just the right amount of moaning from the girl.

Soon he was sweating like a pig from the exertion and his vision was getting blurred. The shortness of breath was starting to slow him down. What the hell, he thought, it was to be expected, twice in ten minutes; well it stood to reason he was going to be a bit winded. The tightness in his chest was something else though; it had started as a feeling of restriction but was now a small but definite pain that was growing inexorably. It spread across his chest up to his left shoulder and into the arm. At the same time he began to feel cold even though the sweating was worse now. Somewhere in his head a voice said, 'How come you are sweating like a pig and cold at the same time?' He noticed his erection failing, but ego made him keep going until finally the pain in his chest was too much and he rolled off the woman gasping, realising at last that this was serious.

The cocaine had been the purest and uncut; she had been surprised at the time it had taken, thinking at first that she might have got the packets the wrong way round, but now she rolled off the bed and stood looking at him in the advance stages of a massive cardiac infarct. He tried to speak, calling for a doctor, and she smiled. 'Only doctor you are going to see is the pathologist that guts you, you bastard.' The eyes reacted, an expression of utter hate there - he had heard her.

The blood stream was now awash with high grade Colombian cocaine and the heart, overloaded and failing fast, started to fibrillate, erratic spasms adding to the already rapidly falling blood pressure. The lips, now covered with spittle, were turning blue; the ears followed and soon the rest of the sweating naked lump that was Neil Bartlett resembled little more than a twitching mass of wet grey-blue flesh. The pupils now fully dilated by the effect of the drug ensured that he could barely see.

She stood there watching, saying no more, but surprisingly turned on by the act of watching a person she had come to loathe slowly die. It took half an hour before she was sure he had gone. She did not want to get too close to him until she was sure he was dead. Cocaine made them very strong she knew. Eventually moving to a position behind the head, she pushed it sideways, then placing her fingers on his neck she felt for a pulse --- nothing.

Still naked she went to her purse and removed a pair of surgical gloves and proceeded to systematically search the place. Only cash was of any use of course. The wallet was the first place to look but by the time she had finished there she was close to ten thousand dollars richer. Not a bad night's work she thought. She went around with a damp cloth she had found in the kitchen and wiped down everything she thought she had touched even the rail on the balcony that she had held on to while he had taken her from behind. Remembering to replace her credit card in her purse she stood looking at her handy work. She was not so naive as to think that a good forensic team would not find some evidence of her being here if they had a mind to. What she wanted was a quick and easy explanation of the death without the more investigative procedures of a murder case. She could easily explain the odd print from the last visit and she had the other girl, Sharon, as evidence of that.

She stood in the middle of the lounge, slowly turning around checking everything. Then moving into the bedroom she did the same thing again, pausing to stare at the cooling body. It had changed. The sweat that had reflected the light and made it look like a piece of fish on a slab had dried now, leaving the cooling mass of flesh dull in the glare of the recessed lighting. The forensic evidence of the sex concerned her but there was not much she could do about that. She had already decided not to shower, and returning to the lounge she carefully dressed making sure that there was nothing that could be used to link her with this place on this night.

Now standing by the main door there was one thing more to do. Lifting the hand piece of the internal phone she called down to the security guard, naming herself as a Mrs Pullman, a woman who, from a quick run through the internet, she knew lived in an apartment two floors below Bartlett's. The security guard answered and she spoke to him with just the right amount of alarm in her voice, saying that she thought somebody was trying to get into her apartment. Initially sceptical she had raised the tone enough to get him to agree to come up and investigate. That done, she quickly opened the door and made her way to the elevator stack and waited, removing the surgical gloves as she did so.

She watched as one of the lifts started to move and then she quickly pressed the down call button. Almost immediately the doors opened as another one arrived and she stepped in. Arriving on the ground floor she walked slowly towards the main door. No one called and chancing a glance at the desk she smiled, it had worked, it was unmanned.

Leaving the building she walked a block before hailing a cab and once settled she made the call. 'Done,' was all she said.

Meldrum replaced the handset, a thin smile on his lips now; I wonder how long it will take for the body to be found. No matter, he had already drafted a eulogy for the inevitable press conference. He would see to it that Neil Bartlett was better liked dead than alive. Not that that was going to be too difficult, he thought.

Sydney New South Wales state police HQ

The Police Commissioner sat chewing on the end of his very expensive pen. The file open in front of him concerned the recent death of one Neil Bartlett, the late CEO of Trans Pacific Airlines, apparently dead from a massive drug overdose, although the forensic people had yet to confirm that.

It was early days but indications were that he had not been alone and that his companion was an unknown female. Predictably the street had gone very quiet and so far all their enquiries had been met with blank stares.

Normally he would not have bothered himself with this. After all the death of one more of these high-profile hopheads was no real loss. This time it might be a bit different though. Subject to the pathology people confirming it, the drug used appeared to be cocaine of the highest quality. Something not seen on the street before if the traces found on a glass table top in the man's apartment were anything to go by. The drug squad people reckoned they may have the beginnings of a new problem.

However his attention had been bought to the case initially, not by this, but by the television news last night in which there was a segment showing that guy Meldrum delivering a eulogy: what a great loss Bartlett's recent departure was; along with a heap of other meaningless platitudes. He had to admit it all sounded very sincere, which only went to show what an accomplished actor this Meldrum character was because his early enquiry with the department whose responsibility it was to keep an eye on big business in the State had unearthed the fact that Meldrum had only recently all but cut Bartlett's corporate balls off. As a result, it was reasonable to assume that there was no love lost between them.

There was little doubt in his mind, therefore, that while Meldrum may appear to regret the loss, Bartlett's departure was something that was going to make his life a lot easier. Especially as subsequent enquiries by his people had come up with the suggestion that Bartlett might have been trying to stage some sort of comeback. It did not take any great piece of police work to come to the conclusion that a combination of drugs death and motive justified a closer look.

He knew full well that most of the drug flow into the city was controlled by the Chinese and in particular one who was a born and bred local, Lee Chin.

Of course, knowing and doing anything about it that would stick were two different things. Especially with a government that cared more about 'protecting' ethnic minorities' sensibilities, than actually recognising that they had their bad apples too, and in this case a very bad apple. If this was the start of yet another major flow, maybe, with a new Premier, he might get them to see that something had to be done.

London

Frobisher and the German had one more meeting at which the required supplies were handed over. The German had spent the last two days watching the target and planning his move. He looked briefly into the small case that contained his requirements... It would do. Tonight he would deal with the car and tomorrow he would finish it and get out.

Having worked on the target vehicle last night, he now stood in the street on the route he knew it would take that morning. There had been one little glitch the night before when it appeared the target had other plans but eventually things had settled down and now it was just a case of waiting. The requirement for collateral damage had been satisfied by his choice of location. A couple of blocks away and on the known route was an entrance to the London Underground and, adjacent to it, a busy bus stop. He had positioned himself so that he was looking down the street in that direction he glanced at his watch, anytime now, yes, here it comes. The car, a late model Audi A6, slowed as it approached the lights at the junction and then on the green it accelerated past him. He waited, finger caressing the button until the car reached the station then applying the briefest pressure. The flash came first, right under the driver's seat; it enveloped the vehicle as it was lifted into the air, then the fuel tank exploded and the flame spread, enveloping the people waiting at the bus stop. The car had been moving quite fast and the forward momentum took it across the pavement into the mouth of the subway station, where the second charge exploded. He watched fascinated. Well, Frobisher had said he wanted collateral damage. Looking at his work he thought there would be plenty of that. No longer interested, he turned and walked away. Not much point in trying for a train or bus now he realised, see if I can get a cab a couple of blocks away later. He sped up, glancing over his shoulder as the first of the police cars screeched to a halt and the occupants began erecting the inevitable cordon of yellow tape.

There was just one more little thing to do. A short walk brought him to the block. Access was easy and he was soon inside the apartment. Quickly locating the safe he had it open in seconds. So much easier with the combination, he smiled. The file was right on top; a quick look through it for confirmation. He was careful not to disturb anything else. There must be no evidence that it had ever even existed.

He got out the way he had come in and soon picked up a cab, using the journey to look through the file. The contents were enough to make him realise they had only just been in time, assuming it was the only copy.

Within an hour he was in Terminal Two at London Heathrow. He had used three cabs to get to the Gloucester Road underground station and once there he had changed in the toilets on the station, using clothing he had left there the day before.

He had got round the fact that the IRA had effectively closed off all the left- luggage lockers on the underground years ago by handing the bag in as lost property the day before, knowing they would keep it for a week. He had ensured that there was enough distinctive stuff inside that would enable him to provide a positive ID when he came to retrieve it.

Now, as he waited for them to call the Swissair flight he started to relax. He had called Frobisher, just the usual one word report. The relief had been very evident in the man's voice. Now all that remained was to ditch the phone and retire for a while. He would do nothing for six months he had decided.

★ ★ ★

The camera slowly scanning the crowd from behind the recessed ceiling passed and then, as it sensed a match, stopped and returned to the seated figure. The discreet warning light flashed. The operator had been idly looking at an attractive female who seemed to be having difficulty convincing an incredibly ugly and very fat woman at the check in desk that her bag was not overweight. Stupid cow, he thought as he slid the seat down to the screen with the light over it, she should have picked a bloke. Tits like that she would have got on for sure. Now, what's this all about?

He looked at the man on the screen. Nothing out of the ordinary that he could see. Looking down he tapped a couple of keys bringing up the images that the computer had matched, or at least as he well knew, 'thought' it had matched because while it did occasionally strike gold, it also had the annoying habit of seeing things that were quite clearly not the same, as a match. Still, it was getting better and as the database built up they said it would eventually be the most valuable tool they had in the never-ending war against terrorism.

However, looking at the three pictures he figured it was having another off day because, while there was a resemblance, it was pushing things to say more than that. No matter, he would log it, file the report and that would be that he reckoned. He hard-copied the four images, the first from three months before, a rather effeminate looking individual, next a businessman in suit and tie, then a rather ancient and tatty looking hippie type and finally this one who was so bland as to be almost completely invisible but was clearly a middle-aged tourist.

He watched as the man, responding to an unheard flight announcement, stood and walked to the boarding gates. Morbid interest made him flick the camera into manual to see which flight 'Mister Lucky,' as he called him, was going to take: Swissair, to Geneva. Okay, he would put it in the report. At least it would show he had been thorough. The fact that Geneva was an unlikely tourist destination for a character dressed like this did not strike him as odd until much later.

★ ★ ★

The news of the explosion had reached the desk of Simon Quartermaine at Special Branch within minutes and the Terrorist Response Team was on its way soon after. He knew the problem would be not lack of evidence but destroyed evidence. With the best will in the world the emergency services had to think of the living casualties first and early reports were that there were quite a few of those. Avoiding the temptation to go himself, he sat with increasing frustration as the news slowly trickled in. The first indicators were confusing; the media was already in the usual terrorist feeding frenzy, but there were a couple of things that made this a bit odd. Not least of these was that this particular area had a relatively large community of Muslims, and to make matters worse there were quite a few Irish as well. The next theory, of a suicide bomber who got it wrong, went out of the window when the trigger device was found. It was a radio trigger, indicating that a remote operator was involved. It should have been consumed in the explosion. That had clearly been the intention, but as luck would have it this little piece of evidence had been blown clear. The other important piece of information yet to be established was the identity of the victim or victims. It was not even clear yet as to how many people were in the car that had apparently been the source of the initial explosion.

He was still at his desk some hours later, trying to concentrate on some unrelated problem, when his secretary came in. He did not look up at first. Only when she had not spoken did he raise his head in mild irritation, immediately squashed when he saw the tears flowing down her cheeks. 'Christ, what is it Angela?' He quickly left his seat and was around the desk in a second, arms around her. 'Come on, love, what is it?' he repeated. 'They have identified one of the people in the car, sir.' He stepped back still holding her shoulders, an increasing sense of foreboding. 'Who?' 'It's your friend Pat Carrington from MI6 sir.' 'What? It can't be. Who the hell even knows him well enough to do that? Bloody hell, he is not even front line. Internal Security is his bag and they are not going to blow up their own are they--?' He stopped. 'I need confirmation on this straight away Angela. Sorry love but you are going to have to save the tears for later. Pat would expect that, if it is him, okay?' She sniffed and pulling a handkerchief from her sleeve she wiped her eyes. 'If you say so sir,' she managed. Just before she reached the door, he remembered. 'Angela, was there anybody else in the car?' She turned back, eyes filling again. 'They think there was a woman in there as well sir.' 'Oh Christ,' he said. Probably the new girlfriend, and then he remembered what else he had heard, who she worked for, and he went cold.

The papers were screaming for blood although they had no idea whose blood. It didn't seem to matter; everybody was getting the blame for it. As one cynic was heard to say, even the 'Salvation' Army was suspect. The politicians, useless as usual, were all wringing hands and muttering the usual ridiculous clichés, 'Britain will not bow to terrorism', 'We must pull together', 'not rest until the murderers are found', all of which amounted to the fact that they had not got a clue. The real problem was--- nor had anybody else.

It was a few days before the first cracks started to appear by which time it had been confirmed that the victims in the car were a Pat Carrington, a mid-level civil servant at MI6, and the female secretary of another mid-level civil servant as yet unnamed. Almost immediately the tabloids were trying to read a sex triangle into this, but the story was still-born when they found that the woman had worked for that dangerous bastard Sir Gerald Frobisher. The idea that Frobisher would ever have any interest in anybody but himself was ridiculous and the story line was quickly dropped. Any cub reporter trying to pursue it was quickly warned off, usually by an editor who had been unfortunate enough to have had personal dealings with Frobisher.

It was the forensic team who were making most progress, particularly with the remains of the trigger. It was a reasonably easy thing to get hold of but specific enough be found in only a few outlets specialising in military and security equipment. In London that meant the few streets radiating to the south from Grosvenor Square. It was here that the outlets specialising in what was rather unusual equipment, had their public faces. Naturally most of them were well known to the intelligence community and the police; they only stayed in business by co-operating with the authorities.

Quartermaine had sent the hardest men he had, to do the questioning. These were the men who lived on the street, usually long overdue for a promotion, which, even if it had been offered, was inevitably refused. They also knew that Carrington had been one of their boss's closest friends; that made him almost family. The answers would be quick, as it turned out very quick, but not much use. The device had been bought from a small place in an alley off South Audley Street. The proprietor, ex army, was only too willing to assist and mildly offended that he should even be suspected of involvement. As he pointed out the item was deemed obsolete and its primary use now was as a replacement for garage door remote controls that had been lost. It no longer had any direct military significance.

Things started to come off the rails when they enquired about the identity of the purchaser. The owner had been off that day and the girl who was on had just gone on holiday to Spain, he was not sure where. She would be back in two weeks. He was very sorry.

Stalled there for the moment, they started on the actual explosive. It was military-grade Semtex, which meant an illegal source or stealing from a legal one. The investigation continued.......

Quartermaine sat at his desk deep in thought, trying desperately to remember exactly what Pat Carrington had said on the telephone at the end of last week and cursing himself for not insisting on an earlier meeting. He realised that Carrington had been worried by something and, given the man's job, the chances were that it was an internal matter.

He was just about to call and arrange a meeting with whoever was doing poor old Pat's job at the moment when his secretary beeped him on the intercom. 'Sir, I have Head of Security from Heathrow here. He would like a word.' Quartermaine frowned; what else could go wrong? 'Okay send him in.' As the door opened he got up from behind the desk and met Harry Carpenter,

Heathrow Head of Security, as he walked in. 'Morning Harry what can I do for you?' 'More what I can do for you really, Simon. Like you to have a look at another set of pictures to go with those we sent you recently and the ones from the CCTV at Hampstead, Okay on the desk?' Quartermaine nodded and the other man spread a group of pictures. 'Now, if you compare these to the others you have I think, like me, you will see an uncanny likeness in the four men. So much so that it is my, and the computers opinion, that they are the same man. If that is the case the next question is why is he taking so much trouble to appear as four different people entering and leaving the UK? Now we have done what we can to tie the face up with a name and, as you would expect, they are all different, as are the passports. Those, incidentally, are all genuine, an interesting fact in itself. However, the really interesting thing is what happens when you compare the days each of these pics was taken to the list of events that we have had in town of late. On at least two occasions, this chap, assuming it is the same man, has either entered or left just before and just after the event. Here I am referring to the creepy lawyer bloke getting it in the Hampstead 'john', which ties in with the CCTV film from the tube there and the Heathrow ones later that night, and then these,' he gestured at the desk, 'Which were taken three days before and then late evening of the day poor old Pat got it.'

Quartermaine pressed the intercom button. 'Angela, bring in that file of photographs we have from Heathrow and the CCTV cameras at Hampstead will you?' He looked at Carpenter 'If you are right Harry you may well have given us the first decent lead in this business.' 'There is a bit more actually Simon,' he continued. 'We then went on to try and match flight numbers and destinations. We got two reasonable guesses and a certainty on the last one.' He paused, smiling, and Quartermaine impatient said 'Christ, you look like the cat with the bloody mouse. What is it?' 'Well all three went to Geneva. Here are the flight numbers and I have taken the liberty of checking with the Swiss and can tell you that our man definitely left the terminal there on the last one. They have him recorded through passport control. Of course it does not mean that he did not re-book to somewhere else, as someone else, but they have done a search and it does not appear so.'

Quartermaine leaned back in his chair expelling the air from his lungs.

'I think I will run all this past Interpol and the US Feds, see if this guy stirs up any matches on their databases. I gather your thinking is that every time he appears here something nasty happens, is that it?' The security man nodded. 'Certainly seems so. While you are at it you could ask the FBI to cross check for any, how shall I put it, 'similar events' that tie in with an appearance of someone resembling this bloke in their back yard.' 'Good idea, Harry, maybe you should think about a change of job, we could use you here you know.' 'No thanks Simon I have quite enough on my plate out there thanks, but I would like to know how it turns out.' He got up to leave and Quartermaine walked him to the door. 'Thanks Harry, we owe you one.' They shook hands and as the door closed Quartermaine walked slowly back to his desk deep in thought.

MI6

A few days later Frobisher sat at his desk, at last he felt he could relax a little. He had managed to get into Carrington's office as soon as the murder had been announced and, given his position, his requirement to access the safe had been complied with without question. Searching quickly through it all had revealed nothing. He was relieved; the copy found at the man's home was the only one.

From the one word telephone call, he now had the name of the interfering sergeant at the Special Branch and he would watch to see if any connections were made that required further action. The German would not like it he knew, but it would be in both their interests to close off this one loose end if it was required.

He also moved quickly to use his influence with Sir Robert Fraser, head of MI6, on the question of selecting Carrington's replacement. After some discussion and his personal recommendation a certain Victoria Manning was chosen. Frobisher had selected her because she was a relative newcomer and as such would be underexposed to the internal intrigue. Soon after her appointment he had called her to his office to offer his support and advice, at the same time implying, in as subtle a way as he could manage, that it would be in her interest to keep him informed and onside.

Nothing too threatening of course but as she left the office he believed he had established their relative positions in the system. She was going to be far more easily controlled than Carrington had ever been. He even felt confident enough of this to raise the subject of the

Special Branch enquiry, suggesting that advice on any further activity in this area should be referred to him.

As she closed the door of the outer office Manning's brow was creased in thought. She was a damn sight smarter than that patronising bastard Frobisher realised and was under no illusions as to what had just taken place. Unfortunately, for Frobisher at least, she had already picked up on the 'office rumour mill' and men like Frobisher and their mutual boss, Fraser, got no good reports from anywhere.

In fact, as soon as she had been summoned she had pulled Frobisher's personal file, something her new position made easy. Before she even went to his office she thought she knew just about everything there was to know about one Gerald Frobisher.

Predictably he had made great store of the fact that she had got the job as a result of his personal recommendation with Fraser, but she was under no illusions as to why. They all knew Fraser was under pressure to increase the number of women in the upper echelons and it was now clear why Frobisher had pushed for her.

She also very quickly realised that Internal Security was the ultimate poison chalice. Even if something unsavoury was discovered, the blame for not discovering it sooner would invariably be laid at the door of the department. Along with her head if they had anything to do with it, she smiled thinly. However she was also well aware that this could be her one real chance on the ladder and she was quietly determined to make this work. Returning to her office, Frobisher's file was still on her desk and she picked it up again idly looking through it when her secretary buzzed her. 'Call for you from

Special Branch Miss Manning, a Chief Superintendent Simon Quartermaine,' the girl said.

Special Branch

Quartermaine had been looking through the file on the CCTV and Heathrow security cameras when his phone rang. The call, from a detective sergeant, was followed by an order to get over here fast. He began his report as soon as he was seated opposite his boss.

'Well it's like this sir,' the Special Branch sergeant began, 'I have a mate at the yard and I was over there a while back just for a chat really. Anyway, he was trolling through a list of telephone numbers that had something to do with that Smith business. You remember that creep that got off from a cast iron case a while back?' Quartermaine nodded, 'Yes, so what?' 'Well, he was a bit puzzled by a couple of the numbers on the list of calls made and received by Smith' slimy mates while he was on remand. These two didn't follow the usual pattern. I looked at them and I thought they seemed familiar so I made a note and checked. I was surprised to find they were a couple of mobiles used at MI6 sir. As you know, they have identifiable sequences. Of course, he didn't know that, hence the confusion. Anyway, and this is really why I came to see you sir, I rang Pat Carrington, incidentally we were at school together. Anyway, I asked him if he knew what it was all about. He said he would look into it for me but he never had a chance to get back. Sorry, it's not much I know sir but Pat sort of looked after me at school, he was a couple of classes ahead, and well, I liked the guy. Probably nothing more than a coincidence but I thought you should know,' he finished lamely. Quartermaine looked at the man with unseeing eyes. Eventually snapping out of it he refocused on the young sergeant. 'And have you told anyone else about this?' The man said nothing, just moving his head. 'Good, well don't, and just watch out for yourself until this is sorted out okay? And sergeant, thank you, it might not seem much but at least it gives us a direction to look in.' He got up and opened the door for him.

Alone, he returned to his desk, deep in thought.

★ ★ ★

A week later the sergeant found himself on an Inspector's Course at the academy, with a fast-tracked posting to Scotland Yard when he was qualified. He did not complain.

Quartermaine spent the next few hours probing around trying to find just who might have had access to the handsets in question. His new contact in MI6 was a Victoria Manning. Recently moved to cover the internal security desk she had been reluctant to talk at first, the old suspicions surfacing, and it was only after he had explained the ramifications of these phones, adding the unfolding data on the mysterious, apparent Swiss, that he started to get somewhere with her.

Eventually the department that had used the units would be identified of course, but even then it could have been one of dozens of people. Right now it seemed poor old Pat had not even had time to run a file on this. Unusual, but Quartermaine put it down to the lack of any real evidence. No doubt he had intended to start one that very week but never got the chance, more's the pity, because it left them almost completely blind.

The one positive thing to come out of the day was that this Manning woman seemed to be on the ball and uncontaminated by the corrosive inter-departmental rivalry that made these investigations so bloody difficult. He made a note to set up a meeting with her on neutral ground as soon as possible.

Chapter Twelve

OP 3

Colonel Raff replaced the handset and looked up at his old friend. 'Chuck Anderson has set it all up; we are using the South Africans this time. I had thought he might opt for an American but having seen the proposed 'venue' he reckons it is a two man job and Jan and Pieter are due in next week from Jo'burg. In the meantime Martin O'Grady has got himself a temp job in the place. Seems the landlord is very much in Smith's shadow but our mad Irishman has managed to get in without arousing any suspicion. He reckons if we had used a local the man would have smelled a rat, as it is he thinks our Martin is just one of the usual 'Paddies' who float around the place looking for work.

He has already confirmed that they have a regular gathering on Thursday nights. Apparently his cronies turn up first, about four of them seems the norm, then Smith and a couple of his heavies join them later. He reckons the early one's case the place to make sure there is no potential threat and then they make a call and the rest turn up. He also said that it is a good job it's not winter because it is very much a local and the trade is known to these people for the most part. The only passing business they get is the odd tourist. I guess the word is out on who drinks there. He said that in winter our two boys would stick out like sore thumbs but that it should be okay now as there are usually a few foreigners around at this time of year.

The 747 had flown direct from Johannesburg. It was a good ten hour flog and the two men were tired. It had been night most of the way and Jan turned to his F\O just before the business of the arrival began. 'You know Pieter I reckon this game is not for the birds like they usually say, it's for bloody bats man, that's what we are. As soon as the sun comes up we should be hanging upside down in some bloody closet somewhere, in the dark.' Pieter smiled, 'Too right, still I'll settle for a bed today. Tonight's the job eh then we are out of here tomorrow, is that how it is?' 'Yep, subject to an okay from the Colonel and the necessary hardware. This Smith bloke is long overdue for disposal.'

The big airplane began its decent on instructions from the London sector controller who was based nowhere near the capital. In fact all operations in the London area were now controlled from a little place called Swanwick on the south coast.

The clearance was the usual, 'Biggin 3Alpha via Tiger for 27 Left'. This was just about as direct as you could expect at this time of the morning and as there did not appear to be too much congestion ahead they were optimistic that it would all be over in twenty minutes or so.

Tired as they were Jan had opted for an automatic landing. They were required to keep themselves current with the procedures and the last thing they wanted was to be caught out in a situation that required a very low-visibility approach when their own recency had run out. Added to which, it was never a bad idea to let the machine do the work when you were stuffed.

The flight management computers were already programmed and all that was required of them was to run the series of checklists and to monitor the aircraft as it followed the required path. Soon they were established on the instrument landing system for 27 Left, capture of the beams was automatic and then, as the speed was reduced, the flaps were extended further and the landing gear lowered. Now back to 170 knots, Jan called for the final stage of flap and the last checklist before touchdown. Flare, touchdown, wheel brakes and runway tracking were all automatic and as the aircraft settled on the runway all Jan had to do was pull in the reverse thrust to assist in slowing it down.

Heathrow tower told them to call ground on 112.9 and Pieter dialled in the new frequency, flicked the selector over and called, telling the new controller they were allocated gate Kilo 17 in the Terminal Three complex.

Within 30 minutes they were clear of the dedicated crew customs and on the road to the city and a well earned rest, although the two pilots had a call to wait for before they could finally get their heads down.

They were sitting in Jan's room drinking a beer when the call came in. A meeting was arranged for 1800 that night, where the things required for the evening's job would be handed over, that done, Pieter went back to his room and they both slept through the day.

By 1800 hours they were back in Jan's room and Martin O'Grady had arrived and handed over the package. As Pieter opened it, Jan had a large scale map of the south bank area open on the bed. The pub had been marked with highlighter. As soon as the job was done they were to exit by the front entrance where a nondescript black cab would be waiting. From the target arriving to them leaving was reckoned to be fifteen minutes max.

The co-pilot pulled the two weapons provided from the box. They were identical Mark 23 Heckler and Koch .45 caliber automatics, with twelve- round magazines and silencers. This was a gun originally ordered by the special forces of the US army, and how and where these two had come from was to remain a mystery. One thing was clear, the Colonels were well connected. There was no doubt that if you got hit with a bullet fired by this thing, the chances are you would not survive. Even though the silencer bought the muzzle velocity down the .45 calibre bullet ensured considerable and almost certainly fatal damage. Two chamois leather shoulder holsters were also provided.

The two men spent half an hour checking the weapons, unloading and loading the magazines and ensuring the actions were free. That done they both screwed on the silencers and slipped the harness of the shoulder holsters on, practicing for ease of extraction. Although both were more than familiar with concealed small arms, you could never check too much. Satisfied, they slipped into the casual jackets of tourists, left the room and, exiting through the main lobby, walked the short distance to the subway.

The pub, located in the shadow of Tower Bridge on the south bank, was awkward to get to but they were in no hurry, they had to give O'Grady time to get there and start his shift first. The nearest tube station was at

London Bridge, so the two men got off there and returned to the surface. Turning east along Tooley Road they passed the great edifice of Tower Bridge and then turned north, back towards the river. From there it was just a few minutes, along the strangely named Shad Thames, to the 'Flying Dutchman'. They recognised it, of course, already aware from the detailed briefing of the layout inside and out. It was a matter of a few minutes before they were sitting at the bar with an ice cold lager each. Both noted that the first four of Smith's men were already there.

These four men had watched as the South Africans sat down. Apparently engaged in idle chat with each other, both were adapting their easily recognisable accent. To the casual observer, while they were obviously foreign, they could have been anything from American, Aussie or Kiwi. Of one thing all the subsequent witnesses agreed, they were not from around here.

They were about half way through the pint when Smith made his entrance preceded by one minder and followed by the other. All three paused in the doorway. The few other customers' conversations slowly stopped and soon it was only the two men at the bar who were talking quietly; neither looked up. Smith glared at the leader of the four men already there, nodding in the direction of the two foreigners. He shrugged his shoulders and indicated that it was okay.

The landlord hurried over to the three as they sat down, adding his reassurance. 'Just tourists Mr Smith,' he fawned. 'Yanks I think, reckon they're a couple of irons,' he added, using the local slang for homosexuals.

The seven men at the table were soon totally absorbed in conversation and the subdued atmosphere in the pub returned.

Eventually Jan slipped off the bar stool muttering, 'Got to take a leak man.' Heading for the gents toilet which, as he well knew, was behind the table occupied by the seven men, Smith glanced up as he went by but the South African ignored him, whistling quietly to himself as he made his way to the door. 'Reckon we could have a bit of fun here boys. How about you two go in there with that bloke and sort him out then we can give his mate a bit of a going over too? Time we livened this place up a bit.' Two of the men got up and followed Jan into the Gents and as they pushed open the second door he was standing by the hand drier. 'What you doing in this part of the world faggot?' the one in front snarled. As he spoke his mate moved out from behind him. Jan said nothing but slowly pulled the HK from under his arm and fired twice. Just two soft 'phut' sounds and the two men slumped to the floor, each with a bullet in the head. He pressed the small transmitter in his pocket twice and Pieter, at the bar, felt the double vibration against his thigh indicating two down. He then pulled a pair of surgical gloves from his pocket and slipped them on.

Swinging round on his stool he looked towards the table where the five remaining men sat leering at him. Slowly, he eased off the stool and walked towards them. As he reached a point about three metres from the table, the door opened and the five men, expecting their friends, turned to look.

To their surprise it was the other foreigner who stood there. As they were taking this in and the slow realisation that he had a gun in his hand and that it was pointed in their direction, Pieter pulled his own HK from beneath his arm and waited for the heads to turn back.

It was Smith who recovered first, frantically trying to pull a weapon from under his coat. Pieter raised his HK and shot him in the shoulder. Smith cried out with pain, the shoulder was shattered. The others looked on in stunned silence not daring to move. Smith started blubbering. 'Who are you? What do you want? I'll pay you twice what you're on.' Jan, who had by now moved around to confront the terrified criminal, leaned forward and said quietly. 'Paid?----- You piece of shit, we aren't being paid, we're doing this as a service to humanity. You remember those poor bastards you had killed and maimed so you could get off once again? Well, unfortunately for you man, they had powerful friends,' he paused 'Us'---- With that he held the HK to the man's head and pulled the trigger.

Standing back, both men looked coldly at the four remaining thugs. Jan moved his gun side to side, 'Any of you pricks feel lucky?' None of them said anything. All had their hands, very still and in sight, on the table. Pieter slowly moved his free hand to the inside pocket of his jacket and removed the card, dropping it onto the table he and Jan backed slowly to the door. No one moved.

As soon as they left the place all hell broke loose and in the confusion the Irishman picked up the two glasses and put them into the dishwasher and then he to slipped quietly away.

The cab driver, who had been waiting outside, said nothing as he pulled out into the traffic and headed west. The two South Africans removed the magazines from the weapons, ejected the live round from each gun, and replaced them in the magazines. They dropped everything into the sports bag they had found on the floor of the passenger compartment. Each of them pulled off his light jacket and reversed it. The colours were now light blue and yellow. They added a pair of sunglasses and then, new identity complete, they sat back and relaxed. The cab driver took them across the city to Chelsea and dropped them off. His only words, as they got out, were a low 'Well done lads.' With that he drove off, leaving them standing on the pavement outside yet another pub only this time on the north side of the river.

They pushed open the door, got a beer, and walked through to the riverside garden. Jan pulled out his mobile and dialed the number. As the line was opened up he said one word 'Done' and pressed the off key. He turned to Pieter. 'No problems there then man.' 'Nope' Pieter agreed. Within a few minutes they had both relaxed, the events of the early evening apparently forgotten as they were joined by three of the girls from the cabin. The senior of the three looked at the two men. 'What have you two been up to? You look like a couple of old tom cats who found a whole bloody dairy.' Pieter smiled, 'Don't know what you mean,' he laughed, 'We only got here a couple of minutes before you.'

The police had arrived at the Flying Dutchman within five minutes, to be met with pandemonium. The four surviving thugs had hastily disappeared leaving their dead boss and the other two there.

It took the law a long time to get any sense out of the rest of the inhabitants of the place. When they did manage to restore some order, the fact that Smith was known to be the boss of this particular manor's crime fraternity made them highly sceptical of the lurid tales of what were either two Yanks, two Aussies or even two

Kiwis. Clearly the South African accent was not well known in these parts.

It was a detective constable who found the card. Sliding it off the table he looked at it without much interest eventually passing it to his inspector. 'Found this on the table Smith was sitting at Guv; funny looking thing.' He handed it over. The Inspector looked at it, said nothing and passed it on to the sergeant who had the evidence bag. Not that there was much evidence: four cartridge cases that looked like a .45 and a card, were not going to lead them anywhere. Somehow he doubted the forensic people would find anything useful either and frankly he was not bothered. However he knew his super would go ape. Just the mention of the word 'Gun' was enough to make the idiot froth at the mouth. The fact that it had been used to do something the police had been failing to do for years would only irritate him more.

His boss, the inspector knew, was far more likely to react to this type of apparent vigilante behaviour than he was to do anything about what the likes of characters like Smith and his mates got up to. These creeps had been doing just about what they liked for as long as this Superintendent had run the division.

Like so many of the new-age managers, he was terrified by the thought that 'Mister Ordinary' might react at last. The idea that society should eventually actually try and defend itself was something he was prepared to stamp out with considerably more zeal than he ever devoted to putting thugs like Smith and his cronies behind bars. Something to do with the fast track promotion system and the degree in pencil sharpening the man had got from some crummy second rate university. The rest of the division was under no illusions about their Super's priorities. He might have a bit of trouble this time though, the Inspector reflected, because as far as he could see this was a thoroughly professional disposal. With the evidence they had so far, he would be lucky to issue a parking ticket.

Smiling to himself, he reckoned that was actually about the level of his ability anyway. He waved at the rest of them 'Okay, leave one uniform here to wait for SOCO. We might as well push off. As far as I can tell we are looking for a couple of blokes in light-coloured jackets and funny accents, which only describes half of this town, but then I would probably want to shake their hand if I did find them anyway.' He turned and the others followed him out of the building.

Simon Quartermaine got the story on the 6 o'clock news, just a clip about a notorious London gangster being gunned down in broad daylight by two unknown assassins. This was followed with a brief and very sanitized synopsis of Smiths activities by some chinless idiot from the local police giving what he obviously thought was a serious and sincere undertaking that no stone would be left unturned to catch these vicious murderers.

This was followed by the Smith widow, immaculately turned out and covered in nine carat gold trinkets, trying hard to weep while at the same time, appear at her best for the camera. She was ranting, in the irritating local estuarine whine, 'that there was going to be 'Real Bovver' until these blokes was caught.' The reporter returned with the comment that Smith's two sons would also have been here had they been able. Of course he forgot to mention that they were both currently serving sentences for violent crime.

The colonel walked across the room and picked up the telephone. 'Looks as though that went off rather well Peter,' he said. 'Ah, good evening Simon, yes I thought so. Those Yarpy lads are very professional. Should be on their way home soon I think.' 'Yes, I suppose they will.' Quartermaine continued, 'Of course the next phase will be the most interesting. I would think there will be one very worried individual in MI6 when they learn about this, whoever they are. Have to say, I am going to be very interested to see if my suspicions are correct. I have a couple of taps in place although I am not optimistic. This guy has got to be aware that we are looking now; I can't see him making that mistake. I have also got a watch on the airports as I think we can anticipate some activity from our Swiss friend. That is assuming things run to what seems to be the pattern with the man.'

Raff agreed and then went on to suggest a weekend at his country cottage for Quartermaine and Fitzroy-Gibbons. Quartermaine looked at his diary; 'Yes I can make that' he said, 'Look forward to it.'

Frobisher's Apartment

Sir Gerald Frobisher had just sat down with the evening gin and tonic as the six o'clock news began. The initial synopsis mentioned only that a notorious criminal had been the victim of what appeared to be gang warfare in south London. Only when the item appeared again later in the bulletin did it grab his attention.

By the time the segment had finished he was sitting paralysed, looking at the set. His drink was untouched on the table beside him the condensation forming a pool on the surface of its glass top. His mind was in turmoil. He was about to telephone the police for more information, only stopping after he had touched the first two numbers. Just in time he realised that it would seem very odd for the Head of the Russia desk at MI6 to be inquiring about the elimination of some low grade London criminal. Cold already, he suddenly realised what the ramifications of Smiths removal could really be and he shivered.

The news had mentioned that the two suspects were apparently foreign. Something there did not fit with the gang warfare idea that was the current media theory he realised. This, coming right on the back of Smiths abortive trial, and then the elimination of the lawyer that followed, was almost certainly going to get the media all fired up again.

He sat there late into the night, trying to convince himself that he had nothing to worry about. If it weren't for those bloody phones and that Special Branch sergeant, none of this would have happened. There would be no way anybody could have made a connection to him.

At least nobody seemed to be connecting any of this with the removal of Carrington and his secretary yet which was something. Even so, he was left with the feeling that he was losing control. Panic was not too far below the surface. Finally he managed to convince himself that the best course of action would be to do nothing until he had some idea of exactly how much they knew, and he was just about to go to bed when the telephone rang.

He looked at it with distaste. No call this late would be good news he was sure. Eventually he picked it up 'Frobisher.' There was a slight delay and then the familiar voice, 'I take it you have seen the BBC news?' 'Yes?' was all he said. 'Do I conclude that we have still got a problem?' Frobisher hesitated and with more confidence than he felt began, 'Look I don't like the idea of you calling here but since you ask, no. I can see no reason for us to be worried. There is nothing to tie either of us to any of this.' The voice interrupted, 'I am afraid I am not sure I agree with you and if a recent conversation I have had with people from somewhere east of here, is anything to go by I am not alone. I am instructed to tell you that they are considering pulling you out. I will be contacting you again in a few days.'

Before Frobisher could say a thing the connection was broken. He was left looking at the hand piece.

Sydney State Police HQ

There had been some developments in the Bartlett case and the commissioner had now taken a personal interest in it given that a tenuous connection to the Chinaman, Lee, had surfaced through one of the woman thought to have been involved.

On the desk in front of him he had the forensic reports from the flat. The labs had confirmed that the cocaine used had been of the highest quality, in fact more pure than any seen on the street to date. That it had also been uncut had assured that Bartlett was a dead man as soon as he sniffed the stuff.

What was even more interesting was the DNA evidence and the statement from the doorman. It was becoming clear that Bartlett had been a very unpleasant individual who got his sex on the street on a regular basis.

The doorman mentioned the two women he had seen with Bartlett a few days before his death.

It was the forensic team who had got a possible lead as to who the mysterious woman on the night of the overdose might be. The doorman was forced to admit that on this occasion he had not seen who she was and he went on to tell them of the abortive call from another tenant. Forensics, having found evidence of the two in the apartment, added that there had been a rather amateurish attempt to destroy prints at some time after that. They had got enough to confirm that Bartlett had entertained at least two women quite recently.

What did get them excited was when they ran the DNA profiles of the hair and skin debris found there against that found on Bartlett's body. To their surprise they got a match with one of the women. As it was reckoned that the man would have had a number of showers between the two events it seemed highly probable that at least one of the women had also been there on the night of his death.

From the description that the doorman gave of the two women he had seen, the vice boys already reckoned they had a pretty fair idea of who they were. It was here that the connection with Lee Chin was first made, because one of them was known to be close to the Chinese.

It did not take a genius to work through the connections. The head of vice was already betting that the DNA found on Bartlett's body would match the older of the two suspects. Of course they had to find her first but it was just a question of time. The word was out and he did not think it would be long.

Sydney Neutral Bay

Shaun's apartment looked out over the harbour and in the evening the three of them usually settled down there and had a few beers together. Jim and the Digger lived within walking distance but neither had the view so this was usually the chosen venue.

They were going over the changes that had occurred since Reg Bartlett's son had died. They agreed that he was no loss but they were glad that their old friend had not lived to see the mess the boy had made of everything. The conversation then moved a little closer to home. Mainwaring, the Chief Pilot had eventually got back to them with an offer and they were surprised that it was actually better than they had expected.

They had all decided to make the transfer and the freight operation was very quickly in action. In fact they had returned that very morning from the new route to Vancouver via Honolulu.

Of course they still had reservations, but at the moment this new bloke, Meldrum, seemed to have injected a bit of life into the company. If it hadn't been for the fact that Mainwaring and people like him were being slipped into the top end of management they agreed they might have actually believed things had changed for the better. As it was, they were still unsure and it was very early days yet.

The call from London had been anticipated, their decision had been reached and when Colonel Raff asked they agreed to join the team. The only concern they had was that if they felt uncomfortable with the proposed case they could refuse. Raff reassured them that there was never any pressure. However he did point out that an operation, once presented to a team, had never been refused. 'The people we remove are always the real scum after all,' he said, 'Once you have seen some of the files you will wonder why it took us so long. Oh! Just for the record, Mr Smith is no longer with us you will be pleased to hear. According to our wonderful media, current thinking is he may have had a falling out with some foreign associates--- no loss,' he chuckled. 'As a matter of fact, when will you be in town again? I may have something that will be of interest to you, can't discuss it here of course.' He paused, Shaun called out to Jim to check the roster and there was a planned London trip in three weeks for him. He told Raff and asked if he wanted them all there. 'Well it would be useful if you could all manage to get here at the same time; save going over it all again. Is that a problem?' 'No, I think we can jig things around a bit. This new freight operation is still in its early stages and the roster people are pretty flexible. We will let you know exact dates as soon as we can, okay.'

The Colonel agreed and went on, 'Been watching the Trans Pac situation of late. That Bartlett business has attracted some attention here, well at least the drug connection part has. It seems pretty clear that your man Meldrum was the big winner in all this, would I be right?' 'Yes, not much doubt about that,' Shaun agreed. 'In fact, seeing as how he has only been in the saddle for a few weeks he has made quite a few changes. The general opinion is that they are for the better. This freight business, for example, has really taken off. Our problem is we have seen this sort of thing before and it is early days yet. One of our main worries is that he seems to be filling the top end with some of the 'dickheads' we know from old and, until things have settled, the boys and I are reserving our judgment.' A few final pleasantries were passed and the connection broken.

Sydney Sussex Street Chinatown

Mary Sinclair was worried. No, more than that, she realised, she was scared stiff. As she sat in the outer office waiting, she had gnawed through both sets of finger nails.

How the hell had they got on to her so quickly, she had been so careful. Of course, the word was that the cops only wanted to question her and her young mate over the first night. But there was something going on, she sensed it. The papers had made a lot of the cocaine business and it was that, and the fact that she needed help to disappear, that had bought her to Lee's office. She had been summoned, and that was what was really worrying her. If that had not been enough, just after she arrived, Tran Van Sah, Lee's Vietnamese deputy, had walked through into the office. He had looked at her with completely dead eyes as he passed, saying nothing.

They called her in eventually and as she sat in the chair opposite Lee she noticed the desk was covered with the newspapers from the previous day. The headlines screamed at her, each one with an opinion on the source and quality of the drug that had caused the death of one of the country's most high profile businessmen. Some had even made the tenuous connection to Chinatown, although none were confident enough to mention names.

Lee Chin said nothing, just stared. Finally gesturing to the pile in front of her, 'What have you got to say then Mary?' Close to tears and visibly trembling she blurted out the story and when she had finished she lowered her head and wept. Eventually, regaining a little of her composure, she looked up. 'I need to get away. Can you help me? It will all die down in a month or two. Please, you owe me that.' 'Mary, I do not owe you anything you have involved me and my business in your messy little game with this Meldrum person. You will notice he is not even mentioned in all the guesswork. You have brought me into the public eye and, as you well know, I do not like that.'

He paused again. 'There may be a way you can balance the books a little.'

The first signs of a way out were there, and she blurted out, 'Anything, what do you want?' Again he waited and she glanced sideways at the Vietnamese, the thin smile she saw rapidly crushing any feeling of relief. 'You will first tell me all you know of this Meldrum. I have a feeling a connection with an airline may well be very useful to us in the future. After that we will discuss you. As you say, I think it desirable that you disappear, for a while at least, perhaps Hong Kong?' Once again the relief rushed through her like a wave and she quickly began to tell them all she knew of Meldrum.

It was not much: the early meetings and the few jobs she had done to ensure the blackmail or disgrace of people he needed to control or felt threatened by. Each occasion had followed the same format, a call, a meeting, the victim identified and the location most likely to produce a contact. It was invariably a hotel while the man or woman was on some business that had taken them out of their home town. Recently the usual sex had included an increasing level of drug taking, something Meldrum encouraged to add to the leverage. The night's activities would, of course, be reported to Meldrum, sometimes with incriminating film and on each occasion the individual was either quickly removed from the equation or brought under control.

She and the younger girl had done about half a dozen such jobs together, for him and she had operated alone on six more she thought. 'And evidence of your 'Arrangement' with Meldrum?' Lee Chin asked. She thought for a minute, 'Well, there isn't any really. All the calls were from a mobile and he has never met the other girl, Sharon. He was always quite specific it was only me he wanted to see and we always met in a different place. Payment was made in the same way and always in cash,' she finished lamely. 'Unfortunate,' he mused. 'Still, we may be able to use it, knowledge is always useful.' He glanced sideways at the Vietnamese who nodded slightly.

'Now,' he continued, 'I want you to go with Tran to your apartment to collect some things and your passport. It must be obvious to all that you have left the country, you understand? He will then take you to the domestic terminal at the airport. They will not be watching the internal side, so you will fly to Brisbane and from there to Hong Kong. I will have people there to meet you and I will tell you when it is safe to return, is that clear? You are sure this other girl knows nothing, you have never mentioned this Meldrum to her?' 'No I paid her off myself she never knew anything about him, or us,' she concluded.

He looked across at the Vietnamese who got to his feet and walked to the door. Opening it he waited and as the girl passed through he glanced back at the desk, a look of enquiry answered with a brief nod from Lee Chin.

She sat in the back with Tran, the driver was alone. They took her to her apartment, waiting just down the street for a few minutes to see if the place was being watched. Satisfied that it was clear, Tran told her she had thirty minutes to get what she needed, reminding her that a passport was essential. Five minutes early she re-appeared at the front of the building and the car moved up to let her in. Tran turned to her, 'We will now collect the tickets. You are booked on the 1200 City Flyer to Brisbane and the 1700 Cathay flight to Hong Kong. The tickets are at my office.' He glanced at his watch and turned to the driver 'Not much time, hurry up,' he ordered.

Tran ran a funeral parlour as part of the extensive collection of businesses required by the organisation to launder the vast amounts of cash the sale of drugs generated. This, and the adjacent pet food factory, also part of the collection, had proved quite useful in the past when a discreet disposal was required.

It was at the office of the former that the car eventually stopped. Tran got out and opened the door for her. 'Hurry' he said. 'We do not have much time.' Without thinking she followed him into the office. Only as the office door closed behind her did the question pop into her mind. Why did he need me to go with him to collect tickets which would normally be available at the airport anyway? Too late, she realised it was a trap; the needle thrust into her neck delivered a massive overdose and quickly caused her collapse. Death followed within minutes.

Three hours later all that remained of Mary Sinclair was a cooling paper trail of her passage through the Domestic Terminal at Sydney Airport and from there to a flight from Brisbane to Hong Kong.

The woman who actually travelled was one of Lee Chin's many drug couriers, well used to any number of identities. She did not know of course but she would not be returning to Australia this time.

The police picked up the younger girl, Sharon, the next day and through her they found Sinclair's address. They watched the place for a couple of days and when there had been no movement they got the required warrants and entered. A quick search made it clear she had gone. This led to the usual enquiries at the usual places and eventually the records of possible travellers through the airports. They soon found the name Sinclair, tracing what they thought was her to the Cathay flight bound for Hong Kong out of Brisbane Queensland. All efforts to get the other girl in their custody to pick Sinclair out on the security camera film records proved useless. An attempt to get a match between the passengers checking in and the name was also a failure. From there the trail went cold, and as it was only a slender lead in the pursuit of the drug cartel anyway, interest soon waned.

The State Police Commissioner sat at his desk some days later. In front of him was the inconsequential file on the Bartlett death with its tenuous links with Lee Chin. Soon his attention had drifted off the case to the meeting he had scheduled with the new State Premier in a few hours.

Thinking about the recent political upheaval brought his mind to the reason for the recent resignation of the man's predecessor, and from there to the meeting with his federal counterpart and finally to what had been revealed there.

Going full circle he looked down at the file on his desk once again. Pretty obvious this is going nowhere, he thought. I wonder if perhaps there is not a better way. Leaning over he picked up the telephone, 'Get me the Federal Police Commissioner in Canberra would you, not urgent, just ask him to give me a ring when he is free please.'

It was only a few minutes before the call was returned and after the usual pleasantries the Federal man asked what he could do for him. 'Well, nothing really, it's just that this Bartlett business is coming to a dead end. I had hoped to establish a connection with Lee Chin and the drug supply. There was a girl who looked as though she would provide us with a direct lead but predictably she has disappeared and as a result the trail is dead. Annoying, as we both know Lee is up to his neck in this. Anyway thought I might send you the file, see if you guys can make anything of it.'

The Fed was puzzled. This new found attitude of cooperation was refreshing, assuming there was no motive. 'Okay,' he replied, 'send it on down. We can have a look at it. Jurisdiction is not going to be a problem is it?' 'Don't see why it should,' the State Commissioner replied 'After all drugs are ultimately a federal issue and your boss is a bit straighter than mine. Don't quote me on that last bit, okay.' The Fed laughed, 'Of course not. Right I will get my people to look at it and see if we can help in anyway.'

The connection was broken and the State policeman leaned back in his chair. Well Mister Lee, he thought, I wonder what the future holds for you. I think I may well have just marked your card for you, he laughed quietly at his little play on words.

Chapter Thirteen
Amport Hampshire UK

The village was some eighty miles west of the city. A fast run down the M3 motorway and then a few miles further on the A303 trunk road with a gentle drive through the beautiful countryside of Hampshire to finish the journey. He had kept a cottage here in the tiny and very picturesque village of Amport for many years. In fact ever since his days as a flying instructor at the main training base of the Army Air Corps, which was a few miles further to the west at the intriguingly named Middle Wallop.

His wife had passed away almost ten years before and since then he had spread his time between the cottage and his London club, of late, more of the latter than he liked. Here at the cottage he was still looked after by the same housekeeper his wife had first employed some twenty-five years before.

As the old Bentley rolled to a stop it was Cathleen who came out to meet him. 'Good evening Colonel, did you have a pleasant journey?' she asked. Try as he might he could not get her to use his first name. She insisted on keeping things formal. She was obviously devoted to him but there were standards to be maintained. 'Mrs Raff would have expected that after all,' she had said to him the last time he had raised the subject.

'Yes, thank you Cathleen. Everything alright here?' he enquired as a matter of courtesy. He knew very well what the answer would be, because Cathleen ran a tight ship and not once had either he or his wife had cause to complain in all the time she had been with them. 'Of course sir, now when will the other gentlemen be arriving? I have three of you for dinner is that correct?' 'Yes, and I think we can expect them both to stay over if that is okay with you. We have a lot to discuss and I doubt either of them will want to drive back to town. Not much point come to think of it, after all it is Friday. I did take the liberty of making the offer. It is Colonel Fitzroy-Gibbons and Chief Superintendent Quartermaine by the way so they will know their way around.' 'Thank you Colonel, I had thought they might so I have made up two rooms for them. Nice to see the gentlemen down here again sir, it's been a long time since we've had guests.' He looked at her as she turned away, sensing the tone and knowing full well that he had just been ticked off. She worried about him spending too much time alone; visitors were to be encouraged she had told him. Sometimes he wondered who was really in charge here. Then smiling to himself he realised the answer was obvious, she was.

He had showered and changed and was sitting with a drink in the large garden that sloped down to the stream, a tributary of the river Test. The evening sun was quite warm and it was very still, the last of the birds were about, he could hear them squabbling as they bedded down for the night to come, the only other noise was the sound of the running water.

He noticed the intrusion eventually. A car was approaching, I wonder if F-G has managed to get Simon to give him a lift, he thought, knowing full well that Alistair would avoid the drive if he could. Sure enough, as he turned the corner of the cottage to meet the arrivals, he saw his old friend sitting next to the policeman in the front of Simon's Jag.

Greetings over and under the direction of a clearly happy Cathleen, the two men were ushered away to change with an instruction that dinner would be in one hour, on the dot.

Soon all three were sitting in the garden and the subject drifted round to recent events. The demise of the two Lebanese in Australia was well executed they agreed, as was the recent removal of Mr Smith. Here, while the media frenzy had not been particularly welcome, it had at least led them all to make the rather tenuous connection to poor old Pat Carrington's murder.

That this lead was proving difficult to follow, and the parallel and equally stalled enquiry into the lawyers termination, was something that was irritating them.

Certainly the disposal of the lawyer had made tracing the suspected leak difficult, but the loss of Carrington and the information he apparently had was disastrous. It was pretty clear that he had been their only link to the individual who had apparently made the calls to Smiths cronies.

The policeman did have some good news though. He had told them of the results from the CCTV surveillance, and the slowly clearing picture of an assassin on the loose was at least somewhere to look. While Smith's disposal had not yet resulted in the hoped for flurry of activity in the Whitehall establishment, it was early days yet and they were reasonably confident that somewhere in the upper echelons of the bureaucracy, there would be one very worried individual.

Raff looked at the other two. 'And where do we go from here? If and when this creature comes to the surface do we think the current administration will prosecute? After all, an election is due in what, eighteen months, and our gallant leader has consistently demonstrated his willingness to circumvent the law when votes are involved. Added to which, if our mysterious he or she is as high up the political pole as we suspect, they are quite likely to come from the same sewer and that would almost guarantee a whitewash.

Even if it did get to court, it is likely to be a rerun of that recent Australian travesty, with a minimal sentence at most. Plenty of tame judges in this neck of the woods too, you know.' 'Quite right Peter, still lets find the bugger first, then we can decide what needs to be done, don't you think?' 'Sorry Alistair, bit ahead of the game there,' Raff apologised and then continued. 'Apart from that, something else has come up.'

He passed each of them a couple of pages of typed foolscap paper. 'Read it later but I will give you something of a précis. It concerns a certain Lee Chin, a citizen of Sydney Australia, of Chinese origin of course, but he is in fact third generation Australian. Apparently his family emigrated to Broome in the far northwest. They were pearl divers in their native China and the growing local industry was attracting a lot of them at that time.

Anyway old man Lee did quite well it seems. Got the next generation educated, something that was continued by his son, this chap's father. Trouble is that it all seems to have gone a bit wrong somewhere there, because it appears there was no way the current Mr Lee was going into the family business. As far as the locals know, he moved to Sydney's 'Chinatown' in the sixties. The chances are he was already involved in the drug trade in a small way, but over the next thirty years or so Lee Chin has risen to the top of a very unpleasant pile.

As well as running a large chunk of the national drug trade, along the way he seems to have built himself some impenetrable defences within the administration. It is reasonable to assume that he has a number of the local 'Establishment' on the payroll. Either that or he has them under control by other means because this guy has never, ever, even been in court. He makes our, late Mr Smith look like a rank amateur, especially as Smith was stupid enough to attract our attention in the end.'

'Well that is until now' he smiled. 'It seems that now the same thing has inadvertently happened to Mister Lee. I would like your opinions on the man and any suggestions you may have as to how we may, how shall I put it, improve the situation. It has been made pretty clear to me by our source that the locals are unlikely to get political support for any official move against this man.'

He paused as they each glanced down at the paper they held. 'As a matter of interest, this little lot has come to us in something of a round about way.'

He went on to explain the connection between the recent death of a Neil Bartlett, late CEO of Trans Pacific Airlines, from a massive drug overdose, his replacement by a certain Francis Meldrum, and an apparent association Lee had with the woman suspected of involvement in Bartlett's demise. She was now suspiciously absent.

'We have been asked by our Australian partner to consider the removal of Mister Lee. Now I know it is our policy to have only one operation running at any time but the Australian end will require some research, and I think we can manage that while we concentrate most of our resources on finding and dealing with the local problem. In the meantime, if an opportunity arises in the Antipodes, I feel we should take it.

There is a new chap running the State now and the word is he is no more trustworthy than the last one. Incidentally, that chappy promptly resigned when the head of the state police dropped a collection of our little messages on his desk. I am thinking a short sharp lesson close to home, might encourage the new boy a little.

What brings this little lot even closer to home of course is that our three newest members are employed by none other than Trans Pacific.'

Before they could discuss anything further, Cathleen appeared and announced that dinner was awaiting them.

Over dinner the three airmen were again the subject for a while. Quartermaine asking most of the questions and entirely satisfied with the answers, he went on to suggest that they might be just what was needed in this new case. After all, they were ideally placed to handle the intelligence gathering required. Raff agreed to get onto it on Monday morning.

The conversation drifted on to more general subjects; the policeman talking most and telling the two retired army officers of the latest fiascos the current government was involved in. It was all something of a pathetic comedy they agreed.

These individuals saw themselves as leaders of the nation but in fact no one, given the choice, would follow them out of anything but curiosity, or as F-G put it, 'I wouldn't breed from the bastards.' The current Prime

Minister, Warren Simpson, was the main but by no means only problem. Quartermaine told them that the wretched man actually believes he talks to God, that is until you try and get a decision out of him, and then it's all committees and camels again.

The rest of the weekend was spent discussing the detail of the two latest contracts while gently strolling around the village and enjoying lunch in the 'locals' that were of quite exceptional quality here. By the time Sunday afternoon arrived two detailed plans had been agreed and, as he bade his friends' farewell, Raff's mind was already on the business of briefing the three airmen in Australia.

He walked slowly back into the house. Cathleen was standing at the door to his study, the evening gin and tonic in her hand, 'A very pleasant weekend sir.' 'Yes,' he smiled, 'Always is with those two, never a bad word or disagreement with either of them you know.' 'I know Colonel. I suppose you will be working late tonight, sir, so if you don't mind I will slip off home?' 'No, that will be fine Cathleen and thank you.' He wondered into his study, his mind already far away.

She closed the door quietly, leaving him alone, but as she left the house a thought crossed her mind: there were at least two very unpleasant people on the planet who would not feel quite so comfortable if they were aware of what had been agreed here this weekend, for Cathleen knew far more about what went on around here than even Colonel Raff realised.

Settled in the study, he took some time to figure out just what time it was on the east coast of Australia. Having experienced the 'delights' of being called from around the globe, by people who consistently failed to grasp the simple fact that the earth was round and that it wasn't daylight everywhere, he was meticulous in trying to avoid doing the same thing to others. The trouble with time zones these days was that the buggers kept changing them. In the current case, for example, it was usually either nine hours or eleven but could, he thought, be ten sometimes. Or had they got that sorted out now? He could not remember.

Finally settling for nine, he dialled the number. After a few rings the bleary voice of Shaun Fitzgerald answered and Raff immediately started to apologise, thinking he had screwed it up. 'No it's okay Colonel, it's eight o'clock here, we just had a bit of a late night is all. What can I do for you?' Raff explained what had been discussed over his own weekend and went on to request some preliminary reconnaissance, to try and establish behavioural patterns. He said he would be sending further details by e-mail just as soon as he had sorted it all out, but for now would they mind just having a look around. 'No problem Colonel, we were wondering where we should go for a bite at lunchtime. Guess you have just solved that for us. Any particular venue owned or even favoured by this guy?' Raff looked at his notes. 'According to this, Shaun, he has an interest in at least two places in Sydney's Chinatown. One is called the Golden Lion, the other The Dragon Pearl. Both seem to be on a Sussex street. We have his home address as a place in Edgcliffe, which I presume is a suburb?' Shuffling the notes, he found the one he wanted and read it out. 'I'll leave it with you then. Oh, one final thing, this will be the limit of your involvement with this, okay. We have someone else in line for the next phase.' 'Right Colonel, got all that. We will be up there soon anyway so

I will let you know what we have found then. Anything I think you need before, I will contact you.' A few final pleasantries and the call was terminated.

Raff leaned back in his seat thinking. 'Well that was the easy one. The other more local and far more complex problem was turning out to be anything but.

M16 Monday

Frobisher had not enjoyed his weekend at all. The call from Moscow, when it came, had been curt and brooked no argument. They seemed well aware of his little business on the side and were none too pleased that it was this that now threatened their primary source in British Intelligence. When he had pointed out that they paid him so little that it had been necessary, the silence that followed had only increased his state of panic. Finally, another voice had come on the line, this time in a more conciliatory tone, telling him that he should make one more sweep of the material available, and that he could expect to be extracted in no more than two weeks, the method and chaperon would be advised. His anxiety became more obvious at this, and the rest of the time was spent assuring him that he would not be disposed of or handed over to his current masters. Ironically, this was something he would have had no compunction in doing had the circumstances been reversed.

Now in the office, he had made discreet enquiries with some of the low-level staff at the Internal Affairs Department and was reassured by the news that the new boss did not seem particularly interested in the issue of the use of a few mobiles. He relaxed a little. Maybe, just maybe, he would be able to weather this.

He did however, put in a requisition order for the file held by Scotland Yard on the matter of Cyril Smith's removal. It was by pure chance that the file, now in the hands of Special Branch, was quickly forwarded to him without question. It was while he was going through it that he came across the card. Turning it over in his hand he was suddenly deep in thought. He had heard or read something about these things some time ago. Suddenly he remembered, and the beginnings of a plan formed in his mind. Removing the card, he quickly closed the file. He made sure he was not indicated on the front as an addressee and passed it to his new secretary with the advice that it was not what he wanted and he would deal with the matter direct.

He then called a contact he had with Scotland Yard and, in as general a way as possible, steered the conversation round to the subject of the Smith case. Again he was reassured; the police were still convinced it was a gangland attack. The card had not aroused any interest there it seemed. A final enquiry with the same man, on the progress of the lawyer murder case, left him feeling almost normal. Apparently here things were cooling nicely. As he had expected the murder of a known sexual deviant and a rent boy bothered nobody and the legal establishment with whom he had been associated was only too happy to let it fizzle out.

He then started going through his own files, deciding just what he should take with him. He had for some time been passing only the occasional pieces of relatively low grade information. Now he had to make it worth Moscow's while to look after him. He knew only too well what had happened with Philby and the others once they had jumped ship and he was determined that he would feed the information to the owners of his new home slowly.

Victoria Manning also sat at her desk. She was looking through the Scotland Yard file on Cyril Smith. She had been a little surprised it had got to her so quickly and out of curiosity checked the requisition list on the front. Curiously she found herself as the first from MI6 to see it but it had apparently already been in the building?

He had been a thoroughly unpleasant piece of work and the world would not miss him. However it was when she got to the details of the trial and the fate of the three jurors that she really started to concentrate, finding it difficult to believe that a high profile source in her agency would be involved in something so bloody sordid. However the evidence was there: the use of the lawyer; the calls to numbers only known to three people, only two of whom were now alive; and then the strange connections being made with the CCTV cameras to this Swiss/German, although she realised that he was quite likely to be neither? What was clear was that whenever he appeared something unpleasant happened.

She had decided right at the beginning of this that she would keep it all to herself; the head of Special Branch had advised as much. He had suggested that there was a bad apple and that until it was found it would be advisable. As he had pointed out, if poor old Pat had done that, he would be alive now.

It was the reference to her predecessor, Pat Carrington, that had started her off on this line because she had come across his diary in the secretary's desk. It included the usual notes and appointments and it was these that had eventually attracted her attention. She was looking at the page covering the week before his murder and two entries caught her eye. It appeared he had gone to see Sir Gerald Frobisher twice in that week and again on the Monday of the week he died. Nothing odd in that of course, except that she could find no other record that the two had even met in the official sense. Obviously there was very little in their individual responsibilities that would lead to any contact, or was there? This and the call she had received from Frobisher so soon after she had taken over started her thinking.

She leaned over and pressed the button on the intercom. As the secretary answered she said 'Would you get hold of Chief Superintendent Quartermaine at Special Branch for me please?' It took about ten minutes to find him and his return call was put through immediately. 'What can I do for you Miss Manning?' 'Well for starters, it's Vicky, and secondly you can take me to lunch,' she said. There was a pause as the policeman got over his surprise 'And why would I do that?' he said a little ungraciously, quickly apologising as he realised just how it had come out, adding, 'Not that I won't of course.' She laughed, 'Because there is something I want to talk through with you on this wretched Carrington business. That's why.' The arrangement was made for the following Wednesday; she left him to pick the venue.

Lake Geneva, Switzerland

The house overlooked the lake, and the city occupied most of the opposite shore. Here, though, there was very little development and surrounded as it was by woodlands it was very isolated. Of course he did not rely on this alone: there was a substantial security system at the perimeter and he always had two of his men in residence, not that there had ever been any need. For the last twenty years he had lived here in peace.

Today his telephone had been running hot, and now as he waited for the Russian to arrive, he sat reflecting on the events of the last few days. He had fully expected to receive an instruction to eliminate Frobisher and he had even been giving some thought as to how. The thought of removing the Englishman did not bother him. Quite the reverse, Frobisher had become a liability and his termination would close off any trail they may have established to him. So, it was something of a surprise when the Russian told him that he was to get the man out. He had protested of course and been quickly told that it was not his place to question orders; it was also made quite clear what would happen if he did again.

What followed was a long and complex briefing session on the extraction plan. By the end of it he had to admit that, if it worked, it would keep the Brits running around in circles for quite a while; more importantly, it would leave him in the clear. The final part of the plan was the real clever piece. Opening the last file he looked at the photograph. Uncanny, he thought; uncanny and unfortunate! He smiled, looked up, and in fluent Russian, asked what the start date for this was to be. He was told that Frobisher had been given ten days from then. He was to be in the UK at least a week before, to establish contact with the man and also to perform the necessary reconnaissance for the last part of the extraction plan. He was to expect that Frobisher would be in a highly nervous state of mind, particularly as they were to leave in the manner described. On hearing this he asked, if an en-route termination became necessary, was this approved. His Russian control looked at him. 'That would be very unfortunate; he will be bringing out information of some importance, here.' He gestured to his own head. 'More than even he realises of course. But we have some special methods of extraction, even in these days of enlightenment,' he laughed. 'However, if all else fails you may terminate and destroy the body.' The German just grunted. At least he had that option.

As soon as he was alone he began to plan.

Sydney Cabramatta, an inner-city suburb

Tran Van Sah sat in the back office of the funeral parlour deep in thought. For some time he had been waiting for an opportunity, this latest fiasco with the woman could well provide it. Lee Chin was losing it, of that he was convinced. His own sources in the local police had confirmed that there was now far more interest being shown in 'their business' than was healthy. He had also received reports from his men that Lee's home and their restaurants and other business premises were under occasional surveillance. An enquiry with his tame police sources had brought the disturbing information that they were not 'State'. The suggestion was that these men might be Federal, which raised the stakes considerably. Until now, the Feds had not been involved and the local drug squad had been manageable, the occasional drug mule sacrificed now and then, the odd bust, agreed beforehand. As long as there was something to show the papers, the local squad was quite happy to leave the main players alone.

Somehow he did not think Canberra would be as easy to get on with.

The tension was raised further when the contact informed them that, the men in question did not appear to be attached to the Federal Drug Enforcement agency either. That they were law enforcement of some sort, he had no doubt, just which department? It was causing him considerable concern. He could take no action until he knew just who he was up against.

However, the time was fast approaching when a change in leadership would be required and he intended that, when it came, he would be it.

The old man was going soft. Certainly, he had finally agreed that the girl had to disappear, but it had taken Tran some time to get even this decision out of him, and the delay had resulted in the other woman being missed. That she seemed to know nothing that could be used against them did not matter in Tran's book. It was a question of lessons and discipline. The sheep had to be shown what happened if they attracted the wrong sort of attention. Of course, he admitted to himself, it was also frustrating to miss the opportunity to dispose of another western woman, something he enjoyed.

His real problem with a takeover was the Chinese. He knew the attitude of Lee's associates to anything or anybody from Vietnam. For a thousand years the Chinese had looked down on his people. As a consequence, he realised that a move to take over would not only involve the disposal of Lee but also a number of his closer associates, and they would have to be dealt with quickly because he could not afford to allow them to regroup and establish an alternative.

Having operated as second in command for some time now, he was well aware from whom the likely opposition would come. It was just a case of getting them all in one place to deal with them at the same time.

One of the first actions he had taken when he had been elevated to his current position, something these very people had all advised against he knew, was to gradually replace the foot soldiers. The people used for the dirty work were all Vietnamese. As a result, he was guaranteed their support in the intended coup. They, at least respected him if only because they knew from the odd example of what happened to those who crossed him that obedience was the only thing that would keep you alive. His problem was much further up the ladder and the solution would have to be a little more subtle than his usual methods.

Having spent most of his early life in the great delta of the Mekong River fighting the cursed Americans his usual methods of disposal could hardly be described as normal. But then the victims were never seen again, unless you counted the contents of a few cans of dog food that they usually ended up as part of. This time though it would have to be different. It was essential that it was classed as an accident. His problem was to avoid attracting any more attention from the already too interested, police. He was pretty sure the demise of Lee Chin would cause no tears with them, what he needed was a period of time after that to consolidate his own position, and he did not need an investigation going on into the 'disposal' while he did it. Little did he realise that all his planning would be unnecessary, his problem would be solved for him.

OP 4

They had watched for two weeks now, the patterns were emerging and one opportunity stood out. The Chinaman had only one regular habit it seemed. Every Wednesday he visited an elderly women they soon found out was his mother. She lived in a quite humble house in the exclusive and expensive harbour suburb of Woollhara. The opportunity occurred on his journey back to the city. Usually he was driven everywhere, but on this one weekly visit, he drove himself. He was in the habit of filling the big white Mercedes up at a particular service station he passed on his way back to the city. This, they then found out, was run on his behalf by one of his men. They figured that the weekly visit gave the old man an opportunity to see for himself how things were going. A plan was put together and the details quickly approved.

★ ★ ★

The airliner from Shanghai touched down at Kingsford Smith airport, having negotiated the protracted arrival procedures. The crew eventually left the customs hall, and the bus contracted by the handling agent stood at the kerbside waiting. Forty minutes later they were in the hotel. The Captain closed the door to his apartment and walked to the window. The view was spectacular, the harbour stretched out to left and right as far as he could see. Normally he would have wasted a few minutes soaking it up, but this time he had other things on his mind.

The call came within minutes and the man was at his door soon after. He handed over a vile in a small box and, indicating that he should take care with the contents, he turned and left. The Captain went and sat at the desk and began to read. The instructions were clear and simple; he looked at his watch, time for a sleep before the evening.

He woke to the alarm at 1800, showered and then, digging into his suitcase, he pulled out the rather tired and none too clean set of overalls he had been advised to bring. Having put them on, his only real problem was getting out of the hotel without being seen by one of his crew. He knew already that the service elevator exited onto the hotel staff car park and from here it was a few minutes walk to the railway station.

Within the hour he was standing on the forecourt of the Edgecliff service station being told his duties by the owner. The job had been got for him through an agency. The owner had specified mainland Chinese and his was the only application - the agency had seen to that. It was Wednesday and his new and very temporary boss gave detailed and specific instructions on his most important customer expected that evening.

Lee arrived, as always, a few minutes after 2300, any surprise he may have had at the new face filling his car was minimised by the fact that the man's English was heavily accented and that he was clearly much more comfortable with Mandarin. Had Lee spent more time in the country of his ancestors he might have realised that a humble service station attendant would not have spoken in such a cultured manner.

The tiny vial and its attached receiver he had been given were quickly slipped into the tank along with a full load of fuel. Lee spent the few minutes required talking with the owner while the new employee went on to busy himself with the windscreen. The man nodded at them to indicate he had finished and Lee climbed back into the white Mercedes and drove away.

The man pressed the button on the transmitter in his pocket and quickly walked off the forecourt to the station. It was fifteen minutes before his now ex boss realised he had gone.

They had been sitting in the taxi a hundred metres back up the road. Hearing the buzz from the receiver, the driver started the engine. As the Mercedes moved out onto the wide six-lane road again, the taxi left the kerb and followed. The next phase would be tricky as collateral damage was unacceptable. This left only one real option and it was important that there were no other vehicles in the area. Soon the road began its climb to the tunnel under the 'red light' district of Kings Cross. The driver in the cab checked the rear mirror, it was empty. Looking to the front there were no cars, other than the Mercedes, there either. The driver grunted, 'That's it' and accelerated to pass the other car, entering the tunnel about fifty metres ahead of it and quickly pulling away. The man in the passenger seat looked back and as soon as Lee's car entered the tunnel he pressed the transmitter. In the tank of the Mercedes the capsule shattered, the nitro quickly mixed with the full load of fuel and exploded. The flame front almost caught the cab now accelerating hard out of the western end of the tunnel. Neither man looked back, the driver quickly slowing to the 60 kph allowed. His partner wound down the window and dropped the card. It was unlikely to be found he thought, but he had his instructions. As soon as a turn allowed, they left the main road and disappeared.

★ ★ ★

The airliner taxied out from the international terminal. He was offered a departure from taxiway Foxtrot some distance from the end of runway 16 Right. The Boeing 777 was well able to handle this and he accepted it. Soon they had made the turn to the south associated with the departure and were established on track to Mount Isa and the north. He sat back and pulled out the paper. The front page was full of an incident in the tunnel at Kings Cross in Sydney. An explosion had totally destroyed a vehicle in there. As yet no evidence of who or what it was had been found. The police were baffled and an appeal for missing persons was being made. It would be some time the paper said, before forensics could even make a guess at the type of vehicle, let alone the occupant.

★ ★ ★

Eventually the identity of the driver was found but only from the dental records as nothing else remained. The victim's identity resulted in two investigations. One a rather half-hearted effort by the State Police, who as far as the street cops were concerned were not, too bothered by the death of one of the city's major criminals and a parallel investigation by the cartel itself.

Tran Van Sah was immediately suspected, but his alibi was watertight and, moreover, all indications were that he was as baffled and concerned as the Chinese. Their only lead, and here they were way ahead of the police, was the service station owner. He, under some rigorous interrogation, admitted he had taken on a new employee that night and that not only had the man attended to Lee's car but he had disappeared soon after. Of this man, detailed and at times violent enquiries in the underworld community brought no information. Both he and the manner of such wholesale destruction remained a mystery.

However, seizing the opportunity, the Vietnamese had systematically divided and eliminated any opposition to his taking over. It had been too easy, all were suspect, and he had the people to deal with each in turn. Within two weeks his position was unassailable, any suggestion of objection simply resulting in another disappearance.

Shaun waited until the evening to make the call, there was nothing to be gained from doing it earlier. Raff answered after the second ring. He had seen the reports.

The local Chinese community was in shock; Lee had been a well-known and very wealthy member of it. His organisation was in disarray it seemed. This, said Fitzgerald, had left the way open for Tran. He then explained that they had watched the Vietnamese over the last week. By now they reckoned Tran would be in total control of the empire. He had clearly used the opportunity provided by the removal of Lee to take over.

There was a pause on the line as Raff thought. 'Okay boys leave it for a while. I will make a few calls to see if the connection you have pointed out has been made. Obviously it would be easier for us to let the official sources handle it if they can build a case. We will put Mister Tran on hold for a bit. It is an unfortunate result and we may have to come back to him later.'

★ ★ ★

In the State Police Headquarters the Commissioner sat looking at the reports, thinking. Well that was bloody quick.

The call he had ordered came through. 'See your little problem seems to have been solved in a rather dramatic way Commissioner,' his Federal counterpart opened up. 'Yes' he said. 'Amazing coincidence, us talking about it just that only recently.' There was a pause. 'Anything turned up as to who and how, yet?' the Fed continued. 'Well we found another of those damned cards, but that's about all, it was lying in the road at the tunnel mouth, other than that, nothing. Of course Lee's organisation is going through something of an upheaval. Quite a few of the faces from the shadows seem to have disappeared. The Vietnamese, Tran, seems to be something of a rising star. Nasty piece of work from what little we know. I have a file on him here but it's a bit thin. I was wondering if you could take a look through your stuff and fill in some of the blanks for us. That is why I called really.' Yes, I bet it was the Fed thought. However, he agreed to look through the records and send anything he found on the Vietnamese up to Sydney.

PART THREE
FINALS

Michael Patrick Collins

Chapter Fourteen
March 2000, Brighton Sussex UK

Arthur Jensen was now in late middle age; his life had been remarkable for one thing only---- nothing, absolutely nothing, had marked his passing. He was a most boring individual. His few friends and they were very few, suffered from a similar ability to clear a room of those more enlightened souls who were familiar with them, as soon as they appeared.

Even his employment with the Brighton Town Council, as the man responsible for arranging the collection of dog waste from the many bins in the place, was hardly a subject likely to be of much interest. He had a wife, and many were surprised that a man such as he could have found some poor wretched female willing to set up shop with him. That is, until they met her. In many ways Mrs Jensen was actually worse than her husband.

However he had one valuable attribute of which even he was unaware. It was this that had bought him to their attention. Of course it had been quite by chance that he had done this, because Arthur Jensen had never attracted anybody's attention by intent.

However having found him, they had watched on an occasional basis for some years now, just in case. In that time more detailed research on the man had been done, again quite without his knowledge. Now they knew just about everything there was to know about Mr and Mrs

Jensen. The file, running to just three pages, dealt mostly with his physiological details. This was really all they were concerned with; fortuitous really, as there was nothing much else anyway.

That the interest in him had now moved up a gear was unnoticed but for the last week his movements had been watched in detail. After day two of intense surveillance, the three watchers were convinced that Jensen was about as predictable as night following day. By day four they were almost beside themselves with boredom.

The German, had arrived and quickly seen this strict adherence to a simple routine as a potential problem. Any variation from it would attract almost immediate attention. It would be necessary to introduce some free radicals into the man's life, before the next phase could proceed.

Very soon a new face appeared in the department and she was allocated a desk next to his. Having introduced herself, she seemed not to notice his ability to cause almost instant slumber. Quite the reverse in fact, she hung on every utterance as though it was the wittiest, most interesting thing she had ever heard. Within a few days Jensen was besotted, and he spent more and more of the day with her. The suggestion of a drink on the way home was initially met with confusion. 'The Missus will be expecting me,' he stammered. But it did not take long for him to agree. 'Just the one though'----- 'of course Arthur,' she said, squeezing his leg as she smiled at him.

Before long the evening drink became two and as Mrs Jensen seemed not to notice, he became bolder, staying longer. The woman made sure they were seen together around the town. Different bars were used and soon the tongues were wagging. Everybody, except Arthur Jensen, seemed to think they knew what was happening.

She made the suggestion as they drove to her home one night, later that week. She had to go along the coast to the small town of Hythe in Kent to consult with a colleague. She would be staying the night. Would he like to come with her? She had thought of everything, she said. He could come as an expert on waste management, she would organise it with the department. He could tell his wife that it was official business. The more he thought on it, the more he wanted it. This was the most exciting thing in his life. It did not take long for him to agree.

He dropped her off at her apartment; she kissed him on the cheek, making an excuse to leave him, knowing he wanted to be invited in. As he drove off she pulled her mobile from her bag and touched the numbers. The circuit opened, 'It's on for Wednesday night next week.' At the other end there was a grunt and the line went dead.

As he arrived at his little semi-detached house he could barely control his excitement. He did not notice the watchers; still there, waiting.

Tuesday 29th March 2000, Frobisher's Apartment

Gerald Frobisher pulled the file from his safe. It had been given to him three years ago. It was the fourth he had received in his career as a spy for the Soviets; each had concerned a different individual. He glanced inside. There was as always a considerable likeness: similar height, weight, colour of eyes. In this case, only the blood group was different, he was A positive, the subject in the file O positive.

It was this and a couple of other little differences that made a file switch necessary. His task was to replace his real file with this, and that might prove a little difficult. Of course, he had access to the computer records and he could modify them quite easily. The problem was that the personnel department at MI6 still insisted on retaining a paper record as well.

He was giving some thought as to how he could make the exchange here. Clearly there was no point in doing one without the other.

As yet the German had not been in contact, not that he had expected it. The plan was clear on that. He was to handle everything up to the point of departure and then the man would arrange the final details, followed by his disappearance. The only meeting he had with them was the result of a call from someone he did not know. He had handed over one of his suits, a pair of shoes and a few other pieces of clothing. They had emphasised that all items should have been freshly laundered. That was two days ago.

At first he had been reluctant to leave. After all, the stories of Kim Philby's exile were not encouraging, and Philby had apparently actually believed all that communist utopia crap, at first anyway. He, on the other hand, was totally apolitical, he thought of nobody but himself. However two more calls from over there had convinced him he had no choice. They had made it quite clear that the net was closing; pointing out the precariousness of his position, at the same time suggesting that it would not be in their interest to let him be taken. That threat took a while to sink in, but eventually he realised the implication. He would deal with this file exchange tomorrow somehow

Wednesday 30th March, MI6

Frobisher had got into the office early; he needed to find out who was where in the building if he was going to make the required change. The call last night had caught him by surprise. He had tried to convince them he needed more time but they were adamant; it was to be tomorrow night.

A quick call to Victoria Manning's department, which was responsible for records, brought the first piece of good news. Her secretary told him that she had called to say she would not be in the office until late afternoon at the earliest, something to do with a working lunch and research. Whilst he was most curious to know what that was about, he knew he could not ask without causing some comment later. He just told her he would try again tomorrow. He then called the records office and told them he was coming down. As head of a department this might seem a little unusual but nobody there was in a position to query it. With Manning away there was nobody to clear it with even if they had wanted to. Added to this, his reputation was such that no one in records was willing to do anything to incur his wrath.

Making the most of the opportunity, he left his office immediately and took the lift to the basement records area, the papers of the replacement information loosely folded in his suit pocket. The switch was far easier than he had anticipated; he was left alone to locate the file. He quickly replaced the data, folded his own details up and placed them in his pocket. He then made a show of checking the computerised files, using the time to confirm that his own modifications of a few days ago were in agreement with the paper information he had just placed in the records.

He ignored the clerk as he left. Returning to his own office, he quickly ran his own personal data through the shredder. Between now, and his departure tomorrow, he would spend the time extracting as much information as he could, to ensure his position with his new masters.

Cavalry Club

Quartermaine had decided to meet Victoria Manning at the Cavalry Club. As an associate member he was well known there and it offered a level of privacy difficult to ensure at more public venues. She arrived and he was called to the lobby to escort her in.

Having never met before, there was a quite natural, initial summing up of one another. For his part Quartermaine was cautiously impressed; Manning, though new to the job, seemed well on top of things so far. Certainly her brush with that bastard Frobisher had not fazed her a bit. In fact it became apparent that it had actually caused her to look at the man more closely and it was what she had found there that was the reason for the meeting.

For her part, she had to admit, the policeman was a formidable individual. Obviously you did not get to run Special Branch if you were an idiot. When she considered some of her own colleagues she was glad she had made the decision to go outside the department with this.

They waited until the lunch was over and they had withdrawn to one of the booths before getting down to the real detail. He ran her through the whole business of the Smith case again, with special emphasis on the question of the use of the mobiles. It was here she smiled slightly. Noticing it, he raised an eyebrow? 'So you have something for me on this then, do you Vicky?'

'As a matter of fact I think I do. I have more or less traced both units used to the offices of your friend and mine, Gerald Frobisher.' He looked disappointed but she continued, 'I have also, more or less, established that it must have been him that used them.' His interest reawakened. Her face clouded over. 'And there is one more thing. I am pretty sure my predecessor had at least one, and possibly two, meetings with Frobisher in the week before he was murdered.'

'What!' he exclaimed. 'Then the chances are he knew that Internal Affairs were getting close, is that what you are saying?' 'That's about the size of it,' she agreed. She waited, watching him think the ramifications of it all through.

"Christ. If what you are saying is proven, it means there is a definite link between Frobisher and that individual we are watching. So far this guy has turned up on at least three occasions before and after a murder as you know. The last two were the elimination of that kerb crawling lawyer involved in the Smith case and then poor old Pat and the girl.' He paused again deep in thought she waited smiling. 'So, we have Frobisher involved in sabotaging the Smith prosecution by tipping off his scumbag associates and getting them to strong arm the witnesses. He then covers up the trail by getting onto this guy,' he passed her the photos. 'Who removes the weak link in a manner designed to deflect our attention. But then, unfortunately for him, one of my lads comes across the phone connection quite by chance, while he was having a chat with an old friend from the 'Yard'.

He then talks to Pat Carrington to see if MI6 have an interest. Pat raises the issue as a query with Frobisher, because the things come from his department. So Frobisher has to eliminate the one connection between that information and him, which was poor old Pat, and his lass, who just happens to be Frobisher's secretary.

'He must have gambled that Pat would want to be sure before he took it any further, but it was clearly a rushed job. Check out the dates on the photos, I bet this guy was none too happy having to come back so soon after the lawyer job. Is that what you think?' Her smile broadened 'Exactly,' she said, 'Frobisher is the only common link with all this. The question I have is, 'Why'. Surely it can't be money. I mean I have looked at his finances and he is, well shall we say --'Well off'. That part does not make sense to me.' Quartermaine then told her of the conversation two of his friends had had on that very subject some time before and the statement from F-G that for some people the very acquisition of money was the thing. The amount was irrelevant. Added to this there was also the power element, the idea of playing God, manipulating and destroying people's lives. 'Still,' he concluded, 'we don't really care about the 'Why' do we; it is just up to us to nail the bastard.' He looked at his watch 'Christ! Is that the time? I must get back. Okay, look Vicky it's Wednesday. I suggest we spend the next few days checking it all over and on Monday we drop this lot into your boss Fraser's lap, it's going to cause a hell of a stink you know. Frobisher spends half his life up the PM's metaphorical butt, and he was supposed to be in line for Fraser's job eventually. Oh Boy! I am going to enjoy this,' he smiled. 'In the meantime, why don't you have a meeting with Frobisher on some pretext or other and casually raise the subject of the phones and the Smith case can't hurt to stir the bastard up a little.' She agreed she would.

South Eastern France TGV northbound

The change of routing annoyed the German. Even though it had been necessary, the need to vary his method of entry had few choices. Flying was out, the only airports serviced from Geneva were Heathrow and Gatwick and he wanted to avoid both. Sixth sense some people called it, he didn't really care what it was, all he knew was that the scar on his head had been hurting like hell of late; and this was an omen he never ignored. Something was wrong and extra care was required. He had felt the need for a firearm this time and that alone ruled out air travel these days.

He was on the TGV northbound to the Gare de Lyon in Paris. He had driven to the French city of Lyon from Geneva. Once in Paris it would be the metro across to the Gare du Nord and then Eurostar to the UK. He would be coming back an entirely different, but equally time consuming way.

As he sat in the train he reflected on the past few years. He had more than enough to retire on. Most of the things he had wanted to do were complete, but as he gently rubbed his forehead he said to himself, most, but not quite all. With the dull hum of high speed on the best railway in the world, he dozed off.

The German had arrived in the small English town of Ashford in Kent in the afternoon. One of the reasons he had chosen to come by train was that Ashford was the only stop Eurostar made in the UK before London Waterloo, the current terminus. He had reasoned that the surveillance here was never going to be as efficient as that in the capital, although he was well aware that the cameras that formed such a major part of security in Britain these days would still be there. With that in mind he had once again subtly changed his appearance although even here he was beginning to run out of alternatives of late. This time he had added some weight at the waist, another change of hair colour and style finished off with a hat and glasses. He felt confident that the best memory in the world would never remember him.

He had been met by one of the watchers and together they drove south back to the coast.

Southern England city of Brighton Council Offices

Arthur Jensen had finished work for the day at 1700, as usual. He left the building through the back door, the Mayor discouraged staff of his level using the main entrance. He still could not believe how little interest his wife had shown when he told her he had to go away for the night on council business. Even when he had dressed in his best suit, she made no comment.

He walked to his little red car, the predictably rather tired old Volvo 440, with the baby on board sign still in the rear window, even though the younger Jensen had long gone. She had told him to pick her up from her apartment. That way they would not be seen, she said.

As he slowly pulled out into the traffic they watched him, and then followed in a black Range Rover.

He stopped outside the apartment and within minutes she opened the front door and walked over to the car. Surprisingly, she went to the driver's side. He got out of the car, she suggested that she drive, it would give him a chance to relax and enjoy the scenery after his hard day at work. He positively glowed at the consideration and the suggestion that his day had been anywhere near hard. Soon she was behind the wheel and they were heading east. The black Range Rover accelerated into the traffic and followed.

Leaving the A27 just north of Eastbourne she turned onto the A259 passing through Hastings. In the passenger seat Jensen was almost beside himself with anticipation. She asked him to light her cigarette then told him to leave the lighter out. In the gathering darkness he did not notice when she turned right on to the narrow country road that would take them, not to Hythe, but out towards the coast again in the direction of the nuclear power station at Dungeness. After the little village of Camber the road passes through largely uninhabited country for some distance, and a few miles beyond the village she pulled over into a lay by. He looked at her, puzzled. 'Just want to stretch my legs a little,' she said. 'Why don't you do the same?' He didn't notice the black Range Rover, lights off, coasting silently into the lay-by behind them. Standing beside the car, looking at her as she moved in front of the vehicle, the two men were right beside him before he could react. One held him while the other hit him twice in the face; he was already unconscious as they carried him back to their vehicle.

They quickly lifted the dead weight that would be Arthur Jensen for a little longer into the back and, after a brief word with the woman; they turned their vehicle around and began the long drive to London.

She stood there in the darkness, finishing the cigarette listening to the sounds of the night for a while, and then got back into the Volvo and headed for Hythe.

Once there, she parked the wretched little car at the back of the car park. It was hidden from the hotel building. She then spent some time removing any trace of her having been there. She collected her overnight bag and his lighter, using gloves to place it into her purse, and went to the hotel. Registering as Mr and Mrs, she told the clerk that her husband would be joining her later; he was on business in the town. Booking for two days, the credit card she used was untraceable. She went to the room and after about an hour in which she showered and changed, she rang room service and ordered dinner for two.

When the knock on the door indicated its arrival she quickly slipped into the bathroom and turned the shower on. The waitress entered and as the tray was placed on the table the woman went over to the bathroom door and called out that dinner was here, he should hurry or it would get cold. Giving the girl a modest tip and closing the door she then turned off the shower.

After eating as much as she wanted, she then took the lighter out of her bag and using sticky tape, lifted Jensen's prints from the metal surface, placing them around one glass and a few other more obvious places in the room. She then emptied the wine bottle into the toilet, together with most of the uneaten food and flushed it away. Moving to the bed she pulled it about such that it looked as though two people had slept there. She did not think it likely that the local police would even bother with this place, but if they did, she was pretty sure they would come to the required conclusion. Arthur Jensen had done a moonlight flit with an unknown girlfriend.

She set her mobile for the agreed time and dozed in a chair. The preset alarm came at three in the morning, she quickly grabbed the bag and slipped out of the hotel unnoticed. The black Ford that was waiting there flashed its lights; she walked over to it and disappeared.

Clapham. A South London Suburb

The bright light woke him. Almost immediately the pain hit him and he would have passed out but for the voice that called out. It was not English and this alone was enough to keep him conscious. Slowly he became aware of figures on the other side of the light. He soon found that he was tied to a chair by a rope around his shoulders. The inevitable query was ignored by his captors but eventually one began to untie him. As soon as he was free, the figure behind the light handed him a pile of clothes and, in heavily accented English, told him to change. The fit was surprisingly good. Not that he noticed of course, but they did. They then pushed him back onto the chair where he was restrained again, once more avoiding any contact of rope against his skin.

Thursday 31st March

It was morning. Arthur Jensen did not know it of course; he was in complete darkness in the cellar. They had come into the room and with the light in his face fed him some unidentifiable slop. As soon as he had finished the light was turned off again and darkness surrounded him. No word was spoken; his repeated and increasingly desperate questions were ignored.

Upstairs the German gave the final instructions to the three men there. Timing was critical. Having reassured himself that they understood this he picked up his bag and left. Driving to the city he pulled over and used the mobile. The final instructions were clear and brief; collection would be at 1800 tonight, one suitcase only.

MI6

Frobisher spent the morning in his office but the tension was getting to him. In fear of attracting attention he called his secretary and told her he was going home early, he felt unwell. As a result, when Vicky Manning called to arrange the meeting suggested by Quartermaine, she missed him.

Once home he re-packed the case (he had already done it three times) and then he paced the apartment. Eventually, at 1800, the call came; he picked up the case and his briefcase, gave the apartment a last look and closed the door. The German was parked right outside and Frobisher quickly threw the bag into the back and got in.

As soon as he had closed the door Frobisher handed over the package. He looked at the German 'They will remember to place the card? It is important that the trail be as muddy as possible and, from the little I know, this should set them off in quite the wrong direction.'

The German said nothing. He drove off, waiting for a while, gauging the man beside him, realising that this was a moment of some magnitude for him. Not that he gave a damn of course, but he was going to be with him for some time now and it was important to ensure that Frobisher did nothing to attract attention to them.

They stopped once, in a quiet street of some inconsequential suburb. A man came to the window and the German handed him the package without a word.

As they left the city Frobisher relaxed a little. Quiet until then, he asked how they were going to exit the country. The German handed him a package. He opened it, inside was a Swiss passport in the name of Schmidt; not very original but as he would only have the identity for a couple of days it didn't matter. There was a sum of money in Euros and Swiss francs and a Swiss driving licence. He already knew Frobisher was fluent in German.

'We are going out through Poole on the midnight Truckline ferry to Cherbourg. This car will be left in Poole and we will pick up another in France. We will then drive across France to my home on Lake Geneva. From there you will be collected by your new friends. We will not be meeting again.'

Special Branch

The pictures arrived on Quartermaine's desk that afternoon. They were from the cameras at the Ashford Eurostar Station exit, and it was from the previous day's collection. He was furious that it had taken nearly twenty- four hours to get to him. The man standing in front of his desk stammered that the matching process had not been completed until last night; that the cameras at this station were not directly linked into the central system and the data had to be downloaded. This was done every six hours or so and it was unfortunate that this train had arrived just after a download. It had been a full six hours before they were even submitted for comparison and it had then taken some time for the possible match with the stored images to occur. They were sorry, he finished lamely.

Quartermaine immediately called the Kent chief constable and got a team down to Ashford to go through everything, including all the CCTV images in the car parks and the surrounding area. It was some time later that the first information started to come in. There were a few rather poor pictures of the suspect getting into a car and heading south out of town, but then nothing. They did have one thing though, most of the number plate and the make of car, a late model Ford Mondeo, dark in colour, possibly blue or dark green. The details were passed to all the forces in the south with an instruction to report and follow. The car was eventually found on film in the car park of the Dover Eurostar station. Once again the CCTV cameras were hastily analysed and the figures of two men were seen to leave it with a woman. The woman continued into the station and was recorded boarding an early morning train to Brussels; the men had left her and returned to the Ford. A similar vehicle was picked up on the M2 motorway heading north as dawn broke. Subsequent inspection of the cameras at the north end of the motorway drew a blank. The suspect vehicle had left the motorway before then. A general alert was put out but Quartermaine knew that the vehicle could be just about anywhere in the time it had taken to get the information.

It was now 1805 and he was still sitting at his desk, trying to figure out what else he could do, when the intercom buzzed. 'It's the head of internal security at 6,

sir,' Angela said. He picked up the receiver. 'Yes Vicky?'
'Hello Simon, just thought you ought to know I tried to
see Frobisher this afternoon and he had gone home early,
sick or something. The secretary said he had been a bit
uptight all morning.' 'That's interesting Vicky. Given
what's going on here at the moment, I think I might just
give him a call myself. Can I get back to you tomorrow?'

He pressed the intercom button for his secretary.
'Angela can you get me Sir Gerald Frobisher, at home
please, we should have his number somewhere.' After a
few minutes she called in. 'I have been calling it, sir, but
there is no answer. Should I try later?' He looked at his
watch, 1815, can't be that bloody sick he thought. 'No,
that's okay Angela, bring the number in and then get off
home, thanks.' She came in and gave it to him 'I can stay
if you want sir,' He looked at her and smiled 'No get off
home, I'll not be too far behind you. See you tomorrow,
and thanks for staying on.'

He sat there thinking for a few minutes, tried
Frobisher's number again and, getting no reply, slowly
cleared his desk and headed home. As he drove away he
reasoned he had done all he could with the information
available. There was an 'all points' out on the foreigner
and an advisory on the dark Ford, but it was all a bit thin.
They needed another break if this was going to be
resolved. He was pretty sure that with this character on
the loose somebody was going to die very soon.

Poole Ferry Port Southern England

They reached the ferry terminal at 2230 and went into
the lounge to wait for the call to board. He had dumped
the car in a side street and they had walked here. Looking

around, it concerned him that there were not very many foot passengers and he instinctively avoided the cameras as best he could. Frobisher, with no sense of field craft, had to be constantly reminded of the danger.

Eventually they were called to board: their tickets were inspected by the ferry company staff but there was no emigration check at all. The German breathed a sigh of relief. If the EEC was good for anything it was the fugitive business. He knew only too well that in the old days his passing would have been noted, even with the immaculate documents they had. As soon as they were on board he hustled Frobisher into the cabin, and began to relax. Only about five hours to go and they would be on the road in France, and soon after he would rid himself of this man.

The ship slipped its moorings and as the dull rumble of the engines picked up, the first sensation of movement was transmitted through the hull. Nothing much yet, they still had to transit Poole harbour, the second biggest in the world. It would not be until they cleared Durlston Head that the Channel swell made its presence felt. Long before that he was asleep; Frobisher, the full magnitude of what he was doing only now sinking in, lay there looking through unseeing eyes at the bulkhead above his head.

Clapham

They had come for Jensen at midnight. He was dragged roughly to his feet. This time they made no effort not to be seen. Holding him up, they looked at his face, still bruised and sore. They pulled the jacket he was wearing open and placed a wallet inside the pocket. Some small change was put in the pants pocket along with a handkerchief and some keys.

Something was said in a foreign language and then one of them held his shoulders while the other stepped back and hit him repeatedly. They kept on with the beating until both eyes were closed and the face was swelling. By then they were beating an unconscious body but that did not stop them. When they stopped eventually, they stood back to examine the man; the face was barely recognisable. They pulled the body to the garage and threw it into the vehicle parked there. There was plenty of room in the rear of the black Range Rover. One of them walked over to the wall and lifted a rope from the hook, it was already knotted.

They made a final check of the inside of the building and then one of them climbed in while the other opened the garage doors. Closing them as the vehicle left, he joined his companion. The street was quiet, hardly surprising at this time of night. Pulling out onto Wandsworth Road they turned left and made for the Albert Embankment on the south side of the river passing the station of Waterloo.

They were eventually in Southwark Street and turning onto the approaches to London Bridge. Here they stopped; the passenger got out and walked out onto the bridge looking over the other side. Satisfied, he pulled a small torch from his pocket and flashed the vehicle. With side lights only, it slowly pulled up to him. Again they paused--- watching.

The streets on both sides of the river were still empty. They moved to the rear of the Range Rover, pulled open the door and dragged the barely conscious man out. One of them grabbed the rope, walked over to the nearest lamp-pole and tied one end to it. The driver had managed to get Jensen to his feet, and between them they pulled him to the edge. The noose was dropped over his head and he was roughly lifted onto the parapet. At the last he must have realised that something was very wrong, because he started to struggle, but it was too late. As they pushed him he rolled to the edge of the parapet and disappeared. The cry of terror was quickly silenced by the dull crack of his neck breaking. They looked over the edge at the body hanging there; satisfied that Mr Jensen had performed his most useful function. The card was placed carefully in a crack in the brickwork next to the pole, just as they had been ordered. Neither knew or cared why. They walked quickly back to the Range Rover and drove away. The body was left swinging gently in the breeze.

Chapter Fifteen
1700 Quartermaine's Office 1st April

His head was aching and he rubbed his temples trying to ease it. So far it had been a shit of a day. The early morning call what seemed an age ago from one of his Sergeant's had been the start of it and it had gone rapidly down hill from then on. The unpleasant surprise of the 'Sweepers' card, given to him this afternoon by the same man, now a newly promoted Inspector, had only added to a day of increasing frustration and concern.

He was waiting for Vicky Manning to appear. The suicide of Sir Gerald Frobisher had caused a hell of a flap across the river and clearly she was having trouble getting away.

To make matters worse he had not been able to find either Colonel Raff or Fitzroy-Gibbons, and the appearance of a card, which had no business being at the scene of the suicide, was bothering him. He needed to clear that up quickly.

So far he had one very dead, head of the Russia desk at MI6, and an assassin, of unknown origin, running around out there somewhere.

He had got his people to check all the airports and ports but nothing had been seen of either that individual or the vehicle since the Ashford and Dover pictures.

The intercom buzzed. 'Colonel Raff sir,' she said. 'At last! Put him through.' 'What's up Simon? I have three messages to call. Got them all together I am afraid.

Sounds like there is a flap on?' 'You could say that Peter. I can't really discuss it over the phone but just reassure me will you; you haven't been involved in anything I don't know about in the UK have you?' There was a pause, 'Certainly not, Simon,' 'And what about those Australian airmen, they are still down south are they not?' 'Yes, not due here for a few days, I am waiting to hear as a matter of fact.' 'Okay, that is all I wanted to know for now. You will see what it is all about if you watch the news. I will need to talk to you and F-G, tonight if possible, usual place okay? I can be there by 2000 I think, if that suits you?' Raff thought for a minute. 'Yes that should be fine. I will get on to Alistair and let him know.' 'Thanks Peter. We do have a problem old chap, there has been a rather awkward development.' The arrangement made, he leaned back in the chair. At least that was good news. Now, if only the rest of the mess would start to unwind.

Angela called again, 'Miss Manning to see you, sir.' 'Send her in and some coffee please, Angela.' The door opened and a very tired looking Head of Internal Security at MI6 walked in. 'Jesus! What a day Simon. That bloody man Fraser is off his head. He is already looking for someone to blame. Nobody seems to know why Frobisher did it. I mean, I know we had our suspicions but he didn't know that did he?

We have been going through his stuff and nothing seems to make sense.' She paused, looking at him, realising how tired he was. 'I'm sorry Simon. What's it been like over here?' 'About the same I guess, except we have the added attraction of a suspected assassin on the loose, just to make things really interesting. I am bloody sure there is a connection but as yet I have not got any idea what it is. I suppose it's conceivable the man topped himself, although it doesn't sound like something the Frobisher I knew would do. The thing I find really puzzling is the state of the body. I mean, he was obviously given a severe beating before he died. We would not have known who he was if were not for the ID. Why was that I wonder? The line I am working on at the moment is that this guy is involved somehow.' He pointed at the CCTV photos of the German. 'It is quite conceivable that, if I am right in my suspicions and there is or was a connection, our friend here might have been doing some housekeeping.'

She looked at the pictures 'Doesn't mean anything to me,' she said. 'Maybe I should run him through our records; we have a better set up for foreigners than you, what do you think?' He got up and walked to the wall, picked the clearest of the photos pulled it off and turned to her. 'Be my guest.'

He sat down again and looked at her. 'Vicky, I am totally buggered and from here, you are too. I suggest we leave this and see what the night brings us, what do you say?' She said nothing, just nodded picked up the photo and her bag and walked to the door. Opening it she turned, 'See you tomorrow then Simon.' He paused before replying, deep in thought. 'Before you go Vicky, stupid question I suppose, but your people have done the basic identity checks on the body?' She paused. 'Yes, first thing I did as a matter of fact. I am afraid it is Frobisher. I went through his bio file and everything matches, blood group, eye colour, don't have his DNA of course. That requirement only kicked in with new hires, five years ago. I suppose it is a relief he has topped himself really,' she continued 'At least we know where he is. I don't think Fraser could stand another Philby.

He waited a few minutes to let her get clear of the building and then he left. He did not go home. The cab dropped him at the Cavalry Club, and as he entered, the steward waived him through. 'Colonel Raff is in the lounge sir,' Quartermaine moved to the staircase, muttering a vague 'Thanks,' as he did so.

Locating Raff, he collapsed into the seat opposite and with pleasantries over, and a large scotch in his hand, he launched into a synopsis of the day. While much of it was already in the public domain, he lowered his voice and went on. 'Thing is Peter, there are a couple of things that have not been released. First up, Frobisher was badly beaten before he jumped, if he jumped. Then this was found stuffed into the stonework next to the point of departure.' He placed the card on the table. 'If that were not enough, that character I mentioned we were keeping a look out for over the lawyer business and a couple of other things, has turned up again. What I needed from you was an assurance that none of your chaps has gone solo, particularly Fitzgerald, he would have more motive than anybody else. As that is not the case, what's your best guess as to how this came to be at the scene?' He tapped the card on the table. Raff picked it up, frowning. 'That is bloody odd,' he said, to nobody in particular. 'Of course, it is none of our people; I can assure you of that Simon. The only ones who are aware of any of Frobisher's past are Fitzgerald and his friends, and they are miles away. I don't expect them here for a few days yet. No one else in the organisation has any idea of the suspicions we have. Not that any of that explains this,' he said, handing the card back.

The two men sat in silence for a while. Eventually Raff looked up. 'As far as I know, only one of these has been placed in the UK lately and that was by the South Africans. Assuming that it was in the police file is it possible that it might have got into the wrong hands?' 'Not likely,' Quartermaine said. 'I will check it out tomorrow though. In the meantime can you check that the Aussies are in fact where they say they are?' 'Certainly,' the Colonel said. Now, can I suggest you get off home - you look stuffed.'

2nd April 0400 Cherbourg

The Truckline ferry slowly backed into the dock. The drivers of the vehicles on the lower deck were already in their cabs. It was a long journey down the Cotentin Peninsula and most of them were expected to be in Paris in time for the business day.

The foot passengers were also disembarking, this time direct from the mid deck and, with Frobisher in tow, the German quickly made his way to the one car hire desk that was manned. He had purposely not booked a car, preferring to leave such things to the last. The girl was half asleep and his Austrian passport and licence were barely looked at. The credit card he used was clean and untraceable, unless the authorities were interested in the middle-aged British tourist who had lost it a week before. Within thirty minutes of docking the two men were on their way. Quickly negotiating the still silent streets of the town, they soon found themselves on E3, the main road off the peninsula. He intended to stay on this and then the E46 to Caen. There he would head south on

N158 to begin the long journey across France to Switzerland.

Neither man had noticed the camera in the car hire office. The images were already being processed by the time the car was negotiating the ring road around Bayeux. Now on E46, the first comparisons were being made. French Customs had installed cameras at all points that were people-sensitive in the ports and the process of scanning and comparing was completely automatic. Only when the computers sensed a match did humans get involved. As the German joined the road to Caen the first light on the screens came on.

The night shift was about to be relieved. It was with a groan of frustration that the operator went to look at what it was that had got 'Felix', their name for the system, so upset.

Without much enthusiasm he checked the apparent match and swore as he saw that the baseline data was a series of photos received from the British Special Branch. Now he would have to do something about it. This one had a red tag on it; to ignore it would be career suicide he knew.

★ ★ ★

As Frobisher and the German completed the circuit of Caen they joined the A13 autoroute. The German intended to stay on the toll-ways until they were approaching the Swiss border. He reckoned it would reduce the journey time by at least two hours and, while he knew there was a risk because vehicles were automatically photographed as they passed through the tolls, he had no reason to think a picture of this car would mean anything to anyone. Frobisher had stayed awake for a while but was now slumped in the right-hand seat, snoring. Good, the German thought, at least I don't have to listen to the man and he can take over in a few hours.

Cherbourg Customs and Immigration

The day shift had arrived at last and the customs officer who had been dealing with the photo match handed over swiftly. He had tried to pass it up the line earlier but no one was interested. The supervisor of the day shift grimaced realising that he would have to contact the British himself.

By the time he had got through to them it was 1000 and even now he was being passed on again.

Eventually the telephone was picked up, 'Quartermaine,' the voice said. The Frenchman's English was excellent and as he completed his story it was with some pleasure that he found himself and his department being congratulated by a rather excited head of the British Special Branch. He was asked to send the pictures over immediately. Would he also check out the details of the vehicle and see if it could be traced? No, it was not to be stopped, it was important to try and figure out where it was headed, and one of the men was dangerous.

Meanwhile the subjects of all the interest were moving rapidly eastwards. Just as the A13 passed Rouen it turned south-east and with the sun now up and in his eyes the German started looking for a service area. Time for a break and a change of driver he thought.

Quartermaine sat in his office waiting impatiently for the French prints to arrive. He had called Vicky Manning, but her secretary had said she was busy at the moment, she would let her know. In turn Colonel Raff had called in; the Aussies were just leaving Sydney on their way north and were well and truly off the hook.

Angela had just bought him a cup of coffee and as she opened the office door it was with some surprise that he saw Vicky Manning standing there. She looked very excited and walked straight into the office. 'Another coffee, thanks Angela.' He glanced at Manning who nodded a thanks. 'Wow' she started, 'Have I got something for you!' 'Ditto,' he said, 'but you first okay.' She smiled 'You remember that picture you gave me last night?' It was his turn to nod. 'Well, I dropped it into the office before I went home and, wonder of wonders, we have a possible match; although if we do, this guy is supposed to have been dead for a long, long while.' She placed a series of pictures on his desk. The original was at the top, followed by a series of much earlier pictures, obviously taken through a long lens. The vehicles in the rest were at least twenty years old and all from the wrong side of the Iron Curtain. Quartermaine looked at them with interest; there was certainly a definite likeness. His man was older, of course, but apart from what looked like some plastic surgery in the forehead area, it could be the same man. He looked up, she was grinning. 'Okay who is he?' She passed over an old and battered looking file, on the front was the name 'Heinz Dietrich'. He opened it. Herr Dietrich, it seemed, was or had been a disposal expert for the long extinct Stasi. He flicked to the end and the few words on the last page suggested that Dietrich had been killed in a bungled incident on the border a long time ago.

His name had been on a list of most wanted after the Berlin wall had come down, but once the Stasi's own files had shown him as deceased and the manner of his departure, interest quickly waned, until now.

She sat down, crossing a very elegant pair of legs, not that he noticed. His mind was racing. 'So you reckon Herr Dietrich has been around all the time and, given his profession with his previous employer, you think he may be a freelance?' She nodded. 'Either that or he is now employed by someone a little further east, could even be a bit of both. There is one other thing,' she said, barely able to contain the rising anticipation. 'Check the date on which he is supposed to have met his maker, does it mean anything to you?' He read the page again and looked up, shaking his head. 'Can't say it does, Vicky I was pretty low on the ladder then.' 'Yes, well; I was still in school myself and I had to run a series of checks so I will let you off.' She smiled, 'On that day, as near as I can tell, there was a rescue operation across the border in Germany. It was supposed to be a Stasi head of station but in the end it turned out to be his daughter who came over. It was done by some lunatic army helicopter pilot called,' she looked down at her notes, 'Fitzgerald'. He got badly shot up for his trouble. The girl also, she was seriously wounded and would have died had it not been for this Fitzgerald character. Unfortunately she proved to be useless as a source of information apparently, gave us nothing. Lost her memory it says, but the general opinion was that it was unlikely she knew anything much anyway. After the dust had settled she----,' there was a pause and when Quartermaine looked up Manning was looking out of the window, 'Well, let's just say she disappeared. Fitzgerald also dropped out of sight around then, it seems he had incurred the wrath of, the powers that be although if you read that and his record, it's difficult to see quite why, I reckon the man should have got a medal or something. Apparently soon after all this he resigned, there were rumours of Vietnam and he probably died there.

'The two most interesting things are the name of the man who was running the op,' she paused again, 'it's at the bottom of the first page.' He glanced down, 'Bloody hell!' He stared at her. 'and the other?' 'Read page two of the pilot's report.' she said. He did, and as he finished he pulled two of the photos towards him. 'You think this Dietrich guy is the man this pilot says he scalped.' He looked again at the recent picture. 'Certainly would explain this.' He ran his finger over the man's forehead. 'And if Frobisher and this guy were associated then,-----' he stopped, thinking. 'Jesus, this is turning into a real can of worms.' The intercom buzzed. 'Yes, what is it Angela?' 'The pictures from Cherbourg have arrived sir. Shall I bring them in?'

He opened the envelope and a series of prints fell onto his desk. None were of particularly good quality but the likeness was unmistakable. He read through the accompanying report, glanced at his watch and frowned. These were over four hours old. He walked over to the map of Europe on the wall as Manning glanced through the pictures. Four hours at an average of, say, 80 kilometres an hour given that there was some urban driving gave a maximum range of 320 kms in any direction. However, if this guy ran true to form, it would be south-east. He called on the intercom. 'Get me the Head of the Surete in Paris please, Angela.' He sat down deep in thought.

At first he didn't hear what she said. 'Simon!' she repeated. 'There is someone with him. Here, look.' Still partially distracted he glanced down at the print she held; sure enough there was another figure there, even less distinct than the main subject, male without doubt, medium build, dressed in nondescript clothes. The next print was a little clearer and they were both suddenly staring intently at the fuzzy image there. 'Bloody hell!' he blurted out. 'Vicky, you will have to check that Frobisher stuff again. Make absolutely sure your body is him.

The intercom buzzed. 'I have the Head of the Surete on the line sir.' He picked up the phone 'Bonjour Philippe,' he began. In fluent French he then very quickly brought his counterpart up to date and concluded by requesting the apprehension of the target vehicle and the two occupants.

Philippe Marcel asked only a few questions, promising to get back to Quartermaine as soon as anything came up. 'One last thing Philippe, these guys are dangerous. In fact one is very dangerous. Tell your people to be careful.' He placed the receiver down. 'This is getting messier by the minute, Vicky can you get on to that body check ASAP. We need to know just who it is we have on the slab. Somehow I do not think it is our much loved civil service colleague after all!'

His intercom buzzed again. 'Yes, Angela?' 'I have had a look through the Smith file you mentioned sir. That card you described---well, there is nothing like that in there, although it is referred to on the list of contents. Do you want me to look further?' 'No, that's okay for now, Angela; I will take it from here. Can you just check whether that file left the building for any reason at all in the last few days?' There was a short pause. 'It went over to MI6 sir it was only seen by Ms Manning then it came back sir.' He thanked her and looked up at Vicky. 'You recall looking at that file on the Smith business?' she nodded, 'well do you remember seeing anything like a business card in there at all? She thought for a minute. 'No nothing like that, why? I do remember being surprised that it was already in the building though. It was on my desk within half an hour of the request. Something I should know?' she waited 'Possibly leave it with me' he finished rather lamely.

Manning left without a word, she was deep in thought. She had an idea. Quartermaine picked up the receiver and punched in a series of numbers. A voice answered. 'Chief Superintendent Quartermaine here Special Branch,' he said 'I want you to go through any reports of missing persons in the last, say three days. Concentrate on the south-east and south first, but do it for the whole country.' A question was asked, 'Yes of course, white male age in the region of 40 to 60.' He went on to give approximate details of the body they had in the morgue.

France

They had traveled for another thirty minutes before a service area appeared. They were now just north of the outer autoroute ring of the capital. Sitting in the cafe the German looked at his passenger. 'You will drive from here.' Frobisher just nodded, the last hour had seen him lapse into moody silence.

It was as they chewed their way through a couple of very ordinary croissants that the German became aware of the policeman. He stood at the door of the restaurant with something in his hand. He was obviously looking for someone, checking with a photo it seemed. He glanced their way, passed on and then returned, checking once again with the image he had. The German acted quickly, whispering, 'Stay here! Do not move.' Frobisher looked alarmed but did as he was told. The German got up and walked slowly to the toilet door at the rear of the place. He had the attention of the officer and as the policeman followed, and passed the table, he glanced down at the Englishman, but said nothing. Frobisher froze, aware at last of the danger.

Inside the toilets the German stood behind the entrance door. He had closed one of the cubicle doors and as the policeman entered he paused then moved towards the closed door. The German moved quickly and silently, he was behind the unsuspecting man. He shot him in the back of the head, the silenced pistol making that soft 'phutt' sound so popular in the movies. Death was instantaneous and, as he fell, the German pushed him through the now open cubicle door. He manoeuvred the body to sit on the toilet placing the feet in the required position. Pulling at the uniform pocket, he found what he was looking for and placed it in his own. He then locked the door from the inside and climbed over the wall into the next cubicle. Briefly checking himself in the mirror, he left. Frobisher was an ashen grey colour. 'What have you done?' he stammered. 'It does not concern you,' was the reply. 'You will do exactly what I say now. Come!'

They stopped in the main entrance. Parked behind their vehicle was a police car of the highway division and in it the dead man's partner sat talking into the radio. The German looked over the nearly empty car park and seeing what he wanted, he pointed. 'See that blue car over there?' Frobisher nodded 'Go and stand by it and wait.' Frobisher moved off slowly and the German walked the other way, approaching the police car from behind and on the right hand side. As he got to the car he tapped lightly on the window. The policeman leaned over and lowered the window, looking to see who it was. The German bent down, raised the pistol and shot the man in the head. As he left he heard the radio crackle. Headquarters were confirming the details of the car they had called in earlier, repeating an instruction that the occupants were dangerous and they should wait for back up before they did anything. It was on the way.

He joined the Englishman, quickly opening the door of the chosen car with one of a selection of quite special keys he had for just such a situation. 'Get in,' he ordered. 'We have to get out of here. I don't know how, but they are on to us. We must leave the autoroute and travel across country; it will be a long difficult and dangerous journey. Do you understand?' Frobisher was stunned, the ramifications slowly sinking in. He just nodded. The German drove the stolen car to the rear of the car park. There was always a private access to these service areas, he knew. It was for the restricted use of the delivery people and the emergency services, it avoided the toll points. Finding it, he flashed the police warrant card, recently acquired, at the disinterested security man and was waved through.

As they joined the country road he heard the first of the police sirens approaching the service area. A narrow escape, he realised. It took a few minutes to see what he had acquired. It was an early-model Volkswagen, the tank was full and the now, ex owner, clearly German by the licence plates had also thoughtfully provided a full set of maps, so far, so good. Now, if only the man was enjoying a long meal followed by a quick nap it would be fine. Somehow he did not think he would be that lucky and the first thoughts of disposing of the main obstacle to his escape passed through his mind. As if sensing this, Frobisher looked at him. 'If you can get me out of this,' he began. 'I will see to it that you are a very rich man. What I have brought for them will ensure their generosity.'

He looked across at the Englishman. 'Verdammt,' he could never resist the thought of money. Right, if he was to keep this odious individual alive he would have to come up with a plan.

Philippe Marcel was in a foul mood. The British Special Branch had called twice to see if the car had been found. The satisfaction that it had was quickly destroyed by the news of the murder of the two police officers. As a result he had made the point to the British that, now, it was a French operation. He had mobilised the Compagnies Republicaines de Securite, the much feared CRS. Heavyweights of the French police force, they were scouring the area. The problem was that, at the moment, they had no idea what type of vehicle the two fugitives were driving, let alone where to. Nobody had reported a stolen car as yet.

He grabbed the handset as the call came in, 'Qui?' 'Simon Quartermaine here, Philippe, I have just heard the bad news. Like to say how sorry we are and offer anything we can to help you. I have arranged for the complete files to be sent over. I am afraid there is not much though; we know very little about this individual as you will see.' The Frenchman rubbed his eyes. 'Merci, Simon. Anything you have will be appreciated. The two officers were both married with kids. It is not something we are prepared to accept. I am sure you understand.' 'Certainly I would hope we would react in the same way here,' he said, though he knew only too well that, under the current administration, the death of two young policemen would never raise much interest, especially if it was suggested that the rights of the perpetrators might be threatened. Fortunately the French had a slightly more sensible attitude. 'One favour, Philippe, if possible could we attend the interrogation when you apprehend these two. We are particularly interested in the other man. I would prefer not to discuss it now, but perhaps I could come over and fill you in on the details sometime?' A meeting was agreed for the next day, by which time the two men would be in custody the Frenchman assured him.

Replacing the handset, Quartermaine looked into space; he was not so sure. Angela beeped him. 'Miss Manning for you sir.' He picked it up again. 'How goes it Vicky?' 'Well,' she said. 'I have to say it gets more and more confusing. I have checked out our rather stiff friend and so far it is definitely Frobisher. All the details confirm it.' There was a pause. 'But?' he said. 'Oh yes, there is always a 'but'-- quite a big one actually. I got them to check the fingerprints and they match our data; however, I then sent a team to his office and, surprise surprise, there is not one match there at all. I then thought I might get a check done on his personnel file, to see if it had been tampered with in any way. There was no record of it having been removed, but then, of course, someone in Frobisher's position could have got round that easily. However, when we checked the file for prints----' 'You got a match?' he interrupted. 'Yes we did, but not with the body. The match we got was with the prints in his office!' 'God! he said 'What the fuck is going on here?' 'There is more Simon. We also did some poking around on the subject of our Teutonic friend, only this time we looked a little further east and it appears our ex Stasi man Heinz Dietrich, might not be as 'ex' as we had thought. Nothing too specific, but there is the suggestion of a semi- freelance doing odd jobs for them. He matches the description of our man. Last known address,' she paused to look at the file, 'Switzerland.'

'Bingo' he almost shouted. 'Have you got any more, like an address or anything?' 'Oh, come on Simon,' she groaned.' I mean, he is not going to be in the bloody phone book is he? We are looking and I have our Swiss people on it right now, okay. Oh, and you owe me another dinner, right.' 'Right,' he said, 'my pleasure, just as soon as this mess is cleared up. I might be popping over to Paris tomorrow to brief Philippe Marcel. His men came within minutes of catching those two bastards and they lost two of their men doing it.' He filled her in on the details finishing with 'Least I can do is pass on most of what we know; not the Frobisher stuff of course.' The light on his intercom flashed, 'another call Vicky, sorry. Keep me posted.' 'Yes Angela?' 'Home Secretary Sir, not happy.' 'Right, he opened the circuit. 'Quartermaine,' he said 'What the hell is going on?' the politician shouted. Once the idiot had settled down, Quartermaine brought him up to date and was promptly told to present himself at the Prime Minister's residence at Number 10--- Now!

10 Downing Street, London: Home of the British Prime Minister

He was the last to arrive as usual, and there had clearly been considerable discussion before he did so. Looking at the gathering, he realised he was the only person in the room from an operational background. The Home Secretary was his usual panicky, indecisive self. His private secretary, typical of the civil service hierarchy was already making excuses, preparing the ground to ensure that the expected sacrificial lamb was not himself or one of his associates.

There were two others in the room who were infinitely more dangerous than the political rubbish. In the corner sat Fraser, the head of MI6, and opposite him Granger from MI5. These two, he knew, would have been fully briefed and, with their own departments to protect, could be relied upon to take a hostile position.

Significantly the PM did not get up, just waved him to a chair looking pointedly at his watch as he did so. 'Glad you could get here Quartermaine, perhaps you would be good enough to tell us just what this is all about?'

It took him about fifteen minutes to give a run down on the state of play, finishing with the latest news from France and his suspicions about the identity of the German assassin's companion. Sixth sense made him leave out the latest revelations of this man's probable past. It was here that Simpson exploded, 'What are you saying? I would remind you that Sir Gerald Frobisher was a close friend of mine. I am still coming to terms with his untimely death. Poor chap must have been under considerable strain, and now you tell me he may not be dead at all and that he might have been a spy. Preposterous allegation! Just what the hell is going on here?'

He stared at Fraser from MI6, who said nothing but was looking increasingly uncomfortable. Granger jumped at the opportunity to 'put the boot in'. 'Actually, Prime Minister, we at MI5 have had our suspicions that there was another leak over there for some time. Never had enough evidence though,' he paused, 'Until now it seems. I must say I think you have been somewhat remiss keeping this to yourself Quartermaine. How long have you known about it? I would remind you that Special Branch shares a mutual responsibility for internal security, as you well know,' he finished smugly.

Before Quartermaine could speak the Home Secretary, wringing his very sweaty hands, started his excuses and between him and his tame civil servant, it did not take long for the first indications of where the blame was to be focused. However, they had reckoned without his experience of this government and the upper levels of the Civil Service. He waited while Fraser added his own interpretations and excuses and then dropped his bombshell.

'Well, gentlemen, I see that you all appear to think my department could have done more. I would remind you that, while that may be true, we have done one hell of a sight more than anybody else in this room and---' he paused. 'I would emphasise that it is not Special Branch that has the problem here. However I am of course quite prepared to hand over the whole case to any of you if you feel it would be in the national interest to do so. Although I should point out that this is getting into the public domain quite quickly now, and the story of yet another leak in one of our military intelligence services will not go down very well with the general public. More especially if it is seen that the original investigators, Special Branch, have been removed from the case for some reason. I can only imagine the effect this will have on the electorate, with the general election not too far away.' Both Fraser and Granger turned a bright red in incandescent fury but neither said a thing. Quartermaine realised that he had just made two more enemies.

The Prime Minister intervened, arms waving in the usual panicky way. The very suggestion of, an adverse electoral effect of yet another political scandal had quickly shifted his attention from any concern for his long- time friend. In fact he spent the next five minutes trying to distance himself from the man, finishing by asking Fraser if there was ever going to be a time when MI6 did not leak like a sieve. He conveniently overlooked the fact that Frobisher's meteoric rise through MI6 had been as a result of his own patronage.

Quartermaine had some difficulty suppressing a smile as the PM turned to him, 'Chief Superintendent, I want you to know I have complete faith in you and I want you to carry on with this, is that clear? However, I cannot impress upon you enough the need for secrecy. Another scandal would do irreparable damage to the political credibility of my government and the establishment. Now, if you will excuse us, we have some other matters to discuss. I will expect regular reports.'

Quartermaine got up and walked to the door. Opening it, he turned, 'And if Frobisher does turn out to be alive and on the run, I presume you will make this public eventually; or do you wish to stick with the body under the bridge scenario? Of course, quite who he really

is, remains to be seen, could be any body.' He left the
words hanging there.

He watched, aware of the faces staring at him: the
Intelligence men with undisguised hatred, the senior civil
servant with the usual self-serving cunning, and the
politicians, with the first signs of relief.

As he left it was clear that he had better get this right.
Those bastards would see him back on the beat if he
didn't.

France, East of Paris

The plan he had come up with was multi-layered.
First he diverted into the next town and, locating the
'Super Marche,' he slowly drove around the car park,
looking. He soon found what he wanted. A Volkswagen
more or less identical to the one he was driving. Parking
as close to it as possible, he waited until they were alone.
He went to the rear of his car and quickly removed the
German licence plate, checking the area again; he then
swapped it with the French plate of the adjacent vehicle.
He knew that while the owner might have noticed the
front plate few people ever looked at the rear one.

Returning to his own vehicle he got back in and drove
for about twenty minutes to the city of Rheims, heading
for the railway station. Here he cruised around for a
while, locating the poorer suburbs. Parking up, he
ordered his now silent companion out. Leaving the key
in the ignition he walked away to the station. Somehow
he didn't think it would be long before one of the locals,
not believing his luck, would be trying to explain how he
came to be driving this vehicle to the police. The
probability of the other vehicle, with the same plate,

getting pulled over somewhere else, should add further to the confusion and give them more time to get out of France. With the Luxembourg border just a few kilometres away, he planned on putting at least two countries between them and what he knew would be an increasingly frustrated and angry French police force.

Ordering the Englishman to wait outside he entered the booking hall and purchased two tickets. Returning, he gave one to Frobisher and told him to get on the train at the other end. As they waited at opposite ends of the station he went over the day, trying to work out quite how they had got on to him.

That there had been a camera somewhere was obvious and his guess was that it had been in the hire car office in Cherbourg. What really worried him though was just why a photo of him on a security camera in the ferry port should have caused any reaction at all. That was causing him real concern. He slowly realised that this had somehow got right out of control.

★ ★ ★

It was another three hours before the next leads in the trail were found. The very angry French housewife, who the police had pulled over in a particularly aggressive manner, was in no mood to explain how she came to be driving a car with both French and German license plates. Having eventually calmed her down it was obvious what had happened and the only result was another hour wasted.

This was soon followed by a high-speed chase in the suburbs of Rheims and at first the authorities were confident that on this occasion they were on to the real thing. When the suspect vehicle was eventually forced off the road, the callow youths inside were manhandled from it by some uncompromising members of the CRS. It was soon clear that once again they were not the men required.

After some rough treatment at the local station the details of how they came to be driving it and where they had found it were extracted. It led nowhere. The only possible link was that the main railway station was within ten minutes of the place where the vehicle had been stolen. Belated enquires there proved useless and, in the estimated three hours it had taken the police to get this far, there had been over thirty trains, local and long distance, through the place. The trail was cold and rapidly disappearing altogether.

It was a very fed up Philippe Marcel who rang Simon Quartermaine late that evening with the news that the two men had disappeared. As he put the phone down the Frenchman was a little puzzled. He had expected the news to be badly received. Surprisingly Quartermaine had been merely sympathetic, saying that he would defer their meeting if that was okay and that he would let him know if Special Branch found anything.

Luxembourg City Railway Station

They had made two changes to get this far and he had seen nothing to indicate that the French had any idea where they were. The few local police evident displayed no interest in anything much. He began to relax. Now, if he could only get over the border to Germany he knew he would be safe. He repeated the exercise that he had used in Rhiems and purchased two tickets on the local train, eventual destination Frankfurt. It would be a slow all night run. The clerk had pointed out a much faster option but he had declined, muttering some drivel about being an enthusiast. The man quickly lost interest and handed the tickets over. Frobisher was now looking decidedly the worse for wear and he led him towards the wash rooms on the station. Feeling a little better for it, he then sent Frobisher to the other end of the platform to wait for the train. Finding an empty compartment he pulled out his mobile and made two calls. He gave each a quick run down of what had happened and arranged a pick up from Frankfurt Hauptbahnhof in the morning with his people.

As the train departed he leant back and closed his eyes, but sleep was impossible. The reaction to the bad news of the recipient of the first call had been unexpected. He had assumed they would want to pick up the Englishman as soon as possible. He had even suggested a collection in Frankfurt. This would have enabled him to meet with his own people there and take a leisurely drive back to Switzerland.

The unwelcome instruction in the first call, that he was to keep Frobisher with him until he was told, was not what he wanted to hear. Nor was the thinly veiled threat that followed this order when he had objected.

The second call to his own people in Switzerland had been to organise the pickup, now for two. A woman, the same one who had lured Jensen to his doom, took the call replaced the receiver and relayed the message to the two men in the room.

She was puzzled. 'I thought the plan was to get rid of this package as soon as possible. Why is he bringing him back here?' One of the men looked up and rather sarcastically suggested she ask the boss. 'There would be a lot of future in that, you know what happens if the orders are questioned. Now, if we are to get to Frankfurt by the morning we had better get moving.' He pointed at the woman. 'You and I will go.' Together they left the house and got into the big Mercedes. It was going to be a long night and day. That was obvious; even if little else was.

Chapter Sixteen
Special Branch 3rd April

Quartermaine had worked until 2200 the night before and the few hours' sleep he had managed left him feeling tired and irritable. He sat at his desk, the first cup of coffee cooling slowly in his hand. He was flicking through the reports that had come in through the night. There was little in them to give much hope of finding the German and his mysterious accomplice now. The trail in France was stone cold; Marcel had called him first thing with the news. They had both contacted the Belgian, Dutch, and German authorities, but borders were non-existent in the EC and neither man was optimistic that the two would be found.

It was the last piece of paper in the pile that stirred some interest. Apparently a woman in Brighton had reported her husband missing. He was supposed to have come home a couple of days ago from a business trip to Kent or something. Anyway, she had reported him missing and the description had caught the eye of a keen young constable, who had actually read the request for information from Special Branch on the board at his local station.

What had increased the young policeman's interest was that the wife was just about as dumb as it was possible to be. Working on the principle that the husband was similarly equipped, he had contacted the man's place of work to find out more about this so called 'business trip'.

It did not take long to confirm that there was no 'trip' and, even if there had been, just about the last person to be selected for it would have been this Arthur Jensen character. Even more interesting was the gossip around the place that he might have gone off with one of the females in the office, on a dirty weekend. Not that they could understand what the hell she saw in him. Still, these foreign women must have different tastes.

He had asked to meet the woman and been told that neither she nor Jensen had been seen since the weekend. He then asked to see her employment file. Her nationality was given as Ukrainian. There was little other detail; she appeared to be just another of the hordes from Eastern Europe that had settled in the South-East of the UK.

He had put it all together and sent it off, as requested, thinking that would be the last he would hear of it.

It was with some surprise therefore, that he found himself talking to the operational head of Special Branch that morning. He was told to get round to the Jensen household and get some stuff from the wife which could be used as an identity check. They would need some clothing and something with his prints on it, and they needed it yesterday, so he was to get the lead out. 'Oh,' the voice concluded, 'and well done.'

Mrs Jensen had gradually realised the significance of the request and tearfully handed over the required items. The young officer could tell her little other than that the request had come from London. This did nothing to ease her concerns and he radioed for a female uniform to come and do what she could; it was not much. He rushed back to the station and arranged for the items to be sent to London in a special car.

A few hours later the package had been delivered to the forensic labs in London. While Quartermaine waited impatiently for the results he had called Victoria Manning with the news and she, for her part, had suggested that they might have a tenuous lead on the mysterious German's whereabouts in Switzerland. Nothing certain, just rumour and second hand gossip, the stuff upon which careers in intelligence are made and as quickly destroyed. The whisper on the street in Geneva of all places, was that there was indeed an individual who, for the right price, would 'take care of' difficult situations in a rather final way. She was following up on the rumour and would let him know. 'If we find them, do you have an opinion on what should happen next?' she concluded. He was non-committal, but as soon as he had replaced the receiver he dialled again, a private number, and a meeting was arranged.

Colonel Raff replaced his receiver in turn and sat there looking at it for a few minutes. Unlike Simon to sound so edgy, I bet he has had another run in with the politicians he thought. This Frobisher business was going to light a few fires, especially as the man had always been known as a close friend and confidant of the PM. The media were well aware of this. Let's see the bloody Guardian put a positive spin on this he thought; he could just imagine the chaos in Number 10, and leaning back he smiled. Serves the bastards right! Make a change for them to sweat a bit.

Still, if Simon needed some help he had better consider the options. He leaned forward and touched the numbers, 'Fitzroy-Gibbons' the voice said. 'Alistair, it's

Peter, are you free for a meeting tonight usual place. It seems there is a flap on over the Frobisher business. Simon has just called.' It was quickly agreed and Raff went on to query the exact whereabouts of a few people he felt they might need. F-G said he would chase them up and put them on notice.

Fitzroy–Gibbons walked over to the wall safe, opened it and rummaged around until he found what he was looking for. Returning to his large ornate desk he began flicking through the pages of the old and rather battered notebook. Finding what he wanted, he picked up the phone and punched in a long series of numbers.

Bangkok

Chuck Anderson groaned. The bloody phone was still ringing; he had tried to ignore it. He looked at his watch, 0100; he had been asleep for one hour only. 'Yeah,' was all he could manage. 'F-G here Chuck did I wake you? Sorry, bit of a flap on it seems.' The voice paused to let the message sink in. Anderson came 'on line' quickly. 'That's okay Colonel, been a long day is all. Awake now, what's up?' 'Well, to be honest I am not quite sure at the moment old boy. Just had a call from Raff and he seems to think we might need you up in this neck of the woods PDQ. Can you be ready to move tomorrow night? probably nothing before then anyway.' Anderson, well used to mysterious instructions in the middle of the night, asked only a couple of questions and replaced the receiver. He thought for a minute or two and, rolling over, was fast asleep soon after. Tomorrow would be soon enough to worry.

Special Branch

The forensic data had eventually been delivered at 1700 and by the pathologist in charge, no less. He emphasised that these were the preliminary results only; the final confirmation would not be available until tomorrow. Quartermaine could barely contain himself, 'Well, man, just who the hell is it you have on that slab of yours?' The pathologist grimaced. 'Well, I can tell you this. It is not Sir Gerald bloody Frobisher. Everything so far points to it being the owner of that stuff you had sent up from Brighton.' He looked at his notes. 'According to this, a certain Arthur Jensen, whoever he may be,' he paused, 'or rather was. Interesting question is just how he came to be dangling from London Bridge in your man Frobisher's tweeds with bits of his stuff in the pockets. Still I imagine I can leave that to you Chief Superintendent.'

When the policeman said nothing he turned to leave, but as he got to the door Quartermaine called out. 'There is a strict security blanket on this Doctor. You keep this to yourself, is that clear?' The man at the door blushed, 'I hope you're not suggesting...' The policeman interrupted, impatient. 'I am not suggesting anything, just making the position quite clear. Now if you don't mind.' He looked down at the pile of paper on the desk as the pathologist left.

Knowing full well that this particular individual leaked like a sieve, he was pretty sure that the whole story would be in tomorrow's papers. There was nothing so likely as to ensure a leak than threatening a known source. He was under no illusions that the head of the pathology department would soon be enjoying a free holiday in the Caribbean as a result of all this.

He rang Manning to give her the news and then braced himself before calling the Home Secretary. Afterwards he had to admit he had quite enjoyed breaking the news to the wretched man that the PM's 'best mate', was not dead after all. Far from it, all indications were that the whole thing had been a very elaborate deception which, if it had not been for the photographic information, would have had them guessing right up to the time Frobisher popped up somewhere unpleasant for HMG. The real question was just where the real Gerald Frobisher was and, more particularly, why. He let the implications of that hang in the air. He figured it would take the politicians a while to ask the question of 'why' and when the probable answers to it all sank in, he was pretty sure they would be racing around like the headless chickens he knew them to be.

He then contacted the young constable in Brighton again. After a brief pat on the back he ordered him to find out all he could about the woman who had disappeared with Jensen. He was not optimistic that there would be anything but establishing any connection between her and the mysterious assassin would help.

Cavalry Club

They arrived individually. Raff was first and he immediately organised a private room for their dinner. As the others arrived they were shown in. As soon as the meal was over F-G ordered a bottle of port and then the door was closed; they were not to be disturbed.

Quartermaine brought them up to date with the latest, including the anticipated leak. He put Raff's mind at rest over the issue of the card found on the bridge near the body. The fact that it was missing from the Smith murder file, and the suspicion that it had been tampered with anyway, explained its appearance on the bridge. They knew that a man in Frobisher's position could easily have got his hands on the file without any record. As to the reason he took it, more disinformation was reason enough and the connection with the dead London gangster provided a convenient link down which the investigation was supposed to lose itself.

Quartermaine then asked the inevitable question, 'So gentlemen, what do we do about this? He has the potential to cause the west, and the UK in particular, a lot of damage. I think we can be sure that it is Frobisher in the car and that he would not be on the run empty-handed. I need not remind you that, as Head of the Russia desk, his knowledge of everything we have over there is just about complete. As to our German friend, it is highly likely that he was behind the murder of Pat Carrington and that more than qualifies him for our attention. Frankly, we have a number of decisions to make. The elimination of the German would seem to me to be highly desirable. As far as Frobisher is concerned, do we want him back or not? The other two sat in silence for a while. Eventually Raff spoke. 'You say this pathologist of yours will almost certainly leak the story, as far as he knows it to the press Simon?' The policeman just nodded. 'Well, in that case I think Frobisher has almost reached his 'use by' date. On the other hand, everything he touched has to be assumed to be compromised so it will all have to be changed anyway, whether he is around or not. My biggest worry, if he is allowed to survive, is that our wonderful Prime Minister and his cronies might find some way of letting him off. However, in the short term, I think Mr Frobisher could still be useful to us for a little longer. I agree that our German friend should be removed but I think Frobisher can be left to the authorities,' he paused 'for the moment.'

'Of course we have to find them first. With luck they will stay together for a few days yet. Now, Simon, assuming tomorrow's papers carry the breaking story, could we ramp up the pressure a little by suggesting to the powers that be, that an official complaint be made to our Russian allies. It just might make them a little more cautious in picking Frobisher up assuming that is where he is bound, after all, so far it has all been quite cleverly disguised and their involvement is only supposition on our part resulting from the German's apparent connection with them post Stasi. Assuming they are involved, and personally I do not doubt it for a minute, they must be aware of the antics in France. That may have made them a little nervous already. Perhaps you could get the Home Office to imply that we are aware of their involvement, even tell them we have been on to him for some time. With a bit of luck they will keep it all at arm's length until they see just how much we really know.' Quartermaine said he would have a chat tomorrow, after the Home Secretary had been given time to read the papers.'

'As to where they will be,' Raff continued. 'Well all signs point to Geneva. We have been getting information indicating the presence of our German friend there. Have to say, it is amazing that we have had no indications before this. Still, the word is out now and our people and those of MI6 are beginning to get results, it seems.

German Autobahn Heidelberg

At 0400 he had called the car. It had been approaching the Frankfurt exit. He told them to change the plan and make for Mainz to the west. It was the last stop before the terminus. He had then walked through the nearly empty carriages and found Frobisher to tell him of the change. His reasoning was that any surveillance would be more likely at the major station. This way he would be able to slip away unseen.

As it turned out, there was indeed a small gathering of police in Frankfurt in response to the French and British requests. He was never going to know how lucky he had been.

Now as he sat in the back on the left side behind his driver he began to relax a little. All that remained was to get rid of Frobisher in Geneva, collect the substantial sum he was due, and then he would slip quietly into the shadows. The journey would take four hours and he would sleep for all of it.

10 Downing Street 1000 4th April

The Home Secretary sat facing the Prime Minister across the large desk. They were alone in the room; the desk was covered with the morning papers. They did not make for pleasant reading. Even the more responsible papers smelt blood in the water. All were asking the same question: just where was the senior civil servant, Sir Gerald Frobisher? The tabloids had even managed to track down a Mrs Jensen, in Brighton, of all places. It was suggested that the man found hanging under London Bridge might be her husband. The questions being asked homed in quickly on the security aspects, and the suggestion of yet another mole in the security services was soon made. The tabloids were also quick to point out that in this case the suspected leak was a close confidant of no less than the Prime Minister himself.

The PM, waving his arms about, was furious. 'Just how the hell does this get out?' he yelled. 'These tabloid rags know as much about this as I do. I want you to find this leak and sack the bastard. I don't care who it is.' He paused for breath. 'And what the hell have you got to add to this; has Quartermaine got anything? And what about our wonderful counter- intelligence people?' The Home Secretary, totally intimidated, managed to stammer that a car suspected of having the PM's friend in it had been found in Rheims, France, but that the French had lost the trail from there on. At this news his boss lost complete control. 'This could destroy me you know,' he screamed, 'and if I go all you bastards will go with me. You had better get out there and do something about this. Find that man and destroy him. He then lapsed into the whining blubbering behaviour known only to his closest confidants. 'How could he do this to me after all I did for him?' He was almost in tears.

The Home Secretary waited for him to regain some control. Then he raised the issue which the head of Special Branch had discussed with him that morning. Grasping at any straw, the idea of complaining to the Russians brought immediate relief and he was authorised to send a stiff note, requiring the Russian Ambassador's presence at the Home Office that very afternoon. Already Simpson's mind was putting a positive spin on the mess, he was framing the words in his mind: 'Decisive PM plugs leak inherited from previous administration. Foreign power warned of dire consequences of any hostile act.' Yes, with just the right amount of sincerity and concern he might just turn this around. Naturally his long association with that swine Frobisher would have to be played down right at the start. So would the fact that his party had been in power for ten years and that Frobisher's rise to the top had occurred entirely during that time.

The Home Office

Mikhail Petrovich, the Russian Ambassador, watched with interest as the Home Secretary delivered his prepared speech. Of course he had seen the morning papers and had a rough idea what this was all about. However, the suggestion that his government was in any way involved was preposterous and, when he got the chance, he said so. His demand for the evidence was predictably ignored. He satisfied himself by stating that, just because this British Government had some difficulty with the loyalty of its employees, there was no reason for it to go around looking for foreign governments to blame. He ended with a firm statement that any action by the British authorities against Russians in the UK would be strongly resisted, finishing with the comment 'We will discuss this in the public forum if required.' The Home Secretary's face paled and the Russian knew he had hit a nerve.

Of course, on his return to the embassy he sought confirmation that they were not involved, from Moscow. This was immediately given. However as news of the query quickly penetrated the dark corridors of Dzerzhinsky Square the effect was somewhat different and eventually a call was made to the embassy in Switzerland. The collection was on hold; Frobisher would be left there for the time being. They were to advise the safe house immediately and in person.

As soon as the Ambassador had left, the Home Secretary called Number 10. The Ambassador's threat to involve the media caused the occupant to cry out in anger and frustration. He could hardly make the face-saving speech he planned if the very people he wanted the media to blame were themselves going to use the media against him.

Geneva, Switzerland

The search had been surprisingly easy, in fact easier than they had any right to expect. The MI6 resident had already told Manning that even if she could find the place at all it could be a month at least and the likelihood of Frobisher still being there after all that time was zero.

As Head of Station she used her authority to place watchers at the three embassies Manning had said were most likely to be linked and it was from the Russian one that the break came. Their man had noted a known KGB operator leaving. She still called it KGB; they may have changed the name to FSB, but for her it would always be that and she loathed them for what they had done to her and her father.

Discreetly following, her agent was led to a large estate on the east bank of the lake. He had waited outside and the Russian had left within a half hour. Calling in she had told him to forget the Russian and stay at the house. He was to watch and, if possible, photograph any activity.

It was later that afternoon as he was beginning to yawn in the warm sunlight when the place showed signs of activity. The large gates at the entrance suddenly opened automatically; clearly something was about to arrive and he quickly got the long lens into position. He was lucky. The man on his side of the car in the back looked directly at him as the late model Mercedes swept round the corner into the drive. He also managed a couple of good shots of the woman in the front right-hand seat. The other two occupants were in shadow.

He called in and she told him to return. They hooked the digital camera up to the computer and looked at his handiwork. None of the faces meant anything to them so she called Manning in the UK. The images were downloaded immediately and Vicky could barely disguise her satisfaction. Bingo! Well done. It seems we have a match. Now, I want you to set up twenty-four hour, two man watches on the place. The man in the picture is to be followed if he leaves. We must know where he is at all times, okay? In the meantime I have another list of requirements for you. I will fax it over as soon as we finish.' She quickly called Quartermaine and as soon as they had finished he called Raff and F-G on a conference line to give them the news.

'Simon,' Raff said, 'do you have any idea just what MI6 intend to do about this? I mean, logic says they snatch him but knowing our wonderful politicians and the tender feelings of the Swiss, the bastard might still get away especially if the press follow up on the story and discovery the PM's man is on the run in company with a suspected assassin with established connections to our Russian friends. If nothing else should demonstrate to the great British public what a complete shit their leader really is. Not that I think there are too many out there who need to be told.'

Quartermaine smiled to himself' There is just such an operation being planned as we speak. Manning is running it off her own bat at this stage. Of course eventually she will have to take it all to her boss, Fraser, but she says she wants it to be in the bag before he, or Simpson for that matter, get a chance to interfere. Must say that lady has balls, this could blow up in her face. Interesting to see what that insufferable prick Fraser says about it when he hears. I will get back to you after I have spoken to her again.'

Geneva. The House

The news that the Russian had brought was not well received by either man. The German had contacted them immediately, complaining bitterly that this had not been part of the deal, that it was attracting dangerous attention, and finally, when he realised that he was getting nowhere, demanding more money. Frobisher, for his part, was appalled that he was still exposed in the West. He had thought that by now he would be safe in Moscow; the idea that he was still in reach of the British government terrified him. The embassy man had listened impassively. Eventually, without raising his voice, he told the German that if he valued his life, let alone his livelihood, he would shut up and make sure that his charge was kept out of harm's way until he was called. He reminded him that this was not 'a deal,' he was in the pay of the FSB. Speaking then to Frobisher he adopted a different approach, seeking to reassure him that the delay was only temporary. The politicians were getting a little nervous but he was still a very valuable commodity to them and they would move him as soon as possible. Frobisher settled down. Later the fact that he had been referred to as a 'commodity' caused his feeling of unease to return.

★ ★ ★

The team had been put together in some haste. The intelligence organisations always had lists of individuals, usually ex Special Forces, on call. On this occasion the four men selected, all French and German speakers, had quickly moved to Geneva in the aircraft it was intended to bring the wandering Whitehall mandarin home in. Their orders were to collect only him. Anybody else was to be eliminated, particularly the suspected assassin.

From the observations so far it was clear that the house was well protected electronically. There appeared to be four other people besides 'the customer'. It was obvious that a frontal assault was out of the question. More subtle means would be required and here the Geneva resident had come up with a plan. When she had finished the briefing they were impressed, particularly when she told them the necessary vehicles were already available.

The watchers called in. There had been no movement from the place except that every morning one man left in one of the cars and went to the local village for fresh bread and anything else needed. This, it was decided, would provide the opportunity.

0700 7th April The House

They had been parked in the lay-by for about half an hour. The car had passed them twenty minutes ago on its outward journey. The return was anticipated at any minute. The four men, all in the uniform of the Swiss police, waited, saying nothing.

Eventually the driver grunted and started the engine in response to the radio call from the watcher further down the road. Set back in the trees their vehicle, a large Audi in the colours of the Swiss police, could not be seen. As the white Mercedes passed he moved the Audi forward, accelerating to a position from which the white car was just in sight. Even if they were noticed, it was unlikely that the driver would be suspicious; it would just be seen as a routine patrol, they reasoned.

It took about twenty minutes to cover the distance to the house gates and, as the target vehicle approached, the large gates swung open as expected.

The fact that the drivers always communicated with the house as they approached the gates had been noticed by the surveillance team and was a deciding factor in the plan.

The Mercedes slowed to make the turn and as it did so the Audi accelerated from behind and quickly followed it through. Before the driver could react, the Audi swung off the drive, accelerated past on the grass and pulled in front. Stopping, the uniformed man in the right-hand seat was out of the car, gun pointing at the windscreen of the now stationary Mercedes, the driver was already opening the door and yelling abuse at the behaviour of people he still thought were the police. He soon focused on the gun and realised something was wrong, but instead of raising his arms as the 'policeman' was yelling for him to do, his hand moved to the inside of his coat. The soft double 'phutt' of the silenced 9mm Russian Makarov pistol ended it, and the now very dead driver slumped to the ground beside the vehicle.

The shooter jumped back into the Audi which accelerated away and within seconds was at the large oak doors to the front of the house. All four men tumbled out and approached the entrance. One pressed the doorbell without much enthusiasm and after a minute or so, with no sign of a reaction from inside, he stood aside and nodded to one of his colleagues. The Browning A5 12 bore self-loading shotgun this man carried had been shortened. It was now very much a close range weapon and with five heavy loads available, the hinges of the door were quickly reduced to scrap. The leader pushed the timber with his foot and the whole thing fell inwards with a resounding crash. Anticipating some reaction, all four men stood back, but nothing happened. The first two entered, one to the left and one to the right, their weapons ready. As they did so, a woman, armed, appeared from a room on the left. No attempt was made to detain her; the man on that side was nearest. He shot her twice in the head, his weapon almost silent. Unfortunately, as she fell backwards her hand tightened on the trigger and, set on full automatic, the full 15 rounds of the 9mm Steyr she carried, riddled the once magnificent chandelier that had been hanging in the centre of the hall.

The four men stood watching for what seemed an age as the room was filled with a rain of glass.

'Well that's fucked up the surprise element I guess,' the leader muttered, then held his hand to the earpiece he wore. A member of the surveillance team outside had seen a man he believed to be the German. He was running for the lakeside boat-shed. The leader turned to two of his men, 'You two outside and nail the bastard. Radio comms from now on, we will clear the house. Back in here when you can, okay? The two men nodded and left.

The leader was call sign 'Zero' and with the last man, 'Zero 4, he began systematically searching the ground floor. By their reckoning, with two down and one running, there should be one more man loose in the place, apart from the target. After all the noise, their presence was hardly going to be a surprise and until he was found, things could get difficult.

It was as they made for the stairs to the second floor that the last man made his play. He caught the leader exposed there and managed to get two shots off before Zero 4 brought him down with half a magazine from his Makarov. The body tumbled down the stairs past the slumped form of the leader. One bullet had caught him in the shoulder. It hurt like hell but as his partner rushed up to him he waved him on. 'Get the bastard first. I'm okay for a while,' he said. Zero 4 pushed past, calling on the radio as he did so. 'All stations, Zero is down; repeat, Zero is down on the staircase. Require back-up'

Alone, he moved to the top of the stairs. With no back- up this was dangerous he knew. Approaching each door he used the A5, always the hinges and always followed by a stun grenade. He had to wait for the room to clear and the process was slow and noisy. It was as he was about to deal with the third room that Zero 3 tapped him on the shoulder. Zero 2 stood on the other side of the corridor, covering the two of them.

The German had apparently made good his escape by boat and alone. They thought they might have winged him but could not be sure. Zero 4 quickly brought them up to speed on this situation and as Zero 2 turned to check out the leader Zero 3 just nodded at the door in front of them. The A5 was used again and, as the door fell in two shots were fired from within, the stun grenade exploded and this time they immediately followed it in. Frobisher, gun in hand, had fallen to the floor eyes closed coughing and begging for his life. The front man kicked him hard in the head and knelt down to pick up the weapon.

Within minutes they had him in the trunk of the Audi. The wounded man was in the rear seat, a large compression bandage shoved inside his blood stained shirt, with another at his shoulder to cover the exit wound.

As they drove, the man beside the driver was talking on the radio. Yes, they had the target; three down, one a woman. One had got away, believed to be the German. Querying what to do with the injured man he was told to head for the private strip where the aircraft waited. A doctor would meet them there.

Within 30 minutes the Learjet was airborne. Frobisher, in a state of total collapse, was tied up and dumped on the floor at the rear of the small cabin. Before departure, the Swiss doctor had cut away the mess of the injured man's shirt and had cleaned and dressed the wound. The bullet had passed through, and the exit hole was proving the more troublesome as usual. He had given him a shot of morphine and the three others had made him as comfortable as possible.

Sixty minutes later the aircraft was handed over to Swanwick Centre. The new controller had quickly pulled the little aircraft out of the airway system and radar vectored them to Northolt, the military airfield just to the north-west of London Heathrow.

As it pulled to a stop on the almost empty apron, one of the three vehicles there moved towards the doorway. The big BMW with darkened windows pulled up at the front door and a tall and distinguished man got out and made to climb into the cabin. The way was blocked by one of the men who stood, stooped, in the narrow doorway. 'Who are you?' was all he said. Flustered and indignant the tall man stood back. 'I'll have you know I am Sir Robert Fraser, Head of MI6, and I have come to pick up the man you were sent to collect. How dare you use that tone with me.' Zero 2, over six foot of red-faced Scotsman, looked at him with utter contempt and pulled the automatic from his belt. 'Aye, well I don't really give a flying fuck who you are. We have a man down here and he goes first. Got it! Now, move your fat Whitehall arse out the way before I do it for you!' Flustered, but still puffing with indignation, Fraser stood aside as the Scotsman waved at the ambulance. The injured man was quickly lifted into the back and, accompanied by one of them, it sped off.

The other two went to the rear of the cabin and roughly pulled Frobisher to his feet, banging his head on the low ceiling as they did so. At the door the Scotsman looked at Fraser. 'This, the piece of shit you wanted?' Frobisher stood in the doorway and looked up. Seeing his old boss, a look of relief flashed across his face until he was unceremoniously pushed out of the door, ending up sprawled on the wet tarmac of the dispersal area.

'Reckon we could have saved the country a stack of cash and whacked the commie bastard over there,' the Scotsman growled.

Fraser signaled to one of the other men in the car and Frobisher was pulled to his feet and pushed into the back seat between them.

As the BMW moved away, the last vehicle eased up to the door and Vicky Manning got out. 'Sorry to see your friend got hurt. Other than that I just wanted to say well done to you all. Debriefing at the usual place in a couple of hours okay?' The Scotsman looked at her and smiled. 'Thanks Miss, he will be okay I think. It will just be the two of us, right?' 'Sure 'she said. Walking slowly back to the car she was already wondering just what was being said in the back of the BMW.

At that very moment it was on the M40 and heading north-west in the direction of Oxford. Not that it went far, leaving at junction seven and moving into the Berkshire countryside. Eventually it turned in through the gates of a large and very discreet manor house; one of a number kept by the security services for just this kind of situation. Nothing had been said in the car but, as soon as they were alone inside, the Head of MI6 began the interrogation. After an hour, Frobisher was handed over to the professionals and within a few days the level of damage had started to become apparent.

The information was routinely passed to Number 10, where an increasingly agitated Prime Minister read the reports. As if sensing this, Frobisher, now fully recovered and showing signs of his usual arrogance, began requesting to see his old friend. The request rapidly ramped up to demands and threats. As this was relayed to the PM, Simpson finally cracked and ordered a car.

Without consulting the security services he went to see the man.

Telling the resident interrogator to leave them, in spite of the man's objections he was eventually alone with the one man who was in a position to destroy him. After an hour the PM reappeared at the door and without saying a word left. His manner was noted as considerably less agitated than when he had arrived. Returning, the interrogator found Frobisher in an equally relaxed state. Later, as he played the tapes back, he found out why. He quickly made two copies and as his shift ended he made a call to an old friend.

The Colonel replaced the handset; teeth clenched tightly together, a look of contempt on his face. Is there nothing that slimy bastard will not stoop to? So be it.' He picked up the phone again. 'We have a problem' was all he said.

The Old Bailey. Central Criminal Court London

The trial had come on quickly, other cases hastily pushed aside. It was held 'in camera' of course, the last thing the politicians or the hierarchy of the intelligence services wanted was the media making the situation worse than it already was. Even now the opposition, smelling a rat, was asking some difficult questions and in spite of the secrecy there was a high level of expectation. The tabloids were all clamouring for a life sentence.

The choice of judge was the key to it all, that and the very private 'plea bargain' that had been agreed between the PM and Frobisher during their private discussion. Very early in that meeting Frobisher had realised that his position was one of considerable power. Warren Simpson was vulnerable and that was something he was skilled at exploiting.

This judge, now sitting in the high court, had been a cocaine addict for many years. Frobisher had learned of his addiction quite by chance while involved in another operation. Predictably he had approached the man who, fearing the worst, had tried to resign. Frobisher, of course, had other ideas and any suggestion of retirement had been stopped dead. He wanted the man exactly where he was and the judge had reluctantly agreed to continue knowing that at some time in the future there would be a price to pay. However, as the years passed and he was left alone, his confidence returned. His addiction, now unofficially sanctioned, continued. Of course the utter hypocrisy of sitting in judgement on drug trials, among others, did not bother him one bit.

The call, when it came was to his home. The conversation was very one sided and lasted for no more than ten minutes. By the end he realised that what he had dreaded for years had arrived at last and from considerably further up the greasy pole than even he had anticipated. The charge, the plea, and most definitely the verdict required, were all made very clear to him; along with the price of not obeying. Replacing the receiver, he would have considered suicide but the caller had even covered that with the promise to publicly destroy his family name should he do so. There was no way out.

In fact the evidence presented was very selective. The word was out that both prosecution and defence had choices to make here and the prospect of a successful career, if the wrong one was made, were not good.

As far as the evidence was concerned, Frobisher's 'erratic' behaviour was to be explained as a nervous breakdown. The sticky point was the corpse found under London Bridge in clothing that had been identified as belonging to Frobisher. The press was on to this and an explanation had to be found. A dry cleaning receipt was presented as evidence for the very suit and when the time came Frobisher, expressing just the right amount of confusion, admitted he may also have mislaid some personal items at around the same time. He could not be sure; the obvious breakdown he had suffered made everything so difficult. It was suggested that theft was the explanation and the subsequent demise of what appeared to be a vagrant was not really relevant to the case. Neither Quartermaine nor Manning were called and, after a two week trial, the verdict was 'innocent of all charges', with an expression of concern for the defendant and the suggestion that a well-earned early retirement on a comfortable pension would be advisable. Frobisher managed to control the smile and humbly thanked the judge.

In his final address the judge castigated Special Branch and the Security forces for the manner in which a loyal servant of the public had been treated.

The three men met in the Cavalry Club that evening, the mood was one of disgust and anger. 'I suppose we all knew that it would come to this in the end,' F-G said. 'We have very little choice now.' Quartermaine nodded his agreement. 'There is one other development,' the policeman said, 'I have an interview with the Home Secretary tomorrow morning and I have a pretty fair idea of what he intends to offer me. Let's just say that I can expect a posting to the Highlands and Islands or some other backwater with the usual threats to help me on my way.' They sat in silence for a few minutes until Raff spoke.

'I think that tomorrow is the time to bring this to a head. It is not a step I take lightly as you will see.' He leant down and picked up the small tape recorder. 'This was passed to me by a very old friend who works as an interrogator for HM Government. Listen.' When it had finished the other two men looked shocked. 'Jesus Christ!' F-G exploded. 'I doubt even He could save the man now, Raff whispered. 'I take it I present a copy of this to that little creep the Home Secretary tomorrow do I?' Quartermaine asked. Raff smiled, 'can't think of a better time Simon, can you? I suggest you play it to him and then tell him that we require an interview with the PM in private, to discuss the terms of his resignation. That should attract their attention!'

Number 10

Warren Simpson sat content behind the large desk. 'An excellent result I think gentlemen. Total containment of the problem, Frobisher shunted into oblivion with no scandal and that troublemaker in Special Branch discredited. Quartermaine wasn't it? About to be put into traffic or something similar.' He glanced sideways at the senior civil servant beside him. 'No sign of the Home Secretary yet?' 'Not as yet, Prime Minister.' The man glanced at the Rolex he wore. 'Should be here any minute I left instructions for him to join us as soon as he got here.'

Simpson, already distracted, turned to the head of the Foreign Office sitting opposite him. 'Of course, all thanks to you Jeremy,' he beamed at the Foreign Secretary. 'Brilliant piece of press manipulation dispatching that infantry battalion to, where was it again? Unfortunate that a couple of the God awful soldiery got themselves killed on the first day. Still, it got the damn press off our backs and I'm sure we can afford to lose a couple of squaddies in a good cause, what?' He laughed. 'Now, Fraser, I trust you will take the appropriate measures to ensure there are no more leaks in your back yard?' Fraser flushed and nodded 'Indeed Prime Minister, the only possible difficulty was the Manning woman, and I have shunted her off to a dead end in corporate espionage. Nothing much ever happens there and I think we have heard the last of her. Of course the interview included a pretty severe reading of the Official Secrets Act, just to remind her of the consequences of a loose mouth now or in the future.'

There was a knock on the door and a woman entered. 'The Home Secretary, sir' she said standing aside and the man entered. Almost immediately all but Simpson realised something was wrong. The look on the man's bloodless face said it all. Simpson ploughed on regardless, finally stopping his self congratulatory waffle when he realised they had all long since ceased to listen to him and were staring at the little man sweating profusely at the end of the table. 'What?' Simpson finally exclaimed. 'What is it? Come on spit it out.' 'I think Prime Minister you would be well advised to hear this on your own,' he eventually managed. 'Nonsense,' Simpson interrupted. 'We are all friends here and I will not have some little glitch in your department spoil the best day I have had for weeks. Spit it out man!' Resigned, he began, 'I have just finished talking to Chief Superintendent Quartermaine, Prime Minister.' Ah I see,' Simpson interrupted, with a guffaw, 'Bloody copper doesn't like the job you offered, eh. What was it, head of traffic on Skye?' He laughed. 'Not quite, Prime minister. He left me this. Are you sure you want to hear it now?' 'What is it? Yes, yes of course. Get on with it.' Resigned the Home Secretary pressed the button.

The resignation occurred two days later, stress of work and ill health cited as the reason. The press release said words to the effect that Prime Minister Warren Simpson had been thinking that it was time to move on for some months and that recent health problems had finally decided the issue.

He was retiring to the Scilly Isles off the tip of Cornwall in the south- west. Like Harold Wilson before him, he sought a life of peace and quiet away from the political spotlight which had been his for so many years.

A week later the date of the general election was announced and a little item buried in the back pages, concerning the apparent suicide of a certain High Court judge, was lost there. Even the suggestion of long and sustained drug addiction had been missed in the feeding frenzy of the political situation. The Scenes of Crime Officer, poking through the evidence bag, had picked up the card and looked at it. Funny looking broom he thought, and threw it into the trash can.

Chapter Seventeen
Sydney Trans Pacific Operations

S haun had called Colonel Raff the night before to tell him they were on their way. He also told him that things with the Lee Chin business had gone very quiet. The police had been poking around and the man who appeared to be the new boss, the Vietnamese Tran Van Sah, had not been seen for some time. As a result, they had pulled back from any surveillance.

The trip was the usual via Bangkok, with a one day slip, then on to London. A couple more days off and then it went into what was officially referred to as a 'flexy roster'. Something which all the line guys knew really meant Operations hadn't got a clue and that they could end up anywhere. It all depended where the next load was sourced. Not that it worried these three. In fact they found the random changes of flying 'Freight' stimulating after years of the rigid stability of passenger operations.

The Colonel had been a little subdued but suggested a meeting sometime during the London slip and Shaun had arranged it for the day after their arrival. Replacing the receiver, Shaun had turned to the other two 'Funny, the old boy was not his usual affable self. Guess he must have something on his mind.'

The next day was the day of departure and it was Shaun's turn in the left- hand seat. As usual he and Jim took it in turns. On this occasion therefore, it was Shaun who was going over the vast amount of paper they were expected to read before making a decision on the required fuel load. In fact they had all been around so long the briefest of glances at the weather, en-route and at the destination, was usually enough. However, today they had with them a rather young and very new Second Officer. Shaun was taking more time than usual, explaining, as he went through the stuff, what was important and what was there to protect the 'Office Wallahs' reputations if something unpleasant came up later. Needless to say, most of it fell into the latter category.

Having gone through it all he called Digger over and introduced him to the lad, with the advice that, This is 'The Digger' and that he was to listen and learn from him, as there was nothing this man did not know about the 747. The first leg would be under Digger's wing, he was told. After that, the mysteries of operations from Southeast Asia to Europe would begin to be revealed.

Digger then discussed a couple of points on the defect list with the young man and, finishing, said, 'Right, you tidy up here and when you have got it all together meet us down in the crew room, right.'

The young pilot's head was spinning. The amount of information he had been given in a very short time was overwhelming. He had already done a couple of trips but the other crews had expected very little from him. Somehow, he figured, this time it was going to be different.

It was with a mixture of anxiety and anticipation that he turned to the dispatcher and asked, 'Christ who are these old guys?' The dispatcher looked at him, a tired smile on his face. 'These Old Guys, as you put it, are something of a legend around here young fella. You will learn more about how this job should really be done from them than just about anybody else around. You may not realise it yet but you are very lucky to score a long trip with them. It's my guess your life is about to change for the better, so make the most of it.' The Second Officer looked surprised at the intensity of the man's reply. 'Yes, thanks, but look, I don't know anything about them, not even their names!' The dispatcher thought for a minute. 'Okay, the one who is operating as Captain on this leg is Shaun Fitzgerald. He's Irish I think, at least that's what one of his passports says, but we're never sure. The tall bloke with him is Jim Kennedy. He and Fitzgerald go all the way back to the Vietnam War. What's more, they take it in turns to sit in the left-hand seat, so don't get smart with either of them okay? The engineer, as you already know, is the Digger. He and Jim Kennedy go back even further than Fitzgerald. Since Meldrum took over and set up the freight operation they mostly fly together. Officially, it shouldn't happen; unofficially, the 'Suits' seem to prefer it. Makes them think they have the three of them under control. Stupid of course, nobody here controls those three--- at all--- ever! Round here we call them 'The Crew'. Like I said, this is your lucky day.' He looked down at the roster, 'Make that lucky two weeks. Now, if I we're you, I would collect all this stuff together and get off down to the crew room. The learning has already started.' The Second Officer collected the large pile of papers together and moved off.

As he left, the dispatcher called him over again. 'Oh, one final piece of advice lad; if they ask you to join them for a drink, go, every time. You will learn as much from those three in a bar as you will on the Line. Got it?' S/O

Sam Wastell walked off in the direction of the crew room, a big smile on his face.

In the crew room the three men sat drinking; Jim and Digger coffee; Shaun, as usual, tea, strong white with one sugar or, as he put it, NATO standard, giving the briefest suggestion of a previous employer. 'Seems a nice young bloke,' Shaun began. 'Good to have some young blood along, eh fellas?' The other two grunted an agreement, there was a pause, then Jim looked up and asked, 'Anybody get his name, I've forgotten it already?' Digger shook his head 'Sam something or other I think.' There was another pause, 'Right,' Jim said, eventually.

The long flight up to London passed in the usual way, with the rather pleasing addition of watching 'young Sam', as he had become known, soaking up the vast quantities of 'gen' the three spent their time giving him.

The keenness and interest he displayed in everything they taught him encouraged them to pass on as much as he was able to absorb.

The Bangkok slip had shown another positive attribute. Young Sam was not afraid to have a beer with the old guys, something that met with unanimous approval, as all three had firm views on the new breed of

'Sensitive new age guys', who wouldn't or in reality probably couldn't handle a beer now and again, young Sam was definitely no SNAG, that was for sure. Digger had had his work cut out keeping him in line.

About two hours out of London with Sam in the right hand seat Shaun turned to him, 'We might have to leave you on your own for a bit when we get there Sam, some business to attend to. Still, there will be some other young blokes in town. Do you good to get out with your own age for a while.' Sam's face fell. 'Give us a rest from you too, we're not as young as we used to be,' he laughed, and the young man brightened up.

The arrival followed the familiar pattern of unhurried professionalism for which Heathrow is famous and they were soon sitting in the car provided, cruising along on the M4 heading for the hotel. As soon as all had signed in, the three older men arranged to meet in Shaun's room at 1800.

They were sitting there sipping a beer each when there was a knock on the door. Shaun got up and opened it. 'Well stuff me! Chuck Anderson, what the hell are you doing in town? We're sitting here waiting for a call from Colonel Raff. The American entered the room and the other two stood up to say 'Hi,' Jim with a little more reserve than Digger. He was still concerned over the involvement of Maria and viewed Anderson with some suspicion.

The American caught the beer the engineer tossed at him, tapped the top to prevent it spraying it all over the place, and sat down. 'The Colonel sent me. He figured the situation warranted the personal touch. There have been some significant developments here while you were on your way up,' he began. 'Yeah' Shaun agreed, 'Looks as though things have been popping, Simpson resigning and all. You fellas have something to do with that?' Anderson smiled but said nothing. Eventually he continued, 'Of most interest to you, Shaun, is that the bastards have let your old friend Frobisher off, in spite of all the evidence that he has been working for the Reds for years. Here, read this little lot.'

He handed the three of them a file each. It took about half an hour to read through it all and at the end Jim, the last to finish, looked up. 'He doesn't get away with this right?' he asked. Anderson said nothing but he lent down and removed another three files from the case, handing one copy to each. 'This is what we propose, and given your man's connection,' he nodded at Shaun, 'we thought you guys might just want to be the ones to clear this up. Read it and see what you think. After a few minutes they had finished and again Jim was the one who spoke, 'Bloody brilliant Chuck,' the early reserve no longer there. 'This, we have to do. Shaun, what do you say?' Shaun, with his usual calm, was less effusive. He looked at his two oldest friends. 'This is my fight boys; you don't have to get involved. You know what it will mean.' Digger exploded, 'Bollocks, mate! This piece of shit is way past his time and you owe him all the way back to that business in Germany. You were right then, and if the pricks had listened none of this would have happened and a lot of good people would still be around. We're in, so get used to it. Right!' Shaun shook his head smiling. 'Thanks,' it was enough.

Anderson continued, 'Okay what we need to know is your movements from here on. There are a couple of details that need to be attended to before this.' He tapped the file on the desk. Shaun walked over to his bag and pulled out the rostered flying plan for the next month. 'Looking at this, we will be back up here some time in the second week in May. How does that suit?' Anderson thought for a minute, 'I'll pass it on to the Colonel but I think that will be just fine. Give us time to do a bit of other housekeeping and prep this up for you.' He got up to leave and Shaun followed him to the door. 'Been a while Chuck. We're just going out for a bite and a few beers, you want to come along?' 'Sorry, old buddy, can't,' he said, 'got to catch a plane. Going to some place called the Scilly Isles, to see a man about a boat ride. Have to say, it's the damndest name for a bunch of islands! See you boys.'

Two weeks later 14th May

Quartermaine sat in his office. As usual he was there early, he was expecting the call. Even so it was something of a surprise because the caller was none other than the recently promoted inspector at Scotland Yard. 'Think I had better come over and see you, sir. There has been another one on London Bridge, only this time it really is Frobisher.' There was a pause '--- I think' he finished. 'Okay,' Quartermaine said, 'later today will do. Don't suppose too many people are interested in that piece of garbage's demise any more.' 'Actually, sir, I think we should meet before that. There is something else I think you should see.'

Within half an hour he stood in front of Quartermaine's desk. 'I thought you should see this sir. I picked it up on the bridge.' He waited a puzzled look on his face. 'Nobody else saw it, but there's something written on the back of this one,' he finished lamely, as he handed it over. Quartermaine looked at the familiar card for some time, before turning it over. Written there was 'For Arthur RIP'. He said nothing and the young Inspector was feeling awkward. 'Thing is, sir, who's this Arthur character?' Quartermaine appeared to be deep in thought; eventually he looked up and smiled at the young policeman. 'I don't think we need to bother with this Inspector. Probably a coincidence - nice card though.

Now, I won't keep you I'm sure you have a stack of work on; I know I do.

As the Inspector left the office he realised that he had left the card and he stopped. 'No, I think I will forget that one,' he said to himself, and walked on.

Epilogue

The old Colonel sat in the sun, listening to the stream at the end of his magnificent garden. It flowed eastwards from here and joined the River Test, finally adding its clear water to one of the most sought after fishing rivers in the country.

I will have to have a go at that sometime he thought. Although, he was none too sure he had the patience for it. F-G was a master of course, sitting for hours waiting for some wretched fish to bite. More of a hand grenade man he admitted to himself, laughing quietly at the consternation such a supreme sacrilege would cause among the local fishing fraternity.

He was waiting for them now: Simon and F-G. This time Chuck Anderson and Martin O'Grady would be with them. It was, after all, something of an occasion and Cathleen had prepared dinner 'al fresco', it was such a beautiful evening.

As he waited he reread the evening paper. It wasn't mentioned in the headlines. It wasn't even on page three. It was buried at the bottom of page eight.

Sir Gerald Frobisher, a recently retired senior officer from MI6, who had left the service because of ill health a few weeks ago, had been found dead that morning having hung himself from London Bridge.

The reporter went on to say that the former civil servant had been depressed as a result of his recent trial for spying at the Old Bailey, in spite of the fact that he had been acquitted. Foul play was not suspected. The reporter then made the connection that this was the second death there in recent times.

In the same paper, again buried deep inside, was the summing up of the enquiry into the recent drowning, off the Scilly Isles, of retired Prime Minister Warren Simpson.

It seemed that he had recently struck up a friendship with a mysterious American who had been on holiday there and they had taken to going out fishing together. On the fateful day nobody could say whether the American stranger had been with Simpson or not and now he had disappeared. There was an appeal from the Devon and Cornwall Police for him to come forward but as yet nothing had been heard. This reporter had tried hard to build the story into something that would attract the attention of his editor but in the end all he could come up with was... 'Islanders express total indifference to the death.'

Clearly the inhabitants of those remote islands were as glad to see the back of the man as was the rest of the country. The only other puzzle in the tale, and the reporter did not even bother to mention it, was the card found on the body. It was an embossed image of a broom with one word on it. Nobody in the local police seemed to feel it was significant and it was soon discarded.

The car arrived on time, Quartermaine driving as usual with F-G beside him. The American and the Irishman were sitting in the back. Cathleen met them at the door and they followed her through to the garden. Raff stood to welcome them and for the next half hour or so they discussed the recent events.

Dinner passed slowly, the suggestion by Raff, of a lull in the operations, occupying most of the conversation.

Eventually, the late afternoon sun gave way to a warm and balmy evening. The frequent lapses in conversation were interrupted only by birds settling in and the low buzz of the insects frantically trying to avoid the predatory attacks of the squadrons of swallows.

There was the noise of another car pulling up and Raff looked up at Cathleen and nodded. She moved quickly into the house, returning in a few minutes followed by a young man in the uniform of an airline captain. He stopped and smiled at the gathering, clearly recognising them all.

He walked over to Raff who stood to greet the newcomer. 'Welcome home Nigel. How did it go?' Very well sir, no problems. There will be no more trouble from that part of the world for a while.' 'Good. Sit down my boy, Cathleen, something to eat for our guest please.' 'Of course Colonel.' She turned and walked back to the house. As she reached it she was smiling. 'Retire? I don't think so, these men could no more sit around and watch injustice and corruption than could I,' she said to herself.

No, she thought, as long as they are able the garbage of humanity will be disposed of and the discovery of a little card close to the scene would be the only clue.

As the night closed in, a few lights started to appear in the little village but none intruded on the sky. Moonless tonight, it was a vast cavern, with only the stars and the last of the dying sun at the very edge of the coming darkness of space.

Slowly, they became aware of the sound; they looked up and found the lone aircraft there, its strobe lights adding brief flashes to the twinkling jewels of the cosmos. The noise, a faint rumble, came from some way behind. It was a heavily laden 747 freighter climbing slowly out of Heathrow, New York bound. The last of the western light flickered briefly off the silver of the wings and was gone.

Raff glanced at his watch and looked up again. Raising his glass he said softly, 'Farewell gentlemen. Thank you and God Speed.'

★ ★ ★

Some eighty miles further east the old tug 'Eful' plodded her weary way up the river. He stood with one hand on the wheel and turned slowly to his nephew. 'Nice night Alf.' The boy, half asleep, nodded, 'Sure is, Uncle Jesse.'

THE END

Authors notes on the tale

With any novel there will always be some unanswered questions. How much is fact, how much fiction? Do these places really exist is that character real or not?

In these notes I have endeavoured to separate one from the other, hopefully stimulating another level of interest in the story.

So to begin

In the early 1960s the Army Air Corps of the British Army did indeed experiment with flying the 'Iron Curtain' patrols with helicopters to back up the light armoured units whose task this more usually was.

The border itself was very un-Germanic. It frequently took turns through as much as ninety degrees for no definable reason. Until one became more familiar with 'the patch' the result was some spectacular and nerve wracking flying displays while trying to get back to our own side, something actively encouraged by the 'Volpo,' the East German border police. They were an unfriendly lot at the best of times and didn't take kindly to this behaviour.

At that time there actually was a Lancer regiment of the British army stationed well forward, patrolling from a camp very similar to that in the story.

Bangkok in the late 60s and 70s was a wide open town. Lucy's Tiger Den was much as described and Tiger Rayling was a very real character. The manner in which he inherited the establishment may of course be legend, although I like to think it happened as written. This was certainly the story doing the rounds at the time.

Bobby's Arms and Club 99 were also very real and the Montien remains the chosen hotel for the Patpong aficionado, being only two minutes from the action.

Bobby's was always the favoured bar of technical aircrew passing through the town. Certainly if a company ever wanted to trace a pilot this was the first place they looked.

Pete, the man from Yorkshire, is a real character and it was when he and his partner moved on that the bar lost its following. Last information received was that the old place still exists at the back of the car park, although now sadly a shadow of its former self the crews no longer adding life and laughter. Bobby, if he is still around, must rue the day they left. Of Pete, word is he is now running a bar in Soi Cowboy, but I cannot be certain.

The Napoleon, was also very real. It was an oasis as described, the working girls were not allowed in, as such, it was an early casualty. It succumbed to Japanese money and was converted to a 'club' for the increasing numbers and exclusive use of tourists from there. The land of Nippon does not like to share it seems.

For background on the sequences on the 'Secret War' in Laos I am indebted to two books on the subject, 'The Ravens' and 'Air America' by Christopher Robbins. I hope my fictional descriptions match the reality.

As to the details of the incident that bought Fitzgerald down to earth over The Plain of Jars. I can state that this is pure 'faction.' It is loosely based on personal experience, not in the venerable Huey but its smaller and much older sister, the Bell 47 and not from enemy fire but something far more sinister in its way.

The technicalities of rotor design and control used by Bell are broadly similar on the two types and therefore the damage described would have had the same result. In this case my old employer had already lost two machines, together with the crews to a manufacturing defect that had caused a separation of the lateral cyclic control run much as described. While I would very much like to claim our survival was the result of my skill, deep down I know 'fate' played the major role. About the only positive thing to come out of this series of real tragedies is that on this occasion someone was alive to point the investigators in the right direction. Up until then each accident had been written off with the all too familiar, 'Pilot Error'. Dead men do not argue. I should point out here that while the machines in question were a Bell design, they had all been manufactured by a contractor and it was to here that the trouble was traced.

The Vietnam War, like all wars, was a terrible period. However I would be less than honest if I did not admit to the excitement of it all. Certainly the veritable plethora of new airlines it gave birth to makes the creation of Trans Pacific an acceptable illusion. Significantly the interference into the times of departure of the trooping flights for 'political reasons' referred to in the text is true. Small wonder so many of us still hold the political animal in such contempt.

Would it have been possible to smuggle a paperless Fernandez out and in, in the manner described? Well the answer is an unequivocal yes. I know of two occasions when something similar occurred, although neither from Bangkok. The first involved a young flight attendant who had rather naively married a Kuwaiti only to find she was now a prisoner, albeit in a gilded cage. Her original employer still operated through the port and, with a borrowed uniform and no papers, she was bought home as a crew member by her friends.

The second involved 'the rescue' of an entire crew stranded in the Balkans in rather awkward circumstances. All were lifted out on an empty aircraft from a different company positioning to their home port. In both cases the crews kept it quiet and the 'pushers of paper' never knew. Such was the brotherhood in those days.

Of 'The Jolly Farmer' and the inimitable Martin O'Grady, well along with 'The Jolly Sailor' this is one of the most popular of names for a British pub and I am sure that somewhere one will have an Irishman in charge. Whether he would take part in such an adventure, who knows?

The Borsch and Tears in South Kensington was and probably still is, real. At the time of the tale it was very popular with the young Irish population of the city. As such the presence of anybody with a tie would not have been well received, at least not on the lower deck.

I have to say that I have done the Chinese community of Sydney a great disservice casting some of them as villains in the tale. They are in fact, some of the most law abiding migrants any young country could wish for and are a credit to their adopted home. More than I can say for some of the others.

Of Sydney, all the locations in this most beautiful and exciting of cities are real. However the headquarters of Trans Pacific Airlines is, in fact, a general office block, in which none of the occupants are involved in aviation.

While the strangely named Shad Thames is certainly there I am afraid 'The Flying Dutchman' is not, probably no bad thing given the clientele.

The village of Amport is very real and as beautiful as one would expect an English country village to be. That Colonel Raff chose to make his home there is understandable. He would have been in good company. Many of his more substantial colleagues in the real world of retired military gentlemen have done so. His cottage is also real; however it would be entirely inappropriate for me to say exactly where.

★ ★ ★

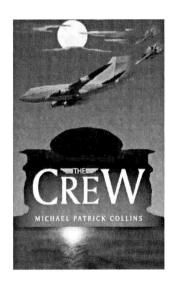

The Crew – Chapter One
Trans-Pacific Airlines
Secret Board Meeting. Sydney, Australia

'We have a problem.'
'You bloody bet we have a problem. This whole crazy idea is falling apart, Meldrum, and I want out. You said we could pick up $5,000,000 each. The way things are we will be lucky to escape the nick unless we do a Skase.'

Mr Skase had been one of a number of Australian high fliers who had walked with the cash when things had got a bit tough in the '80s.

'Belt up, the lot of you. You were all for it when we started, so there's no bloody use whinging about it now. Unless we stick together, we're lost, so shut up and listen.'

Meldrum could be pushy when required and the predictable blast from the senator had needed an early stamp on, if only to stop the rest of them panicking. Not that panic wasn't justified, given the situation they faced.

The director of operations raised his hand as arranged, a nod from Meldrum and he began. 'As I see it, we are up for $25,000,000 at this stage. The problem is a note for this amount is due in the company accounts in two months and we can't cover it. The Bangkok business has collapsed, the properties would be lucky to get five. Any of you got twenty to put in? No? I thought not.'

The whining and grovelling began again, most vocally from the politician, as usual.

'Be quiet,' snapped Meldrum, with more confidence than he felt. 'There has been another development. We have been approached by certain interested parties in Thailand who may be able to help.'

The clamouring for more information and first signs of relief were gratifying. How easy it was to manipulate these bastards. The next bit might not be so easy, of course.

'Certain Thai interests have let it be known that they are aware of our situation and are willing to deal.'

'Deal – deal, how?' from the senator.

'I'm not sure but I am going to Bangkok tonight to meet them and find out. As I see it, we have no choice, so I want a clear agreement from you all that I have a free hand in this. Consider the alternatives before you say anything.'

Slowly the heads nodded assent. Easy, he thought, but Thailand looked anything but.

Bangkok

City of corruption, sex, deviation, all the delights of the flesh! A place where just about anything is possible, no job too big or too small. Here, there was always the man or woman to fix your particular problem. All that was needed was the word. A whisper on the street and eventually a meeting with the problem solver!

Or so it had been back in the heady days of the Vietnam War. It was a wide open town in those days, with fortunes made and lost, almost as fast as lives, and with about as little fuss. For all that, the place hummed and the street crime levels were low. Too many capable people there then, too many, really, had 'seen the elephant' and knew how to handle themselves. No self respecting thug is going to try and mess with a wired up young GI on R & R from 9 months 'over there' against North Vietnam's finest, at least, not more than once. It happened, of course; the boys got pissed, fell over, got robbed and worse. What usually followed ensured that that particular bar changed hands pretty quickly and another unidentified body was found in one of the canals.

In those days you could fix anything: wife giving you trouble, politician in the way, guns, tanks even aircraft wanted. Down to the seamy stuff, little girls, little boys, head jobs, hard jobs, you name it, all you had to do was find the right man or woman.

Things had slowed up after the war, of course, but the fixers were still there and the places of rendezvous. The public image of the place had been cleaned up some, but to those who knew, it was business as usual - a little slower now but 'b.a.u.' just the same.

Lucy's Tiger Den, then on Surawong Road (like a lot of bars in Bangkok it moved about a bit) had become famous during the war as the place to find the man for the awkward job. It was the chosen bar of the hard men. Not surprising, really, as Tiger Rayling, ex-Vietnam veteran had woken up late one morning after a monumental poker game to find he was now the not-so-proud owner of a bar and a girl called Lucy. Having made the switch from trained assassin to entrepreneur, Tiger naturally felt more comfortable with those he knew. While he very soon found his limited number of friends disappearing into the abyss of the war there was a steady flow of like-minded travellers to keep the business profitable.

The bar itself was unique in Bangkok, in that here, the only girls allowed were Lucy and her daughter. Here, peace and quiet was the rule. Conversations were always discreet, the music low, and the booths in relative darkness. In all, an atmosphere of mutual respect that comes from knowing that the other guy has been there. You didn't have to like the man, but this was not the place to settle scores, old or new. The occasional drunken tourist staggering through the door soon realised that the sudden chill in the air was not entirely air conditioning and usually left; with a little encouragement at times, but left just the same.

Francis Meldrum sat quietly in the corner, feeling distinctly uncomfortable. The obviously high levels of testosterone evident in the other customers was bad enough, but the atmosphere was hostile anyway. Already he regretted leaving the choice of venue to the man he was to meet here.

He was, in all senses of the word, a weirdo: 5'6" on a good day, his chromosomes had been a mess from the day of his birth, to the extent that his sexual preferences were bizarre to say the least. This had caused him considerable difficulty at the military academy to which his father had sent him, in a last-ditch attempt to get things straightened out, to no avail. An incident in the showers had brought his already lacklustre military career to an ignominious end, much to the relief of all who knew him, with the possible exception of his father.

Undaunted, the young Meldrum had embarked on a career in business. Already brought up in a strictly religious family, he then joined the local business associations and so, with his now well established 'other connections', he had every base covered and was virtually guaranteed a successful career.

From small trading companies to an equally small airline, he had progressed to insurance, banking and even a government consultancy, making useful contacts on the way. Today found him along with the rat pack of fellow travellers he had collected on his corporate journey, as the chief executive of Trans-Pacific Airlines. He had been called in by the incompetent son of the founder, now deceased, to sort out the mess the airline was in.

As was his way, he had ruthlessly purged the organisation of all who had any idea of how things should be done and who could have asked awkward questions about phase two. This involved ensuring that the fortunes of one F. Meldrum and friends were considerably increased while the exercise in 'reconstruction' took place. Naturally reserves, purchasing, servicing and morale hit the bottom very quickly, but the profits soared and the share price followed.

The shareholders asked no questions about some of the more peculiar practices, in spite of constant rumours that 'something may indeed be a bit smelly in the state of Denmark!' And smelly it was because, for once in his life, Francis was in trouble. He and his cronies had dipped deep into the company cash to fund a large scale resort development in Thailand, with a view to selling it back to the airline as a package holiday deal at considerable profit.

The crash of the so called 'Tiger' economies had found them hopelessly overexposed to the tune of about $25 million. As the meltdown developed, they had become increasingly desperate to the point that they had been willing to consider anything. As is the way in Thailand, desperate situations soon become known and the problem solvers appeared.

He stood as the Thai approached, dwarfed and intimidated by his bulk. His proffered hand was grasped by the man, who unsuccessfully attempted to suppress the revulsion felt at the piece of 'wet fish' he found himself holding.

He sat opposite. 'Your problem, Mr Meldrum, is not insoluble. In fact, if you and your colleagues have the nerve, it can be turned into something quite profitable.' He began. 'You own an airline, I believe?'

'Well, I don't exactly own it, but, yes, we do control it. Why?'

'We have the need to transport large quantities of material around the world from time to time and your assistance in this could be quite lucrative. Obviously, not the full amount you need, at least, not at first, but if you are agreeable we may be able to cover that for you on the understanding that we have a deal.'

'What sort of a deal?'

'I think we should be quite frank with each other, don't you?' The Thai was quite proud of his English and liked to use what he considered sophisticated expressions when he could, although frankness and sophistication were not going to be very high on the agenda in his dealings with this man, he thought. 'Your situation, as we see it, is that having invested $25 million in property here, you now find it is now worth only $5 million. Furthermore, the $25 million was, shall we say, borrowed from the company accounts in a slightly flexible way.'

Francis' mouth was dry. He was, of course, aware that these people must be well informed, but to have their situation laid out like that was not pleasant.

The Thai moved slightly, placing himself in the shadows and leaving Meldrum feeling even more exposed. 'We are prepared to provide you with sufficient funds to retrieve the situation for you and your friends. Of course, we will expect certain considerations in return.'

Here it comes, thought Meldrum. 'What sort of considerations?'

'As the CEO of Trans-Pacific, can we assume you have the ability to arrange the passage of certain items with, shall we say, discretion?

Meldrum said nothing, nodding a brief affirmative.

'In return for our considerable investment in your survival, we would require the movement of particular cargoes of a more sensitive nature from time to time'.

Again, a non-committal nod from Meldrum, but curiosity is a powerful thing and he could not resist it. 'What sort of items?' as if he couldn't guess.

A blank stare from the Thai chilled him. 'It will not be necessary for you to be informed. All that is required of you is that the goods are delivered where and when we say. You do understand that minor inconveniences like customs will have to be avoided?'

A spluttering protest from Meldrum instantly reduced to a strangled croak as the Thai's massive hand closed around his neck.

'You should be aware, Mr Meldrum, that your options here are few; you either cooperate or face oblivion. Do you understand?' Going blue, Francis managed yet another nod. 'Naturally, we would cover ourselves in this, Mr Meldrum. No doubt you and your friends will gather some courage when you return home; it is the usual way of things, we find. With this in mind, I should inform you that each consignment will be made to you personally, so any interception or loss will, of course, be instantly traced back to you.'

As the horror of such an arrangement sunk in, the blood drained from Meldrum's face.

'I see I have impressed you,' murmured the Thai. 'Good, as long as we understand each other! We will now discuss the first shipment.'

Again Meldrum was about to protest, silenced as much by the Thai's raised eyebrow as the slight movement of the hand.

'You have a freighter coming through Bangkok in five days' time. We will require space on that aircraft; one pallet of, shall we say, furniture, for your personal use, of course.' The Thai could not resist a brief smile as the look of alarm spread over the face of his companion. He continued, 'The furniture will be loaded in London. The aircraft will arrive here and experience mechanical trouble. We will arrange this. During that time certain things will occur. You do not need the details. All that is required of you is to ensure the aircraft arrives here and the crew are got out of the way.'

Meldrum, now totally controlled by the Thai, could only whisper that the crew would be no problem as they changed here anyway, and that all that was required was a delay in the call of the new lot.

'Good.' The Thai smiled; no warmth here, more contempt. 'I will leave you now. You are no doubt familiar with this city's red light district in Patpong. Can I suggest the Boy Girl bar in Patpong 3? The little boys are delightful!'

Francis flushed with anger. 'How dare you suggest?'

'We don't suggest, Mr Meldrum, we know. We know all about you. The apartment on your Coast of Gold, the private deals at company expense.'

Francis' jaw dropped and for once he was stuck for words.

'Close that, Francis – in this town it's not a healthy habit!' He got up and left.

Francis took ten minutes to control himself and followed. Where was that bar?

Room 688, Dusit Thani Hotel, Rama 4, Bangkok.

The Thai entered the room and shook hands with the Korean, nodding briefly to the other man.

'So, we have him?' speaking in English, their only common language.

'Yes, he is ours for as long as we need him,' said the Thai. 'I have encouraged him to the bar and the cameras are ready, so we will have influence in two directions. I think we can safely say Mr Meldrum is our man. If the discovery of the drugs is not sufficient, the film will be.'

'This is good! Our friend here, nodding to the man in the shadow, is ready for the other shipment now. When do you expect the aircraft?'

The Thai thought. 'If we proceed as planned and advise the Australian customs official we have of the shipment in, say, 5 days' time. He will approach Meldrum with the news of his imminent arrest in one week. A few hours to sweat and we will then offer the next part of the deal for his perusal; only the rough outline, of course. I will then make his position clear on the next day, with the films of his activities tonight as a further incentive, if required. I shall leave on Thai Airways the day the shipment is due out of here, that is 5 days' time. That way I shall be in Sydney in good time for our meeting.'

The third man, Arab in appearance, moved forward and, in heavily accented English, said, 'We require the items by the end of the month. I trust you can deliver at the agreed fee? Mistakes will not be acceptable.'

The Thai glanced at the man, 'No, four weeks will be sufficient.'

The Arab left and the two Asians settled with a bottle of brandy.

'The ship will arrive in three weeks from North Korea. The equipment will be processed by your people and moved to Utaphao airport. You are sure that the wheels have been oiled? My government will not look well on mistakes and you are already aware of our Arab friend's misgivings.'

The Thai looked balefully at the Korean. These communists were a pain in the arse, he decided, but the years had been good and the money exceptional. It seemed that as long as the Americans and the West were made to look foolish, they were prepared to do anything. This latest deal is really only an extension of years of shipping anything from jeans and condoms to AK47s, aircraft and ammunition to whoever wanted them. All that was required was a mutual hatred of the USA and the West. This deal would, however, probably be the last, he decided. Something this big should set him up for the rest of his life.

The Korean, as though reading his mind, stared at him and for once the Thai felt control slipping. A chill passed over him.

'We will require you to position to Bahrain with the aircraft, you realise that?' he said.

The Thai was surprised. 'But my part in this is over once the aircraft leaves Thailand. Payment was agreed at that point.'

'Things have changed, my friend. For something this big, we require you to see it through to the end.' The tone left no doubt .

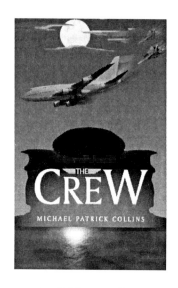

Available now from

All internet booksellers
And to order through good bookshops worldwide